Echo in the Wind

Regan Walker

ECHO IN THE WIND

Paperback ISBN: 978-0-9968495-9-3
Print Edition

Praise For Regan Walker's Work:

"Regan Walker writes great historical romance."

—Virginia Henley, *NY Times bestselling author*

"Ms. Walker has the rare ability to make you forget you are reading a book. The characters become real, the modern world fades away, and all that is left is the intrigue, drama, and romance."

—*Straight from the Library*

"The writing is excellent, the research impeccable, and the love story is epic. You can't ask for more than that."

—*The Book Review*

"Regan Walker is a master of her craft. Her novels instantly draw you in, keep you reading and leave you with a smile on your face."

—*Good Friends, Good Books*

"...an example of 'how to' in good story building... a multilayered novel adding depth and yearning."

—*InD'Tale Magazine*

"Spellbinding and Expertly Crafted"... "The path to true love is never easy, yet Regan Walker leads the reader to an entertaining, realistic and worthy HEA. Walker's characters are complex and well-rounded and in her hands real historical figures merge seamlessly with those from her imagination."

—*A Reader's Review*

"Walker's detailed historical research enhances the time and place of the story without losing sight of what is essential to a romance: chemistry between the leads and hope for the future."

—*Publisher's Weekly*

"... an enthralling story."

—*RT Book Reviews*

Acknowledgements

Many people contribute to bringing a book into the world, but some make special contributions that must be noted. For *Echo in the Wind*, this included some terrific volunteers. My friend Chari Wessel, a doctor of veterinary medicine who, for many years, was the gunner on the schooner *Californian*, a reproduction ship berthed in San Diego, makes sure my ship terminology is correct. This story is sprinkled with French and I must thank Liette Bougie, my beta reader in Québec who checks all my French and adds much more. And lastly, my proofreader *par excellence*, Allison Bullard, who has thankfully joined the team.

You have my undying thanks!

Characters of Note

(Both real and fictional)

Jean Donet, comte de Saintonge and captain of *la Reine Noire*
Lady Joanna West, sister of the Earl of Torrington

At The Harrows in West Sussex:

Richard, Earl of Torrington, Joanna's older brother
Frederick ("Freddie") West, Joanna's younger brother
Lady Matilda ("Tillie") West, Joanna's younger sister
Aunt Hetty and her cat, Aloysius
Zack Barlow, one of the villagers and Joanna's smuggling partner
Nora Barlow, Joanna's maidservant and Zack's sister
William Pitt the Younger, the Prime Minister
Edward Eliot and William Wilberforce, friends of the Prime Minister
Polly Ackerman and her children, Danny, Nate and Briney
Commander James Ellis, captain of the HMS *Orestes* (stationed in Southampton)

On *la Reine Noire*:

Émile Bequel, quartermaster
Lucien Ricard, second mate
Gabriel Chastain, Jean's cabin boy
Franklin, ship's cat

In London:

Cornelia, Lady Danvers, a baroness
John Ingram, Lord Danvers, a baron
Claire Powell (Jean Donet's daughter) and her husband, Captain Simon Powell
Lord Hugh Seymour, former naval officer and friend of Prince George
Higgins, the Danvers' butler

In Lorient and/ or Saintonge:

Pierre Bouchet, physician in Lorient
Noëlle Provot, modiste in Lorient
Vernier, Jean Donet's manservant in Lorient
Rose, housekeeper in Lorient
Gabrielle, lady's maid, acquired in Lorient
Zoé Donet, Jean Donet's young niece
Marguerite Travere, housekeeper in Saintonge
Francis Giroud, *maître du château* (estate manager) in Saintonge
Lefèvre, butler in Saintonge

In Paris:

Flèche, butler and former gunner aboard *la Reine Noire*
Charles Gravier, comte de Vergennes, the Foreign Minister
Louis XVI, King of France and Navarre
Marie Antoinette, Queen of France and Navarre
Prince Charles Philippe, comte d'Artois
Gaspar, former carpenter aboard *la Reine Noire*
Joseph de Vogelsang, Swiss banker

How far away the stars seem,
and how far is our first kiss,
and ah, how old my heart!

—William Butler Yeats
from the poem "Ephemera"

Chapter 1

Bognor, West Sussex, England, April 1784

Except for the small waves rushing to shore, hissing as they raced over the shingles, Bognor's coast was eerily bereft of sound. Lady Joanna West hated the disquiet she always experienced before a smuggling run. Tonight, the blood throbbed in her veins with the anxious pounding of her heart, for this time, she would be dealing with a total stranger.

Would he be fair, this new partner in free trade? Or might he be a feared revenue agent in disguise, ready to cinch a hangman's noose around her slender neck?

The answer lay just offshore, silhouetted against a cobalt blue sky streaked with gold from the setting sun: a black-sided ship, her sails lifted like a lady gathering up her skirts, poised to flee, waited for a signal.

Crouched behind a rock with her younger brother, Joanna hesitated, studying the ship. Eight gun ports marched across the side of the brig, making her wonder at the battles the captain anticipated that he should carry sixteen guns.

She and her men were unarmed. They would be helpless should he decide to cheat them, his barrels full of water instead of brandy, his tea no more than dried weeds.

It had been tried before.

"You are certain Zack speaks for this captain?" she asked Freddie whose dark auburn curls beneath his slouched hat made his boyish face appear younger than his seventeen years. But to one who knew him well, the set of his jaw hinted at the man he would one day become.

"I'll fetch him," Freddie said in a hushed tone, "and you can ask him yourself." He disappeared into the shadows where her men waited among the trees.

Zack appeared, squatting beside her, a giant of a man with a scar on the left side of his face from the war. Like the mastiffs that guarded the grounds of her family's estate, he was big and ugly, fierce with enemies, but gentle with those he was charged to protect.

"Young Frederick here says ye want to know about this ship, m'lady." At her nod, Zack gazed toward the brig. "He used to come here regular with nary a con nor a cheat. He's been gone awhile now. I heard he might have worked up some other business—royal business." He rolled his massive shoulders in a shrug. "In my experience, a tiger doesn't change his stripes. He's a Frog, aye, but I trust the Frenchie's one of us, a free trader still."

She took in a deep breath of the salted air blowing onshore and let it out. "Good." Zack's assurance had been some comfort but not enough to end her concerns. What royal business? For tonight, she need not know. "Give the signal," she directed her brother, "but I intend to see for myself if the cargo is what we ordered."

Without seeking the position, Joanna had become the smugglers' master of the beach, responsible for getting the cargo ashore and away to inland routes and London markets with no revenue man the wiser. She took seriously her role to assure the villagers got what they paid for. Their survival depended upon it.

"Zack, will you row me to the ship?"

"O' course, if 'tis what ye want." The frown over his hazel eyes revealed his displeasure, but Zack knew an order when he heard one, no matter how politely it had been phrased. He would never question her authority in front of the men.

Freddie lifted the lantern from the pebbled beach and slid open the metal cover on one side. A small flame flickered into the Channel, alerting the ship the coast was clear of the Riding Officer. The dying rays of the sun still danced on the rippling water, but the lantern's light would tell the ship's captain all was well.

Joanna got to her feet, tugging her felt hat over her ears and tucking strands of her long red hair beneath the brim. The hat and Freddie's borrowed shirt and breeches rendered her one of the men. Even though his jacket was a bit short, she dare not borrow clothes belonging to her older brother, Richard. He knew nothing of her nightly pursuits and would not approve.

"I'm going with you," said Freddie.

"All right, but stay in the boat." When she'd decided to help the villagers in smuggling goods that kept brandy and tea flowing to England's wealthy and food on the tables of Chichester's poor, her younger brother had insisted on becoming her partner. Still, she tried to keep him from danger.

Out on the water, the ship's crew lowered three longboats into the water, then scurried down manropes slung over the side. Dropping into the boats, they began to accept barrels and chests lowered from the deck.

With a word to her men, Joanna climbed into the small rowing boat at the water's edge. Her two companions followed, and Zack pressed his strength to the oars.

With the first of the longboats loaded, the French crew pulled away from the ship, rowing hard toward the beach. Their boat passed her smaller vessel and she gave them a studying perusal.

Their bright neck scarfs and knitted jerseys, coupled with the set of their caps, rendered them decidedly French.

To a man, their hair was long and loose rather than plaited in pigtails as an English sailor might wear. The knives at their belts, their narrowed eyes and sneers made them appear cutthroats. Of course, to them, she and her brother were no more than young English *"rosbifs"* who had no understanding of a ship like the one on which the Frenchmen served. In that, they would be right.

She shivered and turned away from their harsh glares to fix her eyes on the ship and her mind on the task ahead.

The French brig loomed large as they drew close. A frisson of fear snaked down her spine when she looked up to see an ominous figure standing at the rail.

Like an apparition, he was dressed all in black, his features lost in the shadows beneath his tricorne. Even his hair, tied back at his nape, was black. One side of his coat was pulled back to reveal his hand resting on a pistol. From his waist hung a sword with a golden hilt.

She could not see his eyes, but she felt his penetrating gaze and shuddered. He appeared more pirate than merchant.

Joanna did not like dealing with an unfamiliar captain, but often she had no choice as they contracted for goods through agents. This one's frightening appearance gave her pause, but at least she no longer feared he might be a revenue agent.

Most of England was buying free traded goods but, rich or poor, noble or common, she never forgot smuggling was a hanging offense. It wasn't the typical pastime of an earl's sister, but she had decided long ago to ignore her qualms about her part in the illegal activities.

As soon as they arrived at the ship, Zack steadied their small boat and she reached for the rope ladder. "Stay with the boat," she reminded Freddie.

The climb was mercifully short. A moment later, she stepped onto the deck with Zack right behind her.

A quick glance told her the wood planks of the deck were clean and everything neatly stowed. The ship's crew were busy shifting casks, folding sails and coiling lines. Their wary glances told her the Frenchmen did not trust her and her men. Curious covert glances came her way over a shoulder or around a mast, and just as quickly were turned away.

A thick-chested man approached her. He had swarthy skin and dark russet hair, long to his shoulders.

"Is there a problem, M'sieur?" His voice was rough with a deep French accent. Though his tricorne shadowed most of his face, his downturned mouth exuded suspicion.

Thankful for her deep voice, she summoned her resolve and cast a glance toward the barrels and chests yet to be loaded. "Before I pay, I would see the goods."

"As you wish," the man replied, too politely for his harsh demeanor. He gestured to the casks and chests waiting to be loaded. She turned toward them but did not miss the look of disdain he gave his captain, as if to question a demand for inspection by what appeared to him a beardless youth.

It would not be the first time her authority had been questioned by the crew of a smuggler's ship.

Shrugging in what she intended as a very male gesture, she returned her attention to the goods cast in dim relief against the hull of the ship, for no lantern on deck had been lit.

Zack strode to the chests and lifted one of the lids. Unwrapping an oilskin bag, he pinched a bit of tea between his fingers, first sniffing, then tasting the dried leaves. Nodding his acceptance to her, he moved on to the casks. Drawing his knife, he was about to pry open the lid when the swarthy Frenchman went to the cask and deftly opened it.

Taking a tin cup from the nearby water cask, the Frenchman dipped the cup into the cask and handed it to Zack. "Ye'll find none better in all of France."

Zack sipped the liquid, carefully tasting. It would be clear, because the French did not color their brandy, nor did they dilute it. Only cognac, aged in oak barrels, had the rich cinnamon color.

"Ah," Zack breathed out, licking his lips. "Ye speak the truth. 'Tis fine."

As the examination of the cargo proceeded, the ship's captain never moved from the rail, but kept his attention focused on her. Now that she knew he did not mean to cheat her, that his goods were of fine quality, she ignored his intense perusal.

Nodding to the captain's swarthy mate, she reached into her pocket, lifted out a leather pouch and handed it to him. "We accept the cargo. Thank you for your courtesy." If her tone carried a hint of sarcasm, she did not mind. She hated being underestimated.

The Frenchman accepted the pouch, heavy with coin, and escorted her and Zack to the side of the ship. Zack climbed down the manrope and dropped into the small rowboat. Joanna quickly followed.

A last look up at the deck told her the captain still watched her. But with his face in shadows, she could not tell if his expression was hostile or benign.

"Well?" asked Freddie, looking to Zack as he reached for the oars.

"The cargo is sound." Then, shooting her a glance, Zack added, "'Twas still good we checked."

The ship's crew soon had the remaining barrels and chests loaded into the last of the longboats. They followed Joanna's small boat to shore.

With the end of her task in sight, Joanna's anxiety began to dissipate. Zack pulled the rowing boat up on the beach. Freddie jumped out and went to consult with the men.

By the time the French longboat made it to shore and the crew handed off their cargo, Joanna's men were already loading goods into the two wagons.

Freddie came back to her. "That's all of it, Jo. The wagons are nearly ready."

With a wave to Zack, who would drive one of the wagons, Joanna and Freddie went to where they had left their horses. Mounting up, she looked over her shoulder to see the French crew taking up their boats and preparing to set sail.

The lone figure in black standing at the rail turned to his crew.

Minutes later, the black brig slanted away into the gathering darkness.

Joanna and her men headed up the narrow road leading to Chichester, seven miles north. Tonight they would color and thin the brandy and parcel the tea into smaller pouches. Soon, the storerooms of The Harrows would be bulging with stock.

It had been her idea to use her family's estate near Chichester as a place of temporary storage for the smuggled goods. Wagons and carts frequently came and went unnoticed and Richard's business in the House of Lords often kept him in London.

What had begun with Joanna's baskets of food for the village poor had blossomed into a full-fledged venture in ill-gotten gain. Dangerous though it may be, she was at the center of it all. The need to help the people she cared for compelled her to accept the risks.

She urged her mare to a canter, mindful of the tasks awaiting her. Tomorrow, Richard would host a reception for the Prime Minister and she must be ready. William Pitt's Tories had won the general election, a cause for great celebration. Many in London's nobility would attend. Her brother, the Earl of Torrington, would not be pleased if his hostess were ill prepared.

"Make ready to sail!" Jean Donet shouted, giving Émile a look that spoke of the need for haste. Jean would not linger offshore of Bognor with revenue cutters prowling the waters of the Channel.

"To Chichester Harbor, *Capitaine*?" asked Émile, raising a thick russet brow.

At Jean's curt nod, Émile bellowed over the heads of the crew, "Cross the headsails! On the fore, wear 'round and brace sharp!"

As soon as the words were out of his mouth, the lines surged and the sails flew to their new positions on the port side. Billowing and snapping taut, they emerged into the perfect white curves of a well-trimmed rig.

Jean shared a pleased look with his quartermaster as *la Reine Noire* turned her head and swiftly gathered way, white foam flowing out from under the carved queen on her bow. There was nothing Jean liked so much as being free of the land.

Now that they were under way, he turned to his second mate, Lucien Ricard. The tall sailor was easily identified by his red knit cap and the stray white hairs trying to be free of it. "M'sieur Ricard, take the helm, *s'il vous plaît*, and set a course to Chichester Harbor."

"Oui, Capitaine." Lucien acknowledged the order in a clipped tone as he headed to the quarterdeck. "South around Selsey Bill, then due west till we fetch Hayling Light."

Jean turned to Émile. "Join me for a drink? Our English friends did not get all the brandy we carry. I've a cask of cognac held in reserve."

Émile grinned and followed Jean down the aft companionway to his cabin, his home when he was at sea. He had named his ship the *Black Queen* for Marie Antoinette's spendthrift ways. But no matter her name, Jean loved his brig and knew well every creak emanating from her timbered decks, every sound whispered from the shrouds. Lorient might claim the place as his home, but his ship had his heart.

The captain's cabin was not so elegantly appointed as his hillside home in Lorient or his townhouse in Paris, but it contained all he needed: his charts, his nautical instruments, his books, his weapons and a fine mahogany shelf bed with a velvet cover the same blue as the French royal flag.

Jean stepped over the threshold, his eyes alighting on his cabin boy, Gabriel Chastain, who was busy freshening the finery Jean would don tomorrow. Then he must appear the nobleman he had been forced to become.

"Gabe, two glasses of cognac."

The lad dipped his head. *"Oui, Capitaine."* Brushing dark curls from his plump cheeks, Gabe darted to where the glasses and a flat-bottomed flagon of cognac rested on a fenced tray in the center of the pedestal table.

Gabe had joined the ship during the years Jean had been a privateer in the American War. To his great pleasure, the lad had the instincts of a gentleman's *valet de chambre* and catered to Jean's standards.

Along with the rest of his crew, Gabe had stayed on after the end of the war. A little smuggling on the side in defiance of the English authorities allowed the ship's company the excitement they once knew, and the extra coin kept them content.

When they were not on the ship, many of them lived in Lorient, *la Reine Noire*'s home port in Brittany.

Jean pulled his pistol from his waist and took off his sword. Setting both on the table, he accepted the glass Gabe handed him.

The cat that had been lounging on Jean's bed jumped to the deck, sauntered to Jean's chair and leapt into his lap. He idly stroked the animal's black fur. Franklin began to purr.

Émile dropped into the chair beside him. "Ye've a way with cats, *Capitaine*."

Jean gazed down at the cat whose golden eyes were now closed. "Why, I cannot imagine. I do nothing to encourage them." The feline's purr became loud and rhythmic, ebbing and flowing like the tide.

"I remember the day he followed ye through the streets of Lorient and back to the ship as if ye had summoned him." Émile's mouth twitched up on one side. "Are ye sure ye do not carry a magical pipe?"

Jean chuckled. "The Pied Piper called rats, *mon ami*, not cats."

"Eventually he called children, *non*?"

"So he did. But only for revenge on those who refused to pay him his due. I can hardly blame him. In Franklin's case, I am certain it was cream he wanted when he followed me. He manipulates Cook to get his daily ration as surely as Benjamin Franklin manipulated France into giving him millions. The cat is clever, which is why I gave him the name. Even the most ruthless of my men save the animal bits of fish. He's well on his way to becoming as rotund as his namesake."

The cat pressed his ear into Jean's hand. He obliged the animal by giving it a scratch.

Émile took a draw on his brandy. "Yer mention of Dr. Franklin reminds me. I heard the American has become a champion of that huge air balloon we saw floating over the Tuileries."

Jean remembered the giant balloon from the last time he was in Paris. It was all anyone talked about.

"M'sieur Charles manned that one himself. 'Twas a courageous act. Now that America has her freedom, Dr. Franklin will be looking for things to occupy his mind. I can understand why the inventor would have great interest in M'sieur Montgolfier's curious balloons."

The faint moonlight coming through the stern windows drew Jean's attention as it often did. He tossed the cat from his lap and crossed the cabin, barely noticing the rolling of the ship beneath his feet.

For a moment, he stared out the windows at the moonlight dancing on the waters in the ship's wake. Then looking to the shore they'd just left, his thoughts wandered back to the English smugglers. Something niggled at the back of his mind.

"What did you think of the English smuggler who insisted on seeing our goods?"

"Young and mebbe a trifle arrogant," came Émile's reply, "but I respect him for his caution. Ye would have done the same."

"Probably..." In his mind, Jean pictured the slender form, the well-turned calves and the smooth skin of the young man's cheek revealed beneath the brim of his hat. The voice had been low enough to be a young man, but the more Jean considered what he had seen, the more he became certain this "he" was a "she".

Women sometimes participated in smuggling. Perhaps she was one of the village women aiding her husband, most likely the tall Englishman with the scarred face. But her speech, though terse, sounded genteel. Moreover, English countrywomen did not usually do the talking in smuggling transactions. A mystery he might solve if he decided to make another run on his way to France. He still had a wealth of goods in his warehouse on Guernsey Island to unload.

Gabe came to stand beside him at the window. "Sir, your clothes are ready for the reception. With your leave, I would see Cook about your supper."

"Good lad. Some food would be most welcome." Jean watched the boy as he made his way to the cabin door. Gabe was about the same height as the young English smuggler, but he had a masculine swagger unlike the leader of the smugglers. The difference made him think his suspicion had been correct.

"After Chichester, we sail to London?" inquired Émile from where he sat at the table.

Jean turned from the window, his half-filled glass in hand. "That is still my plan. It has been over a year since my daughter wed the English captain. There have been letters, of course, but tomorrow's reception for their Prime Minister will be the first time I will have the chance to see for myself if Claire is happy."

"Does she know of yer elevation to the title?"

"I sent her a message as soon as I received word."

Émile's smile softened his harsh countenance. "I would like to see the little one." Jean's daughter, whom Émile fondly called "little one", always brought a smile to the quartermaster's craggy face.

Jean took a sip of his cognac. "I thought to accept her invitation to travel with her and her husband to London while you sail *la Reine Noire* to meet me there. You should arrive in time to attend the christening for my namesake."

"*Oui*, I remember the promise her husband made ye."

"The very one." Jean was inwardly pleased the son his daughter had given her English husband would bear Jean's name. Though he had reached the age of forty, he would hardly be a doddering grand-père and could teach the lad much about the sea. "The crew might enjoy some time in London."

Émile nodded. "As long as they can eat on the ship, the crew will not complain. Ye do not serve ordinary seamen's fare, *Capitaine*. They have grown used to brioche for breakfast and French cooking for dinner. The English eat very little bread and call themselves economical because they have no soup or dessert."

"The English dinner is like eternity," Jean remarked. "It has no beginning and no end. And nowhere save England do people drink worse coffee. How they endure such a prodigious quantity of brown water, I shall never know. But we need have no concern when we dine at Claire's table. She wrote to tell me she has finally hired a French cook."

Émile laughed. "I shall look forward to that. And after London, what then?"

Jean patted the pocket of his coat, reminded of the letter from his father's lawyer that had arrived just as they sailed from Lorient. *J'ai le regret de vous informer...*

He let out a breath. "I must return to Saintonge. The funeral for my father and brother will have occurred by then, which is just as well. My father would not have wanted me to attend."

He thought for a moment. "If the *maître du château* is still the same one, he is a capable estate manager. And the servants under him will see all is done as it should be." He smiled to himself. "I wonder how they will react to the disowned younger son becoming the master."

Jean twisted his glass in his hand, brooding over the other matter.

"Something troubles ye?"

His gaze met the deep-set brown eyes of his quartermaster, the man to whom he owed a life debt and his friend for many years. "You know me too well, Émile. *Oui*, there is more. It seems my brother left a child and named me her guardian."

"A child?" Émile asked incredulous. "Was there no wife?"

"There was, but she died some years ago. There is only the young daughter, Zoé. Given our strained relationship and my rather dangerous pursuits these last years, I am surprised Henri would place her in my hands."

Émile shook his head. "Likely he did not expect to die as young as he did. A carriage accident is a bad way to go. Struck down in the road like a stray dog—no valor, no honor, not even a chance to confess."

"But to charge me with seeing to his daughter…"

"Ye have been a good father to Claire, *Capitaine*. He might have remembered that. And now the estate, the vineyards and the wealth of the Saintonges are yers." Émile pursed his lips and lifted his heavy shoulders in a shrug. "Not that ye need 'em."

"I do not even want them," Jean said dismissively. With the *richesse* he had built in the decades since his father had cast him out, he no longer resented the loss of his heritage. "But I cannot refuse to care for my own flesh and blood."

He attributed Claire's good upbringing to her early years with her mother and, after Ariane's death, the teaching of the Ursuline Sisters of Saint-Denis, not to anything he had done.

"There must be something more behind Henri's bequest. My father ordered Henri to break contact with me and he complied, though not happily. A decade ago, he sent me a letter expressing his regret for the family lost to me and telling me his wife had finally conceived." He paused, reflecting. "Still, entrusting me with his only child is more than I could have foreseen."

Émile raised a brow. "So, now that he has, ye're to be a father once again."

Jean gave his quartermaster a sharp glance. "We will see."

Chapter 2

The Harrows, near Chichester, West Sussex

At the bottom of the stairs, the sound of a flute caused Joanna to veer from her intended destination and strike out for the music room.

Her grandfather, the first Earl of Torrington, had built The Harrows as a grand estate for his family. The three-story rectangular house, outbuildings and stables were his creation, but Joanna's parents had changed a charming room in one corner of the house with south-facing windows into a music room for the family. Each of their children had been encouraged to become proficient with an instrument. Joanna could play a fair cello but nothing like the talent her mother had displayed.

"You are late!" Freddie scolded, setting down his flute as she entered. The light from the branched candlestick on the table where he'd propped up his music score set his face aglow.

His auburn hair, darker than hers, was tied back in a queue. It made him appear years older, and his light brown coat made his brown eyes seem darker. Underneath the coat, a thin slice of his moss green waistcoat revealed elaborate gold brocade trim. She smiled to herself thinking of the pains Freddie had taken with his attire.

"At least I am ready," she told him. "What about Tillie?" Her younger sister, Lady Matilda West, nineteen and relishing the idea of her first Season, would be anxious for the evening's celebration. It marked not just the Prime Minister's Tories having swept the general election, but one of the first social events since Tillie's come out. Unlike Joanna, her sister looked forward to balls, house parties and... marriage.

"Tillie popped her head in a few minutes ago but left to look for you. Richard, too, has been asking for you."

"It takes a lady so much longer to dress than a gentleman, Freddie. I'll not bore you with the details, but stays and petticoats are a nuisance, and that does not begin to describe what I must endure to have fashionable hair. Piles of curls must be added to produce this coiffure. Without Nora's skill, I'd not be standing here now."

Joanna smiled at the thought of her maid's fussing, a whole hour of chatter that was as much a part of her toilette as the pulling and poking of hairpins to secure her curls. Nora was Zack's sister, as small and talkative as he was big and taciturn. As if the same litter had produced both a lap spaniel and a mastiff, no two siblings were ever so little alike. Both had brown hair, but Nora's eyes were green, while Zack's were hazel. And Nora was more attractive than her scarred brother would ever be handsome.

Freddie gave her an admiring glance. "Well, you look beautiful, so I suppose your maid deserves your praise." He picked up his flute and gave her a smirk. "'Tis quite a change from last evening."

She curtsied deeply and mirrored his smirk. "Why, thank you, kind sir. And you, little brother, are quite dignified this night."

Freddie smiled, the mouthpiece of his flute paused in front of his lips. "By the bye, where have you been all day?"

"In the village. I had to assure the brandy was properly diluted and doused with burnt sugar. And there were deliveries to arrange." It was only after Joanna's eyes had been opened to the plight of the poor in Chichester that she realized the tea and brandy her family consumed were made reasonable in cost because they were unaccustomed, which is to say smuggled, goods. And some who looked the other way, like the vicar, received his tea at no cost. After a run, there were many to satisfy so that their trade could proceed unhindered.

"The vicar?"

Joanna nodded. "Aye. And the proprietor of the White Horse Inn was running low on his supply of brandy."

"I could have helped." Her brother looked disappointed that she had not included him.

"There was no need. Zack did much of the mixing. Besides, I wanted to look in on the Ackermans. The whole family is ill with the ague; the mother is only now recovering. Nora and I took them some broth, bread and tea, then stayed to see to the children." The worried faces of the younger ones, concerned about their mother since their father had died a year ago, lingered in Joanna's mind. "I will go again tomorrow."

"Be prepared for Richard to expect you in London."

Joanna sighed. "Oh, dear. I was hoping to escape this Season."

"Not likely, but I can keep things going with Zack and the others till you return."

"I will try and avoid London if I can." The back of Joanna's throat began to itch and, with a sudden intake of breath, she sneezed. "Ah choo!"

"Over there," said Freddie in a quieter voice, pointing to a chair in the far corner of the room.

Asleep with her cat, Aloysius, curled up in her lap, Aunt Hetty reclined in a blue-gray gown the color of her eyes, currently hidden beneath closed lids. A swath of white lace graced her bodice and cascaded from her elbows. Her unpowdered silver hair was simply dressed. "You might have told me. What if she'd heard us?"

"No chance of that. She's not likely to be hearing anything."

Casting a glance at her aunt, she noted the steady rise and fall of her chest, satisfied she was truly asleep. "Your flute playing put the old girl to sleep?"

Freddie fought a smile. "I'm sure it helped."

Aunt Hetty had joined their household after their mother's death and brought Aloysius with her. To Joanna's thinking, the white cat seemed an odd-looking creature. One large black splotch covered most of its left side and a black ring circled the base of one ear. Its eyes were a stark gray.

Unlike the cats that frequented the stables, this one made its home inside The Harrows proper where he caused Joanna to sneeze and her eyes to water. "That cat!" She drew a handkerchief from the fold of her gown and dabbed at her eyes. "Before I turn into a puddle of tears and my eyes start burning, I'd best go find Richard and Tillie."

Freddie resumed his flute playing as she sniffed and headed for the door.

"Do not tarry overlong!" she slung over her shoulder. "The guests will soon be here. And bring Aunt Hetty!"

She loved her brothers and her sister, and held them especially close since their parents and eldest brother, William, had died. Both her father and Wills had been soldiers, her brother having served in the Coldstream Guards. Thankfully, neither Richard nor Freddie showed any interest in a military career, their only swords those that formed a part of a gentleman's attire.

As she entered the parlor, a small group of musicians in one corner had begun playing a piece by Mozart. Relieved to see no guests in sight, she scanned the room to make sure all was ready.

The ivory silk brocade chairs and settees had been neatly arranged around the edges of the room, per her instructions, to allow the guests to circulate freely and reveal more of the elegant floral design of the Axminster carpet.

On the walls hung the familiar portraits of her father, mother and grandmother. The room was ablaze with light from the candles set in sconces and the brass chandelier hanging from a medallion in the center of the scrolled ceiling.

On the sideboard, a tray of glasses filled with champagne, brandy and wine awaited the first guests.

The servants had followed her instructions; all was ready.

Checking her appearance in the golden-framed mirror hanging above the sideboard, Joanna touched the narrow band of lace around her bodice and pulled on the lace at her cuffs. She smiled as she recalled her modiste telling her the delicate lace had come from a French smuggler's warehouse on Guernsey.

"'Tis one of 'the French islands'." the woman told her. "Though I cannot imagine why they call them that when they are under the Crown." Joanna was certain the modiste's revelation of the source of the lace had been designed to shock her, but Joanna had not been shocked. Instead, her first thought had been to ask Zack to add lace to their next order.

It had taken her maid much time to fashion Joanna's thick head of hair into something approaching acceptable but, with a parting glance in the mirror, she was pleased to see the denizens of the *ton* would find no fault with her mound of curls. She might spend her nights in breeches, meeting ships carrying brandy and tea, but no one would suspect a darling of English Society—the image she encouraged—had a secret life as a smuggler.

The frippery might be her best disguise.

"There you are!" Richard exclaimed as he strode into the parlor. Tillie was at his side, some of her long red curls dangling to her shoulders. "The guests will be arriving any moment. Where are Frederick and Aunt Hetty?"

"On their way, I expect." She gave her brother a studying perusal. Beneath his fine attire, Richard announced his restlessness by fidgeting with a gold button on his waistcoat. She brushed a speck of lint from the sleeve of his black coat. Trimmed in gold, it complemented well his powdered and queued hair.

Tillie's brown eyes glistened, her smile wide. "Oh, Jo, won't it be glorious to meet the leaders of the new government? I can hardly stand still! Freddie told me Prime Minister Pitt and his friends, Mr. Eliot and Mr. Wilberforce, are all young and unmarried!" Tillie's pink silk gown, heavily adorned with lace and ruffles, rustled with her petticoats. The gilding suited her perfectly and might attract one of those men. Though at nineteen, she could look forward to more than one Season before Richard accepted some swain's proposal.

"Don't let them see your enthusiasm for the leg-shackled state," Richard chided their younger sister, "or you will have them running for the door. Right now, Pitt and his friends care only about politics. If you find you cannot follow their conversation, just look pretty and smile sweetly and you will attract your share of suitors, I've no doubt."

Tillie pouted at Richard and flounced out of the room. Joanna knew her sister would not pout long. Her enthusiasm for her first Season was too great.

Richard frowned at Tillie's departure and then turned to Joanna.

"Do not fret, Brother. All will be well. Tillie is in her element and will, no doubt, charm your guests."

"Joanna," his tone turned serious, "it is not Matilda I would see betrothed this year, but you. I think you should come with me to London now that the Season's on. Aunt Hetty will be acting as chaperone for Matilda, so you can be free to attend the events you desire. Make tonight's reception a beginning. Many men of your rank will soon be arriving. Some will be looking for wives. Do manage to encourage one of them, won't you? At five and twenty, I cannot command you to find a husband as you are of age, but 'tis nevertheless time you wed."

She shook her head, trying to discourage him, but he continued.

"I have it on good authority the family of Lord Hugh Seymour is looking for a bride for him." She listened with one ear.

"Now that peace is here, Seymour has taken up with Prince George and the two are capering about London together. I understand Seymour's family would rather he were settled."

"Capering about with Prince George," she repeated, "no doubt drinking and debauching, for which the prince is famous. Excellent qualifications for a suitor, I'm sure." The last bit she had spoken with intentional sarcasm.

"Well, Lord Hugh will be here tonight and he has much to commend him: he is young, considered handsome of face, well mannered and, as you would prefer, a man of good height. Too, he acquitted himself well as a naval captain in the American War as a part of the Channel Fleet."

"You forgot to mention he is a rake."

A storm was brewing on Richard's face. "He may be that now but, with marriage, he might well reform." At her doubtful look, he added, "If Seymour doesn't appeal, there is Henry, Lord Hood, who is a mere half-dozen years your senior."

"Stop!" She held up a hand. "I will hear no more of your matchmaking."

"Oh, and there is also Henry Bankes, the MP for Corfe and a great friend of Pitt's. He would have you to wife in a minute, were you willing. Just think; you could live in that great mansion he is remodeling. Why, 'tis larger than The Harrows."

"Oh, no you don't." She shook her head. "The Harrows is more than adequate for me. Besides, I consider marriage a dull affair punctuated by moments of misery. I would avoid it, perhaps forever."

Richard gave her an astonished look. "How can you put the epithet 'dull' to a state so many seek?"

"The men you list come to mind, Dear Brother. Besides being dull, marriage in the *ton* is often arranged and, therefore, poses great risk. I have observed the sad state of many women who marry. Few are happy. Many men do not take seriously their vows. Dare I mention Lady Worsley, forced to become a courtesan to survive because her husband, who does not want her, cut her off and will not grant her a divorce? Or my friend, Georgiana, Duchess of Devonshire? A beautiful woman with an indomitable spirit and a quick mind, yet you told me yourself the duke spends his nights at Brook's playing cards. And those are the nights he is not with his mistress. And then there is—"

Richard held up his hand, stopping her diatribe, a pity as she had only begun. The list of poor marriages in the *ton* was a long one.

"I'll not defend the nobility who carry on as if their vows mean little, Joanna, but best not to mention the duchess this evening. Her unwavering support for Fox in the election did not endear her to the Prime Minister."

"I would never do so, Richard, but back to my point, as you are still unwed at seven and twenty, you can hardly wag your finger at me."

"I'll not be a bachelor for long. Now that I have the title, I must wed. I do not seek a love match, but the Earl of Torrington must have an heir."

She let out a sigh. "How romantic." Then with greater enthusiasm, she leaned toward him and smiled conspiratorially. "I shall keep an eye out for a prospective broodmare with good teeth."

His brows drew together. "I can find my own wife!"

She had hoped to amuse, but it was clear she had only irritated him. "Very well," she quipped. "But, in the meantime, you need me at The Harrows." Joanna did not mention that the villagers of Chichester counted upon her, but it was the truth. Seeing to their welfare gave her life more purpose than did all the parties and balls.

Richard let out an exasperated sigh and set his jaw.

Joanna's protests were having no effect. He had become an immovable force. It was so like Richard. Their older brother William, despite his being the heir, had always been "Wills" to the family. Then there were Tillie and Freddie. And she was Jo. Not even their parents had called them by their full Christian names, except for Richard. He had always been "Richard", seemingly too proper to have garnered a nickname. And now he was Torrington. The title fit him like a glove, formal and without the possibility of a sobriquet.

Sensing his growing impatience, she decided to be agreeable. "If it pleases you, Brother, I shall consider marrying when you do."

He opened his mouth to say something when their butler Carter stepped into the room.

"My Lord, the first guests have arrived."

Joanna had met William Pitt before on one of her trips to London, but she had not observed him with his two closest friends, who were also of an age with her. A head taller than William Wilberforce and Edward Eliot, Pitt made a commanding figure in his black frock coat and ivory waistcoat.

Neither Pitt nor Eliot wore wigs, though both had powdered their brown hair. Wilberforce's dark unpowdered hair curled over his forehead and around his ears, the length of it carelessly tied back with a ribbon.

She and Richard greeted the three men and a footman offered them a brandy. Pleasantries exchanged, Pitt and his friends began to recount their travels in France the previous autumn. Eager to hear of their trip to the Continent, Joanna drew close.

Pitt launched in. "We first went to Reims. Only because the letter of introduction we managed to acquire at the last minute named a Monsieur Coustier there. Unbeknownst to us, the man is a grocer who lives behind his shop."

Eliot laughed. "We did well enough until the Lieutenant of the Police discovered our whereabouts and, because of our humble lodgings, thought us English spies in hiding."

Joanna was envious of their trip. Although she spoke French as well as any lady, she had not been to France or anywhere outside of England. Only young men of the aristocracy and wealthy gentry made the Grand Tour of the Continent. Not that a single trip to France was a Grand Tour, she consoled herself, but at least it was some foreign travel.

"Once the lieutenant learned Pitt's father was the Earl of Chatham," chimed in Wilberforce, "we were invited to dine at the palace of the archbishop where we enjoyed a good meal and were finally able to practice our French, which had been one of our goals."

"The abbé, only forty, was most gracious," offered Pitt. "To my delight, I learned the leaders of the French church are not so somber as our clergy. For one thing, they share my love of golf."

Wilberforce rolled his eyes toward Eliot. "We next went to Paris where it seemed the English were in possession of the town. Pitt promptly deserted us to go off stag hunting while Eliot and I took a carriage to Fontainebleau." He smiled at Joanna. "We had a desire to see the French king, who was there at the time."

She well understood. The French Court, about which she had heard much, was more a draw for her than hunting stags in the woods.

"We also had the chance to meet General Lafayette," put in Eliot, "the French aristocrat and celebrated general for the Americans."

"'Tis obvious why," Richard said. "He did them much good. But what was your impression of King Louis?"

Wilberforce exchanged a knowing look with his two companions. They must have heard his thoughts on the French monarch before. "When I first met him, I thought him a clumsy figure in immense boots. But I quite liked the queen. Marie Antoinette welcomed us heartily. As for the French Court, the opulence is overwhelming."

The Prime Minister nodded his agreement. "When I finally

got to Fontainebleau, I, too, was taken with the magnificence of the place. You cannot imagine—"

"And the French were taken with you," said Wilberforce, "crowding around to hear your every word."

Eliot winked at Joanna. "Pitt responded with great spirit, as always."

The Prime Minister looked up, a droll expression on his face. "I paid a visit to Dr. Franklin, the American statesman in Paris. Now, there is an interesting man."

The conversation continued as the men turned to London's politics, still riding on the crest of their victory. "We have much to do," said Pitt. "And being so near the coast tonight, I am reminded of the free traders who keep us afloat in tea. The East India Company complains of lost profits and the government of lost revenue. I shall have to do something about the rise in smuggling."

"Stronger enforcement?" suggested Richard.

Joanna's ears pricked at the suggestion.

Pitt pondered the idea. "I don't think that would change the situation overmuch. There is simply too much coast and too many smugglers. No, something different is called for."

Joanna could not hide her passion for the issue. Despite her inner voice urging caution, she had to speak up. "The East India Company's monopoly on tea keeps the price far too dear for many. That and the high duty only serve to increase the demand for cheaper tea. What more incentive does a starving laborer or an out of work sailor need to become a free trader? They can earn more in one night of smuggling than they can in a week of toiling in the fields or plying their nets."

The four men turned to her, astonished, as if a bird had alighted on her head. She pressed her lips together, knowing she had said too much.

"When did you gain an interest in the price of tea, Sister?" asked Richard, raising a brow.

"I read the newspapers and I am not immune to the talk in the village. 'Tis common knowledge."

Pitt smiled at her. "Your sister is correct. The trade in smuggled tea is so great, the vast majority of the British people drink the smuggled brew. And brandy is no different. Why, even the cognac we drink tonight might be the result of such an enterprise. And without you being aware, Torrington."

Joanna stifled a gasp and took a drink of her Madeira, forcing herself to display a calm appearance as if she was unaware the Prime Minister had just spoken the truth.

Richard sputtered, nearly spewing his drink. "I'm quite certain that is not the case."

"You'll find a way to stop the free traders," Pitt's friend, Eliot, encouraged him.

"First, I must apply myself to reducing the country's debt," said Pitt. "The American War has left our economy in shambles."

Eliot, Wilberforce and her brother nodded, agreeing with Pitt's assessment of the dismal state of the country's economic affairs.

Joanna lost interest, as the men reached for other topics. She sipped her Madeira, glad for the security it represented against what she expected to be a dull evening of polite conversation.

She had already heard the most interesting news.

After a bit, Pitt and his friends were drawn away, leaving her alone with Richard.

Henry Addington, newly elected Member of Parliament for Devizes in Wiltshire, came to join them. "Nice party, Torrington." Like the other men, he dressed in black, offset by a white waistcoat; his hair was powdered a dark gray. Tonight, Addington had arrived without his wife, who he told Richard had remained in London with their young children.

Joanna had met him several times before, as he was a good friend of her brother and a childhood friend of the Prime Minister. She thought him a bit pompous, but her brother appeared relieved to have his friend's approval.

Addington droned on about some new bill he intended to propose. Of an age with her brother, he sounded much older than his years. She was barely listening when a man in a Royal Navy uniform passed them. Joanna considered the tall man with mild interest.

Richard broke off of his conversation with Addington. "Commander Ellis, welcome!"

The commander paused and inclined his head to her brother. He smiled faintly at Joanna. His uniform was that due his rank: a white-lapelled dark blue coat trimmed in gold with gold buttons, a white waistcoat and dark blue breeches with white stockings and gold-buckled shoes. To her mind, he had not yet reached thirty. He had an attractive face framed by dark hair. His eyes were clear blue, and his long aquiline nose was that of an aristocratic Englishman.

"Joanna, may I present Commander James Ellis of His Majesty's Royal Navy?"

She offered her hand and Ellis bowed over it. "Lady Joanna, a pleasure. You grace the room with your beauty."

A flatterer. "Thank you, Commander. Most kind."

Addington greeted Ellis in perfunctory fashion. Richard introduced Addington as the new MP from Devizes.

"I know Devizes," said Commander Ellis. "'Tis just east of Bath."

"What is your ship?" Joanna interjected. "Is it stationed nearby?" She awaited his answer with a sense of foreboding.

The commander turned his blue gaze upon her. "As of this past November, I command the HMS *Orestes*." His pride obvious, he said, "She's an eighteen-gun sloop of war stationed at Southampton. Our mission is to intercept and check smuggling on the south coast."

"Oh." Taken aback, Joanna had never expected to meet the captain of a revenue ship and was surprised at how benign he appeared. But then, he had no idea she was among those he hunted. "And have you encountered many?" she asked innocently.

He indulged her a smile as if addressing a small child. "Why, yes. Some are only small luggers, but other larger ships carry as many guns as we do. At those times, it is much like a battle at sea during war." He gazed beyond her to a group of men surrounding the Prime Minister. "If you will excuse me, my lady, I must speak to Mr. Pitt."

"Of course."

As the captain strode off, Richard whispered into her ear, "He is in his early thirties and yet to wed, Sister."

She whispered back, "No doubt he is married to the sea, *Brother*."

"I do hope William will take on this smuggling menace," offered Addington, having missed her exchange with her brother.

"By his own words, he intends to," Richard replied.

Joanna worried for what it all meant. Between Pitt's determination to deal with smuggling and the good commander's pursuit of the free traders, she and her men were caught in a vise.

Joanna turned her attention to their guests and tried to act the calm hostess, checking the refreshment table where food was served and instructing the footmen as to what might be needed. Once that was taken care of, she went to speak with Aunt Hetty, who sat at one end of the room with two of her friends, ladies as old as herself.

When she inquired as to whether her aunt needed anything, Aunt Hetty replied, "Go see to your guests. I'm content to keep an eye on young Matilda from here."

Joanna followed her aunt's gaze to where Tillie was giggling with one of her friends, no doubt over some young man. "Ah." She smiled at the three ladies. "Then I shall leave you. Have a good evening."

Returning to Richard, she assured him all was well. He thanked her and resumed his conversation with Addington.

Joanna took solace in her wine as she surveyed the parlor's occupants. Everyone seemed to be enjoying themselves. She was pleased with her success as a hostess of the beau monde.

Suddenly, a man appeared at the doorway staring into the parlor with cold detachment. His dark eyes seemed to be searching for someone. His tanned olive skin was a stark contrast to the pasty white complexions of most of the men in the room. He wore his black hair unpowdered and tied back at his nape. His features were bold: a high forehead, black eyebrows, a straight nose and prominent cheekbones.

He cut a striking figure in a dark blue coat edged in cream silk flowers. At his throat and cuffs was a great mound of lace. Beneath the frock coat, an ivory silk waistcoat, embellished in the nattiest of fashion, shimmered.

She knew instantly he could not be English. Such ornate embroidery and so much lace would never be seen in Westminster where the current fashion for men favored a certain austerity. An Englishman attired like this one would be considered a popinjay. But to Joanna, his brooding dark elegance spoke of an uncommon masculine style.

He strode into the parlor, drawing curious glances from the gentlemen and nervous twitters from the ladies. Passing through the crowd, his searching gaze met Joanna's for only a moment yet, in that moment, excitement coursed through her veins. His obsidian eyes flashed with an intensity she had not encountered before. When his gaze moved on, she felt a keen disappointment.

His dark brows lifted as he headed for someone he appeared to recognize.

"Who is he?" she asked her brother.

Richard turned from his conversation with Addington to follow the subject of her attention. "Oh. If I am not mistaken, Sister, that is the new comte de Saintonge."

A French comte. Yes, he quite looked the part.

Addington huffed. "You invited a Heathen Frog to your reception for the Prime Minister?"

"Careful, old boy," chided Richard. "Pitt speaks well of his travels in France and 'tis rumored the comte was once a pirate. You wouldn't want him to get wind of your views or he might slit your throat some starless night."

Addington sputtered.

Richard's face took on a wistful look. "Besides, 'twas Lady Danvers who asked me if she could invite him. I can scarce deny the woman anything, no matter she is Lord Danvers' wife."

Joanna had long believed her older brother had a tendre for her friend, the baron's American wife. Seeing the longing in Richard's eyes as he looked toward Cornelia, she knew it to be truth.

"Well, Lord Hugh might have a different view. After all, he fought the Frenchies in the Channel."

Joanna sighed. Addington could be such a bore. She could not imagine how his wife, Ursula, put up with his rigid views. No wonder the woman had stayed home with their children.

Richard and Addington continued their conversation, but Joanna had stopped listening. Instead, she watched the French nobleman as he arrived in front of a young woman with hair as black as his own and kissed her on each cheek.

Joanna wondered if so elegant a man could, in truth, be a pirate. Still, she could not deny the air of mystery about him or the intense fire in his dark eyes.

'Twas as if Lucifer himself had paid them a visit.

Chapter 3

Jean found his way through the crowded parlor to arrive in front of the two women for whom he'd been searching. He bowed to Lady Danvers and then kissed his daughter's glowing cheeks. Claire appeared to be happy, as happy as he'd ever seen her.

"Please forgive my being late. I was detained."

"Oh, Papa! I am so glad you are here!" Claire took his hands. "I have missed you so."

He looked into his daughter's dark blue eyes, her mother's eyes that had captured him more than two decades ago. *"C'est bien.* The English captain treats you well?"

"Oh, yes." Before Jean could comment, she looked up at him anxiously. "You will come to London, *oui*?"

"How else is your father to attend the christening?" asked Lady Danvers in her American accent. The baroness, in her mid-twenties, was a half dozen years older than his daughter, but her wisdom was beyond her years.

Always smartly gowned, typically in some pinkish color, her dark chestnut hair neatly swept up in a simple style, Jean had noticed her loveliness the first time he'd met her in London when he'd come for his daughter's wedding.

Claire laughed. "You are right, of course, Cornelia." Then turning to him, "But do you sail to London, Papa, or ride in our carriage with us?"

"If you still wish it, I will travel with you. My ship and my quartermaster M'sieur Bequel will meet me in London."

"Yes, of course we still wish it. I will look forward to seeing M'sieur Bequel again. I hope you invited him to the christening."

"I did. You know he will not have it otherwise."

"Wait till you see Jean Nicholas, Papa! He has your black hair and his eyes are changing color now. We think he might ultimately have Simon's golden eyes."

"Jean Nicholas." Jean rolled the name over his tongue. "I like the sound of it."

"A most remarkable babe," offered Lady Danvers. "And before you leave London, Monsieur Donet, I thought to have a soiree to celebrate the end of the war and our new friendship with France. In your honor, as it were. Not that the war stopped me from pursuing French fashion, you understand." She touched the ruffle on her bodice. "By the bye, have you met the Prime Minister? He only recently returned from Paris where he visited your king and my countryman Dr. Franklin."

Jean fought a smile. "I have not met the Prime Minister, but I have met our king and, of course, the American statesman Dr. Franklin." He need not say more. His daughter and Lady Danvers were aware that, with France's agreement, he had become a privateer for America, his letter of marque issued by Franklin himself. But neither knew of his work for Charles Gravier, the comte de Vergennes, France's Foreign Minister.

"Where has that husband of yours gotten to, Claire?" asked Lady Danvers.

"Right here," said a deep voice behind Jean.

Jean turned to see Captain Simon Powell carrying three glasses of champagne. As fair in coloring as Jean was dark, the Englishman and Jean's daughter made a handsome couple.

"I did not wait for the footman to circulate," Powell explained, as if in apology for leaving his wife, "but saw to the ladies' thirst myself."

Claire and Lady Danvers accepted the glasses of bubbling wine.

"I would never leave Claire for long," Powell assured Jean.

"Simon is a most jealous husband!" Claire exclaimed in what Jean took to be feigned annoyance.

Powell kissed her on the cheek and she returned him a smile. Jean was pleased at the affection he saw between them.

"'Tis not jealousy when a man guards what is his," he told Claire. He had once guarded her mother, a woman he had loved more than his own life, only to discover that, while he could protect her from other men, he could not save her from the sickness that had taken her life.

Lady Danvers gave him an assessing look. "An astute observation, Monsieur."

He acknowledged the compliment with an inclination of his head as Powell offered him the third glass of champagne. "Take mine, sir. I will get another."

Accepting the glass, Jean inwardly cringed at the title "sir". When had he crossed the line from youth to an age where a man in his twenties must pay him the respect due one's elders?

Powell left them, heading toward a footman on the other side of the room.

Watching him walk away, Jean sipped his champagne and thought to ask his daughter, "How many ships does Powell have now?"

"He still has the two you are aware of, and he is acquiring another. He wants to have a shipping company one day."

"A laudable ambition," said Jean.

Lady Danvers scanned the room, her gaze pausing on a tall man surrounded by others. "Wait here while I retrieve the Prime Minister. I know he will want to meet you, Monsieur."

Claire had only begun to tell Jean of her life since her marriage when Lady Danvers returned with the tall man on her arm and Lord Danvers at her side.

Since he recognized the baron, Jean acknowledged him. "Lord Danvers."

Lady Danvers introduced Jean to the English Prime Minister, giving Jean's title as the comte de Saintonge.

Jean added his congratulations to the others being expressed to Pitt. "A great victory, Prime Minister."

"Thank you," returned Pitt. "We are most pleased. I was in your country only a few months ago and my companions and I thoroughly enjoyed ourselves. I must ask, do you find France much changed now that the war has ended?"

"Changed?" Jean considered carefully what he might say. He would not speak of the unrest. "Only that France now struggles under a mountain of debt." It was true and all knew it. The decision to aid America had been the right one, but the war had left his country in grave financial trouble.

"France is not alone in that, Monsieur Donet," admitted Pitt.

Lord Danvers nodded his agreement.

"It will be my first task once my cabinet is convened to see what I can do about England's debt."

"I wish you well in that effort," said Jean. "'Twill not be easy. I doubt the common people in either country can bear more taxation."

Pitt gave him a knowing smile. "Then I shall not tax the common people."

Jean raised a brow. "You would tax the aristocracy?"

Pitt's eyes gleamed with purpose. "And the wealthy merchants."

Jean liked the young English Prime Minister and his enthusiasm for what would be a difficult task. "We should do the same in France, but I fear the effort would not be welcomed. Our nobles and clergy remain blithely ignorant of the mounting danger from a people taxed to support their luxurious lifestyle while having no political liberty."

"Monsieur le comte," said Pitt, "I grant that you may have

fewer political liberties in France. But as to civil liberty, from what I observed, the French have more of it than you may suppose. Voltaire was a great defender of such liberty, as I recall."

"You may be correct," offered Jean, "though at the moment, the civil liberty we possess does the French people little good." Jean enjoyed the conversation, but he would say no more. His last trip to Paris suggested a storm was coming. What good was civil liberty when the people had nothing to eat? Jean had been raised the son of a nobleman yet had made his own way the last score of years in a world that favored only the bold. The wealth he had amassed did not come from the noble birth so long denied him.

As the Prime Minister made to leave, he offered his hand to Jean. "Until we meet again, Monsieur. Perhaps in London?"

Jean shook Pitt's hand. "It would be my great pleasure."

Claire's husband returned, a glass of champagne in hand.

Lady Danvers addressed Jean and the Powells. "You must meet our host and his sister."

Lord Danvers agreed. The three of them finished their champagne and followed him and his wife across the room. Judging by the smiles she garnered from those they passed, the American woman had made many friends in the years she had been in England. Jean was unsurprised. She had an unassuming charm the staid English often lacked.

Moments later, Lady Danvers stopped before three auburn-haired young aristocrats.

Joanna watched the French nobleman approach with the black-haired girl and handsome blond gentleman, who, like the comte, had the tanned skin of one who spent much time in the sun. With them were Joanna's friend, Cornelia, and her husband.

"Joanna, my dear friend," said Cornelia, "and Lord Torrington and Mr. Frederick West, may I introduce Jean Donet, comte de

Saintonge, his lovely daughter Claire Powell and her husband Captain Simon Powell?"

Richard inclined his head. "Monsieur de Saintonge and Captain and Mrs. Powell, welcome to The Harrows."

Freddie chimed in, "Yes, welcome."

Joanna was glad Addington had taken his leave, for his views on Catholics might make for an uncomfortable encounter, particularly when the Catholic in question was a French nobleman. Freddie, on the other hand, had no such biases.

She extended her hand to the comte. "Indeed, we welcome you to our home and to England."

With an unmistakable air of distinction, the comte bowed over her hand and returned her greeting. "*Bonsoir*, Lady Joanna. I am at your service."

His hair, clubbed back in a queue and tied with a fancy velvet ribbon, was not solid black as she had once thought, but was threaded with silver, rendering him a very distinguished man in his ivory-filigreed coat. He spoke in a melodious French-accented voice and his lips, she noticed, were seductively curved.

Joanna wondered if the comte had a wife. If he did, she did not attend.

Turning to the couple just introduced, she echoed her eldest brother, "Captain and Mrs. Powell, it is so nice to meet you."

"We'll have none of that," interrupted Cornelia. "Claire is my good friend as are you, Joanna. Amongst us women, I'm afraid it must be Cornelia, Claire and Joanna."

Lord Danvers laughed. To the men, he said, "You see how it is. My darling wife remains the American and will have it her way, formalities be damned."

"We are delighted to be here," Captain Powell graciously put in, "no matter how we are addressed. I was most interested to meet the Prime Minister."

Powell was a tall golden man, so different from his French wife, though he obviously adored her, his amber eyes ever looking her way.

"Pitt is impressive," observed the comte. "Clever, too, I think. I envy you his enthusiasm for change."

Richard nodded his agreement. "England is lucky to have him."

Freddie listened intently, obviously happy to be included.

Captain Powell looked to Richard. "Your home is magnificent. 'Tis not often we get to West Sussex since my ships home port in London."

The comte smiled before he said, "And mine are most often in Lorient."

Ah, he has ships. But then a pirate would. Joanna met his intense gaze. "Are your ships engaged as merchantmen?"

"Often," he said, amusement dancing in his jet eyes.

His cryptic response left Joanna wondering what other business he might be engaged in. Most definitely he was a noble son of France, but she detected a flash of defiance in the depths of his dark eyes, making her wonder if his elegant attire and noble manners were merely a ruse. Beneath them might lurk a beast, tamed for the night, who could well be the pirate Richard had spoken of.

Despite her reservations, she found herself thoroughly fascinated. "Was I correct in addressing you as Monsieur le comte? Or, is it more proper to say Monsieur de Saintonge, Monsieur Donet, or my lord?"

"M'sieur Donet, *s'il vous plaît,*" he responded. "The title is new and unexpected. I am... unused to it. And in France, we do not speak of lords and ladies as you do here. My surname will do."

"Very well." Monsieur le pirate probably would not be well received. Besides, Richard had said it was only a rumor.

"My papa is here for our son's christening," ventured Claire Powell, her eyes lit with excitement. The young woman strongly resembled the comte, save for her blue eyes and feminine features.

He must not have a wife, Joanna thought, for a wife would not miss such an auspicious occasion as a grandchild's christening.

Freddie, only a few years younger than Claire, could not seem to take his eyes off Powell's beautiful young wife.

"The Powells' young son is named after Monsieur Donet," said Lord Danvers. "And he along with my wife and I are to stand as godparents."

"You must see him, Joanna," urged Cornelia. "He's a beautiful baby. We are so proud to be asked to be godparents with Monsieur Donet."

The comte's piercing gaze fixed on her. "Will you be coming to London, Lady Joanna?"

An hour ago, Joanna would have defied her brother's insistence she go with him to London, but meeting the comte's dark eyes the only response that came to her lips was, "Why, yes."

Chapter 4

The village of Chichester

The next morning, Joanna, Freddie and Nora set off for Chichester. Freddie drove the wagon, the three of them sharing the bench seat. The day was sunny and cold and, since they had only a few miles to travel, Joanna had not covered the supplies they were bringing to the Ackerman family.

Chichester had long been a market town, although no more than four thousand souls called it home at present. Joanna had always referred to it as "the village" because of its size in contrast to London. It might be a quiet, unassuming place, but in the center of town stood a great medieval cathedral, its spire visible even from the Channel.

The village had the usual collection of craftsmen, among them carpenters, blacksmiths, gunsmiths, tailors and shoemakers, who did their work in stalls and shops for all to see. And there were bakers, brewers and grocers. But once the American War ended, many sailors were left without jobs; and those who had supplied the ships that had once called Chichester Harbor home struggled to earn a living.

England levied duties on more than tea and brandy. The government taxed everything, including bricks, candles and soap. Farmers were among the poorest. Joanna had known this but until she met the Ackerman family, she had not made the village poor a part of her life. And now that they were, she could not leave for London without looking in on Polly Ackerman and her three children.

Just outside the village, Freddie pulled rein in front of the whitewashed cottage. A humble dwelling to be sure, but Daniel Ackerman had taken great pride in what he had been able to provide his wife and children. Polly had decorated the windows with muslin curtains and their beds with pretty bed covers made from scraps of fabric. She kept a clay vase of wildflowers on their worn table, which brightened the small space. Outside their door, a carpet of bluebells covered the floor of the ancient woodland.

The children seemed happy enough even after their father had died. But when the ague befell the family and their mother took ill, it was as if a cloud descended over the little home. The children, who recovered more rapidly than their mother, worried they might lose their only living parent. Joanna had seen the fear in their eyes and wished to dispel it. If smuggled tea would cheer the small family, she would provide it.

No one was about as Joanna and Nora climbed down from the bench seat. Freddie lifted the baskets from the wagon and handed them down. The wagon also held blankets, clothes and firewood.

Joanna knocked on the wooden door.

It opened almost immediately and the youngest of the Ackerman children, a blonde cherub of four years named Briney, greeted them as she leaned against the doorpost. She had two older brothers, ten-year-old Danny and six-year-old Nate.

Big blue eyes peered up at Joanna from a sweet round face. "Hello, m'lady. Mum's still in bed. Will ye see her?"

"Of course. That is one reason we have come." Taking a tart from the basket, Joanna gave it to the little girl. "I brought this for you. There is one for each of your brothers, too."

The child eagerly reached for the cherry tart and took a bite, smearing cherry juice over her mouth.

Joanna took that opportunity to enter. Behind her, Nora and Freddie followed.

The main room of the cottage was empty. "Where are your brothers?"

The child's expression was glum. "Danny and Nate are gathering wood, but Danny's not well yet."

Joanna and Nora set the baskets on the table in the room that served as parlor, dining room and kitchen. There was no fire in the stone fireplace and the air in the cottage was chilled. Little Briney had a shawl around her slender shoulders but nothing so warm as a woolen cloak. And her feet were bare. Many in the village did not wear shoes.

"We will soon have the cottage warm as bread in the oven," said Joanna, looking at Freddie and inclining her head toward the door.

Freddie gave her a nod and went to fetch the wood. Joanna and Nora began taking things out of the baskets. Sadly, the clay vase in the center of the table was devoid of flowers.

"While Nora sets out food, how about you take me to look in on your mother?"

Briney nodded and glanced toward the door to the bedchamber. The children slept in the loft. The bedchamber in the back that had been their parents' was now Polly's alone.

While still clinging to her half-eaten tart with one hand, Briney took Joanna's hand with the other and together they walked to the bedchamber. Joanna slowly opened the door.

Polly Ackerman lay in bed, her pretty face pale and her blonde hair tucked into a muslin mobcap.

Joanna walked to the bed and sat on the edge. Polly was not yet thirty, but heartbreak, sickness and worry had taken their toll, adding lines to her face. Reaching out her hand, Joanna touched Polly's pale forehead and breathed a sigh of relief. She was only slightly warm. "Has she eaten anything today?"

"Only the tea Danny brought her afore he went out."

Joanna had brought them a good supply of tea and bread when she'd come the day before, but she wanted to encourage Briney, whose sweet face wrinkled with concern. "'Tis good she is sleeping. The rest will help her get well." A smile spread across Briney's face and Joanna drew her into a hug as the child nibbled on her tart. "Don't worry, sweetheart, she will be fine."

Nora peeked her head in the doorway. "Freddie's got the fire going and the cottage will soon be warm. I've put the kettle on for tea."

"Thank you, Nora." Then turning to the child still in her arms, she said, "The boys will be hungry when they return. 'Tis good we brought food, don't you agree?"

Briney nodded her head vigorously. "Danny an' Nate are always hungry."

"Let's let your mother sleep." Joanna rose from the bed, taking Briney's hand that did not hold the tart. She led her back to the main room. Already it was warmer. "If you want to save the rest of your tart, there will soon be tea to go with it."

Briney set what was left of her tart on the table flanked by two long benches. Joanna lifted Briney onto one of them and placed some bread and cheese in front of her. "You can't live on tarts."

Briney nodded. "Yes I can."

Joanna chuckled. "Well, maybe you can, at that. When I was your age, I thought so."

Danny burst into the room carrying a stack of branches and sticks. Nate, at his side, had a bundle of wood under one arm. "Lady Joanna!" Danny exclaimed. "I didn't know you were coming today. Hello Freddie, Nora."

Where Briney and Nate favored their mother with blonde hair and blue eyes, Danny had the brown hair and hazel eyes of their father.

"We came to look in on your mother and to bring more

things for you and your family."

"Thank you, m'lady," said Danny. Only a youth, he had shouldered much responsibility, and Joanna's heart ached for him.

His cheeks were flushed. "Do you still have a fever, Danny?"

"'Tis not bad," he said, making light of it.

Not wishing to embarrass him or worry his siblings, she did not reply. But she was glad she had brought all the children warm jackets and shoes.

The boys laid the wood next to the fireplace where a warm fire now crackled, sending heat into the room.

Respecting Polly's preferences, Joanna reminded the children to wash their hands in the bowl on the sideboard before eating. Freddie added more logs to the fire. Everyone gathered around the table and Nora poured the tea.

The cups they drank from were not the fine porcelain used at The Harrows, but it mattered not to Joanna. Giving to this family was worth more to her than all the porcelain cups she would ever have.

Briney slipped from her chair and crawled into Joanna's lap. "Are you warm enough?" she asked her.

"Now I am," Briney answered in her little girl voice.

"How is Mum?" asked Danny, picking up a piece of cheese and dropping it on a crust of bread. His forehead creased with worry.

"She is only resting," Joanna assured him. "Soon she will be well and it will be summer and you will have months of warm weather."

"We have some things for you," said Nora. "Blankets, linens, clothes and food. The mistress and I will be going to London, but my brother, Zack, will be keeping an eye on you and can help with anything you need."

"Is he the big man?" asked Nate.

Joanna met Nora's gaze and they both laughed. "Aye," said Nora. "The big one."

"I'm not going to London," Freddie put in, "so I will be dropping by from time to time."

Neither she nor Freddie mentioned the smuggling that had produced the tea they had brought or the coins she would send the Ackermans from her share. It was enough they knew she and Freddie wanted to help.

Joanna hugged Briney. "When we are done here and I've seen your mother has something to eat, how would you like to pick some flowers for the table?"

The cherub's eyes lit up and she clapped her cherry-stained hands. "Yes, oh yes!"

On the road from Sussex to London

Lord Torrington had tried to persuade Jean to stay at The Harrows, but he, the Powells and the Danvers had gracefully declined. They did not wish to impose upon their host after the lavish reception he had given for the Prime Minister.

The Danvers had reserved rooms at the White Horse Inn in Chichester for their party, so Jean had thought to have a restful night's sleep. But in the middle of the night, he'd awakened with the face of Lady Joanna West in his mind. Their exchange at the reception had been brief, yet it had led to the momentary impulse to ask her if she would be coming to London. His desire to see her again surprised him.

Shortly after breakfast, they had departed Chichester. Jean, Claire and her husband took one carriage and the Danvers the other.

Travel by carriage, whether from Sussex to London, or from Le Havre to Paris, always reminded Jean of the reason he preferred traveling by ship. He had the changeable nature of the sea to contend with, but the motion was less jarring and the challenge of being in charge of one's own destiny ever appealed.

Powell's carriage was much like the one Jean kept in Paris, a fine, black town coach with good springs and well-padded seats covered in tufted velvet. According to his son-in-law, the roads had improved in the last decade but, even so, the ruts rendered the ride a bumpy one. To his mind, the roads in France were better but not so much they afforded a continuously smooth ride. He was thankful it had not rained, else they would have been mired in mud.

At day's end, after many stops to change horses, they arrived at the Angel Posting House in Guildford in Surrey. The coachman pulled rein and, a moment later, the footmen opened the door.

Jean considered the three-story inn, painted white with black trim, a typical English coach house. He followed Claire and her husband inside to find the Danvers waiting for them amidst a large crowd clustered around the bar, overflowing into the common room. Jean had never been happier to be handed a glass of brandy and thanked Lord Danvers profusely.

"As you see," remarked Cornelia, "spring brings many to London; hence the inn is quite crowded."

"To afford us privacy," said Lord Danvers, "I have reserved a private room in which we might sup once you have seen your rooms."

Soon after, they gathered in the small private room for a meal of English beefsteak, fried potatoes and cheddar cheese, accompanied by a pretty good French Bordeaux. Though a heavier meal than he was used to, it did suffice to sate his appetite after the long day on the road.

"'Tis not French fare, I grant you," said Lord Danvers, "but the brandy and wine are French and perhaps that serves to make up for it."

Jean didn't want the gracious man to think him ungrateful. "The wine is quite good. On my ship, we dine on simple fare. Fish and poultry form the mainstay, of course. But we often pick up supplies from Guernsey. In Lorient and Paris, the meals might be more elaborate, as they would be in London."

Powell spoke up. "Claire taught the Irish cook aboard my schooner the *Fairwinds* a few things about spices and soups, so the crew now asks for the French dishes." He grinned. "I was already enamored by the food."

"Is *the Fairwinds* in London?" asked Lord Danvers.

Powell glanced at his wife before answering. "Aye, but after the christening, I will be taking her out for a short while."

"And your ship, Monsieur Donet, is on its way to London?" asked Cornelia.

"*Oui*, under the command of my quartermaster, M'sieur Bequel. You will meet him at the christening. He is quite fond of my daughter."

"M'sieur Bequel has known me since I was a girl," offered Claire.

Cornelia smiled. "There will be much to do in London now that the Season's on. The christening, of course, but also plays, concerts and a soiree or two."

"Cornelia loves to entertain," put in Danvers.

After supper, they were all of a mind to seek their beds, as a full day of travel awaited them on the morrow.

Jean mused over the possibility of seeing again the intriguing Lady Joanna.

Chapter 5

London

Jean had agreed to stay with his daughter and her husband until his ship arrived, so the morning after their arrival in London he shared brioche and coffee with them in the room where they took their *déjeuner*.

Bathed in light from the many windows looking out on the shimmering waters of the Thames, the yellow-painted room welcomed the morning sun like the mythical Aurora greeting the dawn.

"Did my daughter introduce you to brioche?" he asked his son-in law. Like Jean, Powell had made his own way in the world. Both had spied for their governments during the American War and had battled each other on the Channel. But those days were past. When Powell had promised to care for Claire, the enmity between them had died.

Powell set down his coffee and reached for Claire's hand, meeting her gaze across the table with endearing affection. "Our fondness for brioche was something we shared even before we decided we liked each other."

Claire laughed. "He served it to me for breakfast the first morning I spent on his ship. My mood was most foul. That was the morning I wrecked his cabin."

Powell laughed. "I remember it well. Her temper landed my books and instruments in a pile on the deck of my cabin."

When their meal was finished, Claire asked a footman to have Jean Nicholas' nurse bring him to the table to meet his grandfather.

A moment later, with an air of self-importance, an older woman carried the babe into the room. On her head, she wore a mobcap and around her ample middle was a crisp white apron. At Claire's direction, the nurse placed the babe into Jean's arms.

His sweet face reminded Jean of Claire at that age. Already Jean Nicholas had a head of dark hair.

Memories of a tiny cottage by the sea flooded his mind. Despite the fact he and Ariane had been poor, those had been good years, filled with love.

The babe smiled up at him and latched on to his finger. "He seems an easy-going contented child."

Jean looked up to see Claire returning him a look of mild reproach. "You have yet to witness his black temper, Papa. Whenever his feeding is late or his favorite plaything is moved out of reach, he quickly makes his displeasure known to all."

"You sound surprised," Jean said. "Did you doubt the Donet temper would emerge at some point?"

His daughter frowned. "Humph!"

Powell laughed behind his hand and, putting down his copy of the *Morning Chronicle*, reached for his son.

Jean placed the babe in his father's welcoming arms and glanced at his daughter. "Jean Nicholas will be all the stronger for it, Claire. You will see. A sea captain must not appear weak, as your husband can tell you. A temper applied in proper measure can tell the crew the captain is serious."

Claire's response was to lift her eyes to the ceiling.

Her husband, who had likely observed Claire's temper even after their marriage, merely smiled. The babe must have thought the smile was for him. He let out a squeal of delight.

To Jean, the scene over brioche and coffee had been highly amusing and assured him his daughter fared well with her English husband. It was clear the love the two shared made up for their many differences.

When the nurse reclaimed the baby, Jean stood and wished his daughter and her husband a fine morning. "I am for Oxford Street to buy my grandson, who is also to be my godson, a worthy christening gift."

"We will look for you at dinner," Claire replied. "I am going with my friend the Countess of Huntingdon to hear the Methodist, John Wesley. He is eighty, you know, but has not slowed down."

Jean raised a brow to his son-in-law. The Anglican clergyman who drew large audiences to his preaching was not unknown to Jean, but Claire was Catholic.

Powell shrugged. "My wife and the countess have met with Mr. Wesley before. They admire him greatly. While Claire is with the countess, I will be seeing to my ships, but I will return for dinner."

By the time Jean arrived on Oxford Street, it was already bustling with shoppers, most of them ladies with their parasols lifted to shade their faces from the sun. For London, such weather in April was unusually fine.

He left the hackney at one end of the street and strolled along, tipping his tricorne to the women who offered him their smiles. In his years as a privateer, he had gained an aura of danger and knew it to be a strong lure for many women. But the memory of the blue-eyed woman he had loved long ago kept him from meaningless assignations.

Much negative could be said of London's streets, ever dirty and plagued with foul smelling mud puddles. However, Oxford Street was entirely removed from such prosaic environments.

Though the street itself was packed earth, next to the shops was pavement inlaid with flagstones, allowing shoppers to stop and gaze into shop windows without muddying their shoes. He walked with determination, thankful for the dry pavement beneath his feet, for Gabe had shined Jean's leather boots just before he left the ship.

In the middle of the street, a long row of lacquered coaches awaited their owners.

He passed a watchmaker's shop, then a fabric store and a china shop before he spotted a confectioner's establishment. He could not pass by without purchasing some sweets for Claire. It had been long since he'd indulged her childhood sweet tooth and it cheered him to be able to do so again. Stuffing the packet of sweetmeats into his pocket, he returned to his mission.

For his godson, he wanted something unusual, something that would remind the boy of his destiny, which *naturellement*, must be the sea. A sextant, the essential tool of every sailor, was far too precise an instrument for a child. A silver cup was the traditional gift, but the lad would likely receive many of those from the well wishers invited to the christening. Jean wanted to give his namesake a unique memento of the occasion.

He paused in front of the silversmith's window. The glass projected into the street so that the goods displayed could be seen from three sides. Many well-crafted items were shown to advantage, including an array of silver cups, small boxes and eating utensils. He was about to pass on when his gaze fixed on an item in the center of the window: an extraordinary table clock set upon a small pedestal draped in dark blue velvet.

He had come across a similar planetarium clock in Paris the year before. A work of art, the gilded *Pendulette de table avec planétarium* rested on a base of white marble balanced on three golden hooves. It kept time on its round watch face, white with black hands. Above the watch, inside a crystal globe, a small earth rotated around a larger, golden sun in perfect real time. The other five planets, shown as smaller balls, some silver, some gold, rotated on arms—up, down and around—in relation to the constellations that were precisely etched on the crystal globe.

C'est magnifique!

In Paris, he had stared at the clock for an hour, fascinated by its movement. Now, as if an omen had presented itself, the same clock appeared once again. This time he meant to have it and bestow it upon Jean Nicholas.

A very special gift indeed.

The shop bell jingled as he entered and strode to where the silversmith stood over his counter polishing some silver object.

"Sir?" The gray-haired man looked up as Jean arrived at the counter. "May I show you something?"

"*Oui*, the celestial globe clock in the window."

"Ah, a Frenchman who knows what he wants! Then you must recognize what a rare item the clock is. In England, we call them Orrery chronometers after the Earl of Orrery to whom one was given. I only recently acquired this exquisite specimen from a dealer in Paris."

Jean followed the thin man to the window where he lifted the clock from its pedestal and held it up. Again, the planetarium's movement and the solar system contained in the crystal ball drew his gaze. He did not ask the price for cost mattered not. "*Superbe*. I will take it."

"Very good." The silversmith dipped his head and carried the clock back to the counter.

It was then Jean noticed the two women in the far corner of the shop staring at him. Like a pair of bon bons, one was dressed all in pink and the other in blue, perfectly attired for a spring day.

He recognized the beautiful redhead at once. Lady Joanna West's light blue gown of fine silk adorned with ruffles complemented well her red curls swept off her neck. Atop them she wore a straw hat at a jaunty angle. Next to her stood a younger version of her in pink satin and lace.

Doffing his hat, he inclined his head. "Ladies."

"Monsieur Donet," Lady Joanna returned, coming forward.

"Might you be here on the same errand that brings my sister and me out today?"

Jean had not met the younger redhead but the resemblance was clear. It seemed Torrington and his siblings all bore the same stamp: red hair of one shade or another, brown eyes, pale skin and finely carved features. "That may be, for I seek a gift for the christening of my godson, Jean Nicholas."

"As do we," said Lady Joanna. She stood before him, her sister beside her holding some silver object. "I was so pleased when my friend Cornelia asked if we might attend. How delighted you must be."

"I am, particularly since the child is also my first grandchild."

Her eyes, he realized, were not merely brown like her sister's. They were the color of aged cognac, deep amber pools alight with intelligence, the kind of eyes a man could look at for the rest of his life. Her manner might be direct, but her full lips were enticing and her subtle smile beguiling.

She glanced at the girl in pink and back to him. "I don't recall if you were introduced to my sister at the reception."

He cast a glance at the younger woman and shook his head. "*Je regrette*, I did not have the pleasure." His mouth hitched up in a grin he knew would delight the young miss who was looking at him with an expression of keen interest.

"Well, then," Lady Joanna began, "may I present my sister, Lady Matilda West?"

The girl giggled. Perhaps only a year or two younger than his daughter, Lady Matilda's manner made her seem even younger. But then, Claire had been through much and was now married and the mother of a child—the key to fulfillment for any woman.

He inclined his head. "*Enchanté*."

His greeting drew another giggle from the girl and a chiding "Tillie!" from Lady Joanna.

"I saw you select the clock, Monsieur. I, too, admired the workmanship, but can you not see that giving such a fine clock to a babe in arms is unwise? Would not a silver cup be more appropriate?"

"Now there you'd be wrong, Mademoiselle. Everyone gives a cup. My aim is to fascinate the boy with thoughts of the night sky he will one day see from his ship. 'Tis the perfect gift for a future ship's captain."

Lady Joanna's brows rose in surprise. "But isn't he a bit *young* for such thoughts?"

"Nay, I think not. A child is like a ship. One can never be too young to be steered to the right course."

Her forehead creased in a frown. "Have you considered, Monsieur, that you might have chosen this gift, not because it will please your grandson, but because it will please *you*?"

Jean scowled at her suggestion. What did she know of him that she would impute such a selfish motive to his action? Of course, the clock pleased him. More importantly, it would also please Jean Nicholas.

She looked at him expectantly, beautiful in her defiance, awaiting his answer. Perplexed at his strong reaction to the redhead, he gave her none.

The tension between them hung thick in the air as they stood glaring at each other.

The sister spoke up, sparing an awkward moment. "Ah... we thought to give the baby a silver rattle." She held up a silver toy about five inches long with a whistle at one end and a coral teether at the other and shook it in front of his face. "See?"

Decorated with silver bells, Jean had to admit it made a pleasant jingle. "Quite practical. I am certain my daughter and young Jean Nicholas will be delighted."

"And why not?" Lady Joanna asserted. "Babies need diversion."

From behind him, the shopkeeper spoke. "Your clock is ready, Monsieur."

Jean tipped his hat to the ladies and turned toward the silversmith's counter, glad for the interruption. As he strode to the counter, he could feel the disapproving gaze of Lady Joanna boring into his back. He set his jaw. Jean Nicholas would have the clock whether the lady approved or not.

At the counter, he found his package, tied up with string.

Jean waited until the women had purchased the silver rattle and Lady Joanna bid him a terse, "Good day, Monsieur."

Once they were gone, he leaned over the counter to point to an exquisite silver cup, its handle curved in the shape of the letter S. "I will have that as well, good sir."

"Very good!" the shopkeeper exclaimed, happy to have another sale. "Would Monsieur care to have the cup engraved?"

"Ah, yes. Paper and ink, *s'il vous plaît*."

The silversmith handed him the requested items and Jean penned a line he was fond of, then slid the paper back to the man. "If you could fit this on the front of the cup, I would be most obliged."

The man slid his wire spectacles up his thin nose and read the quote aloud. "It is not that life ashore is distasteful to me. But life at sea is better. Sir Francis Drake."

Dropping his spectacles to the end of his thin nose, he raised his pale blue eyes to Jean. "Well-spoken words by a native son of England. Most appropriate. And should I add a name to the other side?"

"*Oui*. 'Jean Nicholas Powell' and his birth date, 'December 16, 1783'."

"Very good, Monsieur." The man scratched out the request. "You can take the clock today and the cup will be ready tomorrow morning."

He paid the man and picked up his clock, realizing he had just bought a silver cup he had no intention of acquiring all because a beautiful opinionated redhead had thought it appropriate.

Now why, pray tell, was that?

Chapter 6

The sharp sound of Joanna's heels hitting the flagstones echoed in her ears, giving vent to her anger, as she marched down the street toward her carriage, unsure exactly why the French comte's manner had annoyed her so. "What an infuriating man," she muttered.

Holding the brim of her bonnet, Tillie hurried to catch up. "Why do you say that? I thought him ever so handsome." She paused. "He is so... manly with his dark looks. And his French accent is irresistible. Do you not agree?"

Joanna did agree but she would never admit it. That she found Donet attractive, a man who had annoyed her, rankled. "Tillie, do not allow a man's appearance or his seductive voice to sway you. Frenchmen are notorious flirts."

"He can flirt with me anytime he likes," her sister said matter-of-factly. Then, shooting Joanna a sharp glance, she spoke in a sterner voice. "I think you are just disappointed that he did not show the same interest in you as other men do. Perhaps you have become spoiled with all the attention paid you."

"I care not a whit if the comte shows any interest in me, but that clock seemed a frivolous choice for a mere babe and he should have recognized the folly of it."

Joanna felt Tillie's eyes upon her but kept her gaze focused on the carriagc just ahead.

"I rather liked the clock," Tillie said. "You liked it, too, until he wanted it for his godson."

Joanna bit her bottom lip, realizing Tillie had the right of it.

"I'm so glad Lady Danvers invited us to the christening and breakfast after. It should be grand fun! I have only met her friend, Claire Powell, but I like her very much. Claire and I are of an age, you know."

The footman opened the carriage door.

Before Joanna stepped inside, she turned to her sister. "And that means the comte is old enough to be your father."

The next afternoon was cold but sunny. Joanna donned a day gown the color of a London fog, draped a dark green cloak over her shoulders and set a mobcap on her head, covering most of her hair. Satisfied she had dressed plainly enough to get lost in a crowd, she left Tillie practicing the pianoforte in their Mayfair townhouse and took a hackney to the Thames where she had agreed to meet Zack.

The warehouse they had leased some time ago should, by now, be filled with tea and brandy from their last few runs. Joanna was eager to see it for herself.

Most often, Zack took care of this end of things, but she wanted to understand better how the goods were dispatched to the London merchants. Many were glad to have prized goods at a price that made them a good profit yet provided a reasonable cost to their customers.

Avoiding a duty on tea of more than one hundred per cent made everyone rich with coin. The duty on brandy was almost as bad.

The plain black carriage arrived at the busy quay where ships from all over the world were moored. It was home to customs officers, porters, watchmen and thieves, plying their trades among the warehouses and taverns. Not the place for a lady, she knew, but dressed as she was and with Zack by her side, no one would think anything of her being there.

Zack was waiting for her in front of the old warehouse. He wore an anxious expression, which reminded her he did not agree with the risk she took in exposing herself to this part of town.

The two-story building, set among others like it and faded by time, held the goods stored while in transit. A short distance away tied up to the large mooring post, the quay or to each other were tall-masted ships. Above them circled the gulls.

Watermen in their small boats ferried passengers up and down the crowded river.

The excitement infusing the air had always inspired Joanna to think of foreign ports. This, to her, was the real heart of London.

Zack ushered her into the building. "They are just sorting the barrels and chests now."

Inside, windows set high in the wooden structure allowed light to fall on the tall stacks of chests and barrels. Two men organized them into smaller groups. She assumed it was to assist the delivery.

At a desk in the center of the large dust-covered room sat a man poring over a book that looked to be a ledger.

"We keep records?"

"Aye, we must. Else how would we remember who got what?"

"Yes, but records of smuggling present a risk, do they not?"

"I hold the book, m'lady. Ye need not fear its discovery."

Joanna did not share Zack's confidence but held her tongue. They would speak of the ledger again when they returned to Chichester. "I would like to see it."

Zack spoke to the man at the table, a clerk of some sort, and carried the volume back to her. The leather-bound ledger included neat tallies of shipments beginning with their first forays into smuggling.

Zack drew his finger down the columns on the open page. "'Tis all in order. See, here are last month's runs."

"Where did you learn to read?" Most villagers were illiterate. Only a few had ever learned to sign their name.

"Before the war, the vicar taught some of the village boys. I was one. Ye can be sure he is never in want of tea." Pointing to the last entry, he noted, "This here is the tea bound for the tea room at Twinings on the Strand."

"Twinings, really?"

Zack grinned. "Ye don't think all the tea drunk there comes from the East India Company's ships, do ye?" At her raised brow, he added, "We supply a good bit, some might say the best of what they serve."

"I see." Joanna would never sip another cup of tea at Twinings without thinking of her part in it. "I knew the coffee houses bought tea from us, but I can see from this our distribution is wider than I realized."

"Oh, aye, I expect 'tis."

"What about the brandy?" she asked. Stacked high against the walls were barrels and casks of what she assumed was brandy. She knew some of the casks never made it to London. Once diluted and colored, many went to inns and taverns in Chichester. However, she was uncertain of the destination of the casks and barrels stored here.

Zack pointed to entries marked with a "B". "The sugared mixture we sell, the kind the English swells like, goes to taverns around London and some to Vauxhall Gardens in Lambeth on the other side of the river."

Impressed with Zack's efforts, Joanna stayed a while to check more entries and to ask about the wagons that would carry the goods to their various destinations.

Zack told her he would not introduce her to the men he'd hired in London. "The fewer who know who ye are, the better."

When it was time to go, she turned to Zack. "Once the money is in hand, will you see my share goes to the Ackerman family? They need it desperately. The mother has not been able to take in laundry or mending since she fell ill." Joanna never actually received a share of their take, yet Zack went through the fiction so that she could direct her part of the proceeds to those who were the most in need.

"Aye, I'll see to it, m'lady."

"When is our next run?"

"More than a sennight, I expect. I should have the precise day soon."

"Good. Then I shall have time to attend some events with Lady Danvers and return to Chichester. Lord Torrington, Aunt Hetty and my sister will remain here. We will have The Harrows to ourselves which will make our business that much easier." She was glad Aunt Hetty had brought her cat to London. Though she would have to put up with sneezing when the cat returned, at least for the summer, Aloysius would not be there.

Zack walked her to the door and hailed a hackney. As he helped her into the carriage and closed the door, she leaned her head out the open window. "Will you visit Nora before you return to Chichester?"

"O' course. She expects it." And then with a smile, "'Sides, she told me she'd save me one of yer cook's tarts."

Knowing Zack's fondness for fruit tarts, Joanna laughed and waved him goodbye.

By the time Jean arrived at the Thames, his ship was already tied up at the quay. Judging by the scarcity of crew on deck, *la Reine Noire* must have arrived earlier than expected. He expected his crew not on the ship were patronizing the quayside taverns.

Émile stood at the rail as Jean took the gangway in long strides.

"I see you found a good spot."

"*Un coup de chance*," offered Émile, "but I was pleased with such luck for the Pool of London is a tangle today. The ships are crammed in together like herrings in a barrel."

Jean studied the face of his quartermaster. Émile tended to appear stern, even when he wasn't, in part due to his swarthy skin, heavy brows and downturned mouth. But today, he seemed to be in very good spirits.

Navigating the Thames was the worst of the trip to London, but Émile was an experienced quartermaster and their second mate Lucien Ricard was adroit at the wheel. "The trip from Chichester Harbor went well?"

"We had one near call but managed to tack our way around all the *croûtons* in the English soup."

Jean chuckled and scanned the deck. A few of his crew were busy coiling lines and laying out the mooring hawsers. Seeing their attention directed at him, he paused to give them a nod. "You have given the men liberty?"

"Oui, *Capitaine*. All but the few I would not trust to return. Those shall remain on watch with the bos'n to guard the ship."

Jean nodded his agreement. The quay was full of thieves, yet his men, handy with a rigging knife or a belaying pin, were well able to protect the ship. Their cutthroat appearance would discourage all but the most foolhardy.

"By now ye must have seen the little one's babe." Émile's dark eyes burned with curiosity. "What do ye think?"

"A handsome lad with the black hair of the Donets. Claire thinks he will have the amber eyes of his father. You will see him at the christening."

"*Bien*. I had M'sieur Ricard watch the ship for a short time when we first arrived so I could go ashore and buy yer namesake a gift. When Lucien returns tonight, I will be free to attend the christening with ye tomorrow."

"Claire will be pleased to see you. What did you find to give my godson?"

"A brass spyglass. He will no doubt find it amusing as a lad and, if he does not drop it, 'twill be useful when he grows to manhood, *non*?"

Jean chuckled. "It seems you and I had the same thought, *mon ami*. I purchased gifts that will remind him his destiny is the sea. With his father and grandfather both ship's captains, I think we may assume Jean Nicholas will be one as well."

"Aye, the lad has saltwater in his veins. Ye have not mentioned the reception for the Prime Minister. Did ye enjoy yerself surrounded by the English?"

"'Twas an elegant affair. I quite liked the young Mr. Pitt. He is a man of novel ideas. As for the rest, I have been so long among common seamen, even the last few years serving the French Foreign Minister have not made up for a score of years away from my beginnings."

"Ye were a noble son long before ye were a privateer, *Capitaine*. Ye'll get accustomed to them soon enough. 'Tis what ye were raised to be."

Jean allowed himself an uncharacteristic sigh. "*Peut-être*, but with the title also comes a burden. Not just the château but the care of its people who tend the vineyards and my niece, a girl I have yet to meet." He returned his friend a wearisome smile. "I fear my footloose days at sea may be limited, *mon ami*, at least for a while."

"Yer new life may be a better one, *Capitaine*." Émile turned to watch a crewmember. "*Excusez-moi*, I must see to that one before he makes the same mistake again."

Alone for the moment and happy to be back on the deck of his ship, Jean stepped to the rail, hands clasped behind him, and looked toward the quay, his tricorne shading his eyes from the sun. He relished the familiar sounds of shrieking gulls, men joking with each other as they worked on the ships moored nearby, tavern wenches calling to customers and carriages wending their way through the milling crowd.

London had become the busiest port in the world. Each time he sailed into the Pool of London, it seemed more ships vied for space on the river. *La Reine Noire* had, indeed, been fortunate. Other ships tying up next to her were so close one could easily step from one deck to another.

He much preferred the harbor in Lorient.

As he watched the people crowding the quay, a couple emerged from one of the warehouses fronting on the quay. A moment later, a hackney stopped in front of them. The man held the door open for the woman and, drawing her cloak around her, she climbed inside.

Jean recognized the man by his height, his brown hair, his bear-like build and the scar on the side of his face. The English smuggler who had boarded his ship at Bognor. Perhaps the woman was the one who'd assisted him, the one who did the talking. *His wife?*

Jean could not see her face, but when she leaned out of the carriage window, a thick lock of red hair fell from her mobcap. He was certain that profile and hair belonged to only one woman. Of all the colors of red hair Torrington and his siblings possessed, hers was the most distinctive: auburn, threaded with thick strands that turned bright copper in the sun.

Now what was the very proper Lady Joanna West doing with a smuggler on the London quay?

Chapter 7

Joanna and her sister were escorted to a pew near the front of St Martin-in-the-Fields, the parish church where the christening would soon take place. It was her first time in this church. While she thought its exterior of Portland stone daunting with eight Corinthian columns and tall steeple, the interior was beautiful.

Quiet shuffling and subdued voices echoed about the cavernous sanctuary as other guests filed in and found their seats.

As she had some minutes to wait, Joanna shifted her gaze to the tall side windows filling the chamber with cold sunlight. Behind the nave were more magnificent windows of clear glass. Tilting her head back, she looked up to the arched ceiling decorated with gilded scrolled relief. It looked like an ivory sky with scattered lacy clouds.

Tillie nudged her in the ribs. "They are about to begin."

Joanna turned her attention to where the family had gathered in front of the nave before Vicar Hamilton who, according to the invitation, would be conducting the ceremony. Garbed in a white wig, black robe and white bands, he fit well the description of a somber Anglican clergyman.

"Look, Jo, there on the right," Tillie whispered, her eyes darting to where the ebony-haired Claire Powell stood beside her father, the French comte. "It's Monsieur Donet."

Joanna thought she heard her sister sigh, a sure sign Tillie had not lost the tendre she had for the French nobleman. It was one thing for her younger sister to admire the well-dressed French comte and quite another if she were to be vulnerable to his seduction. Joanna would have to make sure her sister did not fall prey to the handsome pirate.

To Joanna, Donet appeared like a black panther that had crept in amongst the sheep. Only grudgingly did she admit to herself that for all his fearsome appearance, he had a noble bearing that announced itself in his erect posture, the proud way he held his head and the French brocade waistcoat of the deepest claret color that spoke of an elegance of a past era.

The pirate—if he ever had been a pirate—had dressed up for what was surely to him a momentous occasion.

To try and turn Tillie from her young girl's affectation, Joanna whispered, "You make too much of what is customary for those participating in a christening. See Lord and Lady Danvers standing next to him? They wear their finery, too. Lord Danvers' silver waistcoat shines beneath his light blue coat. He even sports a wig for the occasion. And while Cornelia wears her customary peach, this gown is adorned with many bows."

Tillie's mouth formed a small pout at being reminded Donet was merely one of the other mortals. "I suppose you have the right of it. Still…"

As they watched, the baby's nurse carried the child down the aisle and placed him in the arms of his mother. Little Jean Nicholas made baby cooing noises as he looked up at Claire. The delightful sounds echoed in the vast stone chamber.

Dressed in a white lace cap and gown extending below his pretty blanket, the babe was well attired for this day. The stone sanctuary, despite being filled with warm bodies, was as cold as when they arrived. Joanna kept her cloak tightly drawn around her and thought well of the baby's nurse for seeing the child was swathed in a blanket.

Mr. Powell moved to the left to allow room for Cornelia to

stand between him and his wife. The two godfathers remained on Claire's right.

A hush fell over the sanctuary as all waited for the vicar to begin.

"Who is the sponsor for this child?" he asked in a voice that boomed the church's authority.

The three godparents silently bowed their heads, acknowledging themselves to be the sponsors.

"And the child's intended name?"

"Jean Nicholas Powell," announced Monsieur Donet in his richly accented voice, tinged, Joanna thought, with pride.

The vicar took the child into his arms and, with a small protest from the babe, baptized him with water from the bowl on a wooden stand while intoning the words that welcomed him into the family of the church.

When the ceremony was over, the vicar returned the babe to his mother's arms, congratulating the parents on their splendid son.

Joanna watched the family file out of the church, irritated with herself for being unable to tear her eyes from the French comte.

Donet's dark gaze fell upon her before he grinned at Tillie and walked on.

Narrowing her eyes at his back, Joanna thought perhaps she was right in thinking he toyed with her sister. He was old enough to be Tillie's father, yet his smoldering gaze seemed to convey some message. Was he a rake, trying to lure Tillie to her downfall? Joanna gritted her teeth, vowing not to allow that to happen.

Outside the church, Joanna spotted the carriage with the Torrington crest, one of several lined up and waiting. Not all of those who attended the christening would be going to the breakfast at the Danvers' mansion in Mayfair. She felt honored to be included.

A short ride later, Joanna and Tillie arrived in front of the familiar gray stone mansion rising three stories into the air. Eight Doric pillars graced the front of the third story. But for the lack of a steeple, it could have been a church.

At the entry to the Danvers' home, a footman took their cloaks. Higgins, the butler Joanna knew from her prior visits, greeted her and her sister.

"Welcome, Lady Joanna, Lady Matilda." His diminutive size and thinning hair made Higgins look older than his thirty some years. Always prim, he wore a gray morning coat, waistcoat and breeches, white shirt and impeccably tied cravat. Not a thread or a hair out of place.

He had never met Tillie, of that Joanna was certain, but Higgins had a reputation for a quick mind beneath his drab appearance. He would know the names of all the invited guests.

She smiled. "Your memory is exceeded only by your efficiency, Higgins. 'Tis good to be in the home of my friend, Lady Danvers." She had often wondered what a butler of strict manners thought of his American mistress who insisted her friends call her Cornelia. And then there was Cornelia's guest, Monsieur Donet. What did the prim butler think of him?

They entered the parlor where two dozen guests had gathered. Standing beside her, Tillie stared wide-eyed at the elegantly appointed room. The Harrows was not so formal. But the cream-colored walls, decorated in raised relief where they joined the ceiling, were a reflection of Cornelia's style. All the colors went well with peach.

A sand-colored carpet with floral designs in colors of deep pink and dark blue covered most of the floor. Blue silk curtains embroidered in gold thread framed the tall windows casting light onto the white brocade sofas and armchairs.

Over the marble fireplace, two gold sconces flanked a large portrait of an older man wearing court attire and a white wig. Cornelia had explained on the occasion of Joanna's first visit that the portrait was of Lord Danvers' father.

Tillie's gaze paused on the ornate crystal chandelier suspended from the ceiling. "What a lovely room."

Joanna agreed. "Yes, and so very much like Cornelia."

In one corner of the large room, a hooded basket set on a stand and lined with white linens had been prepared for the child. Though, at the moment, the babe was being passed from his mother's arms to his grandfather's.

Joanna accepted a glass of champagne from a footman and listened with one ear to Tillie's chatter. "I cannot wait to marry and have a child of my own."

Joanna nodded but her eyes were fixed on the comte's dark head bent to kiss the forehead of his namesake. The tender look on his face stole her breath. The smile he gave little Jean Nicholas was dazzling, rendering him an entirely different man. But then, she reminded herself, Donet is a charmer.

"Jo!" came Tillie's sharp rebuke. "You aren't listening, are you?"

"I'm sorry, Tillie." She turned back to her sister, vaguely recalling what Tillie had said. "It was, indeed, a beautiful ceremony, as I'm sure will be the ones for your children when you have them. But there is no need to rush. You should enjoy your Season."

While Joanna loved to dance, the small talk and rituals of the *ton* often left her eager to return to The Harrows. After three Seasons, she'd refused another. Thankfully, Wills, who was then the Earl of Torrington, had not made an issue of it.

Satisfied she now had Joanna's attention, Tillie said, "I put our gift with the others on the side table." The table, set against one wall, was already laden with gifts, including, Joanna noted, the comte's extravagant clock. Beside it was a lovely silver cup and what looked like a brass spyglass.

Sometimes, only the godparents gave gifts to the christened child. But it seemed many of the guests invited by the Danvers were happy to bestow presents on the babe, for quite an array had accumulated.

Next to the side table on the floor Joanna spotted a beautiful oak cradle carved with flowers and set upon rockers. A large peach-colored bow graced its hood. "That must be the gift from the Danvers."

Tillie nodded. "A beautiful cradle. Any mother would love to have one."

Seeing the comte move away from the Powells, Joanna set her empty glass on a footman's passing tray. "Come, Tillie. Let us pay our respects to the babe's parents."

Simon Powell had retrieved his young son, now falling asleep in his father's arms. Claire, his young wife, gave her husband an adoring look.

"Mr. and Mrs. Powell," Joanna began, "my sister and I are honored to be among the guests Cornelia invited to celebrate your son's christening. As you may have gathered at the reception in Chichester, Cornelia has been a good friend of mine for some years."

"We are so glad you could be with us," Claire Powell said. "And you two must call me Claire. You know Cornelia will insist upon it."

Joanna smiled. "Then it shall be Claire, Joanna and Tillie."

Powell spoke up. "As long as you are in here in London, you must call upon my wife at our home in the Adelphi Terraces. I am often at sea and Claire would love your company."

"'Tis very kind of you," said Joanna. "I will not be here long, but my sister is staying on."

Tillie smiled. "I would be pleased to accept your invitation as I will be here all spring and summer. I am in London for my first Season."

Claire shared a knowing look with her husband. "I never had one, but then, I was raised in France." Her accent was not unlike her father's. "Do not misunderstand me," Claire went on, "I have no regrets." Shooting a glance at her husband, she added, "Even without a Season, I managed to marry a wonderful Englishman."

Simon Powell kissed his wife's cheek and handed the babe back to her. "He's asleep, sweetheart."

Claire excused herself to carry the baby to the hooded basket. When she'd left, Powell leaned in to say, "Actually, I abducted her from a convent near Paris and held her for ransom."

Joanna's eyes widened. "You didn't! Why ever for?"

Powell gave them both a wry smile. "Her father, Monsieur Donet, had seized one of my ships, thinking to trade the crew for American prisoners being held in England at the time. 'Twas the war, you see. Still, I thought it most ungentlemanly of him, don't you agree?" His amber eyes twinkled as he flashed them a brilliant smile.

Joanna couldn't tell how serious he was, but if it had happened as he said and he had at one time been angry, he no longer was. "I do, but then, perhaps to abduct his daughter was a bit ungentlemanly, as well."

He laughed, telling her he carried no grudge. "At the time, it seemed the wisest course."

"And did you get your revenge?" Tillie asked.

"Aye, I did. And more besides, for I kept my ship, my crew and my prize." He welcomed his wife back to his side with another kiss. "Donet's daughter."

Claire appeared amused. She must have heard her husband's last remark.

"'Twas generous of you to name your first son after the man who stole your ship," said Tillie.

Powell wrapped his arm possessively around his wife's shoulder. "A promise I willingly made to secure his blessing for our marriage."

"How romantic!" Tillie sighed.

Joanna smiled at her sister's soft heart. "We had best pay our respects to Cornelia and Lord Danvers."

"Do not be long," said Claire. "You will not want to miss breakfast. Cornelia has planned a feast to rival the one she served for our wedding."

On their way to greet Cornelia and her husband, Tillie walked straight into the path of the comte de Saintonge.

"Oh!" Tillie drew up short and placed her hand over her heart. "Forgive me."

"But of course, Mademoiselle. Good day to you both." The French comte gave Tillie a smile that Joanna feared was designed to lure her sister. Tillie responded with a giggle and a blush.

The comte was not alone. Beside him, his companion stifled a laugh. The stocky fellow appeared to be about the same age as Donet, but a bit shorter and with a less refined appearance even though he dressed in finery fit for the occasion. Here, too, was yet another man who spent his days in the sun.

Inclining his head in a gracious manner, he introduced himself. "M'sieur Bequel at yer service, Mam'zelles."

Joanna looked up at the comte. For a moment, she was lost in his inscrutable midnight eyes. Gathering her wits, she said, "This must be a memorable day for you, Monsieur."

He returned her an impenetrable look. *"Oui, certainement."*

She searched for something to say. "You can congratulate yourself on a fine grandson."

The comte acknowledged her compliment with a nod. Suddenly aware Tillie was staring at Donet with a wondrous look, Joanna took her sister by the arm, wished the men a good day and guided Tillie to where their friends were standing.

As they walked away, Joanna had the feeling she had met Monsieur Bequel on another occasion, though she could not imagine where. Before he had said a word, she knew exactly how his voice would sound.

"The older one is a beautiful woman, *n'est-ce pas*?" asked Émile. "Though, as I think of it, she appeared nervous around ye, *Capitaine*. Do ye frighten her?"

Observing no one close, Jean swept his hand over his waistcoat drawing Émile's attention to his splendid attire. "Dressed as I am with lace spilling over my elaborately embroidered waistcoat, I doubt I would frighten any woman. Do I not appear the French gentleman in all ways? Might not the English even consider me the fop?"

Émile tilted his head back and forth, giving Jean an assessing look, as if trying to decide. "*Oui, je suppose.*" Drawing his heavy brows together, he said, "If a tiger can don the disguise of a kitten and be convincing. But I know ye well, *Capitaine*, and no matter what clothes ye wear today, I see ye all in black standing on the prow of yer ship, yer eyes full of menace, a sword and knife dangling from yer waist and pistols shoved into yer belt."

Jean chuckled, his eyes darting to where Lady Joanna stood speaking to Lord and Lady Danvers. "In any event, *mon ami*, I would not frighten *that* woman. Her younger sister, Lady Matilda, possibly, though with all her giggles, I rather think the young one is fond of me. But her older sister is not easily fooled nor easily frightened. *Au contraire*, for a female, she is quite bold."

The reception before the breakfast had afforded Jean time to study Lady Joanna's profile against his memory of the woman he'd observed on the quay. He was certain the two were one and the same. Strangely, Émile had not recognized her as the smuggler they'd dealt with in Bognor. Perhaps her finery and extravagantly styled auburn curls overwhelmed the quartermaster with her aristocratic status even though the voice demanding to inspect their goods had not changed.

C'est aussi bien. Jean would keep the lovely sharp-tongued vixen's secret for now.

Chapter 8

Joanna took her seat at the breakfast and looked across the table, surprised to see the French comte directly across from her. To her great relief, Tillie had been seated some distance away.

In the center of the table between Joanna and Donet stood a three-tiered dish spilling over with grapes, two pineapples and oranges. Above it, their gazes met.

He smiled and inclined his head. "Lady Joanna."

She returned him a small smile. "Monsieur Donet." Joanna recognized the two women sitting on either side of the comte. Both were attractive widows, older than she by several years. Perhaps Cornelia had decided to dabble in a bit of matchmaking. By the way the two women laughed and flirted with the Frenchman, they were charmed.

Why that annoyed her, she didn't bother to wonder.

Even she had to admit Donet was devilishly handsome and his French-accented voice, seductive and melodious compared to the men around her, could not be ignored.

Forcing herself to focus on her meal, she exchanged pleasantries with the gentlemen sitting on either side of her. They introduced themselves as Jordan Landor, first mate on Simon Powell's ship, the *Fairwinds*, and John Wingate, captain of the *Abundance*, another of Powell's ships. Both had sun-streaked brown hair but Landor's was curly and his eyes were green while

Wingate's hair was straight and his eyes were blue. The sea and sun tended to age a man's face so she could not be certain how old they were. She guessed they might be in their thirties.

Realizing she could have been seated next to some man in the *ton* who thought himself a coveted match, Joanna delighted in the two seafaring men. They laughed easily and seemed unaffected by the elegance around them.

The meal, served on fine Sèvres porcelain, a floral pattern edged in gold, began with a green pea soup. She had just sampled it when Donet broke free of his conversation with the women beside him to greet Mr. Landor.

"Are you still sailing on the *Fairwinds*?"

The curly-haired first mate nodded. "For now, aye, but Captain Powell has asked me to take his new ship."

Donet dipped his head to Landor. "Powell has paid you a great compliment. May I congratulate you?"

Landor smiled broadly. "Aye, you may. I'm rather pleased myself."

Donet turned to the man on her right. "And you, Captain Wingate, are you well?"

Wingate returned Monsieur Donet a small laugh and held one hand to his shoulder. "The wound pains me not. I am entirely healed, thanks to your good surgeon, Monsieur Bouchet."

"I am glad to hear it," said the comte.

The meal continued in lavish style with hot foods served *à la française*—all the dishes on the table at once—presumably in deference to Jean Nicholas' godfather. There would typically be a first course of fish, but with two ship owners and Powell's men in attendance, perhaps Cornelia thought another dish might be more welcome.

They did not lack for choices. Among the dishes on the table were a haunch of venison, roast pork and capons. These were accompanied by plovers' eggs, asparagus, French beans and potatoes served with butter.

Joanna sampled the dishes nearest to her, as was the custom with such meals. What she did eat was well cooked and delicious.

Monsieur Donet had brought Cornelia a gift of brioche, large loaves she shared with her guests. Joanna rather liked the light sweet bread, a welcome change from the plainer English rolls and white wheaten bread they typically ate.

Turning to Captain Wingate, Joanna inquired, "Might I ask how it came to be that you should need Monsieur Donet's surgeon?"

"Have you heard that Donet once seized Captain Powell's ship?"

"Why, yes. Mr. Powell spoke of it earlier today."

"Well, I was wounded in the fracas off Dover and spent some time with my crew as Donet's prisoner in Lorient, tended to by Monsieur Bouchet. He's a fine surgeon, excellent at his profession."

"Were you and your crew treated well?" She imagined them rotting away in some French dungeon presided over by the dark comte.

"Oh, aye. Donet was a fine host. He never intended to keep us, you see, only trade us for American sailors. From what I hear, we fared better in France than the Americans did in England."

Joanna gazed across the table at the comte. His manners were impeccable and he appeared to be listening patiently to the prattling of the two women. Occasionally, he interjected a comment that made the two women laugh. She could not imagine such a nobleman seizing another man's ship, but then, she knew little of his life except for a few salient facts: He had a grown daughter and he owned ships. And somewhere he'd lost a wife.

"Was Monsieur Donet commanding his ship when you were captured?" she asked Landor.

"Nay. 'Twas not *la Reine Noire*, but another ship he'd captured as a prize, a three-masted sloop flying the red ensign of a merchantman. One of his crew acted the captain. We had no idea 'twas Donet's crew until they had slipped over the side in the fog off Dover, speaking in French to each other. My men overheard them saying Donet had given orders not to harm us."

Jordan Landor set down his fork and leaned in. "'Twas war, you must remember, my lady. In truth, it took Captain Powell's marriage to Donet's daughter to bring all to rights."

"I see." She met Donet's intense gaze across the table. His ebony eyes seemed to bore into her, speaking loudly what he did not say in words. Perhaps he had heard some of their conversation for the smile he gave her just then was more of a smirk. She supposed such a man should frighten her but, instead, she was fascinated.

As the dishes were cleared from the table, the footmen delivered desserts: sweetmeats, sugared fruits, jams, jellies and creams.

In front of Claire Powell, who sat adjacent to Cornelia at one end of the table, a footman placed an elaborate white sugar sculpture. A foot high, the plump cherub had a face that resembled her babe, Jean Nicholas.

"Oh my!" Claire exclaimed.

Conversation came to a halt as everyone paused to admire the work of art. Another sugar sculpture, just like it, was set before Simon Powell, sitting adjacent to Lord Danvers at the other end of the table.

"Amazing, that," said Captain Wingate. "I've never seen the like."

Joanna had viewed sugar sculptures before, but they were smaller, lords and ladies circling the top of a grand cake.

She admired any artist who could work in such a medium to sculpt such wondrous figures. "They are quite remarkable, but then Cornelia has a penchant for the unusual."

With the desserts, the footmen also served wine, port, brandy and chocolate.

Joanna accepted a glass of wine. She noted Donet drank brandy but ate no dessert.

"Lady Danvers is a superb hostess," she observed to her dining companions. At the men's nods between bites of sweetmeats, her mind drifted back to Chichester and the villagers who scraped out a living as best they could.

Guilt assailed her as she thought of how much she and her aristocratic friends had in contrast to the poor, who existed mostly on bread and gruel. Because they lived near the coast, the villagers in Chichester ate fish, too. She thought of the Ackerman family and hoped the money she had sent with Zack would carry them through the summer.

When the guests began to take their leave, the comte stood. "Did you enjoy yourself, Lady Joanna?"

She rose from her chair. "I did. 'Twas a marvelous breakfast and my companions entertained me with some interesting tales." With a smile, she added, "You featured prominently in them."

He laughed. It sounded nothing like a nobleman's laugh, but the hearty laughter of a lusty pirate. "I can only imagine."

She shivered. The man's presence was disconcerting.

He bowed and departed, telling her he would see her again and soon. She watched him walk away wondering what he could mean.

She and Tillie thanked Cornelia for a delightful morning and then returned to Richard's townhouse. Tillie went up to her room.

Richard, who had been waiting for Joanna, asked her to follow him into his study.

Once there, he poured himself a brandy, offered her a glass of claret, which she declined, and presented her with an envelope.

Before she could open it, he said, "It seems Lady Danvers is having a party for Monsieur Donet. Did she mention it?"

"No, but at the reception for Pitt she did say she'd be having parties when she came to London." Joanna opened the invitation and began to read. The words confirmed Richard's description and the reason behind the comte's telling her he would see her again. "Might you and Tillie attend without me? I will only be in London for a few more days."

Aunt Hetty could act as chaperone for their sister for one evening. It would be good practice. But as Joanna thought more of it, she decided perhaps it was best she attend to guard her sister. Tillie was too enamored of Donet to resist him and Aunt Hetty would not be much of a hindrance should he lead Tillie to a darkened terrace.

Richard frowned. "I had been hoping you would stay for the Season."

"I cannot spend months in London, but I will attend the soiree. Then I must see about returning to my work in the village. Besides, Freddie is at The Harrows alone while you are here. And, if I stay overlong, I will be subjected to bouts of sneezing from Aunt Hetty's cat. At least at The Harrows I am free of that for a while."

"Oh, very well," said Richard. "If it must be only one party, make it this one. I believe Lord Hugh will attend. There might be an opportunity for you to catch his eye."

Joanna lifted her gaze to the ceiling and let out a sigh. "I hardly think we would suit, but since it will ease my return to Chichester, I will go." She looked again at the invitation. "It's tomorrow."

"Yes, plenty of time for you and Tillie to decide which of your gowns to wear."

"I have some shopping to do tomorrow morning. If you have no objection, while Tillie and Aunt Hetty make their afternoon calls, I will see to those tasks." Joanna's shopping, ostensibly for Freddie, would allow her to buy some better-fitting breeches than the ones she had borrowed from her younger brother. "The day after tomorrow, Cornelia has asked me to go with her for some adventure."

Richard's shoulders relaxed. "I've no objection; however, I

have a request. Nay, a condition."

She looked at him expectantly.

"Before the party, Lady Danvers has asked us to attend a concert with her and Lord Danvers. More like *the* concert of the Season. With the invitation for the soiree, she sent three tickets for you, Matilda and me to attend the Commemoration of Handel at the Pantheon."

At that, Joanna's ears perked up. She loved Handel's music.

"This is much like the performance recently held at Westminster Abbey that all of London is talking about. You know how involved Lady Danvers is with her charities. This performance at the Pantheon will benefit several of those for musicians." Richard did not wait for her to answer. "I have already sent her our grateful acceptance. The soiree will occur immediately after."

Raised to love music, Joanna answered quite truthfully. "I would love to attend." That the comte would likely be there as well added to her excitement and her trepidation.

The next morning, mist settled over the waters of the Thames and flowed across the deck of *la Reine Noire*, rendering it near impossible for Jean to see the other ships, much less the people on the quay, though he could hear them.

Émile had arranged an appointment for the two of them with an agent at The Devil's Tavern. Determined to reach it on foot, Jean stuffed his hands in his coat pockets and headed down the gangplank with Émile at his side.

Once on the quay, the heels of their boots made a sharp sound on the paved surface, echoing back to them in the thick fog.

For this meeting, Jean wore all black and had foregone his morning shave, allowing his rough appearance to speak of the pirate he had once been. 'Twould be a mistake to look the nobleman where they were going.

Émile hunched down in his heavy wool great coat, his collar meeting his tricorne. "The London fog is the worst, as thick as gutter mud."

"I remember it well from the last time we were here," said Jean. "Lucien was at the helm and almost ran into another ship."

"Worse than rain in Paris," added Émile, clutching his coat to his chest. "At least in Paris, the rain washes away the stench of raw sewage. Here, I can still smell it."

Jean drew his collar up against the sodden murk, his mind on the meeting ahead. "What do you know of this agent?"

"'Tis an acquaintance of the go-between who arranged our last delivery. His message said the goods were for Bognor, same as before."

Bognor. Perhaps he would see again Lady Joanna acting the smuggler.

"Only this time," Émile continued, "the English customer wants lace as well as brandy and tea. I thought it best ye and I meet this new agent rather than send one of the crew."

So she wants lace, does she? "And how are we to find the agent in a crowded tavern?"

Émile pulled a small leather-bound volume from his coat pocket and held it up. "He'll be looking for two Frenchmen, one carrying a book."

"Very clever." Jean admired his quartermaster's plan. "There are many countries' ships in the Thames, but it's unlikely any man in this tavern would be carrying a book."

Émile returned him a satisfied smile. "I borrowed it from one of yer shelves."

Jean glanced at the book's cover. "You chose well. *Gulliver's Travels* is one the English would recognize in the unlikely event any in the tavern can read."

"My reading is confined to ship's matters, but I knew 'twas English."

Jean had a sudden thought. The English seamen by and large

didn't like the French any more than his crew liked the English. "You don't suppose because we are French this new agent thinks to have the goods at a bargain?"

Émile gave him a side-glance. "*Je ne sais pas*. But when he sees ye, he'll soon drop any such notion. Still, it brings me comfort to feel my weapons beneath my coat. Some of the crew know this place and told me 'tis known to serve smugglers, thieves and pirates. They offered to come along as *chiens de garde*."

Jean laughed, peering ahead into the mist as they strode along. "The day you and I need a guard dog to see our way out of a tavern fight would be a sad day, indeed. 'Tis more likely we will be greeting some of our old friends."

"I was of a similar mind and highly offended when M'sieur Ricard offered to come along."

Jean raised a brow and inclined his head to Émile. "Does Lucien worry we are not up to a fight?"

"*Non*. 'Tis only that the men have become very fond of their *capitaine* and would not like ye to lose yer life in some squalid London tavern."

Jean smiled to himself but said nothing.

A quarter of an hour later, they neared the tavern. The mist had begun to clear and the fingers of fog were pulling back from the ships tied up at the quay. Riding the tide, their hulls caused the river to slap against the wooden piles.

Jean stopped in front of the door. Hanging over the entrance to the building, looming over the waterfront like a slumbering stone giant, was a sign. In gold letters lavishly painted on blackened wood were the words The Devil's Tavern. Above the sign, silhouetted in skillfully worked iron, snaked a long lean dragon, its open mouth breathing out black flames.

A bell on the door jingled as they entered, telling everyone inside a new customer had arrived. Jean was certain the ensuing silence, as heavy as the earlier fog, had likely been boisterous conversation a moment before.

He paused in the shadows, scanning the smoke-filled room. Half the tables were occupied by what appeared to be the crews of various ships, men hardened by the sea, sun-browned, weather-creased and lined with salt and tar. They stared back at him with scrutinizing looks. He recognized no one. After a minute, the men turned back to their conversations.

To his left, stretching into the murky depths of the tavern, was a pewter-topped bar. Every stool was occupied, the men focused on their drinks or engaged in hushed conversations.

To his right, a dozen feet away, paned windows looked out on the quay and ships tied up on the Thames. Directly in front of him was a huge stone fireplace at least five feet long where a fire blazed.

In the corner, between the fireplace and the windows, Jean spotted an empty table. Catching the eye of the serving wench approaching from the bar, Jean jerked his head toward the table and, with Émile at his side, crossed the flagstone floor to settle into one of the chairs. With his back to the corner, the light from the windows fell over his shoulder so that anyone looking in his direction would be staring into the glare of the gray light outside.

Émile slid his brawny frame into the chair adjacent to Jean's as the dark-haired serving wench sidled up to the table. "What'll ye be havin', gents?"

Jean looked toward Émile, who nodded once. "Two brandies, please."

"Ye're French," she remarked, sounding surprised. "And such a handsome one." Drawing close, she pressed her ample hip against Jean's arm. "Would ye like anything else, Lovey?" The invitation was clear and expected. 'Twas often how such women earned extra coin.

"*Non*. Just the brandy, *merci*."

"And yer friend?" she asked, looking at Émile.

The quartermaster sputtered. "*Non*."

She sauntered away, a frown on her face, clearly disappointed to have lost the shillings either of their company would have brought her.

"She's none too pretty, *Capitaine*, but she appears to like Frenchmen."

"And what about you?" Jean asked. "She seemed quite willing."

"I do not think she really liked me."

Jean's quartermaster liked to tease, this being yet another instance. "In *her* business, Émile, she would like anyone in breeches. 'Twas best you declined, for we are here for *our* business. My own taste does not run to seasoned tavern whores with soot on their cheeks and God knows what disease under their skirts."

"Mark my words, *Capitaine*. One of these days, ye'll find a woman ye cannot say '*non*' to."

"If you are speaking of marriage, *mon ami*, 'tis highly unlikely. You will remember I have been down that road before."

Émile smirked. "As ye would say, we will see."

The crackling fire soon warmed Jean and he began to relax, ignoring the familiar smells of sour ale, unwashed bodies and the stinking tidal mud of the Thames.

The serving wench returned with their drinks. Jean laid a coin on the table and resigned himself to a poor version of the drink he loved best. Taking a sip, he tried not to wince. "We are expecting a man to join us," he told her. "When he does, return for his order."

"It'd be me pleasure." She flung her dark hair over her shoulder and slowly walked away. She might have been pretty if one looked past the smears of soot on her cheeks and the shadows beneath her eyes. A tavern wench's life was a hard one, but some girls had little choice.

Émile placed the book on the table next to his brandy.

Jean had just taken another sip of his drink when a man left his stool at the bar and came toward them. He was not dressed in sailor's slops, but more like a merchant with a dark brown coat over green waistcoat and brown breeches. His boots were not scuffed but shined and his tricorne well shaped. A man who did not mind Jean knowing he was reasonably successful.

"C'est lui," muttered Émile.

The agent stopped when he reached their table. "Might ye be from the French ship, the *Black Queen*?"

"Oui," said Émile, gesturing for the man to sit. "Join us."

The man pulled out a chair and sat. The serving wench dutifully returned.

"What will you have?" Jean asked the agent.

The man lifted his eyes to the girl. "Another ale."

While they waited for the drink to arrive, Jean inquired as to the man himself. "Are you from London?"

The man looked directly into Jean's eyes, making him think the answer would be truth. "Nay. I am from Sussex, come to town only to assist with the trade. I represent many clients."

Sussex had a long coast so Jean did not doubt the agent could service many smugglers.

"Ye have an order for us?" asked Émile.

"Aye." The agent pulled a piece of paper from his waistcoat and slid it across the table to Émile. "For Bognor one week hence."

While his quartermaster read the list, Jean studied the agent. Somewhere in his thirties, but his clean-shaven face had lines enough to suggest experience. His dark hair was neatly tied back at his nape, but not a braided pigtail, the badge of pride for the English sailor. A former officer, perhaps, or a village merchant who had carved himself out a role in the lucrative free trade business. He would have to be trustworthy to have gained such a position, for his compensation would come from the one placing the order only after acceptable goods were delivered.

"We can handle the order," offered Émile, "but we require more time. We do not leave London immediately, and the lace will require a stop in another port. A fortnight should be sufficient."

The agent nodded. "That is acceptable. I will advise my client." He stood and offered his hand. Jean took it, noting the man's firm grip.

The agent picked up his ale and walked back to the bar where he reclaimed his stool.

Jean turned to his quartermaster. "Our business here is done, *mon ami*. Finish your drink."

Émile pushed his half-filled glass away and stood. "'Tis not worth finishing."

Jean cast a glance at his own glass. "My sentiment as well." He got to his feet and the two of them wound their way through the other tables as they headed toward the door.

Jean reached for the handle and a seaman in grease-smeared slops stepped in front of him. "Me mate was killed by one of ye Frenchies!" The man's words were slurred.

"We have all lost mates," said Émile in a calm but firm voice, "some of us brothers. But the war is over."

The drunken seaman pulled a knife from his waist, not the blunted rigging knife of a sailor, but a landsman's blade, long and thin, with a wicked point. "Not fer me, t'ain't," he snarled.

Jean stepped back and slid his sword from his belt. The metal glistened in the light of the fire behind him. The conversations in the tavern died away. "You may wish to reconsider, *mon ami*."

Perhaps it was the edge to Jean's voice or the intensity of his gaze, but the man backed away.

Jean sheathed his sword, turning again to the door. He sensed a movement behind him just as Émile shouted, "*Capitaine*!"

Jean whipped around and hit the drunken man's wrist, sending the blade he held flying across the room to land on the flagstone floor where it skidded to a stop. Drawing his own knife, a deadly weapon from his pirate days, Jean grabbed the man by his coat and held the blade to his throat.

His frown and narrowed eyes had the sailor trembling. "Only a coward attacks a man's back," Jean hissed, his voice dripping disdain. He slipped his knife into his belt, then drew his fist back and slammed it into the man's jaw.

The seaman dropped to the floor.

Beside him, Émile looked glumly at his pistol. "Ye took all the joy out of it, *Capitaine*. I had no chance to fire my pistol."

Jean chuckled and laid his arm over Émile's shoulder as they walked through the open door. "There will be other opportunities, *mon ami*, I am certain."

Chapter 9

Joanna considered the Pantheon one of the most elegant assembly rooms in London with its great domed ceiling. The large room beneath the dome was sixty feet on each side. She had once attended a masquerade there and enjoyed herself immensely. To see it adorned for the concert in commemoration of the composer, George Frideric Handel, would be a once-in-a-lifetime event.

She regretted that Freddie was not in London to attend with her. Already there was much talk of the earlier concert held at Westminster Abbey where hundreds had vied for too few seats. And because this would be the first concert held in the Pantheon, the royal family would attend.

She had just decided upon her gown when Tillie, looking quite frantic, appeared at her bedchamber door. "What should I wear?"

Remembering her own first Season, Joanna gave her sister a look of sympathy. "Since Cornelia is having a soiree after the concert, I rather think a gown that will serve both purposes would be best." She thought for a moment, mentally sorting through Tillie's gowns purchased for the Season. "The satin gown that is the color of butter with the Verona green ribbon crisscrossing the bodice and lace at the elbows would suit the occasion. 'Tis truly the most eye-catching of all your new gowns. The evening will be warm, so you will not need a cloak."

"Oh, yes! The yellow gown is perfect."

"And a welcome change from pink," muttered Joanna.

Tillie flounced farther into Joanna's room, one hand on her hip. "You cannot fault me for preferring one color above another. Your friend, Cornelia, almost always wears peach. You told me so yourself. And she looks marvelous in it."

"She does. But still, for you, I think the yellow satin will do nicely."

Mollified for the moment, Tillie asked, "And what will you wear, Jo?"

Joanna was tempted to say her new breeches in which she delighted, but Tillie had no idea of her unladylike pursuits and would not find the prospect amusing. Instead, Joanna had chosen a gown that looked like it had been crafted in Paris.

"I thought I might wear the *robe à l'Anglaise*." At Tillie's puzzled look, Joanna said, "The striped one with the ivory satin petticoat." She gestured to the gown lying on her bed. "When the modiste first suggested it, I thought it most unusual."

Tillie walked to the bed and touched the silk gown, shining in the candlelight. "Isn't this the one the modiste modeled after a fashion doll from Paris?"

"It might be." The close-bodied gown with its fringed ivory satin petticoat, around which hugged the blue-green and ivory striped silk, had become her favorite. Unfortunately, it was too fancy to wear most evenings and the neck dipped precariously low for practical wear. She hoped it was low enough to distract a certain French comte from her sister.

"That will be lovely on you. But first, can you come to my room and help me? I can't find Nora anywhere."

Joanna followed Tillie to her bedchamber and retrieved the yellow gown from her sister's clothes press. "Now that you're out, we will need to find you a maid of your own. Perhaps one of the girls Richard employs here in London might appeal."

"There is one I like and she is my age."

"If you think she will suit, she can be trained as a lady's maid."

"I'll ask Nora about her." Tillie smiled, obviously happy to finally have her own maid. Then, taking the gown from Joanna, she said, "I'm glad you suggested the yellow one, Jo. I had forgotten it has sequins. I love how they sparkle."

Tillie laid the gown on her bed, took a seat at her dressing table and picked up a brush.

Joanna reached for it. "Here, I can do that."

Tillie sat, looking into the mirror at her hair, a lighter shade of red than Joanna's and with more curls. As she pulled the brush through Tillie's long hair, Joanna's thoughts turned to their family.

So much had changed.

Their father had died early in the American War and, two years past, they had lost their mother to illness. Joanna had become as much a mother to Tillie, then seventeen, as a sister. The whole family had mourned deeply, but it was worse for Tillie and Freddie because they had relied so much on their mother.

They had barely finished mourning their mother's death when the next year, their eldest brother Wills was killed in Italy. Richard became earl, steeling himself against the pain, and Joanna had become his hostess, running the household and guiding her younger siblings. That Freddie had joined her in smuggling still caused her much guilt.

Tillie met Joanna's gaze in the mirror. "I wonder if we might see Monsieur Donet tonight."

"I expect we will, for Cornelia is giving a party in his honor after the concert and we are invited."

Tillie's eyes lit up. "I shall look forward to that."

Inwardly Joanna groaned. It would be a long evening for Aunt Hetty would be staying home and Richard was seemingly unconcerned with Tillie's infatuation.

Nora came into Tillie's room just then. Seeing Joanna brushing her sister's hair, the maid reached for the brush. "Let me, mistress."

Joanna relinquished the job to more capable hands. "When you are done here, Nora, can you help me dress?"

"Yes, of course, my lady." The petite Nora had been a stalwart soul during the days the family had mourned the passing of so many members. Joanna was grateful for both her and her brother Zack. The two Barlow siblings were like family.

She returned to her bedchamber and sat at her own dressing table, pulling the pins from her thick hair and rubbing her scalp. As she brushed her hair, her gaze was drawn to the porcelain figurine her mother had given her a decade earlier. Ironically, it portrayed a young woman wearing the court dress of France with an elaborate white wig.

The figurine made Joanna think of the comte, part of her wanting very much to see him and another, saner part of her wanting him back in France.

A short while later, Nora appeared at her door. "Lady Matilda is dressed and has gone down to meet his lordship."

"Thank you for helping her, Nora. Did she mention she has thought of a girl who might serve as her maid?"

"She did. I agree the young woman is a good choice."

Once Joanna was dressed, Nora turned to Joanna's hair. With expert fingers, her maid drew Joanna's long hair back from her face and added a hairpiece of the same color hair. Soon, a mound of curls was piled high on her head with a few left to dangle on one shoulder.

"Did Zack pay you a visit?" she asked her maid.

"Oh, yes, and he ate several of Cook's tarts. He also gave me a message for you, m'lady."

Joanna glanced at her maid in the mirror.

Lowering her voice, Nora said, "There will be another run in a fortnight. And you shall have your lace."

Joanna smiled, pleased. "The modistes will be happy and the villagers will have more coin to feed their families."

"You take great risks for us, m'lady."

"I couldn't live with myself if I did not do what I could to help the families of the seamen without work and the farmers struggling to pay taxes. Besides," she added in a lighter vein, "what would the vicar do without his tea?"

Nora laughed. "Oh, yes, the vicar. But do you worry about the Excise Officers?"

"Yes, but I am careful." Joanna loathed the violence that had accompanied some of the earlier smuggling in Sussex so, at her insistence, the men she led carried no weapons.

"I know Zack watches over you, my lady."

"I count upon him, Nora. And now he's watching over Polly Ackerman and her children while I am gone."

"He won't mind. Zack has always been responsible."

With her hair in a fine style, Joanna bid Nora a good evening and went to find her siblings.

Shortly after, the three set out for the Pantheon. Joanna and Tillie sat in the carriage looking forward and Richard took the seat across from them. In black and gold, he appeared the elegant young earl.

"You're looking dapper this evening, Richard." With his handsome face and burnished red hair neatly queued, he would catch the eye of many young women, especially those who were aware he was a wealthy earl in need of a wife. Joanna hoped he would choose well, not only for his sake but also for their family and The Harrows. She had no desire to live with a harpy.

Richard smiled at them. "And you, Sisters, are a vision."

Their carriage crawled down Oxford Street.

Joanna glanced out the open window at the long line of carriages ahead of them, all making their way to the Pantheon. The street had become clogged with vehicles, slowing their travel.

People on foot flooded the street, their destination the same place.

Richard strained his head out the other window. "What a

crush. We might have done better to walk."

"After the acclaim the Westminster performance received, I am not surprised," said Joanna. "Cornelia told me that between the Abbey and Pantheon performances, three thousand tickets have been sold."

Tillie was so excited she practically bounced on the seat. "I expect all of London Society will be here tonight. I never thought to attend such a grand concert in my first Season."

Richard sat back and met Joanna's gaze. "The concert does not begin until eight, but as the doors opened at six, I thought it best we came early. Just getting to Cornelia's box will take us an hour at the rate we are moving."

As it turned out, Richard had been correct. It was almost seven before they had worked their way through the mob of aristocrats, gentry and others fortunate enough to have a ticket. Once inside the theater, they located the Danvers' box midway down on the second level of the galleries. Two benches provided seating for eight but, at the moment, the only occupants were Cornelia and her husband.

Cornelia rose to greet them. "I am so glad you have arrived. I have been worried you would be lost in that great horde of people pressing to enter. She gestured into the rotunda floor below. "Already hundreds of musicians and the choir gather, filling the open area. Only the platform at the front remains for the soloists."

Lord Danvers welcomed Joanna and her sister and offered Richard his hand. "Soon, not one bench in the galleries will be left unfilled." Dressed in a suit of blue silk with his hair powdered dark gray, the baron appeared every bit the English lord.

Cornelia, too, had dressed for the occasion. "You look lovely," Joanna told her. The baroness had worn a gown of shimmering peach silk embroidered with delicate white flowers and lace edging the bodice and the sleeves. Her chestnut hair was piled high but simply styled as always. Cornelia did not like to powder her hair any more than did Joanna. The powder made her sneeze.

"Your *peach* gown is beautiful," remarked Tillie to Cornelia, casting Joanna a sharp glance, reminding her of their earlier conversation. Joanna did not begrudge Tillie her fondness for pink, but she did like to tease her into wearing other colors.

Cornelia smiled at them. "You two will draw the eyes of many suitors."

Joanna gave her friend a knowing smirk. "You may leave me out of that, Cornelia."

"My sister's not interested in gaining a husband," said Tillie.

Cornelia opened her fan and fluttered it before her face. "Neither was I until I met Lord Danvers on my first trip to London. Much to the regret of my family in Baltimore, he convinced me to stay."

Danvers, who'd been conversing with Richard, stepped to his wife and kissed her cheek. "And wasn't I glad she was made to see reason?"

Joanna shook her head. "I see I cannot argue with you two and expect to prevail." She took her seat on Cornelia's left. Tilting her head back, she looked up to the great dome above the rotunda, shining with many oil lamps. The splendor of the Pantheon was unequaled tonight.

Tillie took her place on Cornelia's right while Lord Danvers and Richard claimed the rear bench where they proceeded to catch up on matters before the House of Lords.

Joanna's ears perked up when Danvers mentioned a piece of legislation Pitt had introduced in the House of Commons. "'Tis called the Commutation Act," he said to Richard. "If it passes, 'twill bring an end to the smuggling of tea."

Joanna would hate to lose the money their free trade in tea brought to the village, but she quickly thought of other goods that could make up for. Brandy, lace, silk and even tobacco were much in demand. The Prime Minister would have to cut the duty on all to destroy smuggling altogether.

When the men's conversation turned to Pitt's India Act and

Tillie began telling Cornelia of her plans for the Season, Joanna watched the floor below.

The orchestra area, enlarged for the concert, teemed with musicians tuning their instruments to the oboes. The vocalists and the choir were filing into the raised areas allotted them in front of the orchestra. The two floors of galleries on each side of the theater contained benches like the ones in the Danvers' box. From every entrance, people streamed in to take their seats.

Joanna looked across to the galleries on the other side of the rotunda and recognized a few of Richard's fellow peers.

A gallery erected over the main entrance to her left housed an opulent royal box on a level with the box assigned to the Danvers. The seating area for the royal family faced the orchestra and choir. It was lined with crimson satin and mirrors and draped in crimson damask, distinguishing it from all the other boxes.

"The entire Pantheon has been made into a grand theater royal," Cornelia remarked, joining Joanna to watch the activity below them. Cornelia looked toward the place where the royal family would sit. "King George will have a truly splendid view."

"I rather like our view," said Joanna. Halfway between the royal box and the soloists' platform, it gave those in the Danvers' box a broad perspective. "We may have to turn our heads to see the soloists, but we will be closer to them than the king."

"I wonder who from the royal family will attend," mused Tillie.

"Well, at the Abbey performance," Cornelia replied, "'twas their Majesties, King George and Queen Charlotte, and Prince Edward, Charlotte, the Princess Royal, and Princesses Augusta, Sophia and Elizabeth. Regrettably, the Prince of Wales did not attend."

Noting the look of disapproval on Cornelia's face, Joanna wondered if the prince had been too busy cavorting with Lord Hugh Seymour to join the king and queen for what might have been the concert of the century. But wanting to encourage her friend, she said, "Perhaps the prince will attend this one."

Lord Danvers leaned forward. "My dear wife has been most pleased that every ticket has been sold."

Cornelia looked over her shoulder and smiled at her husband sitting behind her. "The charities for the musicians will be greatly benefited, my lord, and that does please me."

"You are expecting more guests, are you not?" Joanna asked.

"Oh yes!" exclaimed Cornelia. "Claire and her husband, Captain Powell, are coming, as well as Monsieur Donet, Claire's father. I cannot think what has happened to them."

On the other side of Cornelia, Tillie grinned.

"Simon Powell is a resourceful type," said Lord Danvers. "He would make it through the crowd even if no one else did. And from what I know of Monsieur Donet, he is cut from similar cloth."

Joanna was a bundle of conflicting emotions. Donet would be sitting directly behind her and Tillie. And then there would be the soiree to follow. There was simply no getting away from the French rogue. Yet even as she thought it, the prospect of his being so close made her heart race in anticipation.

Jean kept Claire between him and her husband as they worked their way through the crowd, afraid she might be crushed in the throng of people clamoring to get inside the Pantheon.

Used to vast blue skies and empty horizons of the sea, he hated events where bodies were crammed together. But he was determined to spend his last evening in London with his daughter, else he would have stayed on his ship.

He thought Claire's sapphire silk gown a good choice, for it matched her eyes. And he was pleased to see his son-in-law had a protective arm about his young wife.

Making their way up the many steps to the second level galleries, they finally managed to locate the Danvers' box.

Lord Danvers stood as they entered. "Ah, our remaining guests have arrived. Welcome to the event of the Season!"

"It was good of you to invite us," said Claire.

Jean bowed to the other ladies and complimented them on their gowns: Cornelia in her usual peach color, young Matilda in yellow, and Lady Joanna in a delectable striped affair.

The smuggler had turned into a genteel woman of retiring delicacy, her gown a French confection made to satisfy a man's sweet tooth. The mounds of her breasts were, for the first time, revealed in diverting fashion. As a lady of English Society, she was alluring, but as the rebel who lurked beneath the silk and satin, she intrigued him.

He had to work hard not to chuckle when he met her cool gaze. She fooled many, but she had not fooled him. For all her finery, she remained a vixen.

After the exchange of greetings, he and Powell settled on the second bench, Danvers and Torrington between them. Jean purposely chose the seat behind Lady Joanna.

From the floor of what was possibly the most elegant structure in England came the sounds of the orchestra warming up. The audience's collective hush had him turning his head toward the royal box. The king and queen had arrived.

"Oh, look!" whispered Lady Danvers. "The prince is here."

"I don't see him with the royal family," remarked Lady Joanna. "I see only the king and queen, Prince Edward and the princesses."

Lady Danvers shifted her gaze to the gallery across from them. "He's not with the family. See? The prince sits with his friend, Lord Hugh, attending as a private gentleman." Facing Lady Joanna, the baroness said, "Seymour has been invited to the soiree."

Jean cared little whether the prince attended the concert or Lord Hugh would come to the soiree to follow. At the moment, his eyes were fixed on Lady Joanna's slender neck, recalling her appearance on the deck of his ship in the dim light that evening off the coast of Bognor. Why would she risk so lovely a neck when she obviously had no need of coin?

From what Jean had learned, Torrington did well with his lands in Chichester and their home bespoke of family wealth. Was she just another bored aristocrat?

The sound of the orchestra striking up brought his musing to an end. Jean glanced at the program he held as the orchestra set a sublime mood for the concert.

The Pantheon had a daunting resemblance to a great church, which was only enhanced by Handel's music brilliantly played. He crossed his legs and prepared his mind for the music as the stirring sounds reverberated around the large chamber.

After the opening piece, the choir sang the chorus from *Ye Sons of Israel*, their two hundred voices rising to the dome. Jean watched the hundred violins playing in perfect accord. Never had he heard such a sound. *Quelle musique sublime*!

He closed his eyes, hearing only the sound of the strings. The music of the German composer who had lived most of his life in England had been a favorite of Jean's from his youth, and the violins brought back memories from happier days.

By the time the performers began the second part, the *Fifth Grand Concerto*, the theater had grown stiflingly hot. Jean fanned himself with his program, regretting having worn the velvet coat and the waistcoat, heavy with embroidery.

Lady Danvers opened her fan and fluttered it before her face.

In front of him, Lady Joanna maintained her calm appearance, but tiny beads of moisture formed on her fair skin, like drops of seawater on an oyster's pearl. In the moist heat, a few strands of auburn hair curled against the back of her neck. He had the unexplainable urge to press his lips to the very spot, to taste her skin, to send shivers down her back, knowing he was the cause.

Not since Ariane had he experienced such desire for a woman.

Surprised by his reaction to the English vixen, he forced his ears once again to the music of the violins that summoned the passions of his soul and not his flesh.

The loud applause that immediately followed the *Grand Concerto* abruptly pulled Joanna from the magical state into which her mind had drifted. Rising from the bench, she joined the rest of the audience in acclaiming the performance.

Cornelia leaned toward her, speaking over the appreciative clapping. "Wasn't Pacchierotti's voice fine in the "Alma del gran Pompeo" from *Julius Caesar*?"

"Yes, he was magnificent, but nothing could exceed the grandeur of the chorus from *Israel in Egypt*. The crash of instruments, the response of the great choir and the immense torrent of sound were almost too much for my senses." Her heart sped as she remembered the exhilaration she had experienced.

"In other words, my lady," said Donet from behind her, "you loved it."

She turned to meet his disquieting gaze. "Why, yes, I did."

When the applause died, Cornelia asked Monsieur Donet, "What was your favorite part?"

He did not hesitate. "The violins."

Joanna puzzled over his answer, seeing something in his face she had not seen before. A brightening of his countenance, perhaps even a look of bliss.

"Too, I liked the choir's rendition of 'hail-stones for rain and fire, mingled with the hail'," he added, smiling at Cornelia. "The orchestra's great volume of sound accompanying so many voices raised in song reminded me of a storm at sea. *Tout était magnifique*, Lady Danvers."

Cornelia seemed pleased. "I am delighted you enjoyed it, Monsieur."

"The crowd is flowing out the doors," observed Lord Danvers to his wife. "We can make our escape. As it is, some of our guests may arrive at our home before we do!"

Tillie rushed up to Donet, effusive in her telling him of her joy of the concert. The comte smiled delightedly and, agreeing with her remarks, offered his arm to escort her from the box. She smiled up at him as she placed her hand on his arm and the two filed out with the others, leaving Joanna with Richard.

"The comte has made a conquest in our sister."

"I have noticed, Brother. But do not fear, I will be watching to make sure he does not take advantage."

"I cannot imagine he would, Sister. Donet is a gentleman. A Frenchman, yes, but also a man of noble birth."

"Whom you once described as a pirate," she reminded him.

Richard chortled. "I only said that for Addington's benefit. He is biased against the French and the Catholics. I like goading him. I remind you 'tis only a rumor Donet acted the pirate."

She took Richard's arm and they descended the steps behind the rest of their party.

At the Danvers' mansion in Mayfair, the party was well underway when Joanna and her siblings arrived. In the elegant parlor, a cacophony of voices rose in boisterous conversation. Beyond them in the large hall, where Cornelia had told her there would be dancing, Joanna heard music.

Footmen circulated among the guests with trays of champagne and small *hors d'oeuvres*.

Hungry after so many hours, Joanna happily accepted both a glass of the sparkling wine and a small bit of food. She had just taken her first swallow when Richard approached with Lord Hugh Seymour, each holding a glass of whiskey.

"Look who I found mingling about!" said Richard.

Seymour inclined his head. "Lady Joanna, how lovely you look. Torrington tells me you were at the concert. I am sorry to have missed you, but the crowd was daunting."

"It was," she said, sure this meeting had been arranged by her brother. "A splendid display of Handel's music, though."

Muttering an excuse, Richard left them, winking at her behind Seymour's back. Silently, she vowed to have her revenge upon him later.

Seymour's hazel eyes glistened. He was, as Richard had described him, handsome of face, well mannered and of good height. In her mind, she saw him in his captain's uniform with martial bearing.

"Will you be in London for a while?" he asked with avid interest. "I would love to call upon you."

"Only for two more days. Then I must return to Sussex."

"Might I talk you into a ride in Hyde Park tomorrow?"

She laughed, drawing her hand to her throat. "You overwhelm me, good sir. But it cannot be tomorrow. I have promised to go with Lady Danvers on some adventure."

"Very well, but you must grant me a ride before you go. The day after then? If the weather holds, it should be quite pleasant."

He was trying hard. "You persuade me, good sir. The day after tomorrow it is. But might it be morning? I will need to pack in the afternoon and spend the evening with Torrington and my sister."

"Of course. I shall call upon you at ten of the morning. You do have a horse here in London?"

"Oh yes. Torrington keeps a good stable even here."

Lord Hugh bid her a good evening and, taking his leave, was soon lost in the crowd.

Joanna cast her gaze about the room, wondering to whom she should speak next. Tillie was talking to Claire Powell and her husband, and Cornelia appeared engrossed in conversation with several gentlemen. In truth, the concert had run long, till midnight, and Joanna was beginning to feel the fatigue of the long day. Perhaps she might retire—

Monsieur Donet stepped in front of her, interrupting her

thoughts. "I see you are in want of champagne."

Joanna looked down at the empty glass in her hand.

"Should I call for another, my lady?" the comte asked.

"No, thank you. One was enough."

"That being the case, will you grant me the honor of a dance? In the room beyond, the couples gather for a *contredanse*."

"I would rather watch, I think."

She expected him to hie off and seek another partner but, leaning closer than was proper, he whispered in her ear in his sensual French-accented voice, "Dance with me, Lady Joanna, or I will seek out your sister. You and I both know she will not turn me away."

He stepped back, his face bearing an enigmatic smile.

"You rogue!"

"I do not deny it. In my experience, some of the best times are to be found in the company of scoundrels, rogues and, dare I add, smugglers." His mouth twitched up in a grin.

She blanched at his words. "You say that to shock me."

"I do not think much would shock you, my lady."

Joanna narrowed her eyes. "And why, Monsieur, would you say that?"

"Why, based solely upon my intuition." Before she could answer, he offered his arm. "Come, let us dance."

Seeing no alternative but to leave Tillie vulnerable to the too attractive comte, Joanna stifled the retort welling up inside her and placed her hand upon his arm.

He led her to the next room where a line of ladies faced a line of gentlemen in preparation for the next dance.

Angry that he had forced her into dancing with him and mystified as to why he should want to seek her out when it was Tillie he had been flirting with, Joanna thought to provoke him. "Is it true what they say about you, Monsieur?"

He adroitly stepped through the motions of the dance and, when next they came together, asked, "And what is it they say, my lady?" His midnight eyes twinkled with mirth as his warm hand took hers, sending a strange and not unpleasant sensation rippling though her.

"That you have been both a pirate and a privateer," she flung the words at him in a voice low enough only he would hear.

"Ah, now that would be telling and I won't do that. Instead, I shall leave you to wonder if there be any truth to such tales."

"You would have fun at my expense, good sir?"

"*Peut-être* I would. You are quite beautiful when cross."

"And for that compliment, I will say, you may be a pirate, but you dance like a nobleman."

"A return compliment from the austere Lady Joanna? I shall savor it!"

Of a certain, he was having fun at her expense. With every move of the dance, he touched her and smiled. His masculine presence was not to be dismissed. His coat sleeve slid across her arm, making her heart speed. The room suddenly grew overwarm.

The image came to her of a panther clothed in velvet with the smile of a predator, leaving her to wonder if she hadn't ventured into waters far beyond her depth.

At his insistence, she danced a second time with him. At the end of it, he bowed before her. "My lady, it has been a pleasure."

"Monsieur Donet, before you go, tell me one thing."

He stood proudly before her. "*Oui*?"

"Where exactly is Saintonge in France?'

"So curious, you are," he said with a look of wonderment. "It is in the far west, south of Bretagne. That would be Brittany to you."

"It must be beautiful there—and warm." She meant it sincerely. With rare exception, London had been cold this spring.

"I assure you, it is most pleasant."

"When do you return?"

"I leave tomorrow with the tide, but I am certain we will

meet again."

She did not think so, unless he came to England, but she would wish him well all the same. "Godspeed, Monsieur."

Joanna chided herself for the sadness she felt as he strode away. She had never before encountered a more exciting man and yet, at times, for no good reason, he could infuriate her. All the same, there was something about him that inexorably drew her. But at least with his going, Tillie would be safe from his advances. Though, as she thought of it, he had not approached her sister all evening. Could she have been wrong about the object of his intentions?

Might that object be her?

Chapter 10

In his cabin, Jean looked up from the chart, feeling the ship surge against its moorings as it responded to the rising tide. Setting aside the chart, he headed for the weather deck.

A blast of cold wet wind hit him as he emerged from the aft hatch. Above him, dark clouds hovered over the Thames, the same gray color as the waters of the river.

He scanned the deck for his quartermaster and found Émile amidships, his back to Jean, watching the crew preparing to set sail.

Jean acknowledged Lucien Ricard's salute from the helm and strode to meet his second in command. "Tide's turned, *mon ami,*" he said to Émile. "Have the crew clear the moorings and take her out."

"*Oui, Capitaine,*" came Émile's rough voice. "The men are anxious to exchange the stink of London for the flowers of Guernsey and the *agréable* harbor of St. Peter Port."

Guernsey was a favorite place of Jean's. Neither English nor French, the island had been an *entrepôt* for goods, particularly smuggled goods, for a very long time. While not as warm as Lorient, Guernsey was pleasantly mild, bringing to mind cliffs blanketed in flowers.

It might be a dependency of the English Crown, but Guernsey was independently governed with its own laws and its own way of looking at things. Being a free port, the British Parliament had no right to levy taxes there. Which made it home to many privateers. Not surprisingly, much of the island's businesses were French. After all, the island was closer to France than to England.

In short, Guernsey was an ideal spot for his warehouse.

Émile relayed the commands and the crew cast off the lines.

M'sieur Ricard maneuvered the ship through the sluggish traffic on the Thames to ride the outgoing tide to the Channel.

Jean watched the quay fall away, wondering what he would do when next he encountered the fetching auburn-haired smuggler, who by then would have exchanged her silk gowns for a man's breeches. He looked forward to that sight.

Cornelia had refused to say much about their destination to Joanna, telling her only to "dress simply for town." So, to account for all contingencies, Joanna had chosen a modest skirt of indigo linen paired with a white shirt and cravat like a man's. Over the shirt, she donned a close fitting jacket of the same blue fabric as her skirt. Dressed thusly, she could go most anywhere.

"Where are you off to?" Tillie asked from where she leaned against the doorpost of Joanna's bedchamber.

"Cornelia gave no particulars. She said only that I would find the excursion most interesting."

"You had best take a cloak. 'Tis a gray day, windy and cold."

Observing Tillie's chiffon gown of Celadonite green, Joanna asked, "And where might you be off to?"

Her sister's eyes grew bright. "Aunt Hetty is taking me to my first garden party. The event is being given by the young Countess of Claremont, who Aunt Hetty tells me is a most gracious hostess."

"Oh yes, she is. You will like her. Everyone likes Muriel. And, if the weather fails to improve, I imagine you will be inside. She and the earl have a large orangery which is quite suitable for such a party."

"That is not all," Tillie said. "Afterward, Aunt Hetty and I are paying a call on Claire Powell at the Adelphi Terraces. I am anxious to see Claire's home. She has promised to introduce me to her neighbor, the widow of the famous actor, Mr. Garrick. And tonight, another ball—"

"A busy day, indeed, but then such is the Season."

Joanna bid her sister a good day and reached for her dark blue woolen cloak before heading downstairs.

The Danvers' carriage was waiting for her when she stepped outside.

The footman opened the door. Inside, Cornelia beamed at Joanna, her eyes alight with excitement. "Hurry, Jo, we must not be late!"

Drawing her cloak around her, Joanna climbed in and took a seat next to Cornelia. Beneath the baroness' brown cloak, she had donned a simple peach-colored gown.

With the crack of a whip, the carriage lurched forward.

"Why, pray tell, are we in such a hurry?"

Cornelia looked smug. "Prepare yourself. No shopping today. No ride in the park. No calling on friends. We are off to see a trial at the Old Bailey!"

The vehicle bumped along over London's streets as Joanna considered Cornelia's words. This was something she had only heard described. She had always been curious to see a trial in the great Justice Hall and now she would. "Another adventure?"

"Most assuredly and, I imagine, one we will not soon forget." Cornelia gave Joanna a sidelong glance, for they had shared many adventures.

"I have not forgotten any of our excursions," said Joanna. "Without you, my trips to London would be dull, indeed."

Cornelia laughed, owning the remark. "Well, I have no children and you have no husband so we have the time when you are here. How long are you in London?"

"Only tomorrow. The day after I must return to The Harrows."

"I will miss your company but I am glad we have this day. I did not get a chance to ask you at the concert or the soiree after, did you enjoy the christening?"

"I did. And the breakfast you gave was incredible, as are all your parties."

"What did you think of Claire's father, the comte de Saintonge? You have seen him a few times, yes?"

Joanna took a deep breath and let it out, turning to look into Cornelia's dark brown eyes, twinkling with anticipation. "Actually, more times than that. Tillie and I encountered him in the silversmith's when we were selecting a gift for your godson. I know you expect me to say that Donet is a most handsome man and elegant of manner. A bit dangerous, too, perhaps."

"And? Is it not so?"

"I suppose." Joanna looked down at her hands. "But Richard says it is only a rumor he was a pirate."

"'Tis no rumor, Jo. He *was* a pirate, or at least a privateer without letter of marque, which is the same thing. But once he gained his letter of marque from Benjamin Franklin, the American statesman in Paris, with France's blessing, Donet entered the war on America's side. He became famous for eluding English frigates in the Channel and capturing many prizes. He was decorated by both America and France. Of course, that did not please my husband, but it did please me. I wanted America to be free."

Joanna tried to match the description with the man. Yes, she could see the comte doing all that. His manners were elegant, yet his eyes spoke of daring and danger.

"That is how Claire met her husband, you know," Cornelia went on. "Monsieur Donet captured Simon Powell's schooner. To regain his ship, Simon abducted Claire from the convent near Paris where she was a student."

"Mr. Powell told us the story after the christening." Joanna did not find it surprising Donet had taken to the seas without sanction of any country or that he had seized Simon Powell's ship. That he had become a decorated hero in the process did. "I find the comte to be rather mysterious. I am unable to decipher him as I am most men." Recalling the incident in the silver shop when he rejected her advice and then at the soiree when he insisted she dance with him, she added, "And he is stubborn."

Cornelia raised her brows. "O ho! 'Said the pot to the kettle, you are black!'"

Joanna felt her cheeks heat and lowered her eyes. "You have caught me."

"Do not fret, Jo. You know I love that you are not a weak sister. I am well aware of my own faults, for which my gracious husband forgives me, thank the Good Lord."

"You and Danvers have an exceptional marriage, like my own parents. Not many women in the *ton* are so fortunate."

Cornelia took Joanna's hand. "I know you think never to wed because of the bad matches you have witnessed, but do not lose hope. The man you will love, Joanna—and I am certain there will be one—will not be like those men. He will love you for the strong woman of character you are. And he will be faithful."

"Or I will kill him?"

Cornelia laughed. "Indeed."

Joanna allowed herself a smile. "I am fortunate to have you for a friend, Cornelia." She sat back on the tufted velvet seat, amused. "One who shares with me her many interests."

Her friend's eyes twinkled. "You are the only one who will follow me anywhere."

"I enjoy your company." She thought of the question she'd been meaning to ask. "Tell me, how did Monsieur Donet lose his wife? I assume he is not married or he would not have come alone to the christening."

"He was widowed when Claire was quite young. The man

was devoted to his wife, or so Claire tells me. He was born the son of a comte, but his father disowned him when he insisted on marrying the woman he loved. Since her death, Donet has taken no wife. Not even a mistress that I know of."

"A man still in love with his dead wife?"

"Possibly. I have known such men."

"Most interesting," muttered Joanna, as she stared out the window. A man who would give up his noble birth for a woman was not a shallow man. In London Society where marriages were often arranged and women forced into loveless unions, Donet's behavior appealed to her woman's heart.

A half-hour later, the carriage stopped before the Old Bailey.

"Wait for us," Cornelia told her driver.

Joanna looked up at the three-story edifice that included the main Justice Hall and an attached wing on either side. She shuddered. Made of stone blocks, it appeared formidable. To one accused by the Crown of a hanging offense it would be frightening. She had ridden by it many times but had never been inside.

"An imposing structure. I can almost hear the wheels of justice grinding."

Cornelia nodded. "I agree 'tis a somber place. Come, let us go in. We will sit in the gallery above the court where we can see all."

Joanna followed Cornelia through a narrow opening and up the stairs to the main floor where they were directed up more stairs to the spectators' gallery. Others were already there, seated on long benches looking into the huge courtroom below.

She and Cornelia found seats on one end of a bench just as the proceedings were getting underway. The others on the bench were all women, save for one young man. From their anxious faces, she thought they might be the family of the accused.

On one side of the court, to their right, the judge sat on an elevated platform, his high seat reminding all of his authority. His white wig of curls hung long to his shoulders, and his face was round and his cheeks reddened. Over his ponderous girth, he wore a black robe and white bands.

Beneath the judge's raised platform was a long table with bewigged men in black robes. "Those are the barristers who will argue the case," whispered Cornelia. Clearly, these men were not in awe of the proceedings as she was. They shuffled through papers and flipped pages of open books, occasionally commenting to each other about something or other.

The twelve men of the jury were in a closed off section on the floor below the gallery where Joanna and Cornelia sat. Joanna could look down upon their heads. The jurymen wore gentlemen's clothing, which did not surprise her, for she knew they had to meet a property qualification in order to serve. All would be from the middling ranks of society, unlike most of those whose guilt or innocence they decided.

Facing the judge in an elevated box stood the prisoner, a man of middle years. His brown coat and black waistcoat were not so neat as those worn by the jury and his shirt appeared soiled. But then, like other prisoners awaiting trial, he would most likely have been in Newgate for months. His dark hair was loose and fell just short of his shoulders. With his hands gripping the edge of the railing in front of him, he looked anxiously about the large courtroom. Whatever charge he faced, it must be grave.

With a word from the judge, a clerk at the end of the counsel table stood and began to read from a paper.

"The prisoner, one John Shelley, is accused of disturbing of the peace of our Lord the King on the nineteenth of November last. With firearms and other weapons, including bludgeons, a blunderbuss, a pistol and a sword called a cutlass, he did unlawfully, riotously and feloniously assault officers of the king. He and ten other persons took away three hundred pounds weight of tea, being unaccustomed goods liable to pay duties, and which duties had not been paid."

"A smuggling case!" Cornelia exclaimed in a whisper to Joanna. At the mention of "unaccustomed goods" Joanna had known the nature of the case they were to hear. Her stomach was already tied in knots at the thought of what lay ahead.

The clerk paused and then began again. "The prisoner is charged with another count for forcibly assaulting, hindering, obstructing and opposing said officers."

Looking up from the paper he held, he asked the accused, "How do you plead?"

The man responded from where he cowered behind the wooden railing. "Not guilty." By the look on his face, Mr. Shelley well understood he faced the possibility of execution.

A man Cornelia identified as Mr. Wilson, Counsel for the Crown, opened the case. He explained the offense had been made a capital felony and described in some detail what had occurred.

Then a tall bewigged man sprang up from his chair. "'Tis Mr. Garrow, the prisoner's counsel," said Cornelia. "I've heard he is a very clever barrister."

Mr. Garrow asked that the witnesses might go out of the court until they were called, which they did.

Mr. Wilson then gave a more detailed description of the crime. He explained the tea had been seized in Apperton and the officers were transporting it in a cart to London. On the way, the prisoner and a group of men attacked them, bludgeoning one of the king's officers.

William Fillery, a witness, was called and sworn, taking the stand at the opposite end of the room facing the jury. Joanna looked directly at the slight man dressed in well-fitting clothes.

The courtroom grew quiet as Mr. Silvester, identified as one of the prosecutors, rose to question the witness. He asked about the man's identity and his purpose on the day of the crime.

"I am an officer of the Excise," Mr. Fillery explained. "I went with the other officers to a place called Apperton, at the sign of the Fox and Goose. Our purpose was to seize some smuggled tea."

"When you came there what did you find?"

"We looked into the outbuildings. In one of them we found twelve bags of tea hidden beneath some boards."

The judge leaned over his desk. "Were they all in the same sort of packages?"

Mr. Fillery said, "All in similar packages, yes. A paper bag, a canvas bag, an oilskin bag and a sailcloth bag sewed up. But they were different sorts of tea."

Mr. Silvester asked, "How far is Apperton from London?"

"About seven miles and a half. We had hired a cart for the purpose. On our way to London we met two men on horseback. One is that gentleman." He pointed to the prisoner. "He was on horseback and turned to look at us."

"Was anything said?"

"Not a word," replied Mr. Fillery. "We proceeded on farther till we came to Broad Street in St. Giles. I was walking along the pavement when somebody knocked me down."

At this point, the courtroom erupted in chaos and loud protests sounded from the jury, appalled at what they had heard. Joanna had known juries frequently expressed their opinion of the proceedings but to witness such an outburst given the crime at issue made her uncomfortable. She suspected the further testimony would only tell a worse tale.

The women sitting on the bench next to Joanna nervously twisted their handkerchiefs in their hands. Looking at them, she felt a sudden dread for the fate of the prisoner, a fate that could one day be her own and that of her brother and Zack.

When order was restored, the witness continued. "I tried to get up but somebody knocked me down again. When I finally got up, I leaned against a post. I saw the prisoner among the group of people, fifteen or twenty."

"Had he anything in his hand?"

"I cannot say; the people that were with him had sticks. He might have had one, but I cannot say. Three of them tried to take my weapon from me."

"What weapon had you?"

"A small cutlass. Two men took hold of the blade and swore if I did not give it to them they would shoot me. One of the men, who held a blunderbuss, said, 'Damn your eyes, take care, or I will blow your brains out.'"

"How were these men armed?"

"All with sticks, good sized walking sticks with knobs on them. They snapped the blunderbuss, but it did not fire. I made an attempt to strike at the man with my cutlass, but several of them prevented me. Then they beat me."

The jury broke out in loud cries of anger at hearing this, their feelings made clear to all. One raised his fist in the air, shouting, "He beat an Excise Officer!"

The women sitting on the bench covered their mouths with their hands. The young man pressed his face into the shoulder of the woman sitting next to him.

Joanna, too, was grieved at the actions of the smugglers and wondered what they could have been thinking to have attacked the revenue officers.

The judge slammed his gavel down, restoring order.

Mr. Fillery proceeded to speak. "Somebody struck at me with a stick, but he missed me and hit the doorpost of the house where I had run to. I had not been in the house more than a minute when three men with their sticks took the cart and horse. They beat the horse."

Again, the jury went wild. Most of them owned horses, Joanna was sure. The idea of beating a defenseless horse repulsed Joanna, too, especially since horses at The Harrows were pampered.

Cornelia must have had the same reaction as she squeezed Joanna's hand, whispering, "Oh, my."

The witness continued. "There was a great mob, a hundred or more all shouting as they drove the cart up the street and into

Bloomsbury Square."

When the witness paused to draw breath, Mr. Silvester asked him, "What happened next?"

Joanna was sitting on the edge of the bench, straining to hear.

"At the end of Dyot Street, I heard somebody cry, 'Let him go, let him go!' and I saw one John Cook with the prisoner in his arms. I jumped up and told the prisoner if he did not go quietly, I would run him through with my cutlass. He struggled a good deal, but there were many people who came and assisted us so we were able to take him."

The questioning proceeded, the witness being asked about what he saw of the prisoner, which it seemed, was not much, having initially been hit from behind. It sickened Joanna hearing it. Cornelia still held Joanna's hand. Tension permeated the court.

Joanna swallowed hard, suppressing an urge to scream. There was no need for such horrible treatment of the officers and the horse merely to recover smuggled tea. Guilt overwhelmed her until she reminded herself that she and her men never carried weapons and would not use force to regain seized goods. She would have been relieved to get away.

The next witness, Thomas Buckland, a short man with a stout body, was called and sworn. Mr. Wilson questioned him.

"I am an officer in the Excise," said Mr. Buckland, his cheeks red under his wiry fair hair. "I was with the last witness and went to Apperton with him and the other officers. We seized twelve bags of tea and made our way toward London. The prisoner passed us on horseback."

"Are you sure it was the same man?"

"Yes. There was another with him. As we came near the Excise Office, a large mob met us."

The judge interjected, "Had they anything in their hands?"

"Bludgeons, sir. I saw nothing but bludgeons. They attacked us and I defended myself as best I could. I lost sight of the horse and cart and my comrades but, as soon as I could, I went in pursuit of them, and the goods were retaken."

Mr. Garrow cross-examined. "How far were you behind the cart at the time you were attacked?"

Joanna was struck by the barrister's elegant, soft-spoken manner.

"I was close to it," the witness said. "The greatest part of the mob was before me."

"You could see distinctly, I take it?"

The witness nodded. "There was a great mob I could see from all quarters."

"What sort of bludgeons did they carry?" Mr. Garrow asked thoughtfully.

"They were large sticks."

Pondering for a minute, Mr. Garrow then asked, "Were they common walking sticks or were they bludgeons?"

"They were what you'd call bludgeons or clubs."

"Do you mean to swear that?"

"I will swear they were sticks."

The judge intervened, scolding the prisoner's counsel. "Mr. Garrow, it does not matter whether they were sticks or bludgeons!"

The witness, Mr. Buckland, spoke up eagerly. "I will swear they were large uncommon sticks." If the matter had not been so serious, Joanna would have laughed at their banter about sticks. She agreed with the judge. What did it matter what the weapons were called when they were used to beat a man senseless? She was repulsed by the violence. Only foolish men would fight revenue officers when they could have fled and been free.

The trial went on with more witnesses testifying as to what transpired that day. One witness for the prosecution remained in Joanna's mind because he was a soldier.

John Chatterton testified, "I am a soldier. I was with the other witnesses. I saw the prisoner that day about half a mile from the place where the seizure took place. There was a large noisy mob there and I asked the officer, Simpson, what was the matter. He said he did not know. Then three or four of the mob came up and struck him as hard as they could."

The jury groaned as one.

The judge asked, "With what?"

"Large bludgeons, very large sticks. They knocked Mr. Simpson off the cart; he tumbled on top of me."

"Did you see the prisoner do anything?"

"He struck me with a stick and knocked me down, and said to the mob, 'Damn him, kill him, knock him on the head.' I had nothing to defend myself with. I had lost my weapon. In the scuffle, I had lost the blunderbuss I had under my coat. I do not know what became of the horse and cart. I was so knocked about, I lost sight of them."

The judge narrowed his eyes on Chatterton. "You are sure that Shelley, the prisoner at the bar, was the man who knocked you down with the stick?"

The witness straightened. "I am quite sure of it."

Mr. Garrow cross-examined. "Were you in your soldier's dress?"

"No, sir, I was not. I had on a brown great coat." That fact stuck with Joanna. How were the smugglers to know Mr. Chatterton was with the revenue service if he wore a common man's clothing? Perhaps that had been Mr. Garrow's point.

"So you took this blunderbuss in order to fire it?"

"Yes, for my own defense."

"Was there any other blunderbuss there?" Mr. Garrow asked.

"I did not see any," said Mr. Chatterton. "There might have been, but I could not have seen them. I was knocked down and had no idea where I was."

The men of the jury sent up a great hue and cry at the soldier's dilemma and the prisoner's having beaten him. The woman sitting closest to Joanna chewed on her knuckles.

More witnesses testified, including those for the defense, until

Joanna was nauseated from the descriptions. At the end of it, Mr. Garrow made a long speech, part of which focused on an issue he felt had not been addressed.

Arguing to the judge, he said, "My Lord, I humbly submit that the goods must be unaccustomed; they must be liable for the payment of duties. Can the gentlemen upon their oaths say that the duties on this tea were never paid? Not at all! Why then, I say, the Crown has not proven they are unaccustomed goods."

The judge gave him a skeptical look.

Undaunted, Garrow continued, "There is no evidence the package was peculiar to smugglers. It may have been carried to Apperton under permit. Shall the prisoner not defend his property? Even a constable may be lawfully resisted unless he is a known constable or produces his warrant."

Joanna thought it a clever argument, but with witnesses describing the manner in which the tea had been hidden before being seized by the excise officers, she had no doubt the goods were smuggled. Besides, all of England was drinking smuggled tea. One did not need to hide tea on which a duty had been paid.

After some argument by the Crown's counsel, the judge addressed Mr. Garrow's objection. "Whether the goods were unaccustomed is a matter for the jury. But people are not called upon to make positive proof of negative propositions. They can prove that the tea was concealed and in what sort of packages. Upon all the facts, the jury must form a judgment, whether or not it amounts to proof that they were unaccustomed goods. I am of the opinion that the prisoner ought to go on with his defense."

More witnesses were called for the defense, testifying to different aspects of the attack on the revenue officers.

At the end of the cross-examination, the judge addressed the jury. "Gentlemen of the jury, this indictment is founded on an act of Parliament in order to repress the daring conduct and behavior of the smugglers, who endeavored not only to violate the laws, but to resist them with force. It is for your consideration whether the facts and circumstances fail to show these goods were unaccustomed." Adding to his final instructions, the judge said, "If a person is stopped and apprehended, and tells a false story, that is evidence of guilt."

After the judge set forth the evidence and listed the questions for the jury, the group of men retired to consider what they had heard.

Cornelia leaned to Joanna. "I cannot imagine the man will go free, can you?"

"No, I cannot." Awash in guilt for her part in smuggling that might have led to such an encounter, she vowed to remind her men never to resist should they be captured. They might face gaol but not death. At the back of her mind was the thought she must find a way to help the poor of Chichester without engaging in illegal trade.

The jury returned shortly and the foreman faced the judge. In a loud voice, he proclaimed, "Guilty, death."

The woman sitting on the bench next to Joanna screamed and the young man shouted, "No!" A loud tumult sounded from the rest of the observers in the gallery, all save Joanna and Cornelia who remained gravely silent.

Joanna's attention turned to the prisoner, who had been reduced to a pathetic wretch. He brushed away tears from his cheeks and looked up to the gallery where the women and the young man sat next to Joanna. Shaking his head, he looked down at his hands, gripping the railing.

When the noise in the court died down, the foreman of the jury, still standing, added, "My Lord, it is the unanimous and earnest wish of the jury that the prisoner may be humbly recommended as an object of His Majesty's mercy."

Joanna doubted, based on the case presented, the prisoner would ever see that mercy.

The whole experience had shaken her. To think she, too, could face such a trial, that Freddie could be in that box where

John Shelley stood, made her stomach roil and her heart pound in her chest.

She let out a deep sigh.

One more run. They had committed to one more and then she must find another way to help the villagers. She never wanted to see them at the Old Bailey. She never wanted to be there herself.

The prisoner was led away and the gallery began to empty. The women who had watched the trial beside them were dabbing at their eyes with handkerchiefs as they stood to leave.

Once they were gone, Cornelia abruptly stood. "Tea, I think, is in order. Twinings?"

Joanna got to her feet, her shoulders sagging with the weight of what she had witnessed. "Some refreshment after that is welcome, though I shouldn't wonder if we ought to drink something stronger than tea." Particularly if it were tea she knew might very well be smuggled. But then, so was most of England's brandy.

Chapter 11

Despite tossing all night with dreams of smuggler John Shelley facing the noose, the next morning Joanna was up early. Fortified with coffee and dressed in her cinnamon-colored riding habit and feathered hat, she was prepared for the arrival of Lord Hugh Seymour.

Up half the night from the ball she had attended, Tillie still slept, so Joanna did not have to answer her younger sister's prying questions as to why she would ride in Hyde Park with a man rumored to be one of London's rakes.

As promised, Lord Hugh arrived promptly at ten. She expected no less of a former naval officer, no matter he and the Prince of Wales might have been up all night drinking and gambling in the golden halls of London's gentlemen's clubs.

She met him at the door with a cheerful smile. "Good morning, Lord Hugh." Behind him, a sunny morning presented itself.

He stood tall in his fine set of dark brown riding clothes, his riding boots well polished. Under his beaver tricorne, his nut-brown hair was neatly queued at his nape. Indeed, she had to agree with Richard, the man cut a handsome figure.

He looked her up and down with an approving smile. "By God, I will be the envy of every man on the Row!"

"You flatter me, good sir, but I will take your compliment and say 'thank you'. Shall we go?"

Outside, Seymour's chestnut gelding stood next to her white mare that she had earlier asked the groom to bring around to the front.

"We shall have good weather," he remarked, as he helped her to mount.

Mayfair was only a few streets from Hyde Park, so they were soon trotting down the broad sand-covered road that was once called *Route du Roi*, now simply known as Rotten Row.

Since it would be a few hours before the *ton* appeared *en masse* at midday, they mostly had the park to themselves. From the tall trees on either side of them, robins greeted the cool sun-filled day with vigorous songs.

She glanced across at Lord Hugh and noticed his eyes drooping. "Up late with Prince George?"

He smiled sheepishly. "More like we greeted the dawn together."

She laughed. "At times, Lord Hugh, you must miss the sea. At least as a captain of one of His Majesty's ships, you had regular hours."

"At times I do, my lady, though plying the waters of the Channel can become boring. It is not exactly a battle on the sea of great import. When the Channel is all you see for days, any excuse to sail into port is a good one. I am happy for the change, particularly as I am aware war is never far away." At her raised brow, he went on. "The climate in France bodes ill. 'Tis a rising tide of discontent. We who are attuned to such matters watch it closely."

"Is it so bad?" she asked, concerned.

"It is. The French queen is not popular with the people and now that America has her independence, the peasants clamor for their own freedom. There have been eruptions of violence in the countryside, and in Paris, riots for the lack of bread."

"Oh, I didn't know, but what you say makes sense. Even the common man in England is none too happy with the increase in taxes to pay for an unpopular war. Our countrymen's situation deteriorates along with the French."

"Just so. 'Tis why I keep my uniform at the ready should I be called upon to serve once again. My life, as it is now, may be only a brief respite, an interlude between wars, if you will. So I am determined to enjoy it."

She smiled, realizing there was more to this man than his rakish habits. "Then I shall not begrudge you your pleasure while you may take it, but perhaps I can help bring you awake this morning. Let us take the Row in a race!" She flicked her mare with her riding crop and plunged ahead, galloping away.

Seymour followed, his horse's hooves pounding the dirt path as he shouted encouragement. "On! I say onward, my lady!"

At the end of the Row, a mile long, Joanna pulled up, out of breath and heart pounding. She loved the thrill of such a mad race, the exhilaration and the wind on her face.

Lord Hugh drew even with her. "Why, Lady Joanna, you are a fierce horsewoman! And you have a mind to go with that beautiful face. I only wish you might come to London more often."

"What? And force you to rise before noon? Nay, not while you are partnered with Prince George. You need your sleep!"

He laughed heartily. "Of a certainty, I will miss you, Lady Joanna."

She smiled up at him. "That is most kind of you to say." He looked long into her eyes, seeing what, she had no idea. "Is something amiss, Lord Hugh?"

"No... No, it just occurred to me you would, indeed, make an ideal wife."

Narrowing her eyes, she studied him, suspicious at this sudden thought. "Did Torrington put you up to this?"

"Your brother? Why no... Well, he may have suggested... But no."

"I see. Truly, Lord Hugh, I am not the woman you seek."

He waggled his eyebrows. "I can be persistent, you know."

"I fear it would be a wasted effort," she said, then softened her words with a smile.

He seemed to accept her answer. "All right," he said, disappointed.

They walked their horses back down the Row and then to Mayfair, speaking of the London Season, of the Handel concert and Seymour's escapades with the prince.

She enjoyed Lord Hugh's company and their easy banter, but she could never imagine him as more than a friend. Their conversation lacked the edge she had come to appreciate when she was in the company of the mysterious comte de Saintonge. The Frenchman was unpredictable, amusing and his masculine presence excited her in a way this man never could.

As she waved goodbye to Lord Hugh, she pondered what Donet might be doing now. Was he on his way to France where an unhappy populace fomented discontent?

North of Guernsey Island, in the English Channel off the coast of Normandy

Midmorning, Jean stood at the rail, wind whipping his hair free from its queue. It was a blustery day in the Channel as they headed south.

Off the larboard, twenty-six miles to the east, the hills of Normandy's Cotentin peninsula boldly emerged from the white-capped waters. Off the starboard, he could see the three lighthouses standing sentinel on the Casquets, the huge cluster of rocks off Alderney Island. The familiar landmark told him they were not far from Guernsey.

With a northeasterly wind and full sail above him, they would soon arrive in the harbor of St. Peter Port.

"The weather has been kind to us, *Capitaine*," said Émile,

suddenly appearing at his side. Jean turned to see the rough outline of his quartermaster's face, shadowed with his back to the sun.

"We should reach St. Peter Port in time for supper," raising his voice to be heard over the wind.

Émile smiled. "As I remember, Lidstone's on the quay serves a tolerable veal."

"Supper at Lidstone's appeals." Seeing his quartermaster's weary look, he added, "We might enjoy an evening to ourselves."

"And the men would enjoy an evening in port, *Capitaine*."

"I have no objection. We need only enough men for a harbor watch to guard the ship."

"I will see to it. And, if ye agree, I would propose to load the ship tomorrow."

Jean nodded. "*Très bien*, as long as those ashore tonight return by morning."

"Any special orders for Cook for provisions?"

Jean reflected on the foods he favored from St. Peter Port. "A few. Along with our usual supplies, see that Cook takes on a good supply of honey and some cream and cheese. After a fortnight of English bread, some pastries and brioche from the *pâtisserie* on High Street would be welcome, too." He thought for a moment, then added, "And some of those sausages from Philippe's *boucherie*, I think. Enough for all the men."

Émile rubbed his belly. "Ye're making me hungry, *Capitaine*. What shall I tell the men ye want from the warehouse tomorrow? Anything besides the brandy, tea and lace ye promised the agent in London?"

Jean tried to remember all that was stored in his warehouse on Guernsey. He was constantly adding to it. Thinking of his recent acquisitions, his mind settled on an idea. "As I recall, the warehouse contains several lengths of silk from our last trip to Paris."

Émile crossed his arms and nodded. "*C'est vrai.*"

"*Parfait*. Make certain the crew fetches the vermilion brocade and a few other lengths of silk. I have a notion our customer in Bognor would be pleased to have some."

"Oui, *Capitaine*. I shall see it added to the order." He winked. "Silk and lace often go together, *non*?"

"In this case, the silk will be a gift, a test of sorts."

"*Capitaine*?" Émile's furrowed brow bespoke his confusion. "Ye would give away that silk? Why, 'tis a quality even Marie Antoinette would covet."

"I have a reason, *mon ami*."

"*Très bien*, I will instruct the men."

Once M'sieur Ricard had adroitly navigated the granite rocks and islets around Guernsey, Jean concentrated on their approach to the harbor.

Sailing into St. Peter Port presented its challenges. Shifting tides and changeable winds meant he must give the ship and her sails his constant attention. He knew the familiar charts well and was pleased they would have a strong northeast wind to aid them.

His crew, familiar with the island's proclivities, quickly moved to comply with his orders. Soon, they sailed into the harbor and the ship drifted slowly to her moorings.

His spirits lifted as they always did when *la Reine Noire* was tied up to the solid granite of the north pier, busy this afternoon with several ships. The faces of his men and their easy joking spoke of their eagerness for an evening ashore on the island.

An hour later, Jean and his quartermaster walked along the quay, enjoying the warm evening as they headed into town toward Lidstone's Hotel.

A fine meal followed, consisting of *soupe à la reine*, roast veal spiced with sage and thyme, fried potatoes in sherry sauce and a *ragoût* of French beans. Jean was just licking the last of the sherry sauce from his lips when Émile suggested a glass of brandy at the Crown & Anchor.

"*Excellente idée*," said Jean. "After that meal, a walk appeals."

They left the hotel and strolled along the cobblestone street on their way to the tavern.

The setting sun peeked out between clouds to light the evening sky with a golden glow, shimmering in the waters of the harbor.

On the other side of the harbor, the dark hulk of Castle Cornet loomed against the golden sky. The landmark sat atop a rocky islet off Guernsey's coast. The castle, a granite fort that had guarded the harbor for five centuries, had long been a prison.

Jean stepped through the door of the Crown & Anchor followed by his quartermaster. The large tavern was crowded this night, noisy and smoke-filled. Every table was filled. Several of the crew of *la Reine Noire* were among those drinking ale.

Slurred shouts of "*Capitaine*!" rose from throats that obviously had been imbibing for some time.

Jean waved to them and looked about, hoping to find a place he and Émile could sit by themselves. Because of the great volume of French wine and brandy flowing though Guernsey, he did not doubt there would be a fine cognac to be had.

Wending his way through the wooden tables, heading toward the back of the tavern, a serving girl waved to him from a table off to one side.

He obliged her with a gesture of his head and strode in that direction. As he drew close, he saw she had a head of copper-colored curls and beautiful green eyes.

Returning her smile, he ordered a bottle of cognac and two glasses before taking his seat. Émile slipped in next to him.

She tossed her long red hair over her shoulder. "I'm Annie."

At first glance, she reminded him of a certain auburn-haired lady he would soon see off the coast of Bognor, but the comparison did not hold. Annie, albeit a pretty girl, was a pale shadow of the woman Jean could not dismiss from his mind.

Her gaze roved over his black coat, waistcoat and breeches. Reaching out a long-fingered hand, she lifted the white lace at his throat.

Gently, he brushed away her hand but smiled to soften the dismissal. *"Non, merci."* She was young and attractive. Her rounded breasts rising above her loose-fitting bodice would have tempted most men, perhaps even him were he not consumed with thoughts of Lady Joanna West.

Undiscouraged, the girl trailed her fingers over his hair he'd worn long to his shoulders. "'Tis a shame, what with ye being such a fair looker. But I'll be back." She returned him a wicked smile. "Maybe ye'll think of something more I can get ye." Flipping him a smile, she sauntered away.

Beside him, Émile's gaze slid to another table where something had garnered his interest. Jean looked in that direction to see a brute of a man glaring at him.

"Ye seem to have drawn the ire of one of her admirers, *Capitaine.*"

The man had the look of a sailor off an Italian ship, a swarthy man of rough countenance with a knit cap shoved down over his forehead to just above his dark hooded eyes and prominent nose. His upper lip sported a wide dark mustache and he wore a gray-striped shirt like the kind Jean had seen on the crew of Italian ships. A sash of bright yellow circled his waist to which he had secured a long knife with a wide blade.

Jean turned his face away from the man's angry stare. It was not as if he wanted the girl. But if he had, the Italian sailor would not have stopped him from having her.

A bottle and two glasses appeared on the table. Jean poured the brandy and handed one glass to Émile. The color of the cognac reminded Jean of Lady Joanna's eyes. Would he ever drink cognac again without thinking of the darling of the *ton* who made smuggling her pastime?

She was not alone in her pursuit. Lady Holderness had smuggled over one hundred French silk gowns into England, but that embarrassment to the English had been many years ago.

Émile nudged Jean's elbow, interrupting his musings. Slowly, he became aware of a hovering presence. The serving girl stood beside him.

Inclining his head, he looked up at her green eyes.

"Well?" she asked. "Any second thoughts?"

Before Jean could answer, she plopped into his lap, her breasts served up before his face like a meal. She wrapped her arms around his neck and smiled coyly.

Beside him, Émile sputtered, spewing his drink.

Jean had had enough. Placing his hands on her waist, he lifted the girl from his lap, rising from his chair as he did so.

The sound of wood scraping over the floor caused Jean to swivel his head to look behind him.

The huge Italian sailor got to his feet, knocking over his chair. The tavern suddenly grew quiet. "Hands offa *mia ragazza*, Frenchie!"

Jean dropped his hands.

Annie shot the Italian sailor a scathing look. "Don't mind him. I'm not *his* girl."

"*Se na vada*!" the Italian roared and stomped toward Jean.

Émile grabbed the bottle of cognac and backed away. "This one's all yers, *Capitaine*." To the Italian, the quartermaster said, "Consider yerself warned."

"Out of the way, Annie." Jean gestured the girl away from what was soon to be a fight. Turning to the sailor, Jean tried to calm the man. "There has been no harm done, *mon ami*. I make no claim on the lady."

"I'm not yer *amico*, Frenchie," said the Italian. He drew his wide blade from his waist and waved it threateningly in front of Jean's face. "I carve you like a roast and feed you to the dogs. I hear they love frog." He bellowed his laughter, his friends joining in. They shouted their encouragement to their fellow sailor.

Jean sized up the Italian as patrons backed away, dragging their tables and drinks with them. Much heavier than Jean, the

Italian would be slow and possibly lumbering.

"Best leave off, Antonio," yelled a voice Jean recognized as one of his crew. "The *capitaine* is fierce with a blade."

"*Quel piccolo*? This little one?" The Italian sailor sneered and spat, clearly not impressed. His ignorance would be his downfall. In Jean's experience, bullies who preyed upon others weaker than themselves were cowards. This one was just bigger than most.

Jean pulled his sword from his belt, the blade gleaming. "*Très bien*, if you insist." The Italian had longer arms and a longer reach, but the length of Jean's weapon made up for the disparity. And then there was the matter of skill. Jean's father had arranged for Jean and Henri to be trained by the best fencing master in France. After that, there had been years of practice wielding his weapon as a privateer.

Shouts went up from the men and one of his crew urged the onlookers to pick a favorite. Jean's men loved a good fight, especially on the rare occasion their *capitaine* was involved.

Taking up the challenge, money quickly changed hands as the men placed their bets.

The Italian lunged for Jean, but with a quick turn, he evaded the long knife.

With a flourish of his sword, Jean met his opponent's blade and forced him back. The Italian must have been counting on brute strength. He swung hard, but Jean slipped under his blade and cut a swath across the man's gray shirt. A thin line of red appeared on the cloth.

The Italian howled, looking down at the blood. "*Bastardo*!" Mad with anger, he lunged at Jean.

Jean kicked out his boot, hitting the Italian in his side. He grunted and shot Jean a harsh glare.

Jean danced away from the knife. Making the man angry had been part of his strategy. Soon, the Italian would strike without thinking at all.

"*Fermati*! Stop moving!" Antonio yelled, his sweat-stained face betraying his frustration. With an angry grunt, he swung his blade in a reckless attempt to catch Jean off guard.

Jean easily parried the blade. "I wouldn't want to make it look too easy for your sake, *mon ami*." This time Jean crossed blades with the man, then tripped him with one of his feet.

The Italian stumbled and Jean brought his sword hilt down on the back of the sailor's head.

Antonio fell, splayed out on the floor, his eyes closed.

A cheer went up from the crew of *la Reine Noire* as they began to collect their winnings. "*Vive le capitaine*! *Vive le capitaine*!"

"Come," Jean said to Émile, "let us away while this one sleeps."

Holding the cognac bottle close to his chest, Émile joined him.

Jean bowed to Annie, whose face bore a look of regret. As he left, he tossed a pound sterling to the proprietor standing behind the bar for his trouble.

"Yer usual evening ashore, eh *Capitaine*?"

Jean returned his friend an amused look. "An all too familiar scene, *mon ami*. But at least you rescued the brandy. Shall we finish it in my cabin?"

As they strolled back to the ship, Jean reflected on his fight with the jealous Italian. Perhaps 'twas his age, but the brawls of years past did not hold the same excitement for him they once did. His rough unanchored life that had him dealing with tavern bullies whenever he sat down for a drink with a friend had become less satisfying. His imagination whispered of a different life, one more settled and with a woman who was more than a friend.

When they arrived at the ship, it became clear that some of the crew had raced back to bring exaggerated tales to those who'd remained onboard, regaling them with the story of their *capitaine*'s bravery in the face of a much larger foe.

Jean dismissed them all with a shake of his head and ordered them back to work.

The next day, the crew loaded the cargo from the warehouse. And that night, Jean and Émile dined onboard, letting M'sieur Ricard have the evening free. Their supper of oysters and roast capon, thanks to their cook from Marseilles, was as fine as any meal in Paris.

The Harrows near Chichester, West Sussex

Joanna was delighted to be home, *sans* older brother, younger sister and Aunt Hetty and her cat. She had committed to one last run and it was best not to be worried about nosey siblings asking questions. Her smuggling partner Freddie being the exception, of course.

Her guilt for involving him had not lessened, particularly after her outing to the Old Bailey. She had once tried to convince Freddie to stay home, but he would have none of it. He explained he had plenty of time for other pursuits since his schooling was done. His flute and Richard's discourses on how to manage The Harrows hardly filled his days. How could she deprive him of a bit of adventure to punctuate such tedium?

Joanna prepared for the evening ahead by donning her new better-fitting waistcoat and brown wool breeches, over which she wore a jacket of the wool. Dressed as a lad, she met Zack and Freddie in front of the stables.

"This is the same ship as last time?"

Zack adjusted his slouched hat over his forehead, shadowing his eyes. "Aye, and the same order 'cept for the lace."

She cast a glance at Freddie. "I will want to inspect the lace since 'tis the first we have ordered."

Freddie opened his mouth to speak. She shook her head. "You can go with me in the rowing boat but not on board the ship."

"Aw, Jo," he groaned in protest. When she did not relent, he gave her a reluctant nod.

She and Freddie mounted their horses while Zack climbed into the seat on the large open wagon. A brown oilcloth lay in the back, ready to cover the goods once they loaded them at the shore.

"Nate will meet us on the beach with the other wagon," Zack said. He looked up at the scattered clouds. "The sun will be down soon."

Joanna's palms grew moist and her mouth dry. Though she was committed to the run before her, she did not dismiss the danger inherent in what they were doing. Nor had she forgotten the trial of John Shelley or its end in his sentence of death.

"I'm thinking this will be our last run," she told them. "We need to find a better way to help the people of Chichester."

Zack and her brother gave her an incredulous look.

"We can talk about it tomorrow," she said. "There's no time tonight."

Chapter 12

Bognor, West Sussex

Jean sailed *la Reine Noire* to Bognor and gave the order to heave to just offshore. The cold wind chilled him where he stood amidships, his eyes scanning the beach. The twilight sky, a brilliant lavender streaked with pink, cast a faint light on the shore.

On deck, his men stood ready to deliver the goods to the beach or flee as the circumstances warranted.

Jean thought only of seeing Lady Joanna, once again costumed as a lad. As one who had donned many disguises, he admired a good one. Hers was not so well done as to hide her feminine curves but, still, as disguises went, it was passably fair. Émile had yet to discover the leader of the Bognor smugglers was not only a lady, but the sister of an English earl and the object of Jean's interest.

One day, Jean would tell Lady Joanna he had known from the beginning she was the slender English smuggler, but perhaps not tonight.

"I expect they will want to examine the lace," he told Émile, who stood nearby, his feet apart and his hands clasped behind him, looking toward shore.

His quartermaster gestured to one of the chests on deck. "The lace is just there, *Capitaine*."

Lined with linen, the chest was one they had used before to transport the delicate needlework. Machine-made lace was available, but the fine bobbin lace he had brought Lady Joanna was meticulously handmade. An aristocrat such as she would know the difference.

The signal flame flashed from the beach and he gave the order to lower the longboats. Adept at their task, the crew quickly had the boats in the water and were busy handing down chests of tea and casks of brandy. The lace he kept on deck, expecting Lady Joanna would want to check the new goods as she had the tea and brandy before. The silk would be his surprise.

As the longboats cut through the water toward the beach, a small rowing boat carrying three figures launched from the shore. The largest of the three did the rowing. Jean assumed this was the same scarred man he'd seen on their last run to Bognor and then again in London on the quay. All three wore hats pulled down over their heads, their features hidden in shadows.

Minutes later, the scarred man clambered over the rail and his smaller companion followed. The third remained below in the boat.

Jean acknowledged the two who had come aboard with a nod and looked over the side. To his surprise, gazing up from the boat, his face no longer obscured by his hat, was Lady Joanna's younger brother, Frederick, who Jean recognized from the Pitt reception.

Torrington could have no idea of his siblings' involvement in the Bognor smuggling ring or the danger they courted, danger to their family's good name and to their very lives. One might assume such a risk to feed one's family as he had done long ago, but Lady Joanna and her brother? What need had they?

Jean's men reached the beach and were unloading the goods. One boat was already returning to the ship.

Lady Joanna and her companion watched Émile as he knelt and opened the chest, then peeled back the linen to reveal the fine lace.

Lady Joanna gave a sharp intake of breath. "This is exceptional," she remarked in a low voice, as she lifted the lace and draped it over her fingers.

"That is not everything," said Émile. "Should ye be interested, we also have French silk." He opened another chest revealing lengths of brocade silk in sapphire blue, vermilion and ivory.

The ivory silk, embroidered with roses, reminded Jean of Claire's wedding gown he'd had made for her in Paris.

Lady Joanna's wide grin spoke loudly of her pleasure at the quality of the silk. "This is exquisite!" she exclaimed, giving away her woman's knowledge of the finest silk brocade.

Jean watched his quartermaster carefully and noted a frown on his rough-featured face his tricorne did not hide. Émile had not expected a young smuggler to recognize the finest quality. After all, what would a young villager know of silk?

Lady Joanna shifted her gaze to Émile. "It must be dear. I cannot pay more than the prices agreed by my agent."

"'Twill cost ye nothing." Then looking toward Jean leaning against the rail, Émile added, "The *capitaine* would make ye a gift of the silk."

Aware his quartermaster thought him insane, Jean merely nodded. He wanted to see what the lady would do. Would she covet the silk for herself? He had included the vermilion because it would go well with her coloring. Or, might she reject the gift, suspicious he would bestow anything so valuable on a fellow smuggler?

Her head jerked from Émile to Jean. "Why?" Suspicion dripped from the word.

Jean nodded to Émile. With his face shadowed by his tricorne in the dim light of the fading sky, he was confident she did not recognize him.

"The *capitaine* is feeling generous."

"Most generous, Monsieur," she said, rising from where she

had knelt next to the chest. "Very well. We accept your gift of the silk as a seal on our partnership and accept the lace, brandy and tea as agreed."

Her companion, the scarred man, was about to lift the chest of lace, but Émile ordered some of the crew to take the chest down to the rowing boat. Once the lace was loaded, the giant climbed over the rail and lowered himself down the manrope to the small boat.

Jean's crew had returned from the shore and were winching the longboats onboard.

Lady Joanna handed Émile a pouch of coins. At Émile's direction, a crewmember hefted the chest of silk and waited for her. She turned to Jean, standing a mere stone's throw away. "I will not forget your generosity, Monsieur. I can assure you, the proceeds from the silk will be used to feed families in dire need."

He touched his tricorne, but said nothing. So, she was not a bored aristocrat out for a bit of nonsense, as he had once thought, but a well meaning, although perhaps misguided, lady wanting to help others. Nevertheless, if he had anything to say about it, she would not persist in this dangerous business better left to men like him.

"Sail, ho!" shouted his lookout.

"Where away?" yelled Lucien from the helm.

"Off the larboard quarter, coming on hard!"

Jean reached for his spyglass and peered through the lens to see a revenue cutter under full sail bearing down upon them from the west.

Lady Joanna cried, "I must go!"

Jean shouted out the orders. "Run out the starboard battery! And get underway!"

He turned to see Lady Joanna staring at him open mouthed, as if seeing him for the first time. "Monsieur Donet?"

"*Oui*, Mademoiselle, it is I."

The guns rumbled as they were moved into place. His crew

let go of the lines they'd been holding and the ship veered away from shore, heading into the Channel with the gun ports thrown open and the guns run out.

Off the starboard bow, Jean saw the English cutter coming closer.

Lady Joanna lurched for the rail. "My brother!"

"Too late for that!" he roared, pulling her back. He pointed to the aft hatch. "Get below decks where you will be safe."

She backed away, again going for the rail. "Freddie!" she yelled.

"Stubborn woman," he muttered. Striding to the rail, he looked over the side. A short distance from the ship, the rowing boat bobbed in the water, its occupants staring at him with a look of shock. "Get to shore!" Jean shouted. "I will take care of her!"

"'Tis the comte!" Frederick cried to his large companion. With that, the scarred man bent to the oars and rowed hard for shore.

Jean faced Lady Joanna. "Your brother will be safe. The two ships will soon pass. Do as I say and get below!"

He turned from her to see the revenue cutter hoisting her signals, the red ensign flying from the gaff visible even in the fading twilight.

The English ship fired a single musket shot, an order for *la Reine Noire* to heave to.

Jean took no notice. He had no intention of doing as the English captain wished. He would not deliver his ship or his aristocratic passenger into the hands of English Customs.

Émile stepped up to him. "Yer orders, *Capitaine*?"

"As soon as the cutter is in range, fire a warning over her bow."

Émile saluted and stepped to one of the starboard guns. "*Hé, le gars*! Let us give this English dog a warning bark to show him we, too, can bite."

As the ships began to pass before each other, *la Reine Noire* sailing west and the revenue cutter heading east, Jean read the name on the English ship: HMS *Orestes*.

Behind him, Lady Joanna shouted, "'Tis Captain Ellis' ship!"

Shocked she had disobeyed him, he turned and scowled. "Right now, I care not, Mademoiselle. You must go below! The cutter has no idea I have a female on board. You are fair game like the rest of us." He turned to his nearest crewmember. "Baudin, get this one to my cabin."

The bos'n grabbed Lady Joanna's arm and turned her toward the aft hatch. This time, she did not protest.

Émile shouted, "Fire!" The starboard gun belched flame and smoke, blazing away.

On the deck of the *Orestes*, a biscuit toss away, red-jacketed Marines raised their muskets and fired, the snap and whine of the shots echoing over the water.

Smoke billowed in the air and balls flew across *la Reine Noire's* deck. Jean's crew yelled as they scampered to avoid them. His sailmaker let out a groan and dropped to the deck not far away.

Chaos reigned all around him for a moment, but his well-trained crew quickly moved into battle positions and readied the guns.

Jean shouted orders and the deck crew jumped to obey. The square sails filled with a "thump" and the yards creaked as the ship picked up speed, lunging ahead. "The English ship will have to turn to give chase," he yelled to Émile, who hurried to Jean's side. "But with more guns, the cutter is a laboring ox. They'll not catch us."

He turned to be certain his passenger had gone below. To his horror, just short of the aft hatch, the bos'n stood looking down at Lady Joanna lying unconscious on the deck. Her hat had come off, leaving her beautiful auburn hair splayed out around her. Dark red blood seeped from her belly and flowed to the wooden planks.

"*Seigneur Dieu*!" he cried and rushed to her, crouching down to sweep her into his arms. He shouted to Émile, "The ship is yours. Make for Lorient!"

The quartermaster, his face frozen in shock, stared at the woman Jean held in his arms. *"Oui, Capitaine."*

Jean disappeared down the hatch. At his open cabin door, he passed Gabe and laid Lady Joanna on his bed. "Quickly, Gabe, more light, warm sea water and bandages! I fear the lady has been gravely wounded."

Sitting on the edge of the bed, Jean grabbed one of his shirts lying on top of the cover and pressed it to the front of Lady Joanna's blood-soaked breeches. Out of the corner of his eye, Jean saw Gabe pause to look.

"No time to gawk. *Maintenant!*"

"Oui, Capitaine." The lad scurried to do as ordered, lighting another lantern and placing it on the table near Jean. Then Gabe dashed to one of Jean's chests for the bandages. Heating sea water would take longer for the boy would have to go to the galley.

The ship's carpenter handled minor injuries and could even dig out musket balls when necessary, but Jean's miracle-working surgeon, Pierre Bouchet, remained in Lorient, stubbornly refusing to go to sea. Jean would allow no one, except him or his surgeon, to touch Lady Joanna. He clenched his teeth, determined to do whatever he must to see her through this.

The blood seeping from her breeches soon soaked through the shirt he held to her body. He could see no alternative but to remove her clothes.

His cabin boy brought him the bandages.

"Drying cloths, Gabe!" Jean ordered, reaching out his hand so the boy need not approach.

The cabin boy placed the requested cloths in his hand. "I will see to the water, *Capitaine.*"

The cabin door slammed shut as boy left for the galley.

Jean ripped open Lady Joanna's waistcoat, sending buttons flying, then more cautiously lifted her shirt. He did not allow his gaze to linger on her beautiful breasts, but covered them with one of the cloths. Then he carefully opened her blood-soaked breeches and slid them off, tossing them to the deck. He had tried not to look at the auburn curls at the juncture of her thighs but so alluring a sight was impossible to avoid. As if Neptune had washed a sea goddess up on Jean's deck, her pale ivory skin and long auburn hair made her appear an ethereal creature.

He ripped the rest of her shirt from her and placed another drying cloth over the thatch of auburn curls. With only her belly bared, he turned his attention to the damage done by the musket.

She had worn no stays under her man's clothing, so he was seeing her marred naked flesh. The ball had sliced across her abdomen, from one side to the other. Thankfully, the resulting gash was not deep. If none of her organs were affected, as he hoped, she would have a good chance of surviving. Even so, she could die from fever or blood loss.

His cabin door sprung open and Gabe stood there holding a metal container. "Are ye ready for the sea water, *Capitaine*?"

"Oui, set it there." He pointed to the stool next to his shelf bed. Gabe placed the container on the stool, together with another drying cloth.

"At least she is unconscious," Jean muttered as he set about cleaning the wound, "or this would be agony for her."

He tried to remember what Bouchet had done when treating flesh ripped open by musket balls. He glanced at the decanter on the table. "Bring me that brandy, Gabe."

The boy held out the brandy. Once Jean had cleaned the wound of fibers and blood, he doused it with the liquor, something he'd seen Bouchet do countless times.

Holding a cloth over the wound, he said to Gabe, "Ask Cook for some of that clover honey we acquired in Guernsey, *s'il vous plaît*. A small jar will do."

While he waited for the honey, another substance Bouchet used liberally, Jean brooded over the grisly wound on so fair a skin. "*Quel sacrilège*," he hissed under his breath. Silently, he prayed she would heal. Her skin would be marked, but he was not a man to care about a woman's jagged scar. He had scars of his own to match any left on her.

A lock of her hair had fallen over her forehead and he reached out to brush it from her beautiful face. A long auburn curl lying on the pillow drew his attention. He picked it up and rubbed it between his finger and thumb. He had admired her hair from afar more than once and, now, it was in his hand. In the light of the lantern, he saw more clearly the strands of burnished copper ribboned in auburn locks.

More than her beauty, it had been her spirit that drew him. Lady Joanna was bold, independent and unafraid. Seeing her like this, broken and struggling to live, flooded him with tender feelings and a desire to protect her.

He could love such a woman if he allowed himself, but his last venture down that path had nearly destroyed him. He could not again risk so much. And she might not be willing. Despite what must have been many offers for her hand, she had accepted none. Then too, they came from different worlds, even different faiths.

But if he had anything to say about it, she would be a smuggler no more.

He took her hand and gently squeezed. "'Twill be all right, Lady Joanna," he whispered. "I will not allow you to die."

A few minutes later, Gabe returned with the honey.

"Good lad. Now, a clean shirt if you will." Once he had bandaged her wound, the shirt would serve as a *chemise de nuit* for her.

The boy took one of Jean's shirts from a chest under the stern windows and brought it to the bed, laying it at her feet.

"Ask Cook to make some willow bark tea." The tea could have waited, but Jean wanted to be alone with Lady Joanna for what he had to do next.

Gabe did as bid and turned toward the cabin door.

Jean poured a bit of honey on her wound, just enough to

cover and seal the gaping flesh. Removing the cloth that covered her breasts, he lifted her with one arm and wrapped the length of bandage around her belly with the other. He repeated the action three times before laying her back against the pillow.

As carefully as he could, Jean slipped the shirt over her head and worked her arms into the sleeves, then inched the shirt down her body. Unable to resist, he bent over her and touched his lips to her forehead. Her skin was still cool. Then he covered her and sat back.

"Voilà, c'est fait."

If by sheer force of his will he could compel her to live, she would.

Chapter 13

Joanna's thoughts swirled in a misty fog as she and her companions waited on the beach for a smuggler's ship expected off Bognor. Near darkness surrounded them as hours passed, the only sound the waves racing over the shingles. The ship had not appeared as expected. She fretted, a sinking feeling coming over her. What has happened?

Finally, a ship emerged out of the fog, heaving to just offshore. Its sails seemed to glow in the light of the full moon peeking through the mist.

Anxiety washed over her. Something was amiss.

Suddenly, an Excise cutter broke through the darkness, guns blazing flames, illuminating the smoke-filled air. Shot sliced through the sheets of the smuggler's ship.

Men grunted as they fell; others raced to the guns to return fire.

The air exploded around them.

"No!" she screamed, her heart pounding in her chest.

A cool cloth brushed over her forehead and the images faded. She awoke to pain and nausea and a vague sense of motion like being rocked in a cradle. Someone held her hand.

Where was she?

"'Tis all right, Lady Joanna. You are safe."

She rolled her head toward the voice she recognized as belonging to the French comte and slowly opened her eyes.

Haunted black eyes looked back at her. He was not the fashionably attired comte she remembered in his crisp white shirt garnished with lace, claret waistcoat and black velvet coat. He was not even the ship's captain clothed all in black, his features shadowed beneath his tricorne. Here was an entirely different man.

Haggard in appearance, his ebony hair, shot with silver, hung disheveled and unconfined, long to his shoulders. His wrinkled shirt gaped open at the neck, revealing a scattering of black hair on his tanned chest. Here was the pirate she had only heard about, a seductive Frenchman who must have broken many hearts.

"Ah, you are awake. I am greatly relieved. Were you to die on my ship, Torrington would be most displeased."

Joanna detected amusement in his words. It would be like him to try and humor her even in this. But his dark eyes revealed only concern.

"We cannot have that," she croaked. Her gaze reached behind him seeing moving reflections filtering through the stern windows. The rocking motion suggested she might be on a ship. "Where am I?"

"In my cabin, Mademoiselle, aboard my ship and sailing to Lorient."

With his free hand, he again wiped her forehead with a cool cloth. "My surgeon, Pierre Bouchet, is in Lorient and I want him to see your wound. The musket ball grazed you. 'Twas clean, but you lost a great deal of blood. I have done all I can, but I do not possess Bouchet's skill."

She struggled to rise. The pain in her abdomen pierced like a knife. She subsided onto the pillow with a heavy sigh. Donet placed his hands gently on her shoulders, holding her down.

"You must not move overmuch, Mademoiselle. I believe you are out of danger, but your body needs time to mend and that will take weeks."

She could not go to France. She must go home! Freddie would be worried. *Freddie!* What had become of him and Zack? In her mind, she heard echoes of muskets firing, felt the searing pain in her belly and the hard deck rising up to meet her as she fell. "Freddie and Zack… Were they hurt?"

"Your brother is safe and he knows you are with me. The large man with the scarred face—the one you call Zack—rowed them both to shore. The cutter can't pursue them on land, of course, but your Commander Ellis will be plying the waters off Bognor more frequently now."

Joanna let out a breath, relieved to hear they had gotten away. "Did they know I was injured?" She settled into the soft bed, trying to ignore the throbbing in her belly.

"I do not think so."

"Oh." In a way, that was worse, for Freddie and Zack would wonder, if she were well, why she remained with the comte. "I must return to England, Monsieur. My family will worry."

"I do not believe your younger brother will expect you anytime soon. And, after the encounter with your Commander Ellis, I cannot sail *la Reine Noire* back to England, at least not for some time. They might seize my ship. The English authorities cannot summon me to England for trial, but I must consider what they would do to you. I'd not see you face the hangman's noose."

He watched her closely. Did he expect her to panic? She would not. She met his steady gaze with her own. "You have other ships, I trust?"

He smiled. "I do."

"Perhaps you would be so good as to return me to England in one of those?"

"Eventually, *oui*. But not until you are well and I am free to do so."

His voice was that of a captain in command of his ship. It would do little good to confront him in her weakened condition. She took in a breath and slowly let it out, trying to ignore the pain. "I shall try to recover quickly. You have my thanks for seeing to Freddie and Zack."

"You are welcome, my lady."

She looked toward the stern windows. "What time is it?"

"'Tis afternoon but the sky is clouded over, hence the dim light in my cabin. We may soon be into rough seas. I should be on deck."

Another thought occurred to Joanna causing her to shut her eyes tight. If word got out she had remained on a ship full of men with no chaperone, her family would face scorn. But there was no help for it. She could not very well swim back to England. She had always believed she would live an unusual life, but she had not imagined all of London would gossip about her as a fallen woman.

Once she recovered, she would somehow find her way back to The Harrows. Richard was rigid in many ways, but he would never turn her out. Perhaps the comte might take her to England in another of his ships. If she were lucky, she would return before Richard, Tillie and Aunt Hetty left London. Parliament had been called into session in the middle of May, so the Lords would not be released until sometime in August. She had time.

She opened her eyes as Donet laid his hand on her forehead. His calloused palm was warm on her skin. His touch was gentle but too intimate to be proper. Of course, she felt certain he had touched her in more intimate ways than that in tending her wound.

"You have been fevered, my lady, but *Dieu merci* the fever has finally broken."

"How long was I… unconscious?"

"Two days or more, though you were not so much unconscious as delirious. Last night, I gave you laudanum to help you sleep. It seems to have worked."

She slipped one hand beneath the cover and realized only a thin cloth covered her naked body. "Who?"

"It was I who removed your clothes. It was necessary. Of course, my attention was directed at your wound. You wear one of my shirts, which is long enough to serve as a lady's shift."

Hardly decent. But she could not complain under the circumstances. Still, imagining the comte seeing her naked caused a deep blush to creep up her face and heat to spread across her breasts, the same breasts he must have seen no matter how *focused* he was on her wound. What about her personal needs? She could not bear to think of the comte tending to those. Moreover, she had no intention of raining the subject. Instead, she took a deep breath and asked, "You are a smuggler then?"

"At times." Then he smiled broadly and laughed. His laughter warmed her. "It seems we both dabble in free trade, *non*?"

"So it seems, Monsieur," she said, resigned to his knowing what she could no longer deny.

He frowned. "You engage in the business with some misguided notion of helping the poor, I believe."

"I am not misguided. Half of Chichester starves and I am determined to see them fed."

"Would not a ladies' charity be more appropriate for the sister of an English peer? And less dangerous?"

For some reason, she wanted him to understand. "It started with a basket of food I delivered to a poor family barely surviving. The husband had been killed in the war. There were three children. When I learned many of the villagers—even the brother of my own maid—had become smugglers to feed their families, I offered to help. One thing led to another and, well, here I am."

"*Oui*, and where is that?" His gaze traveled over her body, bandaged beneath the bed cover, a body he had obviously perused at some length. "You're wounded and lying on a smuggler's ship."

"I did what I could. Foolish, it may have been, but it improved the lives of the villagers."

"I would not argue with you in your weakened condition. We will discuss your future in smuggling when you have recovered. *À présent*, I must see you fed. Some broth, I think." Over his shoulder, he said, "Gabe, fetch more of Cook's chicken broth for our guest, this time with some bits of meat."

Gabe must be his cabin boy. She did not realize the lad had been hovering in the shadows.

"*Oui, Capitaine,*" the boy replied. The cabin door opened and shut.

"You should know Gabe has been my able assistant in your care."

The comte still held her hand, its strength and warmth bringing her comfort. How long, she wondered, had he done so? She had a vague memory of her hazy fevered state in which she floated somewhere above the bed. Always she had been tethered to a hand gripping hers. He had held her to reality, to earth, perhaps even to life. She could not fail to show her gratitude.

"I am grateful, Monsieur, to you and your cabin boy for all you have done for me."

The boy returned with a bowl and spoon. "*Bonjour*, Mademoiselle."

She smiled at the boy. Donet let go of her hand and helped her to sit against the pillows. The pain knifed through her belly, causing her to wince.

His brow furrowed. "You can thank me by being a good patient, eating your broth, and doing as I instruct."

"So, I am now subject to your orders?"

"As is everyone on my ship, Mademoiselle. Would you like some brandy with the broth? It might help dull the pain."

She let out a breath, resigned for the moment to complying with the arrogant captain's demands. After all, he had likely saved her life. "Perhaps that would be wise," she agreed.

The comte took the brandy from his table and poured some in the bowl of broth Gabe held. Then Donet took the bowl and brought a spoonful of the broth to her lips.

She sipped, the burn in her throat distracting her from the pain in her belly. She had tasted brandy before, of course, but it was not a lady's drink and not usually mixed with broth.

When she'd finished all of the broth, Donet gently laid her

back on the pillow. How many times had he done so over the last few days?

"I will see you have some laudanum tonight so that you can sleep."

"A small amount, perhaps. From the look of you, Monsieur, you also need some. Did you not sleep?"

"I will now that you are out of danger."

A sudden movement at the foot of the bed drew her attention. Huge golden eyes peered at her from glossy black fur. "A cat?"

"'Tis the ship's cat, M'sieur Franklin, named after the American statesman who provided my letter of marque in the war. He is well beloved in France."

The cat rose from the bed and stalked toward her. It was the largest cat she had ever seen. "Has the cat been here all this time?"

"*Oui*, he has not left your side but to catch his dinner in the days you have lain here."

"And I have not sneezed?"

"Sneezed? *Non*, not once."

The cat came closer. She reached out to stroke its glossy fur. The huge animal began to purr and curled up beside her. "Aunt Hetty's cat always makes me sneeze. How odd this one does not."

Donet grinned. "It seems *mon chat* is pleased with your touch."

Jean trudged up the companionway, forcing his eyes to stay open, still thinking of Lady Joanna's fingers running through Franklin's fur. He had imagined those same fingers running through his hair. He shook his head to clear his thinking. After going so long without sleep, even longer without a woman, his mind had conjured something that could never be.

Emerging onto the weather deck, he breathed in the fresh sea air and yawned. The white caps on a gray sea beneath heavy dark clouds told him a storm was coming. The growing wind blew his hair into his face. Taking a ribbon from his waist, he tied it back.

Émile glanced toward Jean standing near the helm. The quartermaster's face was set in grim lines as he marched toward Jean from amidships.

"Well?" said Émile, arriving at Jean's side. "After so long and very few reports from yer lad, the whole crew wonders if the English smuggler has survived. Or their *capitaine* for that matter."

"She lives. I have remained with her because I was worried. The wound was not a simple one. She lost much blood. Then the fever consumed her." He met Émile's gaze. "For a while, it was close, *mon ami*, but I think she will recover."

"*Mon Dieu*, *Capitaine*, what would ye have done had she died? This smuggler is not only a woman, but Lady Joanna West!"

"Yes, yes, I know." He crossed his arms over his chest. Standing with his feet apart, he searched the ship for signs of damage. "I have known all along."

Émile inclined his head. "Ye have?"

"You don't think her breeches could hide her woman's shape from me, do you? It took only a little more information for me to ascertain her precise identity. I have been wondering how long it would take *you* to realize the truth of it."

Émile pressed his lips tightly together and scowled.

"'Tis true. Lady Joanna leads the Bognor smugglers."

Émile shook his head. "The crew won't like having a woman aboard. We both know 'tis bad luck to have a woman on the ship, especially one they can't touch."

"Most will accept it. You may tell them she is my lady. And those few who do not accept her I will replace in Lorient." In the long nights he had watched over her, Jean had sorted through the crew in his mind, deciding which ones might present a problem.

"How fares the ship? Gabe's reports were rather vague, but I knew if the damage were severe, you'd have sent for me."

His quartermaster looked aloft. "The English dog got off a lucky shot that sheared the main peak halyard. The bos'n and his mates rigged a jury splice that's holding for now. The spanker boom and stern are cut up some, but nothing serious." Facing Jean, he said, "The carpentry can wait until we reach port, but meanwhile, what'll ye do with *her, Capitaine*?"

"Lady Joanna will sail with us to Lorient, of course. 'Tis not far from there to Saintonge. I would not send her back to England until she is well. Nor would I allow anyone other than myself to see her safely home. Since I cannot sail *la Reine Noire* to England any time soon and my sloop in Lorient needs some alterations to be readied, the lady will be with us for some time."

"Does she know her sojourn in France will be longer than she might expect?"

Jean shook his head. "After she made her displeasure known to me at being forced to sail to Lorient, I thought to wait till we arrive before telling her she will be seeing more of France."

His quartermaster gave Jean a lingering perusal. "Ye don't seem bothered by the prospect of having her with ye."

Jean gave his friend a sidelong glance. "Oddly, I am not."

"I see."

Perhaps Émile saw more than Jean intended. But he was too weary to think of it. He closed his eyes, swaying with the movement of the ship. He could fall asleep where he stood.

"If ye don't mind my saying so, *Capitaine,* ye look like a whore's bed. Why not get something to eat and a few hours of sleep?"

Jean's head ached and his eyes burned. "That was my plan, but I could not sleep without a damage report and seeing to our passenger. Wake me should the storm turn out to be more than a small squall."

"And where will ye be sleeping?" asked Émile.

He fought a yawn. "Oh, did I forget to say? Since yours is the largest of the officers' cabins and the only one with two bunks, I thought to share with you."

Émile smirked. "Ye may recall there's a reason few would share my cabin."

Jean furrowed his brow.

"I snore."

He shrugged. "I doubt if any noise will keep me awake tonight. But if the sea turns ugly, Lady Joanna might become frightened, so wake me. I've kept Gabe out of the cabin for most of the last days. He is putting it to rights now. He's to bring her food if she is up to it, but no one, save me, may tend her wound."

Émile muttered an oath under his breath, unhappy, Jean knew, for having the lady aboard. "*Oui*, it will be done as ye say."

Jean, on the other hand, had no such qualms. With the vixen onboard, life was bound to be interesting.

Joanna watched Gabe move about the captain's cabin, cleaning up the mess created by her presence. During the two days she had lain in the throes of the fever, Donet must have denied the boy his usual duties.

Everything was in disarray, her bloodstained clothes in one corner where Donet had apparently thrown them, books scattered on the table and charts strewn across his desk. Even the leavings from his hastily eaten meals were evident.

Thoughts of the comte's care for her, especially his removing her clothes, made her cheeks flush with heat. He must have seen all of her.

The boy fussed as he cleaned the cabin, giving her the feeling he had no tolerance for disorder in his captain's domain. He set the empty chamber pot next to the bed.

Before the night was out, she would need to use it. Perhaps the brandy he had left on the stool nearby would dull the pain so that she could get out of the bed on her own.

Awake for the first time in days, she thought to engage the boy in conversation. "Gabe, I want to thank you for helping the captain attend my wound."

He looked down at his feet. "I only did as ordered."

"Even so," she began and then thought better of it. "You speak English well. Have you served the captain long?"

He straightened. "The last three years of the American War, Mademoiselle."

He must have been eight or nine when he joined Donet's crew. He had the swarthy complexion of a Breton, yet his face still possessed the soft curves of a boy beneath his wavy brown hair. Circling his neck was a red handkerchief. Over his shirt, he wore a light blue jacket. Like most of the crew, his breeches were wide-kneed "slops". Some of the crew, she had noticed, went barefoot, but Gabe wore white hose and leather shoes.

The boy reshelved two leather-bound volumes that had been lying open on the table, night reading for the comte, perhaps.

"Monsieur Donet is a good captain?"

"*Le meilleur.*" Then, possibly because he did not know she spoke French well, he added, "the best."

His hurried movements implied he felt awkward in her presence. "I imagine you would rather I did not occupy his cabin."

The boy shrugged. "'Tis what the *capitaine* wishes."

Curious, she ventured to ask, "Am I the first woman to be in his cabin?"

He turned and faced her, his stance proud. "No woman has ever stepped foot in his cabin while I have served him."

Tempted to laugh, she smiled instead. "Then I shall try not to be a burden. Once I am better able to move about, perhaps the captain can assign me another cabin."

The boy's face appeared to take on a pleased expression as he considered her words. Loyal, this one, and she admired him for it.

Gabe left the cabin saying he would return shortly. Now was her chance to use the chamber pot. Fortified with another gulp of brandy, she eased off the bed. The cabin swam before her. Slumping back on the bed, she waited until the cabin settled and the only movement was the pitch and roll of the ship.

With one hand on the bed, she gingerly slipped her feet to the deck and reached for the chamber pot, an action that brought a knifing pain to her belly. She clenched her teeth and waited for the wave of pain to pass. She had yet to see what lay under her bandages and was none too eager to glimpse the damage inflicted by Commander Ellis' Marines.

Since she could not very well crouch, she leaned to the left, stretching out her hand, and grasped the edge of the metal container. Taking a deep breath, she brought the pot up under the captain's shirt that fell to her mid-thighs and let nature do the rest. "Ah," she sighed in relief.

Still lightheaded, Joanna slowly slid the chamber pot to the deck and sagged back on the bed. The roll of the ship as it sliced through the gray sea she glimpsed out the windows only added to her unstable feeling. It wasn't the seasickness some experienced, rather a kind of weakness. It might be due to her lack of food or the loss of blood, or both.

She rested her head on the pillow and slowly pulled the blue cover over her. Her new friend, Franklin, whom she had decided to call "Ben", curled up beside her and promptly went to sleep, purring like a warm clockwork.

Had the comte really stayed with her for more than two days? She would never have thought him capable of so much tender care.

Her gaze drifted about his cabin, alighting on the pedestal table and, beyond it, the mahogany desk and bookcase, its treasured volumes secured with strips of wood. Cobalt blue velvet curtains framed the windows, the same fabric as the bed cover. The large well-appointed cabin spoke of a man who wanted his comforts while at sea.

It felt improperly intimate to be in his bed and in his private domain.

Her courage flagged as she considered her situation. She had sailed away from her home and family on a foreign ship to a country she'd never seen under the command of a captain who'd once been a pirate, not to mention his cutthroat crew. Yet Donet had tended her wound and held her hand through her fevered days and nights. Perhaps because of that, despite all the strangeness and uncertainty around her, she felt no fear. Instead, she felt protected and safe.

But what did she really know of him? A pirate turned nobleman, Donet was entering his fourth decade; she was in her second. She'd been five years old and sneaking treats from the kitchen when he'd defied his father to marry the woman he loved. When she was taking cello lessons and learning how to dance, he had become a privateer, capturing English ships and gaining accolades from two countries. He had experienced much of life when her life had only begun. Yet smuggling had brought them together and now her life was in his hands.

It could be worse, she supposed. She could have been killed. And how would Monsieur Donet, comte de Saintonge and captain of the sixteen-gun *la Reine Noire*, have explained *that* to Richard? She smiled to herself as her eyes began to grow heavy.

Perhaps pirates—or former pirates—never had to explain anything at all.

Chapter 14

Bay of Biscay, off the coast of Brittany, France

Another three days and they were past the storm and heading south by southeast, closing on Lorient. Jean felt much better for having had some sleep, though Émile's loud snoring was making him eager to return to his own bed. Not likely that. It would belong to Lady Joanna for as long as she was aboard.

Each night, he fell into the narrow bunk, imagining her curled up in his larger bunk with his cat, a very inviting scene. He had an overwhelming desire to replace the cat in her bed though he knew it could never be a simple affair with a woman like that.

After checking with M'sieur Ricard at the helm, he headed below decks. He had taken to joining Lady Joanna for his *déjeuner* and dinner since he was accustomed to eating in his cabin. Émile had dined with them once, but the quartermaster fumbled with his knife and fork, still awkward in her presence and uncomfortable with her lad's attire.

Arriving at his cabin door, Jean hesitated before knocking. He shouldn't have to knock to enter his own cabin, but gallantry required he do so.

Gabe opened the cabin door and greeted him with a terse "*Capitaine*." He supposed the lad didn't like having a woman aboard any more than did Émile, but both had accepted their captain's orders and were treating her like a guest.

Jean scanned the table. The lad had laid a fine repast of brioche, smoked fish, fruit and cheese. His mouth watered and he inhaled deeply the aroma of hot coffee wafting through the air. His first cup of the day was always most welcome.

Sunlight streamed in through the stern windows touching all in his cabin, including the vixen sitting at his table. He shut the cabin door and accepted the coffee from Gabe.

The cabin boy begged leave to go to the galley to see to his own breakfast. Jean nodded and waved him on his way.

He sipped his coffee watching his guest. She sat straight in her chair as if she had just paid a morning call on Lady Danvers and they were sharing tea in her London parlor. Her attire, however, one of his shirts and a pair of Gabe's breeches, spoke of an entirely different setting. After she had awakened from the fever, she had insisted on changing her own bandages, depriving him of a glimpse of her glorious body, but he had not forgotten what lay beneath her male attire.

"Won't you join me?" she asked.

He pulled out a chair and sat. "You do better as each day passes."

"I do, don't I?"

Franklin sidled to the table and disappeared under it. Jean inclined his head to see the cat rubbing against her leg. "My cat has become quite attached to you."

The cat purred and she reached down to scratch his ears.

"Ben and I have become friends; he likes to sleep next to me."

"Ben?"

Her cognac eyes glistened with her smile. "I think the shorter name suits him, don't you? In any event, he doesn't seem to mind."

"Hmm..." Jean set down his coffee and picked up a piece of brioche. The vixen continued to stroke the cat's fur. He wouldn't mind what she called him either if he could sleep next to her and she petted him the way she was petting the cat.

Since his wife died, he had indulged in only a few liaisons with women, finding them unsatisfying. Yet he still had desires and the stirrings her presence caused brought to mind feelings long forgotten, emotions he thought never to have again. Fear licked at the wounds he had hidden for years.

Lady Joanna lavished honey on her brioche and then licked it off. Watching her pink tongue reach out to taste the sweet nectar made his loins harden.

He remembered spreading honey on her belly but, at the time, licking it from her skin had not occurred to him so focused had he been on saving her life. But now, he wanted to kiss those honeyed lips, to take her full breasts in his hands and lick her all over before sending his hard body pounding into her softness. Clamping down on his rising desire, he broke off another piece of brioche and brought it to his mouth.

"'Tis a bit like painting the lily to add honey to the sweet bread, don't you think?"

She grinned. "Since I am forced to be your *guest*, Monsieur Donet, I should think I might eat the brioche any way I like. Besides, your cabin boy offered me the honey and 'tis quite good."

"It comes from Guernsey." He lifted his coffee to his mouth and swallowed the dark liquid, ordering his body to calm. "A place I think you would like very much. I have a warehouse there full of tea, brandy and... other things. That is where the silk was stored."

"I remember the silk," she said with a sigh. "Brocade such as I have never seen."

"I chose the vermilion because I knew it would go well with your hair."

Her eyes flashed a look of surprise before focusing on her coffee. "I do recall you telling me you have known from the beginning I was a smuggler. 'Tis embarrassing to think my disguise so transparent."

"Only to me. My quartermaster, M'sieur Bequel, with whom

you spoke, never suspected. Nor did any of my crew."

She smiled at him over her brioche and swept her tongue over her honey-sweetened lips. The sunlight had rendered her long auburn curls a waterfall of burnished copper. The innocence in her eyes told him she was unaware of her seductive effect.

Her eyes seemed to scrutinize him as she bit her bottom lip. "So, you keep secrets?"

"Many," he said.

"A man who keeps secrets is unusual. And one who knows ladies' fashion is most rare. You, Captain Donet, are a rare and unusual man."

He laughed. "I am French, Mademoiselle. I once had a wife and still have a daughter, and I have been to Versailles, which may explain my familiarity with silk and ladies' fashions. As for the other, you must know that pirates and spies, both of which I have been, must frequently keep secrets."

"I knew you had been a pirate, but a spy?"

"In the war, *oui*. Ostensibly for America's Mr. Franklin, but our Foreign Minister, Charles Gravier, comte de Vergennes, was his partner in all."

She merely shrugged at his past pursuits, then blithely licked honey from another piece of brioche. Many women would be horrified. Not this one.

He liked looking at her across his table and would regret the day he must return her to her brother. But until then, he would enjoy her company. "Once we are anchored in Lorient, I will take you to my home. It overlooks the harbor. You will be more comfortable there. I will, of course, provide you with a maid." He didn't expect to find a lady's maid at the château in Saintonge since both his brother and father had been widowers at the time of their deaths.

"How long will we be in Lorient?"

"Only a few days." He did not tell her they would be going on from there to Saintonge. She would know soon enough. "If

M'sieur Bouchet assures me you are on your way to a full recovery, I will take you to a modiste I know who can make up some gowns. At my expense, of course."

"'Tis very generous, Monsieur, but it hardly seems fitting for you to buy clothes for a lady who is not your wife, your sister or your daughter."

"If it bothers you, I can seek recompense from Torrington, but I would prefer the gowns and other garments you will require be my gift for your trouble. I can hardly send you back to England in breeches."

Her cheeks flushed scarlet. At that moment, sitting there with her auburn hair falling down her back and honey glistening on her lips, he had no desire to return her to England or, indeed, to send her anywhere he did not plan to go.

Stifling an urge to tumble her to his bed, he set his napkin on the table and stood. "I must see my ship safely into Lorient. When that is accomplished, I will come for you."

Joanna drank the last of her coffee, which was quite good, though she found it ironic Donet did not offer her tea when he must have plenty of it stashed in his hold. Or, maybe he no longer did, having unloaded his goods at Bognor. All but the silk, she reminded herself. That was still aboard. He had known she would like the vermilion silk. The man had very good taste.

Slowly, she rose, flinching only a little at the pull of her damaged but healing skin and walked to the stern windows. She felt quite accomplished now that she could cross the cabin while the ship was under way without holding on to the edge of the table.

Gazing out at the sun dancing on the waters roiling in the ship's wake, she drifted into a contented state and her mind turned to the mysterious Captain Donet.

She had no trouble picturing him as a spy. There had always

been an air of danger and mystery about him. The way he had shouted orders to his crew as the revenue cutter sailed straight toward them proved he was calm in the face of danger.

He had said she would be staying at his home in Lorient. 'Twould be scandalous if it were known she had been alone with him in his home, but the prospect appealed all the same. He had been a gentleman for all she had feared him a rogue. And she believed he would keep his word and return her to England. Truth be told, she enjoyed being with him, perhaps too much for her own good.

Behind her, she heard the cabin door open and turned to see Gabe returning. "Good morning."

"*Bonjour*, my lady." He set about clearing the table and straightening the cabin.

Joanna turned back to gaze out the large windows. The coastline of Brittany lay off one side of the ship. As the ship turned eastward, land came into view off the stern she had not noticed before. "Is that an island?"

Without looking out the window, the cabin boy said, "*Île de Groix*, the island Groix. It marks the place where the ship turns into the channel leading to the harbor of Lorient."

The small island seemed to float above the blue waters. Above its sea-battered cliffs, white clouds drifted in an azure sky. She would have liked to see the island from the main deck, but Donet had not allowed her out of his cabin. At first, the pain from her wound would not permit her to climb the ladder or to walk so far. Now, she believed his order to stay below had more to do with his men. They must know he kept a woman in his cabin, but did they believe she was an injured English smuggler who had masqueraded as a man? Or did they think he had made her his mistress?

She toyed with the wicked thought for a moment, allowing her imagination to sweep her into his arms. He was the first man to ever make her think of such things. But perhaps he did not find her attractive, particularly in her men's clothing. After all, he had been more polite than anything. He did not even flirt with her like other men did.

When he came for her, ready to disembark, she might be able to discern from the faces of his crew what they believed about her. M'sieur Bequel, the quartermaster, gave no hint of his feelings when he had joined her and Donet for dinner. A gruff man, he had nevertheless been gracious in his manners, recalling to mind his attendance at the christening. Even then, she had thought there was something familiar about Bequel.

Gabe came up beside her. "The *capitaine* asked me to give you one of his cloaks to wear. I have placed it just there." He gestured to a black cloak flung over the back of one of the chairs. "It will be too large, I fear, but at least you can cover yourself. It has a hood."

"*Merci*, Gabe. If he insists, I will wear it, but I expect today is too warm for a cloak. From what I can see, it will be a lovely day in Lorient."

"*Oui*. Lorient is a very fine place." He gave her a sidelong glance. "Many privateers and smugglers sail from there."

She smiled to herself at the boy's remark. Yes, she was a smuggler. Just like his captain.

Lorient, France

Draped in the ridiculously large cloak, Joanna followed Donet out of his cabin, grateful for his assistance in scaling the ladder to the weather deck. His touch, as ever, made her body come alive. She would have liked to turn in his arms and see if he would kiss her, but he acted only the gentleman.

With the hood drawn over her head, she crossed the deck behind Donet, his crew turning to stare, but not uttering a single jeer or rude comment.

With a few words to M'sieur Bequel, Donet took her elbow

and led her down the gangway to the quay, the long cloak trailing behind her.

Once on the quay, she paused to scan the immense harbor, noting the many ships were not crowded together as they were on the Thames.

"So many ships," she remarked.

"Lorient trades with Africa, India, America and the French colonies, so there are merchantmen as well as Indiamen here. And the Royal Navy of France uses Lorient. The port is always busy."

Joanna thought it a splendid place. She had always loved the energy surrounding London's port on the Thames. This port had the same feel.

One of Donet's crew hailed a carriage and, soon, they were traveling away from the harbor. "The town is a half-mile from the port. 'Tis where M'sieur Bouchet has his practice."

Joanna turned toward the open window, enjoying the breeze on her face after so many days below decks. The horses' hooves clattered on the cobblestones as the carriage briskly moved along.

Lorient's streets were broad and well paved with white stone houses and buildings on either side. Beyond the harbor lay wooded hills with scattered homes visible among the trees. Might he live in one of those?

He gazed out the window, pointing to the distant streets. "The main streets diverge in rays from the city gate. The others cross them at right angles. All is very orderly and clean, as you can see."

She looked at him askance. Amusement danced in his dark gaze. She would not rise to the bait. All knew London had dirty streets. "And where do you live?"

"In the hills above the town. But first, we must pay a visit to M'sieur Bouchet. I dispatched one of my crew to let him know to expect us."

They arrived at a small storefront with paned glass windows looking out on the street. Over the carved wooden door hung a gilded sign with the name "M. Bouchet" painted in script and beneath it "*Chirurgien*".

The surgeon was nothing like Joanna expected.

A man of small stature with thinning gray hair, his green eyes sparkled behind his spectacles. "My lady, I have been expecting you."

He wore simple but well-made clothing: a moss green velvet coat over black waistcoat and breeches. His cravat was devoid of lace but well tied. His manner was confidant yet oddly humble for a man so well thought of. *So this is the miracle-working surgeon.*

After Donet introduced them, Bouchet glanced at her briefly before waving her into the room where he examined his patients.

When Donet tried to follow, Bouchet stopped him with his outstretched hand. "I can see you are anxious, *Capitaine*, but you must allow me to do my work. Once I am finished with the mademoiselle, you will have my report."

It occurred to Joanna that no one addressed him as the comte de Saintonge or Monsieur le comte, not on his ship, nor here in Lorient. All seemed to identify him with his ships and the sea, not the lands that went with his title. A nobleman engaged in business would be thought odd in England. Likely, it was the same in France, yet all accepted Donet no matter his role.

She followed the small surgeon into the room. One wall of his office was covered by a large mahogany cabinet filled with bottles and leather-bound books. The bottles were all neatly labeled though she could not read them from where she stood.

She turned to face him, uncertain as to what she should do.

"Show me the wound, if you will, Mademoiselle."

Even though she knew him to be a surgeon greatly respected by the comte, to her, Bouchet was still a strange man. Nevertheless, she did as he asked and lifted her shirt and opened her breeches to bare her wounded flesh for his examination. She had given up the bandages this day knowing she was to see him.

He touched the large scab stretching across her belly, studying the skin around the healing wound. "You are fortunate 'twas M'sieur Donet who treated the wound, for he has watched me patch up his crew over the years and has obviously been paying close attention."

He stood and wiped his hands on a cloth. "You will have a scar, but none so grievous as you might have had if another had tended you."

Joanna believed she lived because of Donet's efforts. Here was confirmation.

Monsieur Bouchet eyed her over his spectacles. "You may restore your clothes, Mademoiselle, such as they are. I expect the *capitaine* will replace them with proper attire for a lady."

She felt her cheeks heat and tucked the captain's shirt into her breeches. "He has told me he intends to do so."

"I don't suppose it would do any good to inquire as to how you came by the wound."

"Does it matter, sir?" She would rather not admit she and the captain were smugglers, pursued by one of His Majesty's revenue cutters.

"Perhaps not. Keep the wound clean and give it fresh air." He handed her a small pot with a cork stuck in it. "Here is some salve. You will need it, for the wound will itch as it heals. Once you have a lady's clothing, do not bind your stays or lace your gowns as tightly as you might otherwise."

"Yes, sir," she said, accepting his salve and his advice.

He paused as if considering what next to say. "I am very fond of the impudent *capitaine*, Mademoiselle, and since he has brought you to me, concern for you seeping from his every pore, I can only assume he is very fond of you. Know this: He bears wounds only seen with the heart, and the scars that have formed over the years still pain him. Tread carefully."

The surgeon's manner was in earnest, his counsel sincere and given for a purpose. She would remember it. "Thank you for telling me."

He returned her a small smile and, with his words still echoing in her mind, she followed him out of the room. In the entry, Donet paced before the door.

When he looked up, brows raised in question, Bouchet said, "The wound heals nicely. You have done well, *Capitaine*, though you would have done better to have prevented the lady's wound in the first place."

"You are right, of course," said Donet with uncharacteristic humility. "I will endeavor to assure *la Reine Noire* is not again exposed to the muskets of England's Royal Marines."

Joanna cringed. 'Twas the very information she had hoped to conceal.

The surgeon chuckled. "I recall hearing similar words from you before."

Donet reached into his pocket and pulled out some coins. Bouchet waved him off. "You have given me enough money over the years to pay for my lodgings for the next decade. I would rather you spent your gold on proper garments for the lady."

Joanna offered her hand to the surgeon, whom she was coming to like very much. Anyone who stood up to Donet earned her respect. "Thank you, Monsieur."

"My pleasure," he replied, bowing over her hand. Then he winked at Donet and went back into his office, closing the door.

They returned to the street and Donet assisted her into the waiting carriage.

"He is a surgeon of great skill?"

"He has saved the life of more than one of my crew. We hold him in the highest regard but, unfortunately, I have not been able to persuade him to sail with me."

"Your talk of Royal Marines firing on your ship would not convince him to leave France?"

He chuckled. "You are probably correct. He knows well the hazards of the sea, particularly on a privateer's ship. Even as a merchantman, my decks are not always free of danger. I take it you did not tell him?"

"I said nothing of how I came by the wound."

"Well, Bouchet has seen enough to recognize yours for what it is. Given his optimistic words of your recovery, if you are willing, I would take you next to the modiste."

"I cannot follow you about Lorient dressed like this." She opened the cloak to reveal her male attire. "Yes, by all means, the modiste's."

"*Parfait.*" He leaned out the window and shouted an address to the coachman.

The carriage lurched forward, picking up speed as it rumbled over the cobblestones. Joanna looked out the window, aware the comte's eyes still rested upon her. She had been keenly aware of his penetrating gaze that first night in Bognor. And now, sitting across from him, her heart beat excitedly. She kept her eyes on the passing shops, unwilling for him to see how he affected her.

The shops they passed were of different sizes but close together and all neatly trimmed out. Many of the doors were painted in bright colors.

A few streets on, the carriage rolled to a stop in front of a shop with a bay window. Over the bright blue door was a sign that read "Mme Provot".

Donet helped her down. "Noëlle Provot is the finest modiste in Lorient. She learned her trade in Paris and returned home to marry M'sieur Provot, one of my business partners."

Joanna gave him a sidelong glance, resisting the urge to ask what business that might be. It seemed the pirate had friends at all levels of society, both in London and in France. Unconfined to one class, he could move in all, seamlessly blending in with whatever group he deigned to join. Perhaps he had done so as a spy.

Donet opened the door and gestured her inside.

Joanna stared in wonder. Shelves from counter to ceiling graced the walls of the antechamber, filled with bolts of fabric in a rainbow of colors. Some were shimmering satins and silks, others fine woolens. She had frequented many shops in London with Cornelia searching for silks, satins and velvets. This establishment competed well with those in the selection offered.

"*Capitaine* Donet!" exclaimed a petite woman, who rushed from behind the counter toward him. "You return!" The modiste had a natural grace that reminded Joanna of Donet's daughter Claire. Perhaps it came with being French.

He placed a kiss on each of the woman's cheeks. "Madame, not only have I returned, but I have brought you a new customer."

The woman's blue eyes regarded Joanna with interest, the cloak she wore, her boy's shoes and her long auburn hair falling about her shoulders now that she'd doffed the hood. What a ragtag she must appear to this elegant French modiste.

The woman, older than Joanna by a decade, had a pleasant demeanor. Her cinnamon silk gown was simply styled with the merest bit of white lace at her cuffs. She wore her dark brown hair swept off her narrow face and twisted into a knot at her nape with a wooden pencil piercing it through. A very functional embellishment.

Without taking her eyes from Joanna, Madame Provot asked Donet, "Can this be the daughter for whom I have sewed so many gowns?"

Joanna stifled a gasp and glanced at Donet.

He covered his mouth with his hand and cleared his throat. "*Non*, this is not Claire, Madame. Allow me to introduce Lady Joanna West."

Joanna had yet to speak, which would have told the modiste she was English, not French, but now she did. "I am most grateful to meet you, Madame Provot. As you can see," she held open the cloak, "I am in dire need of a lady's clothing."

"*Oui, je vois bien cela*!" the modiste exclaimed, her expression conveying her shock at what Joanna wore. "I will see to it immediately." With a pointed glance at Donet, she chided, "Wherever have you taken the lady that she would need to wear such clothes? They do not even fit her." When he began to speak, the modiste waved him off. "*Non, non*, do not tell me. I do not wish to know."

"The lady will require more than gowns," said Donet. "In truth, a wardrobe is required and all that goes with it. The lady has some fine bolts of silk, which will be delivered to you later today from my ship, but you and she are free to select whatever fabric appeals. The bill is mine to pay. And if you could manage to find a gown for her to wear now, it would be much appreciated."

The modiste's eyes perked up. Joanna was certain Donet's "appreciation" translated into more coin. "*Entendu*. It shall be done as you wish, *Capitaine*." She looked at Joanna as if measuring her. "There is a gown that is nearly finished. I think it might suit you well. My assistant can alter it quickly."

"That would be fine." For once, Joanna was glad to doff breeches for a lady's gown.

From his expression, Donet seemed pleased with the speed at which the woman was moving. But then, she was probably used to the demanding captain.

The modiste showed Joanna into a large inner room decorated in cream walls, one of which was covered in mirrors. Facing the mirrors on the far side of the room were two Louis XIV chairs upholstered in blue silk brocade. On the floor was an Aubusson carpet that reminded Joanna of Cornelia with its wide peach border. In the center, there was a ring of blue, spread like an open fan and surrounded with flowers. The effect was graceful and feminine like the woman who reigned over the shop.

Madame Provot called for her assistant, a girl she called "Flavie", at the same time she reached for a silk gown in Verona green hanging on one of several pegs artfully arranged on one wall. The gown's styling was tasteful, the bodice adorned with minimal lace and only a few bows. She could wear it most anywhere.

A young woman wearing a pink gown decorated with a blue gauze fichu and a mobcap over her blonde hair entered through a partly open door to what must have been a workshop. "Flavie," said Madame Provot, "this is Lady Joanna, a friend of *Capitaine* Donet."

The girl curtsied and, taking note of Joanna's clothing, blinked twice as if to clear the image from her mind.

"We will be making several gowns for her," Madame Provot continued, "a pelisse, a cloak and a bed robe. Since there is no time for a new one, the pale green brocade robe we keep for special clients will do. I will be back shortly to measure but, in the meanwhile, find her some undergarments and help her try on this gown. I believe it will fit with minor tailoring. You must finish it promptly as she will wear it today. She will also need a *chemise de nuit*."

Flavie dipped a small curtsy. "*Oui*, Madame."

The modiste faced Joanna. "If you will excuse me, my lady, I shall return in a moment."

"Thank you." Her gaze followed Madame Provot as she hurried out of the room, leaving Joanna with the distinct impression "the *capitaine*" was about to be pelted with questions.

Chapter 15

Jean watched Noëlle close the door to the inner room and walk toward him in determined fashion. He waited for the questions he knew would come.

"And what have we here, *Capitaine*? Plunder from one of your raids?"

He smiled. "You know me better than that, Noëlle. Have I ever brought home a woman from any of my trips?"

She pursed her lips and brought one hand to her chin. "*Non*, but I see the way you look at this one. Am I designing clothes for a new mistress *peut-être*?" With a smile, she moved her hand to her hip. "One who likes to wear the trousers, eh?"

"*Non*. Despite her appearance, Lady Joanna is the sister of a prominent English earl."

Taken aback, she asked, "How did such a woman end up with you unchaperoned in Lorient?"

He let out an exasperated breath, supposing he would have to tell the tale more than once before it was done. "You recall that your husband and I sometimes invest in merchandise intended for English appetites?"

"*Oui*, but what has this lady to do with that?"

"Let's just say one of those trips to deliver the merchandise led to an altercation with the revenue authorities while the mademoiselle was on my ship—in disguise, of course. Unfortunately, a musket ball found its way to her flesh."

Noëlle's expression became one of alarm. He attempted to assure her. "She has been wounded, *oui*, but she is healing. Which reminds me, when you fit her for the gowns, do not constrict her overmuch so that it pains her."

"Am I to know *where* she is wounded?"

"I suppose you must. She may tell you herself, but the musket ball cut across her belly."

"*Mon Dieu.*" She shook her head. "I will not ask how you know that, M'sieur. But do not worry for her. I will take the greatest of care. Skirts are typically full and we will not use a stomacher nor lace her gown overmuch." She held her hands in front of her. "Now, tell me. Am I designing gowns for Lorient or somewhere else you have yet to go? Paris, as you are aware, requires more formal gowns than here."

"For now, it will be Lorient and then on to Saintonge, but the lady does not know of the latter destination, so please do not mention it."

"Ah yes, I had heard our favorite *capitaine* now has a title. Your father's, *oui*?"

He nodded.

"I am sorry for your loss."

If Jean mourned at all it was for his brother. Their youth spent together had brought them close. "It has been many years since I have seen either of them, Noëlle. The title matters little to me. And to you, I am still '*Capitaine*'."

"*Très bien, Capitaine*. I will have the one gown for her before you leave today along with some nightclothes. The rest will follow in two days' time."

"That is all the time we have, I'm afraid. If you can have them sewn faster, I will pay for the additional seamstresses."

"*Très bien*. It shall be done. The gowns shall be delivered to you the day after tomorrow. Should they require adjustments, there will be time before you depart."

She turned toward the fitting room and then paused, looking back at him. "Am I wrong in assuming you wish to watch as I fit the lady?"

"*Non*, you are quite correct."

Since the girl had to supply Joanna with stays and a petticoat, it took a few minutes before she had donned those over a thin shift. Flavie was just slipping the green gown over Joanna's head when the door opened and Madame Provot briskly strode inside, her skirts swishing noisily as she cried for pins and a tape to measure with.

Flavie quickly tied Joanna's laces and then scampered off to find the requested items.

Behind the modiste, Donet walked in and took one of the chairs, crossing his arms and legs as if he meant to stay and watch.

Surely not! Joanna met his intense gaze in the mirror with one of her own. "Monsieur Donet, do you intend to remain while I am fitted?"

He grinned like the pirate he had once been. "I do."

Joanna did not like his impertinence one bit, but since she was fully clothed, she merely let out a "humph". In the mirror she could see his dark eyes devouring her.

Even from that distance his presence had a powerful effect. She imagined his hands coming around her to stroke her breasts, his lips kissing her neck. Beneath the gown, her nipples hardened. She flushed scarlet.

Catching another glimpse of him in the mirror, she wondered if it had been his intention to turn her into a mass of quivering flesh.

Be he pirate or nobleman, Donet was a virile man, confident in his appeal. She was no simpering debutante, but she was unschooled and untried in the ways of a man with a woman. And this was no ordinary man she could banter with and then ignore.

Like the mighty sea he sailed, Donet was a force to be reckoned with, and she was inexorably drawn to him.

Madame Provot began pinning in the waist. Flavie, having returned, knelt at Joanna's feet to pin up the hem.

The bodice fit perfectly, revealing only the edge of her rounded breasts. Joanna held still, not wishing to be stuck with an errant pin.

"There." The modiste stood back, hands on her hips, assessing the temporary adjustments she had made. "What do you think, *Capitaine*? Is she not lovely in this gown?"

Joanna looked in the mirror seeing the slow smile spread across the comte's face. "Lady Joanna is lovely in any gown. Even in breeches, she draws a man's eye."

"Just as I thought," said the modiste, shooting Donet a look that only made his smile broaden.

Joanna felt heat rise in her cheeks. She thought back over their encounters since she had first met him at the reception, those times when he had been most polite. Had he looked at her then the way he did now? She had been so worried for her sister's virtue, had she failed to see her own was at risk?

Madame Provot began unlacing the gown. "Now for the measurements."

Joanna held the gown to her. "Monsieur Donet, you cannot stay for this!"

He shrugged and got to his feet. "I could and Noëlle would not object if I did. But since you do, I will wait outside." As he turned to go, she breathed a sigh of relief. He may have seen her naked when treating her wound, but she had not been conscious then.

"Thank you."

He gave her a parting look before slipping through the door.

The modiste let the gown fall and Joanna stepped out of it, leaving her in stays, a single petticoat and shift. Madame Provot then began measuring her. "The *Capitaine* is a most attractive man, *n'est-ce pas*?"

How could Joanna fail to admit to another woman what none could deny? "He is."

"Many women in Lorient desire him but, until now, he has held himself apart from all. You are *très* unique."

"He didn't really have a choice except to bring me. I was unconscious and bleeding on his deck."

"Ah, *oui*, the wound. He mentioned it. He was most concerned I not impair your healing. You must tell me if any of the garments I give you are too tight." The modiste slipped the tape around her waist. "You are slender and your waist is small enough without having to cinch you in. The only place you possess true fullness is in the one place men desire to see more flesh."

"If that was a compliment, Madame, I thank you, though truly I had nothing to do with it. My mother was the same."

"Your mother no longer lives?"

"She died two years ago and my father five years before that." Joanna did not mention her older brother who died last year. The four siblings did not often speak of Wills. They all missed him terribly.

"Then you and the *capitaine* have that in common, Mademoiselle. Both of his parents are dead."

"Is that how he came into the title?"

"*Non.*" The modiste took the last measurement and looked up at her. "He had an older brother, Henri. Both he and the *capitaine*'s father were killed not long ago in a terrible carriage accident."

"How awful to lose them like that."

"They were not close, but the *capitaine* will have to tell you the story."

The modiste walked to the back room door, opened it and called for another assistant. A woman in a mobcap poked her head in the opening. "I need some silk fabric," said Madame Provot.

"Some of that sapphire and a length of the gold. The emerald brocade and lemon yellow silk with embroidered edges will do nicely as well. *Capitaine* Donet will be having more silk delivered this afternoon."

The girl left for the antechamber. Once Flavie returned with the green gown, she and the modiste helped Joanna to dress.

Standing back to view her creation, Madame Provot exclaimed, "*C'est parfait*!

A man of action, Jean hated to linger anywhere without good cause, but knowing the woman he waited for only increased his anticipation. He wanted to see her dressed as a lady again and looked forward to showing her his home in Lorient.

After what seemed like an hour, which he attributed to the ladies' chatter as well as the selection of fabric and measuring, Lady Joanna emerged from the fitting room in the lovely green silk gown, now tailored to her enticing curves. It was not unlike the one she had worn the night he'd first met her at the reception in Chichester. However, this was more of a day gown and the color more subdued than the emerald green she had worn that night.

"Do you like the hat?" Lady Joanna asked, tipping the brim of the straw hat to an angle that drew his attention to her eyes. "Madame Provot insisted I wear it."

Her auburn curls had been drawn away from her face and simply tied with a ribbon. She looked very young and very pretty with it styled that way, reminding him how much older he was than she. Had she lived, his wife, Ariane, would have been a decade older than Lady Joanna.

The English vixen was a bold adventuress. Ariane had been shy, sweet and retiring. His wife had been horrified at the risks his smuggling brought. Had she lived to see his privateering, she would have known great fear. The two women were both ladies but so very different.

"Noëlle has excellent taste," he said. "The hat becomes you." To Noëlle, who had followed Lady Joanna into the shop's antechamber, he said, "You have done well."

The modiste's assistant hurried to place a package in her mistress' arms. Noëlle passed it to him. "She will need this before she has the rest of the gowns."

"I owe you my thanks, Madame." With that, he tipped his tricorne to the modiste and offered his arm to Lady Joanna. As they left, he had the oddest feeling his world was about to change. 'Twas the same feeling he got whenever a squall threatened his ship.

The carriage wound its way into the hills above the harbor. Joanna gripped the strap to avoid falling into the comte as the vehicle careened around the curves. The carriage seat was narrow, bringing his body close to hers. When his thigh touched her gown, she forced herself to look out the window and not at him.

Many ships were anchored in the harbor's cerulean blue waters. Several appeared to be merchantmen, but there were also men-of-war and smaller boats.

In the distance, fishing boats were returning with the afternoon tide.

On one side of the harbor was a huge round tower that looked to be a hundred feet high. Made of white stone, it had a railed gallery at the top.

"Can that tower be a lighthouse?" she asked Donet.

"*Non*, though it does look a bit like a very tall one. In recent years, lightning has damaged it, so pieces are missing. 'Tis the signal tower, built as a watchtower to monitor the approach of the ships belonging to the Company of the Indies. And to discourage smuggling."

"Oh."

"Do not worry, my lady. The king's grandfather, Louis XV, bought the buildings and properties for the Royal Navy when the Company went bankrupt some years ago. Smuggling ships destined for England now operate quite unimpeded to the benefit of France."

"Is that why you live here?" she asked, turning to face him.

"In part. When Claire was born, Lorient became our refuge. Neither my father nor Ariane's approved of our marriage. We were cast out without a *sou*. It was here a friend put me in touch with the smugglers. And it was here I first went to sea as a smuggler myself to feed my family. It took years, but eventually I gained my own ship."

Ariane. His wife's name. Joanna had so many conflicting emotions running through her just then. She felt sad for the plight of the young family and a nobleman's son forced to turn to smuggling to buy bread, but his hard life had made him the man he had become. Not the soft French nobleman he might have been, but a man of the sea, a man of great inner strength whose crew snapped to follow his commands. Perhaps, there was little difference between what he had done and what the villagers of Chichester did to keep from starving.

"It must have been a hard time."

His look turned wistful. "In many ways, it was the very best of times."

She attributed the look in his eyes to his love for his wife. Perhaps he still loved her. Joanna sighed. One could vie with another woman for a man's affection, but how did one compete with a ghost given the status of a saint?

Looking out the window again, she searched for another subject, a happier one. "Can you see your ship from here?"

He reached across her to point to a black-hulled ship. "Just there." His body pressed into hers and she leaned into his heat, melting like wax put to a flame. She recalled another time his touch had affected her so. The night they had danced in London.

"Lorient trades with both India and China," he said, sitting back on the seat. "'Tis a profitable business. Privateers, too, sailed from here, especially during the American War."

"How many ships do you have?" she asked, curious.

"Three now, but I often held more during the war. They were English ships I seized for M'sieur Franklin, their crews exchanged for American sailors imprisoned in England. One of the three ships I own now is currently in the West Indies. Only my sloop and *la Reine Noire* are here in Lorient."

Climbing a small rise, the carriage stopped in front of a well-kept white stone house of two stories nestled among the trees. Behind the house in the distance, she glimpsed the harbor. A profusion of pink and lavender flowers grew in neat rows against the front of the house.

Sunlight filtered through the branches to fall upon the front door. Painted black, like the shutters, it had a large doorknocker of polished brass. A glistening shell sat on top of the rounded knocker and wave-like embellishments curved all around.

She counted eight windows across the front of the house, four on each story. Delicate lace curtains hung in the windows. It was not the home she would have pictured for a widowed sea captain much less a pirate.

"*Voilà*, we have arrived." He stepped down from the carriage and turned to assist her with one hand while he held the package the modiste had given him in the other.

The front door opened, and a man and woman stepped out. The plump woman waited by the door, but the slender man came to Donet's side.

"*Bienvenue*, Monsieur. Your crew sent word from Guernsey that you would be along, but we were unsure when to expect you."

"I wasn't certain myself, Vernier." Donet turned to Joanna. "Allow me to introduce my valet, Vernier.

To Joanna, the man appeared a dour but efficient sort, the kind she'd encountered in many homes of the English aristocracy. Her brother's valet had the same air about him. "*Bonjour*, Vernier."

"This is Lady Joanna West, Vernier. She will be my guest while I am in Lorient."

The valet bowed. "At your service, Mademoiselle."

Donet leaned in to share with her a salient fact. "Like Bouchet, Vernier chooses not to go to sea and Gabe is happy to take his place."

"'Tis the *mal de mer*," the valet muttered in explanation.

Donet handed the package he carried to the valet. "For Mademoiselle's bedchamber." Then he pressed his hand into the small of her back and urged her forward. "The harbor views are best seen from the rear of the house." His warm hand touching her back had its effect, making her sensitive to his touch as he guided her toward the door.

The woman who waited smiled at the approach of her master.

He took the woman's large upper arms in his hands and gave her a resounding kiss on each cheek.

The woman blushed and covered her mouth. "Oh, Monsieur." Then shyly she looked up at him. "'Tis good to have you back."

"Rose, meet my guest, Lady Joanna West."

The woman curtsied, holding her skirts. "Mademoiselle."

"Rose is my housekeeper in Lorient," said Donet. "Her cooking is something to anticipate."

Again, the woman blushed, clearly enthralled with her master.

Joanna returned the housekeeper a smile and, guided by Donet, passed through the open door. The servants followed.

Once inside, Donet unbelted his sword and doffed his tricorne, handing both to his valet.

"Would you and the lady be wanting some refreshment?" Rose asked.

Donet glanced at Joanna. "Some tea, *peut-être*?"

She nodded. On one side of the entry, she glimpsed a large parlor and on the other side a dining table. Directly ahead, a staircase led to the second story.

"I'll see you are served in the parlor," said the housekeeper, before ducking behind the stairway. Joanna assumed it must be a passage to the kitchen.

Donet offered her his arm. "Allow me to show you to your chamber."

She lifted her skirts and placed her hand on his arm. They climbed the stairs.

"The house is not large, but it meets my needs when I am here, and there are rooms for guests."

When they reached the top of the stairs, he directed her to the left. Midway down the corridor, they stopped at a door on the right. He turned the handle and gestured her inside.

Immediately before her was a row of windows looking out on the harbor in the distance. "What a lovely view!" she exclaimed going to them.

He spoke from behind her. "The view is what convinced me to purchase this house."

She turned to see his eyes on her. Her heart fluttered in her chest like a skittish colt. Donet was simply too handsome, too virile to trust herself alone with him, particularly in a bedchamber. Tearing her gaze from his, she glanced about the room.

On her right, she saw a dressing table, mirror and side table. To her left stood a magnificent four-poster, its cover, headboard and curtains all done up in azure blue velvet. Next to it was a fireplace with a white marble mantel.

She walked to the bed and ran her fingers over the soft blue velvet.

"The bed linens you see are the same color as the waters off Guernsey. I like the colors of the sky and the sea in my home."

"I can see why. Guernsey must be a beautiful place."

"I said you would like it. I do not think I am wrong."

She turned to face him. "I doubt you are ever wrong, are you?"

"Not often. Not about you."

That he should have such confidence in knowing her rankled, but then he had been the only one to see through her disguise. She had to give him that. Turning toward the door, she said, "Perhaps it is time for tea?"

He chuckled as if he had read her mind and gestured her out of the room.

While they waited for tea, Joanna looked around the parlor. Like her bedchamber, it was decorated in shades of blue. The curtains framing the lace-covered windows were a deep shade of Prussian blue. The two sofas that faced each other in front of the fireplace were a blue toile with white figures of a girl and a boy.

The housekeeper brought tea on an oval tray and set it on the small table between the sofas. Joanna poured, feeling Donet's eyes on her as she did.

She sat on one sofa and he on the other. Behind him, she spotted a large ball hanging from the ceiling in one corner of the room. "Is that a globe?"

"It is."

She set down her teacup and walked to the globe, turning it slowly. "I have never seen one hanging from the ceiling."

"I thought it unique when I first saw it, like the planetarium clock I bought in London."

She turned from the globe to see his wry smile. "I will grant you that both are truly unusual." She was certain neither of them wanted to do battle again over a clock.

After they finished their tea, Joanna begged leave to rest.

Though her wound no longer pained her, all the twisting and changing at Madame Provot's left her in need of a rest before supper.

"I must see to some matters of business and my quartermaster will be by this afternoon, so I would not be good company in any event. By all means, do have a rest."

Joanna returned to her bedchamber. A fire had been laid. Perhaps the housekeeper had a lad to help with such tasks. The air in the room was cool. She imagined the night might present a chill. A fire would be welcome.

On the bed was the package Madame Provot had given Donet. She took off her hat and managed to unlace her gown and slide it from her shoulders. She laid it across the chair sitting next to the fireplace. Until she had others, she would need to treat this gown with care.

She didn't bother to remove her stays and petticoat. Inside the package, she found a shift-like garment decorated with delicate lace and pale green ribbon. She recalled the modiste had spoken of a *chemise de nuit*. Folded underneath was a lovely robe in green brocade silk. She set aside the chemise and donned the loose robe. Pulling back the velvet cover, she slipped between the soft sheets.

A moment later, she drifted to sleep with visions of a dark pirate standing on the deck of his ship gazing toward a dark shore.

"Rose, I need a maid for Lady Joanna, one who is free to travel with us to Saintonge. Do you know of a girl in Lorient who might be qualified for such a position?"

"*Oui, Capitaine*. My niece is training to be a lady's maid and would leap at the opportunity. She is good with hair and even speaks a bit of English."

"Excellent. Have her come around tomorrow morning so Lady Joanna can meet her to see if they suit."

"*Oui*, Monsieur." The housekeeper bowed and left as Vernier entered the study.

"Monsieur Bequel is here," his valet announced.

"Show him in." Jean set aside the ledgers he had been working on and greeted his quartermaster. "All goes well on the ship?"

Émile grinned. "*Tout va bien, Capitaine*."

"Did you replace the one sailor?"

"*Oui*. The rest have no problem with a woman sailing with us. And they are happy to have a few days at home. Has yer time spent with the English lady been agreeable?"

"It has and thanks to Madame Provot, the earl's sister has returned to a lady's attire. Lady Joanna is resting or I would ask her to join us." Jean reached for the decanter of brandy sitting on a small table. "Would you share a brandy?"

"I will and gladly."

Jean poured them each a glass and handed one to his quartermaster, inviting him to sit in one of the chairs flanking the fireplace. His study at the rear of the house, on the other side of the parlor, was his favorite room of the house. Like the breakfast room, it had a view of the harbor.

"Have ye told her yet of yer plans to sail to Saintonge?"

"*Non*, I will leave that news till tomorrow. I suspect she will not be pleased, but I am already late to see to my obligations there. I fear my niece will think she's been abandoned."

"The ship will be ready to sail with the tide, *Capitaine*. I have brought ye the charts ye wanted and some messages that awaited yer return from England. The men are loading fresh water and provisions as we speak."

"*Excellent*." He handed his quartermaster an envelope. "See that M'sieur Ricard gets this to the crew on the sloop in Lorient. 'Tis instructions for some alterations." Émile nodded and stuffed the envelope into his coat pocket. "Will you stay for the evening meal?" Jean asked.

"*Non, merci*. I have a lady to see and a meal to eat at my favorite restaurant. But I will be on *la Reine Noire* when ye arrive with the English lady." With a gleam in his eye, Émile asked, "Are we to be sharing a cabin again?"

"Much as I regret to say, I will be enduring your snoring for the foreseeable future." What he had told Émile was true, but that didn't mean he wouldn't be thinking of the vixen who slept in his bed.

With his cat.

Chapter 16

Joanna woke to a knock on the door. Roused from a deep sleep, she opened her eyes, disoriented. It took her a moment to realize she was in Donet's home in Lorient.

She sat up and slid her legs over the side of the bed. "Come in," she said, rubbing her eyes.

Donet's housekeeper peered around the door. "The *capitaine* sent me. He expressed concern and asked me to see how you were doing."

He worried for her? The wound had healed but the scabs that had formed itched. She was thankful for Bouchet's salve. "I must have needed that nap, but I am fine."

"Supper will soon be ready. Have you an appetite?"

"Oh, yes." She ran her fingers through her long hair, trying to sort out the tangles. "I look forward to tasting your cooking that Monsieur Donet praises so."

Rose smiled and beckoned Joanna to the dressing table. "Come sit here. I am not a lady's maid but, if you like, I will see what I can do with your hair."

"I am sure you are too busy to tend my hair, Rose. I will leave it simply styled, but you can help me with the gown." She slipped off the robe. "The laces are easier to undo than to tighten."

The housekeeper picked up the gown and slid it over Joanna's head, tying the laces.

"That reminds me," said Rose, "the *capitaine* has asked me to suggest a lady's maid for you. Tomorrow, my niece Gabrielle will come and you can see how you like her."

"How thoughtful of him." He had promised her a maid and it cheered her he had not forgotten.

"There is no better man than the *capitaine*, my lady."

"Did you know his wife?" Joanna had an abiding curiosity about the woman he had given up all to wed.

"For the last years of her life, *oui*. A gentle soul, that one. He loved her deeply."

Since the housekeeper did not seem inclined to say more, Joanna did not ask. Once she was dressed, she dismissed Rose to her more important duties and went to sit at the dressing table. The image that met her in the mirror presented a woman who'd left the frippery of London far behind.

A brush had been laid on the linen cloth covering the surface. She wondered to whom it had belonged as it looked to be new. She brushed out her curls, her imagination spinning tales, each more fanciful than the next, of Donet's having entertained ladies of the night in his home, providing each a new brush.

Tonight, she would dine with him, perhaps alone. The prospect was exciting, yet along with the excitement she felt a twinge of fear. She was more vulnerable to this man than any before him. And one did not cajole a pirate.

Descending the stairs, she looked first in the dining room. The table was set with fine china and crystal but seeing no one there, she turned away and went to the parlor.

Donet stood with one hand braced upon the mantel and the other holding a glass of what looked to be brandy as he stared into the flames. Once again, he appeared the nobleman in black velvet and ivory.

He was so deep in thought he did not notice her standing in the doorway.

"*Bonsoir*, Monsieur Donet."

He turned, his eyes fixing her with an assessing gaze.

"Did I disrupt your thoughts?"

"Lady Joanna, I believe it is your destiny to disrupt my thoughts, though I cannot say I regret the inevitability. Would you care for a glass of sherry?"

She wondered at his meaning. "Yes, that would be lovely."

Once he had poured the golden liquid, she accepted the small glass from his hand. His fingers slid against hers leaving a trail of shivers moving up her arm. Needing fortification for the evening ahead, she downed the sherry in three gulps.

"How are you feeling?" Genuine concern was etched on his olive skin, a dark gold in the light of the fire.

"Almost like new after my nap. I did not mean to sleep so long. Being on land once again I am a bit unstable on my feet and seem to tire more easily. At times, I feel like I am still on the ship."

He gave her a sympathetic look. "It may take you a while to get used to firm ground. Even I have to cope with legs that still think they're at sea when I am first off the ship. 'Tis the *mal de débarquement*."

She raised her brows.

"Land sickness."

"Ah, and I suppose I will recover only to board your ship again."

"Yes," he said, but his gaze flitted away as if he would say more and did not.

"I *am* boarding your ship again, aren't I? You told Madame Provot as much."

"Oh, yes, I did, and you are."

Rose appeared in the doorway. "Supper is served, *Capitaine*. It's your favorite chicken dish, a *fricassée* cooked in a broth of white wine and grapes and served with fried veal balls and fresh vegetables."

"That sounds perfect." He offered Joanna his arm. "Rose maintains a small garden on one side of the house that rewards her tender care with fine vegetables."

The dining table could seat eight, but as there were only the two of them, he suggested they dine at one end.

This room did not face the harbor. Through the windows, she glimpsed trees, dark silhouettes against the indigo sky.

Once the claret wine was poured and the dishes served, Donet dismissed the housekeeper, leaving them alone. Candles flickered from silver stands set in a row in the center of the table. It struck her as a too intimate setting for an English spinster, even one who had gained that status by choice, yet she had no desire to leave him.

The aroma of the chicken wafted in the air, making her mouth water. She took a bite, tasting a rich blend of herbs and butter. "The chicken has an unusual flavor, 'tis the best I've ever tasted."

He watched her closely. "'Tis the spices. Rose comes from Provence and her sister, who is still there, sends her herbs to use in her cooking."

In the candlelight, his olive skin glowed, his black brows and hair striking. On his forehead was the beginning of a frown.

She sipped her wine. "Something worries you?"

He met her gaze. "You are most perceptive, my lady. I do worry, but not for my ship. The repairs are under way." Cutting into his chicken, he said, "Some messages I received today tell me conditions in my country are worsening. I will not know how bad the situation is until I get to Paris." He looked up. "I fear the revolution in America has laid the foundation for another in France."

"But France is not a colony suffering under unfair laws and heavy taxes," she observed.

"*Non*, but we have the Crown and the clergy, both of which benefit from the peasant class bearing the burden of taxes and tithes. It cannot go on, but convincing the king that change is needed may not be easy. Or even possible."

Joanna finished her chicken and he poured her another glass of wine. She had just lifted her wine to her lips when he asked, "Would you take your wine with me in the parlor? The fire is better situated there to warm us both."

Sated with good food, she readily agreed. "Of course."

He stood and offered his hand. They carried their glasses to the parlor and went to stand in front of the crackling fire. He set his glass on the mantel and, using a poker, stirred the fire to greater life. "The nights can be cool."

They finished their wine in amiable silence. "If you are willing," he offered, "I would show you the harbor and the stars above it."

"I would like that."

He took her hand and led her through a door that connected to a study at the back of the house. His warm hand held hers, anchoring her unstable legs to the floor. It occurred to her that being unused to walking on land, her drinking might not have been wise.

As they passed through the study, she noticed a painting of a black-hulled ship hanging over the fireplace. "Is it your ship?"

He paused to admire the painting, letting go of her hand to touch the gilded frame. "*Oui*, I had it commissioned the year I bought *la Reine Noire*."

"The name in English means 'the Black Queen'. Did you have a particular one in mind?"

"Queen Marie Antoinette. Beautiful and charming, but indifferent to the needs of her people, as is the king. They were raised to believe they rule by Divine Right, so they are blind to the storm that may soon be upon them."

Casting her gaze around the room, she spotted a chess set in one corner. "You play chess?"

"I do. And you?"

"Yes, but not very often. My oldest brother Wills and I used to play." She dismissed the pang of regret at the memory and turned back to Donet.

Taking her hand, he said, "Come, the stars above the harbor await us."

He led her through a door to a patio running alongside the rear of the home. The light was too faint to see clearly, but the heady smell of roses told her the flowers surrounded them.

Lights from the quayside taverns and lanterns on the ships dotted the harbor, competing with the glorious array of stars above them. She walked to the edge of the patio and gazed into the distance. "I have never seen anything so beautiful. The lights in the harbor are like jewels in a dark setting. The stars above are a wondrous complement." Feeling the chill of the night air, she wrapped her arms around her midriff.

"You are cold," he said, stepping close behind her and encircling her in his arms. "Let me warm you."

At first, his bold touch alarmed her. But she found his rich French-accented voice intoxicating, lulling her to contentment within the circle of his arms. He knew precisely how to warm a woman.

If it had been any other man, she would have pulled away, but this was Jean Donet for whom she had developed a strong attraction. And the more she knew of him, the more her respect for him had grown. Many men had pursued her, but here was the first man who had ever made her want to escape not from him but to him.

Leaning into the warmth of his chest, she turned her face to the side where his lips met her temple, his breath warm on her skin. She deeply inhaled his rich, masculine scent that spoke of the sea. It was not the wine she had consumed that made her feel lightheaded; it was he.

"If you would allow it, I would kiss you, my lady," he whispered, pressing his lips to her temple.

She turned in his arms to meet his midnight gaze. "It seems to me, Monsieur, you already have."

His mouth curved in a slow sensuous grin, his brilliant smile visible in the faint light. "That was hardly a kiss. I assure you I can do better." Bending his head, he brought his lips to hers.

She closed her eyes and opened to his kiss, enveloped in his arms and the heat of his body. Instinctively, she raised her hands to his nape, entwining her fingers in his silky hair.

He slanted his mouth over hers and joined their tongues in a slow dance as his hands stroked her back. She had never kissed a man in such a way. It seemed unduly intimate but, because it was him she was kissing, her body responded to his mouth and his hands. Soon, her breasts became sensitive and an ache grew in her woman's center. Perhaps he sensed her innocence in such matters, for he did not hurry.

As the kiss went on, Joanna became his willing partner, learning from him how to move her tongue against his.

He responded by kissing her more fervently. All she could feel, all she could think about was him. In her mind, she whispered his name, "Jean", over and over.

She would have kissed him long into the night but, suddenly, he pulled his lips from hers. She kept her eyes closed, savoring his kiss. She didn't want it to end.

Breathing heavily, he kissed her again, this time more forcefully. She knew a moment of fear at the power of his urgent demanding kiss with his hands on her hips, pressing her belly into his hardened flesh. But, as her desire grew, her fear diminished.

Ripping his mouth away, he pressed his forehead to hers, breathing harder than before. "If we do not part now, my lady, I fear the morning light will find us lying together in twisted sheets."

She had no idea what to say. He was right, of course. In one brief span of time, everything had changed. To wake next to him in those tangled sheets seemed a very real possibility.

She blurted out the first thing that entered her mind. "Why do you have to be French?"

His laughter was a rich melodious sound as he stepped back. "Ah, my lady, don't you see? It is precisely because I am French that I could reach beneath the thin veneer of your aristocratic English upbringing and kiss the smuggler lurking there."

And quite suddenly, Joanna was envious of his dead wife, the young woman who had shared his kisses, his bed and made a child with him.

He took her trembling hand and led her back inside. "I will see you to your chamber where you have my word I will leave you there to sleep alone this night."

Only the growing darkness prevented him from seeing her frown.

Jean had known it was only a matter of time before he kissed Lady Joanna. Not since Ariane had he desired a woman like he did her. But he had not expected his hunger for her to be so great.

The sleepless night that followed the kiss came as no surprise, his mind conjuring thoughts of what might have happened had he succumbed to the temptation she presented.

He would have to be careful in the future not to allow the passion between them to have its predictable end or he would make an English earl's sister his mistress. Marriage between them was out of the question.

He had loved Ariane with a fervor that had not died in the years they were together. Her death had rent his soul. For years, he was no more than an empty shell. He could not again risk such a loss. He still bore a weight of guilt for the times he had left his young wife.

At first, he had taken to the sea to meet their needs, but it soon became a love affair of a different sort. The sea became his mistress, stealing time from the family he loved. The risks he took excited him, but Ariane only feared she might lose him in a storm at sea or a battle in the Channel. Ironically, in the end, he had been the one to lose her. He was not even in Lorient when she died, a fact he deeply regretted for she must have felt afraid and very alone. And after, he had not given up the sea even though it meant sending Claire to the Sisters of Saint-Denis for her education when he could have educated her at home.

When light finally crept into his bedchamber, he rose and dressed, not bothering to summon his valet. Wearing only his breeches and shirt, he silently padded down the stairs.

Musing on the past always put him in a morose mood. He wandered into the parlor, knowing he would find there the one thing that would soothe his soul.

The rising sun filled the room with light, exposing to his seeking eye the object he had left sitting on the cabinet. He went to the familiar case and lifted the lid. The fine wood instrument called to him. He lifted it to his shoulder, drawing the bow across the strings.

Joanna woke to the mournful sound of a solitary violin. Lying in bed, she listened, wondering who could be making such ethereal music. It sounded to her like the sorrowful cry of a tormented heart and yet so beautiful as to fill her with awe.

Being as yet without a maid, she donned the pale green gown, tying the laces as best she could, determined to find the source of the music.

At the dressing table, she ran the brush through her hair and tied it back with a ribbon. A brief glance at herself in the mirror told her she had changed.

The woman who looked back at her had knowing eyes and cheeks flushed with remembered passion. Donet had awakened in her a new desire, a new longing. She wanted to see him, to be with him. Was it mere infatuation? Or could it be more?

She hurried from the bedchamber.

At the bottom of the stairs, she met the housekeeper. "Oh, Mademoiselle, I did not know you were up. Did the master's violin wake you?"

"Monsieur Donet is the one playing?"

"*Oui*, in the parlor." She gestured to her right.

Joanna whispered, "Can you tie my laces?"

The housekeeper hastily complied. Joanna thanked her and stepped into the parlor.

Donet's back was to her as he stood before the windows playing to the trees outside. He wore one of his fancy shirts with lace falling over his wrists and snug black breeches that emphasized his lean muscular thighs. She had never seen him barefoot before and it brought to mind the image of a pirate climbing the rigging.

Quietly, she sat on one of the sofas to listen, enraptured with the music. Her mind drifted to the Handel concert in London. No wonder he had loved the violins. She recognized the piece as another of the great composer. She thought it might be from the opera *Xerxes*.

After a while, he played a lighter piece she had never heard before.

He must have become aware of her, because he stopped playing and turned, his midnight eyes intense as they confronted her.

"Don't stop on my account. I am enjoying your music."

He shrugged. "I don't play often, not anymore." He returned the violin to its case.

"What was that last piece?" she asked. "It is new to me."

"'Tis the music of Viotti, an Italian court musician at Versailles. I heard him two years ago when I was there."

She went to join him. "I had no idea you could play, but I should have known your fondness for the violins at the Handel concert had its roots in a knowledge of the instrument. You play very well."

"Do you play an instrument, Lady Joanna?"

She lowered her eyes. Compared to his talent, she had none. "The cello, but not well."

He smiled as he stepped closer. "I should like to hear you play sometime."

Neither of them acknowledged the tension flowing between them, but it was there in his eyes and she supposed it was in hers. She could not stop looking at his lips. The kiss had taken them from grudging friends to something more. Something neither wanted to discuss.

"Perhaps that can be arranged," she said. "I need only a cello." Behind him, she glimpsed again the globe hanging from the ceiling and walked toward it. "This continues to fascinate me."

Joining her in front of the globe, he twirled it around. "I like to know where I am going. Charts, maps, even this globe, provide certainty as to where one is headed."

Her gaze fixed on his sensual lips and the black hair peeking out from his white shirt, open at the neck. "I find it difficult to know where life will take me, no matter the plans I make or the maps I consult. See where it has taken me now?"

"That may not be life directing your steps, Mademoiselle, as much as it is you setting your own course."

"Yes, I suppose," she reluctantly agreed. It had been her choice to engage in the smuggling that had led her here.

He offered his hand. "I think this conversation is better carried out over a leisurely *déjeuner*. You will join me, *oui*? I am certain, by now, Rose has set the table in the breakfast room."

Without hesitation, she placed her hand in his. It was like coming home.

He escorted Lady Joanna to the small room at the back of the house off the main dining room where the table had been laid with the foods he liked to eat in the morning: fresh eggs, salty sweet Gruyère cheese, some *petit pains* and a dish of butter. In the center of the table was a bowl of strawberries. And for the lady, *chocolat*.

Next to his place, Rose had set a small pitcher of sweet cream for his *café au lait*. The aroma of the rich dark brew drew him. After his sleepless night, he needed the coffee.

He pulled out a chair for her facing the view of the harbor. "I see Rose has thoughtfully included tea and chocolate for you, my lady. Do you mind my dining as I am, without even a waistcoat?"

"Not at all," she said, taking her seat. "You look as I imagine a pirate might when eating his breakfast."

He laughed. "A pirate would not wear so much lace, I assure you. Is the food to your liking? Perhaps I should ask for some honey?" He had not forgotten her pink tongue licking the golden nectar from her luscious lips.

"With all this, I do not need honey. Your housekeeper is a wonder."

They ate in amiable silence for some minutes, Jean enjoying the quiet. He liked that she was not given to constant chatter, as were some females. He peered at her over his coffee. This morning, wearing the simple morning gown, her lovely hair tied back with a ribbon, she appeared a beguiling creature as she bit into a strawberry. But young, he reminded himself.

He should not have kissed her, because now he very much wanted to do it again. Clearing his mind of such thoughts, Jean picked up the *Journal de Paris* Rose had placed on the table and read a bit of the article by Benjamin Franklin. He sat back and laughed.

"What is it?" Lady Joanna asked, setting down her chocolate.

"If Benjamin Franklin were a sailor, he would have made this discovery long ago." Seeing he had piqued her interest, he went on. "It seems Franklin's servant forgot to close his master's drapes.

Awakened at six o'clock by a noise, Franklin was surprised to find his bedchamber filled with sunlight. The statesman had no idea the sun came up so early in June."

"Hardly a revelation."

Jean could not resist a smile. "You must remember, this is Franklin the scientist. His discovery got him to thinking how many candles the city of Paris could save if the French would merely arise and retire at an earlier hour."

Lady Joanna screwed up her face in an enchanting manner and shook her head. "How could he be so smart, such a clever inventor, and yet not have realized that before?"

"Well, the article indicates it is his habit to retire several hours after midnight and then sleep until noon so he never sees the sun rise and, seeing it, his brilliant mind began to consider the possibilities." Jean looked again to the article, his finger following one of the lines. "Among other things, he proposes that every morning, as soon as the sun rises, all the bells in every church should be rung. And if that is not sufficient, cannons should be fired in every street to wake the sluggards."

Lady Joanna shook her head and licked the berry juice from her now red lips. "I cannot see that becoming a popular idea."

"He has one thing correct," Jean said, trying to focus on the article and not her enticing lips. "He claims the heavy taxes imposed upon the people by the necessities of state provide abundant reasons to be economical."

"Somehow, I think the poor do not have to try and rise or retire early. Their work requires it."

"'Tis true. I remember my life in Saintonge as a youth. The workers were in the vineyards early."

"You were raised in Saintonge?"

"*Oui*. Except for excursions to Paris, I lived there until I was twenty. Which reminds me, we sail tomorrow, but not for England. I must first go to Saintonge."

"What? But I thought—"

"Yes, I know, but Saintonge is closer, and I have not been there since I learned of the deaths of my father and brother. It is imperative I go now."

The vixen brooded for a moment.

He smiled, trying to coax her to consenting. "Would you not like to see the vineyards that produce all that brandy you and your fellow smugglers sell in London? What matters it if you do not return till summer's end? If by being with me, you are ruined, a delay of some weeks will not alter the fact." He gave her a wry smile, hoping the rebel in her would rise to the occasion. "I will give you quill and paper to write a letter to your brother. You can tell him the pirate holds you captive but is treating you well."

He was certain the smile that crossed her face just then was a reluctant one. "I suppose it would do no good to protest."

"None at all, Mademoiselle."

Rose entered with more coffee, which he gladly poured.

"My niece has arrived, *Capitaine*, if the lady would like to meet her."

Jean glanced at his guest whose face bore a scowl. Better she should meet her prospective maid than argue with him over something she could not change.

He picked up his coffee and rose to leave. To his housekeeper, he said, "Bring her in."

Conflicting emotions warred within Joanna. She was angry with Donet for having misled her into thinking she would be going home from Lorient. But she did not want to leave him just yet and, in truth, she did have a desire to see more of the land of his youth. Besides, if she were to travel as a lady, she would need a maid.

"You are Gabrielle?" Donet asked the dark-haired girl. Nearly a foot taller than Nora, Gabrielle had thick dark hair, confined to a knot at her nape, and expressive blue eyes.

"*Oui*, Monsieur," she said curtsying before him.

"Lady Joanna, I will leave you two for a bit so you can get acquainted. If she meets your needs, she has indicated to her aunt she is willing to serve you and travel with us to Saintonge. There will be room in my cabin for the two of you."

So, he had known from the beginning she would be sailing to Saintonge. Very well, she would go along with his arrangements. "You do think of everything, Monsieur."

One side of his mouth hitched up in a bit of a grin. "I try."

After he left, Joanna turned to the girl. "Please have a seat. Do you speak English, Gabrielle?"

The girl sat in the chair vacated by Donet. "*Oui*, Mademoiselle, some."

"And I speak French, though not as well as Monsieur Donet. Between us, perhaps we will be able to communicate nicely. Tell me what you know of being a lady's maid."

With some particularity, the girl described her training and her talents. She was not an accomplished maid like Nora, but she could style hair and knew enough about a lady's dress to satisfy. Importantly for Joanna, the girl was French which, given Joanna's immediate future, would be a great help to her. And the pretty girl had a pleasant manner.

She poured Gabrielle a cup of chocolate. While they drank, they exchanged stories about their families. The maid was the youngest of three children with two older brothers. Joanna talked of her two surviving brothers and her younger sister. Of an age with Tillie, but more mature, Joanna thought Gabrielle would serve admirably.

"If you would like the position, Gabrielle, it is yours for as long as I am in France."

"Oh yes, Mademoiselle. I would like it very much." The girl was already making an effort to speak more English, which impressed Joanna. They would do well together.

The housekeeper returned. "The *capitaine* is asking for you, Mademoiselle. Madame Provot has arrived with her assistant and many boxes."

"Come, Gabrielle," said Joanna. "You can begin now helping with my new gowns."

Many hours later, Joanna had a new wardrobe. The lovely French gowns were as elegant as those she had at The Harrows, perhaps more so. Madame Provot's flair for lace, ribbon and bows reminded her why the English modeled their fashions after the French.

That night, after dining with Donet, Joanna wrote Freddie a letter to explain her injury and recovery. She told him her return would be delayed, but not to worry, that Monsieur Donet was being the perfect gentleman and had retained a maid for her.

Donet promised to see the letter delivered. She did not doubt he had ways to see it done.

Chapter 17

La Rochelle, France

It had taken them two days sailing southeast in the Bay of Biscay to reach La Rochelle, a port near Saintonge. Jean stood in the stern, his mind filled with memories, both pleasant and bitter. Two decades had passed since he'd left Saintonge under a cloud. More than a decade since he'd lost Ariane. Soon, he would see again his family's estate and confront the ghosts dwelling there.

They sailed into the harbor just as the sun was setting behind the tall buildings lining the quay. The golden cloud-filled sky gave the water the same glorious hue making it appear like a great river descended from Heaven.

Lady Joanna, her auburn hair tinged with the same golden light, stood amidships gripping the rail as she watched the activity in the harbor, her gaze fixed on the small boats and large ships.

Looking over her shoulder, she tossed Jean a smile, her enthusiasm for what lay ahead clearly outweighing her annoyance at his failing to return her to London.

On the deck beside her sat the ship's cat licking his paw, unconcerned. "Ben", as she called him, had become her constant companion, causing much speculation among his superstitious crew. While they worried for having a woman aboard—even more so one who had red hair—the constant presence of the black cat, a sign of good luck, had managed to neutralize their misgivings.

One day, he must return her home, but it would not be easy, for he had grown attached to the vixen. Dining together and sharing quips about the aristocracy and his life at sea had brought them together. Neither spoke of the kiss they had shared but, sometimes, when their gazes met over the table, she would lick her bottom lip and then it would take all of his self-control not to drag her to his bed.

Now that she had the gowns from Noëlle and Gabrielle to style her hair, she not only spoke like an aristocrat but looked very much like the earl's sister she was. In the afternoons, she would venture on deck, drawing the eyes of his crew. Believing she was the *capitaine*'s woman, they did not openly leer, but their surreptitious glances told him much. Neither he nor Émile had let it be known she slept in his cabin alone with her maid.

Émile came up beside him. "Am I to join ye onshore, *Capitaine*?"

"Unless you would rather stay in La Rochelle with the ship, I would have you with me."

"Then I shall come. Who knows what ye will face in Saintonge?" His quartermaster frowned. "Like as not, 'twill be a bunch of glowering servants who thought ye dead. 'Sides, I still have yet to see those vineyards ye boast of."

Jean smiled as much to himself as to his friend. "Even I have not seen them for a very long time, *mon ami*."

"Do we disembark tonight?"

"*Non*." Jean had no desire to travel the roads by night. Though safer than some of England's highways, he was not about to expose Lady Joanna to robbers lurking behind trees. "I think 'twould be best for the lady if we spent the night aboard ship and depart for Saintonge on the morrow."

Émile nodded. "As soon as we dock, I'll have one of the crew arrange for a carriage."

Jean gave the orders that moored the ship at the quay where *la Reine Noire* joined a long line of merchantmen.

The province of Saintonge, France

The carriage bumped along on the dirt roads, which narrowed as they ventured deeper into the countryside. The rough jarring made Joanna glad she was nearly healed. Next to her, Gabrielle slept, leaning against the side of the carriage.

Out the window, Joanna glimpsed rows and rows of grapevines covering rolling hills as far as the eye could see. On the top of the vines, the sun turned the green leaves gold. The stalks bore long bunches of green grapes. Never having seen such a place, she was enchanted. So this is the land that produced the amber liquor all of England craves. The same land that produced Jean Donet.

Seeing the sun on the gnarled vines gave her a new appreciation for the brandy she and the villagers of Chichester smuggled into England. And a new appreciation for the man sitting across from her.

She sneaked a glance at Donet as he stared out at the vineyard, a melancholy expression on his handsome face. Was he remembering the past? For him, this was coming back to a home that had once rejected him. "Has it been very long since you were here?"

He turned to face her and, seeing the longing in his eyes, her heart reached out to him. "*Oui*, Mademoiselle, a very long time."

"Has it changed much from what you remember?" She grabbed the strap and he braced his boot against the base of her seat as they swung around a curve. Gabrielle stirred and then went back to sleep.

"*Non*, not at all," he said with thoughtful inflection. "The odd thing is that I had expected it to."

"Perhaps that is because 'tis *you* who has changed in all the years that have passed."

He laughed. "Well, that is certainly true."

The nonchalant manner in which his body easily adapted to every curve in the road told her he did as well in a swaying carriage as he did on the deck of his ship.

"You did not expect to return," she said. With all she knew of him, she believed it to be true.

"Very perceptive, Mademoiselle. I did not." He returned his gaze to the vines.

Even if the world stood still, Donet never would. Forced to give up one dream, he had pursued another. She admired that about him. And she trusted him, even with her life. The life he saved, she reminded herself.

What would it be like to be married to such a man? She thought of his past, his privateering for America and his daring escapades. It would be like marrying adventure itself. He would never be dull like so many men in the *ton*. And while he was very attractive to women, he was no Jack among the maids. He had been faithful to his wife. Perhaps he was even now.

Joanna no longer believed he found her unattractive. What she had seen in his eyes, what she had felt in his kiss told her otherwise. He wanted her, that much was clear, but as what? He, more than she, held himself away. Why? Did he worry for her virtue? Or was it the love he still harbored for his dead wife?

The carriage slowed and she peered out the window to see a grand château set back from the road. As they neared, it seemed to grow larger, rising before them, a stone palace with a slate mansard roof pierced by eight dormer windows.

More than twenty large windows graced the front of the edifice. On either side of the main building stood a wing with a high pavilion. "Why, 'tis enormous," she said, her voice reflecting the awe she felt.

"As a child, I imagined it went on forever," said Donet. "On rainy days, my brother and I played games in the great hall."

Gabrielle woke and looked out the window, her eyes growing wide.

The carriage stopped and Donet's quartermaster, who'd been riding on top with the coachman, opened the door. "Ye failed to mention a few details about yer ancestral home, *Capitaine*."

The comte stepped down and helped her and Gabrielle to alight. "Should I have said it is quite large?" He paused to examine the château as if seeing it for the first time. "Even so, it is larger than when I last saw it. Why my father felt a need to add to the monstrosity, I do not know. Come, let us see who is here."

Before the four of them reached the front door, it flew open and a young girl in a white gown with a wide blue sash ran out, her dark hair flying behind her. "Papa, Papa!" she cried, hurling herself at the comte and hugging his waist. "Oh, Papa," she cried, shutting her eyes.

Joanna shifted her gaze to Donet. As far as she knew he had only one daughter, and that one was grown and living in London.

Donet gently placed his hand on the girl's head. "You must be Zoé."

The girl pulled back, her brow furrowed. "You are not Papa, are you?" Her young face conveyed her terrible disappointment. For a moment, she stared up at Donet. "I hoped he had returned."

A woman hurried out of the same door the child had come through. "Zoé!" she shouted, a look of despair on her face. The girl turned to look at the woman but held on to Donet as if afraid he might disappear. The short woman wore a ruffled mobcap on top of gray curls. Her careworn face bore an anxious look. Wiping her hands on her apron, she frowned at the girl. "Mademoiselle Zoé," she said in a kindly tone. "*Ce n'est pas votre papa.*"

The girl had thought Donet was her father? But why?

As if to answer Joanna's question, the girl raised her eyes to Donet. "But he looks so like Papa, I wanted it to be true."

The woman in the mobcap lifted her gaze to Donet and gasped.

"Marguerite," said the comte. "It is you, is it not?" To Joanna, Donet muttered, "My older brother Henri and I always looked much alike. Marguerite knew me as a younger man."

"Master?" The woman's wrinkled face stared up at the comte in wonder. "You have come!"

Donet leaned forward and kissed her on both cheeks. "I have and I must beg your forgiveness for my delay in doing so. I had intended to be here earlier, but my presence was required in London." Crouching down in front of the girl, he said, "Zoé, I am *ton oncle* Jean."

The girl touched his face as if to assure herself he was real. "*Mon oncle*? You have come to stay?"

He stood and patted the girl's head. "We will see." To Joanna, he said, "Allow me to introduce you to our housekeeper Madame Travere and to my niece, Mademoiselle Zoé Donet."

The woman curtsied and Joanna returned her a smile.

His niece greeted Joanna. "*Bonjour.*"

To the woman he had called Marguerite, he explained, "My guest is Lady Joanna West. She brings her maid, Gabrielle, who is also the niece of my housekeeper in Lorient."

Gabrielle dipped a small curtsy to the older woman.

"And lastly, here is my quartermaster and good friend Émile Bequel."

M'sieur Bequel bowed before the housekeeper. "At yer service, Madame."

The housekeeper smiled at the gruff man, not put off in the least by his harsh countenance and rough appearance. "Come inside," she said to them. "You must be tired from your journey, and we have much to discuss."

Taking Donet's hand, Zoé walked beside them as they headed toward the door.

Inside, a young dark-haired maid hurried toward the housekeeper. "Some refreshments for *Monsieur le comte*, Sophie."

The maid gave Donet a startled glance and curtsied before

rushing through a door on the other side of the entry.

The entry hall was large, its floor black and white marble tiles that reminded Joanna of a checkerboard. Because of the many windows, no candles would be required during the day, but a huge crystal chandelier hung above them with candles ready to be lit.

In front of her, a wide curving staircase led to the next level.

"Where is the butler?" Donet asked, looking around. "And the footmen?"

"The butler, Lefèvre, retained by your brother, is around somewhere. A most unusual man, that one, but efficient. And there are still a few footmen, maids and, of course, the groom and stable boys. But after the funeral, some of the servants left. Alas, the child's governess has gone as well."

"I did not like that one," said Zoé, still holding Donet's hand. "She was very strict."

As if in explanation, the housekeeper said, "Like you, Monsieur, the child has a mind of her own."

Donet smiled with approval at the child. Joanna had no doubt that Donet, as a child, possessed a strong will for he did to this day. Perhaps this niece of his would be the same. Someone should warn the men of France in years to come.

Marguerite continued. "You will remember the old *maître du château*." Donet nodded. "Monsieur Giroud is just now inspecting the vines with one of the workers."

"Well," Donet said to M'sieur Bequel, "it appears we have much to do."

To their right, a parlor beckoned and Donet led them to it. "We might as well make ourselves at home. You will see about rooms for my guests, Marguerite?"

She dipped her head. "*Oui*, Monsieur."

The parlor was not unlike those in fine London homes but reflected more of antiquity. The walls were high and much of them covered with large tapestries, bucolic scenes of people enjoying themselves beneath trees in the countryside. Over the fireplace's mantel of white marble hung a tall mirror between crystal sconces.

Scattered around the room, she counted six chairs and two sofas. On one end of the room sat a pedestal table holding a bouquet of pink and white roses in a large vase.

The floor was inlaid parquet, small squares of oak set at angles to each other, making a beautiful pattern around the edges of the cream and rose carpet.

Observing her interest in the polished floor, Donet said, "There is much of it at Versailles. The parquet is easier to maintain than tile."

A man appeared at the doorway dressed in a suit of bright orange brocade, his stockings white silk above his silver-buckled black shoes. His hair was the color of walnuts and his face looked ancient, his leathery skin wrinkled like a prune. Joanna could not tell if he was a guest or part of the household.

When he saw Donet, he stared as if in shock. Then, in a flourish, he bowed. "Monsieur le comte, I am your butler, Lefèvre. The maid told me you had arrived, but I must say I am astounded. You look so like your brother, it is as if he were here with us again. Welcome to your home."

"Lefèvre," Donet said, returning the butler a small smile, "it is good to meet you. I have brought guests. My quartermaster M'sieur Bequel and Lady Joanna West. Her maid, Gabrielle, accompanies her."

The butler dipped his head to the quartermaster and bowed before Joanna.

"Do you require anything, Monsieur?" he asked Donet.

"Nothing now, but later I would like to go over the accounts with you."

"As you wish, Monsieur. I am at your service." Lefèvre bowed again and disappeared through the doorway.

Jean escorted Joanna to a chair as Sophie returned with a tray of wine, bread, cheese and fruit. After they were served, Madame Travere asked the maid to show Gabrielle to the room for Joanna and to make ready the rooms for the other guests. "Sophie can show you the servants' quarters as well," she said to Gabrielle.

With a nod from Joanna, Gabrielle followed Sophie out of the room.

Donet, M'sieur Bequel and Joanna sat in chairs facing the housekeeper. Little Zoé chose to stand next to Donet, a gesture Joanna found endearing. Obviously, the girl had loved her papa very much and now that his equal was here, she was not letting him out of her sight.

Zoé could have passed for Donet's child, a pretty little thing with hair almost as dark as the comte's, but she had lighter eyes.

Jean looked into the face of the housekeeper he had known as a youth, thankful for her presence at this difficult time. Though older and her face lined from the years, she remained the stalwart soul she had always been, a safe harbor in a storm. Even when his father had cast him out, she had been sympathetic. "Marguerite, what can you tell me about the death of my father and brother?"

The housekeeper glanced first at his niece, but Jean could see no reason to hide the facts from her.

"Where the accident occurred is not far from the château," she said. "The day was warm, the sun strong. Since the sky was clear, the comte had asked the carriage top be left down. He and the driver had exchanged words that morning over one of the horses, but 'twas not unusual for them to do so."

Marguerite looked again at the girl, but Donet said, "Go on."

"When the accident was discovered, Monsieur Giroud had the carriage brought back to the château. It is the one your father kept for his trips through the vineyards. From what Giroud said, the carriage upset going around that curve where the road dips. It ended up in the ditch. Your father was thrown out and killed, but your brother lingered awhile."

"I thought Papa was sick," Zoé put in, her eyes brimming with tears. "But he didn't get well. I know he is gone, but sometimes I pretend he did not die."

Jean put his arm around his niece and drew her close. "You are not alone any longer, *ma petite*."

Sitting beside him, Lady Joanna gave Zoé a look of empathy. Understanding came to him as he recalled Cornelia telling him that years after Torrington lost his father, he lost his mother and then his older brother. Lady Joanna knew what it was to lose close family.

"What became of the driver?" Jean asked, curious.

The housekeeper shook her head. "We don't know. He must have leapt to safety and, seeing the comte was dead, ran away for fear of what might happen to him. We have not heard from him since."

"And the funeral?"

"The funeral was attended by a few friends, some neighboring landowners, the servants and the priest, of course. It was a solemn affair. Since then, we have tried to keep the estate running."

"Is there a lack of funds?"

"*Non*, Monsieur. The lawyer has made funds available, but the workers who tend the vines do so halfheartedly. Your brother was well liked by them. And others are angry at their circumstances, which concerns Monsieur Giroud."

"I will have a talk with him and see what can be done." Jean looked to his quartermaster, glad he had decided to come. Above Émile's deep-set dark eyes, his heavy brows drew together. Before they left Saintonge, they must set the estate to rights.

When they had finished the small repast, Jean got to his feet. "Zoé, would you show my friend Lady Joanna to her room? I will join you both for dinner."

Though he knew she was reluctant to leave him, his niece

nodded and took the lady's hand. "I will show you upstairs, Mademoiselle."

Lady Joanna smiled at Jean. "It seems I have a guide." The two of them left the room hand in hand. When they were gone, he said to Émile, "Let us have a look at that carriage."

"Before you go, Monsieur," said Marguerite, "I have something for you." She walked to the side table and pulled out a drawer. Reaching inside, she drew out a small box and removed something from it. Grasping it in her hand, she came back to him. "This is yours by right, now." Into his open palm, she placed his father's heavy silver ring with the Saintonge crest, three *fleurs-de-lis* and a bishop's hat for Saint Eutrope, first Bishop of Saintes.

He slid the ring on his finger, wondering if he would leave it there. So much went with it he did not want. "Thank you, Marguerite."

"I never thought to see it on your hand, Monsieur, but now that it is there, I see God's hand in it all along. The younger son, scorned by his father, has returned to command all." She crossed herself. "By His hand, 'twas meant to be."

Jean waited until the housekeeper had gone and, with a heavy sigh, looked to Émile and jerked his head toward the door.

The room to which Zoé brought Joanna was in the east wing of the château. Greater in size than her bedchamber at The Harrows, it contained not only a four-poster and dressing table, but a wash stand and a sitting area with a settee and a small table and two chairs set in front of the gilded fireplace. The walls were painted a robin's egg blue, the raised panels gilded like the fireplace.

On the parquet floors lay a carpet in the same blue but with elaborate gold scrollwork throughout. In one corner of the room, near a window, sat a small gilded writing desk, inlaid with white enamel painted with flowers.

The bed cover and bed curtains were a lovely shade of blue, paler than the walls.

She turned in a circle, astounded at the opulence of it all. *A lady's room.* Perhaps it had once been the bedchamber of Donet's mother, the comtesse de Saintonge. Funny, she had never thought of him as having a mother but, of course, he had. What must she have been like?

Joanna took off her hat and gloves and set them on the bed.

"After *ma mère* died," said Zoé, "Grand-père reserved this chamber for special guests. It is my favorite of all the bedchambers."

"And why is that?" Joanna asked with a smile, for the girl was enchanting.

Zoé ran to the large paned windows and placed her palms on the glass, looking out. "From here, you can see *le jardin*—'tis the most marvelous garden!"

Joanna walked to the windows and gazed below at the pink and white roses, lavender just starting to bloom and boxed topiary, all circled by well-trimmed boxwood hedges. Beyond the sculpted gardens was a small field of wildflowers and beyond that, hedges and trees. Someone had tended it all with great care. "I see why you love it so. Is the gardener still here, then?"

"*Oui*, Old François would never leave. He thinks the plants are his children. He even talks to them!"

"We have one like that at my home in England. I dearly love him." Casting her gaze to the left of the gardens, Joanna glimpsed Donet and his quartermaster rounding a building. Throwing open the wide wooden doors, the two men went inside. "Whatever are they doing?" she muttered.

Zoé narrowed her eyes as she looked out the window. "Oh, that is where they took the broken carriage. I don't like to go there."

Joanna laid her arm across Zoé's shoulder. "I would feel the same if I had lost my father that way. Mine died on the battlefield."

With a worried glance, the girl looked up at Joanna. "Will my uncle take care of me now?"

Joanna smiled down at the pretty child. "I am certain he will. Monsieur Donet treats his daughter very well. Did you know you have a cousin named Claire?"

"*Oui*, my father once told me of her, but we have never met. Does she look like me?"

"She is very beautiful, just as you will be when you grow up. Like you, she has very dark hair, but her eyes are blue where yours are a lovely gray."

Zoé smiled broadly, making Joanna think this young girl had missed the encouragement of a mother. At least Joanna's mother had been alive as she was growing into womanhood. But Zoé's mother had not been there and the governess had not seen fit to fill the role.

"You would like Claire," she told the girl. "Her husband is a ship's captain like your uncle." Well, maybe not exactly like Donet, Joanna thought. As far as she knew, Simon Powell had never been a smuggler or a pirate.

Chapter 18

Jean walked around the remains of the carriage, studying the damage. The conveyance lay on its side. "It must have rolled as it left the road." The top was crushed on one side, a door was torn off and a wheel had come loose.

"Does look like it was pulled from a ditch," observed Émile, who stood to one side, his arms crossed over his chest.

"It bears enough mud to suggest that," Jean replied, examining the axle.

"What are ye looking for, *Capitaine*?"

"Something out of the ordinary, something that should not be here. I only thought to examine the carriage more closely when Marguerite mentioned the driver had argued with my father and has not been seen since the accident."

He stood and faced Émile. "You had to know him, *mon ami*, to understand. The late comte de Saintonge was a difficult man. Smart and clever, *certainement*, but, at times, he could be cruel. Coupled with the Donet temper, he was formidable. I don't doubt he treated the driver harshly. How Henri endured him all those years, I have no idea."

Crouching again beside the axle, Jean ran his fingers over the wood.

"Sounds like ye were well off to have been dismissed as ye were."

"I have thought the same thing many times." Jean reached out to touch the break in the wooden axle. "The driver could have been angry and taking the road too fast. Accidents sometimes happen that way." He paused, encountering something he had not expected. The splintered wood would be common in an axle break but not the sharp cut his finger touched just before the break. "Or, this could be the result not of an accident, but of something more foul."

"What? Show me." Émile bent his head to look.

"See here." Jean pointed to the cut. "The wood has been partially sawed through, weakening the axle and allowing it to break more easily." Rising from his crouch, he faced a somber Émile. "This was no accident, *mon ami*, but murder."

"*Sacrebleu*! What beast would do such a thing?"

"I do not know, but I intend to find out. If there are those who wanted the former comte dead, when they discover there is a new one, they may want me dead as well." He thought about what he should do in light of that possibility. "While I seek the answers, Émile, I do not wish to advertise my presence."

His quartermaster's forehead creased in a harsh frown. "Ye'll need to be watchful."

"My father would have kept a town carriage in addition to this one he used when inspecting the vineyard. But that one will have the family crest. For the time being, I would rather ride in an unmarked one when not on horseback. See if our driver is willing to serve me for a while longer. I will pay him well."

"It shall be as ye wish, *Capitaine*."

Because the air was quite warm in the château, Joanna dressed for supper in a white *chemise à la reine*. Madame Provot had told her the style of gown was a favorite of the queen and very popular at the French Court. It was made very simply, the fabric the lightest of muslin. It felt like something she would wear under a gown. Its only decoration was a wide pink sash at the waist and a bit of lace at the cuffs.

The brim of the straw hat, circled by a pink ribbon, made her think of Tillie. How her sister would have teased her to see Joanna wearing the color Tillie had claimed as her own.

As Gabrielle dressed her hair, Joanna thought of her siblings in England. She didn't worry for Tillie, enjoying her first Season, or Richard, consumed with the business of the Lords, but she did worry about Freddie, alone at The Harrows with only Zack and servants for company.

Had he yet received her letter telling him she was safe with the French comte? And what would he make of that? Since Freddie was master of The Harrows for the summer, he would have much to occupy his time. Perhaps he would not worry about her. She could only hope he and Zack did not pursue another smuggling run. With Commander Ellis angry for losing one smuggler's ship, he would be eager to seize another. The smugglers on the beach would also be in danger.

She thought of Polly Ackerman and her children and worried for their situation. But at those times, she reminded herself Zack and Freddie could be trusted to watch over them.

"You look lovely, Mademoiselle," said Gabrielle, "and so French."

"All due to your talent. I do hope you are enjoying your position as my maid."

"Oh yes, Mademoiselle, *beaucoup*."

Pleased, Joanna smiled at the girl and picked up her straw hat, carrying it with her as she left her chamber. She reached the bottom of the stairs and saw the butler standing to one side of the entry.

"Mademoiselle," Lefèvre said, inclining his head. With a sweep of his arm, he gestured her toward a large dining room. "Monsieur le comte is waiting for you."

She nodded and entered a room as grand as the parlor. Its large crystal chandelier hung above a long and highly polished walnut table. A sideboard of the same wood held a silver tea set. On the table were several branched candlesticks, their flames flickering.

Donet rose from where he was sitting adjacent to his niece. "Lady Joanna, won't you join us?"

"Thank you, I would love to." She set her hat on one of the side chairs and took the seat he held out for her.

Zoé appeared in a good mood, her face brighter than when Joanna had last seen it. "I hope you are hungry, my lady."

The quartermaster came into the room then, shared a meaningful glance with Donet, and took a seat next to the girl.

The meal of veal, turkey, artichokes and a salad was welcome after the long day of travel. Donet's quartermaster, who ate much, kept them entertained with tales. Zoé seemed delighted and encouraged M'sieur Bequel to tell her more.

Joanna stole glances at Donet, who appeared preoccupied as he sliced his turkey. He ate little, brooding over his meal, and said even less.

"Did you really sail an English ship to Dover and hide in the fog?" asked Zoé, her gray eyes huge in her young face.

"*Oui*." The quartermaster puffed out his large chest and waved his fork in the air. "And them Jack-tars were none the wiser till we slid over the side of their ship."

Joanna cleared her throat.

The quartermaster, apparently remembering she was English, gave her a sheepish look. "*Pardonnez-moi*."

She smiled, shaking her head. "I suppose I should be flattered you have forgotten I am not French, Monsieur."

After dinner, Joanna savored one of the fresh plums served for dessert, a bit of the cheese and a fine Bordeaux wine Donet told her had come from vineyards south of Saintonge.

Once she had finished the plum, he leaned in. "Mademoiselle, forgive me. I have been a terrible host. Would you like to take your tea in the garden? We might as well take advantage of the long June day."

Remembering the garden she had glimpsed from her room and hoping she might learn what troubled him, she gladly accepted. "I would."

"And you, Zoé?" he asked his niece.

"I want to hear more of M'sieur Bequel's stories. But I will come after that." Then looking up at Donet, she added, "If it's all right with you, *Oncle* Jean."

Donet shook his head, smiling at his niece and his quartermaster. "You two are like old salts sharing tales, half of which bear no resemblance to the truth, but since you are enjoying yourself, *bien sûr*, you may stay, Zoé." He then asked Sophie, who stood in one corner, to serve tea in the garden terrace.

"*Oui*, Monsieur." She dipped her head and left the room. To Joanna, the girl appeared to be enamored of her master. Perhaps it was his likeness to the older brother. But surely the maid would notice a difference. The air of confidence he had gained in a score of years at sea would set him apart from most aristocrats, even one who looked very much like him.

Joanna took her straw hat from the side chair where she had left it and set it on her head. "I am ready."

Donet held out his arm and she took it. It seemed so natural to be with him, to follow him to the gardens. There was so much she loved about this man, no matter he was a French Catholic and a former pirate. He exuded a strength that made her feel safe. He was charming and he could make her laugh.

They did not sit to take tea when it was served. At Donet's suggestion, they picked up their cups and followed the line of rose bushes. Every now and then, they would pause to take a sip from their cups, admiring some flower.

Seeing a large pink rose, Joanna bent to smell the heady fragrance.

"Dressed as you are, Mademoiselle, you grace the roses."

She turned to see him smiling. "I grant you, Monsieur, breeches are more comfortable, but I have had enough of those for a while."

He laughed. "I shall always remember you as you were when I first saw you. It took but a moment of careful perusal to realize you were no lad."

"I suppose I should take that as a compliment." She did not tell him she had thought him the devil himself the first night she'd seen him.

They walked along companionably for a time, sipping their tea and meandering among the roses.

Seeing no one about, she asked, "Something has been weighing on you, Monsieur. Might you confide in me?"

His expression turned serious. "I expect you will know soon enough. The accident that took the lives of my father and brother was no accident. Someone tampered with the axle."

For a moment, she just stared, shocked. "But who would have done such a horrible thing—and why?"

"'Tis hard to say. Even when I was living here, my father was not popular with the people of Saintonge, especially his own workers. Add to that the unhappy state of the French people and you can see how it might have happened. So far as I know, there have been no riots in Saintonge, but there is always the possibility."

"What will you do?"

"While I am here, I will investigate, ask questions. Someone is bound to talk." He took her empty teacup from her hand and set it next to his own on a nearby bench. "Come, the sky is still blue and 'tis unusually warm. Let us speak of more pleasant things and enjoy the evening."

Jean did not wish to speak of death, not with the beautiful vixen walking beside him. A soft and feminine woman with an inner strength he admired. With her, he wanted only to embrace life. Since that night in Lorient when he'd given in to temptation and kissed her, he had desperately wanted to do it again.

Not since Ariane had a woman reached inside him and taken hold of his heart like this one. Lady Joanna made him want things he thought never to have again. She made him want to love again. But what if he did, only to lose her? France was becoming more dangerous. With the attack on his family, perhaps England might be the best place for her.

He had only to look at her and his body responded with an overwhelming desire. But would she want him without marriage? Would such a woman, a lady of noble birth, give herself to him? That he even considered the possibility troubled him, for what would he do with her if she did? She hardly fit into his life, which, he reminded himself, grew more complicated by the day. Still, the thought tempted him as never before.

She walked ahead of him, the path narrowing between the tall hedges. The pink sash tied in a bow at the back of her small waist drew him like a banner. Her auburn hair fell in curls to her shoulders beneath her straw hat. He pictured it splayed out on his pillow.

"You should be leading me," she said. "I am likely to get us lost."

"I am only too happy to oblige," he said. "If I remember correctly, there is a stone bench not far on." Drawing up behind her, he inhaled her lovely floral scent and turned sideways to pass. She turned as well, toward him, bringing them face-to-face on the path.

She tilted her chin up and he gazed into her cognac-colored eyes. He had only to dip his head to bring their lips close. No longer fighting the desire welling up inside him, he brushed his lips across hers. "As you are destined ever to tempt me, Mademoiselle, I am destined always to succumb."

She did not protest, but closed her eyes as their lips met. He reached his hands to her waist and she slid her palms up his arms.

Her lips soft and welcoming, she tasted of the plum she had eaten and the honey she had added to her tea. Intoxicated with her scent and her taste, he held her tightly, then kissed her deeply.

Drawn by the slender neck he had observed so often but had never dared touch, he left her lips to kiss the warm column. With a small moan, she tilted her head to expose the span of ivory skin to his lips.

When he slid his tongue over her ear, she melted into his body.

He did not release her until his mouth returned to hers and she had been thoroughly kissed. Finally, he raised his head.

Slowly, she opened her eyes.

He smiled. "'Tis a prelude to more if you want it, my lady."

"I do," she said in a husky whisper.

Taking a leap into an uncertain future, as he had done so many times in his life, he said, "I give you leave to change your mind. I do not forget you are a lady. But if you still feel the same when night falls and the household is asleep, come to my bedchamber. 'Tis the one next to yours. You do not need to knock. I will be waiting."

Staring into his eyes, she slowly nodded.

"*Oncle* Jean!" came Zoé's voice from somewhere close. "Where are you?"

He let go of Lady Joanna and moved beyond her. "Over here!" Then reaching for Lady Joanna's hand, he pulled her along to the bench he had remembered. He invited her to sit while he stood. It seemed a more appropriate scene for his niece to come upon. He was glad his coat hid his body's reaction to the exchange of kisses.

"There you are!" Zoé said. "I'd forgotten about this old bench. It's quiet here." His niece turned in a circle in the small space. "I should come here to read. I like to listen to the birds." Then pointing to the white flowers, she said, "Oh, see? Old François has been tending the wood sorrel."

"We have wood sorrel in Sussex," offered Lady Joanna.

Her mention of the flower that grew near her home reminded Jean of her expectation to return. If he made her his, would she still want to leave? Could he let her go?

Joanna sat on the edge of the bed, brushing her hair and listening for the sounds of footsteps in the corridor. The candle on the small bedside table flickered in the breeze coming through the lace curtains that hung over her open window. Outside, the stars glistened in the midnight sky.

In the bedchamber next door, he waited.

Since their kiss in the garden, her ardor had calmed enough for her to carefully consider the choice he had offered her. There would be no turning back if she went to him.

If she declined his offer, she could return to England, untouched. One day, she might marry an Englishman, even a peer. But she had never believed that would be her fate. And there was the matter of her reputation, which might, even now, be in tatters.

Still, she was not running from that life as much as embracing another. Jean Donet had shown her there was another choice, another path.

She did not believe his invitation was due solely to a moment's passion. A man who had loved only one woman and taken no mistress since her death would not casually invite a woman to his bed. She had glimpsed the desire, the amusement and the admiration in his eyes so many times, she knew his offer was based on something more.

To be with a man as free as the wind that filled the sails of his ship, as wild as the raging sea he had conquered and, at times, as fierce as a storm, that would be her fate if she accepted his invitation.

He was not like any other man she had known. He was a man she could love. Might already love. That he had not spoken to her of love or marriage did not surprise her. Given the torch he carried for his dead wife, he might never do so. But even if he never said the words, never asked for her hand, to be with him would be enough.

She had never known a man the way she would know him. To give herself to him was to risk her heart. A man of his experience would know that. But he had asked it of her, which told her he would not cast her aside once they were lovers. He would be faithful. That meant more to her than a loveless marriage that might await her in England.

Would she stay in France as his mistress if there were no marriage? She might, especially if she were to conceive a child. She remembered the way he had looked at the babe Jean Nicholas. One day, it could be her child he smiled at.

Her mind made up, dressed only in her *chemise de nuit* and green silk robe, she laid aside her brush and padded to the door. As she opened it, the light from her bedchamber flooded the corridor showing her which door was his. She listened for sounds and heard none.

Silently, she crept from her chamber, closing the door behind her, and walked to his door. With shaking hand, she opened it. The light from a single candle cast shadows on the massive four-poster hung with burgundy velvet curtains tied back at the posts.

The bed cover was rolled back and, in the center of the bed, Donet indolently reclined on white pillows, his tanned, muscled chest bare and a sheet pulled up to his waist. His black hair, threaded with silver, hung long to his shoulders.

His black eyes fixed on her. On his lips was a faint smile. Had he expected her not to come?

He spoke not a word, but his eyes followed her as she took tentative steps across the thick carpet. She knew instinctively he would not help her, would not reach for her.

This was a chasm she alone had to cross. He had extended the invitation; she must be the one to accept it.

Arriving at the edge of his bed, she let her robe slip to the carpet. Then, gathering her courage and keeping her eyes on him, she reached for the sheet.

He smiled and raised his hand to her face, cupping her cheek. His touch on her face was warm and calmed her fears a bit. Perhaps he knew she needed that. His expression told her he was pleased.

"Come," he said at last, drawing her onto the bed.

She was glorious in her brave display, her dark red hair a waterfall over her skin, glowing like alabaster in the candlelight.

The vixen had come this far. He would do the rest. Soon, by her own choice, she would be his.

He pulled her into his arms. Only her thin chemise lay between them. Her beautiful breasts he remembered so well pressed into his chest, stirring his loins. He slid his palm over her rounded buttocks, firm beneath the silk, and stroked her back to calm her rapidly beating heart.

Burying his head in her neck, he inhaled deeply her floral scent.

She would be frightened of what lay ahead, but Lady Joanna had a brave heart. She had chosen this course and would not shrink from it. And he would show her he could be tender.

Holding her tightly to him, tying together their heated limbs, he kissed her with all the passion he felt, emotion and desire he had suppressed for so long.

She was everything he had thought she would be and more.

Though as yet untutored in the ways of love, she showed her willingness to learn, reaching her hands to his nape and holding him to her.

"Let's get rid of this," he said, pulling up her chemise. "It's not as if I haven't seen you before. And I so want to see all of you again."

She raised her arms and he lifted the thin chemise over her head.

Taking one rounded breast into his hand, he gently cupped the ripe mound, coaxing a moan from her throat. "You are just as I thought you would be, my lady, soft to the touch, sweet to the taste."

"Joanna," she whispered, grasping his shoulders.

"Joanna," he returned, loving the sound of it on his lips, "you will be mine this night."

"Yes…" she whispered.

"Trust me with this."

She splayed her hand on his chest and ran her fingers through the black curls. "'Tis soft."

He heard the nervous tenor in her voice, her touch that of a virgin's first acquaintance with a man's body. Yet she seemed to delight in learning it. "Beneath your skin I feel hard muscle."

She had no idea.

Pulling back, she moved her fingers over his ribs and down his side. "There is a scar, more than one. Wounds from a sword, Sir Pirate?"

"And other pursuits," he said with a chuckle. He placed her hand on his rigid flesh. "Your touch affects me, my lady."

"Joanna," she murmured and, with tentative strokes, moved her fingers gently over his hard length. Her delicate touch inflamed his desire for her.

"If you keep touching me like that 'twill soon be over. You have much to learn. Let me initiate you in the ways of lovemaking."

Propping himself up on one elbow, he slid his hand down her belly, touching gingerly the scarred flesh. Then he pulled her to him and tenderly kissed and licked her breasts. The musky scent of her skin mixed with the floral smell was a heady mixture, making his blood pound in his veins.

She made small noises that told him her body was responding. He had been ready for her since she walked through his door. But he would be patient this night, allowing her fear to be consumed by her rising passion.

He held her close, keeping her warm as he slid his hand past the scarred flesh to the nest of red curls he had glimpsed when she lay wounded on his bed. He felt her shiver at his touch. "Open your legs for me."

When she complied, he dipped his finger into her center, wet with honey he would taste before the night was through. Slowly, he circled the place that would bring her to her peak if he allowed it, but he had other plans. For her first time, he wanted to be inside her when the moment of ecstasy came.

She panted out her breaths, matching his own, and moved her hips against his hand. Her nails sank into his back, her body telling him she was ready. On her own, she let her knees fall to the side, making way for him.

He kissed her as he centered himself above her. With a single thrust, he was past the barrier and deep into her core.

She shuddered and tensed. He stilled, their tongues entwined as their bodies.

She was so close to her peak her muscles were already beginning to clench around him. He retreated, then advanced, coaxing her passion to its crest.

Their bodies grew slick against each other.

"Ah..." she moaned, raising her hips to meet him as he drove deep, her core pulsing around him.

The storm came upon him, violent in its power. He rode the crest of the wave until, with a groan, he gave into its depths.

Locked in her arms, he allowed himself to drift, feeling a fierce possessiveness for this woman. He did not sleep nor did he roll from her, but stayed inside her, kissing the damp, salty skin of her neck, prolonging their union as long as he could.

He was still hungry for her.

The sun had not yet risen when Joanna stirred in his arms, slowly coming awake. The candle had burned to a nub and the room was cast in shades of gray. She turned her face on the pillow to see him, feeling his warm breath on her face. Still asleep, his face was partly covered by his long black hair. She brushed an errant strand from his forehead and thought of their long night of love when her fingers had been tangled in those same locks.

A pang of guilt rose up to accuse her for what she had done. She was now one of the fallen. Yet she would not have missed Jean Donet for anything. What would he think of her now? He had known her as a smuggler, then a lady, but what was she to him now? Merely a conquest?

She had loved his body, his touch and their joining, surprised at how little pain there had been. She had no one to compare him to, of course, but she couldn't imagine a more considerate lover. He had been tender, even romantic. She had felt… loved.

He had made her a woman, giving her a night she would never forget. In turn, she had given him her body and, she was quite sure, her heart. In the hours he had taught her about the physical side of love, she sensed his feelings, though unspoken, were there in his touch. Surely he felt more than mere lust. It was all very well to be desired, but even a mistress would want a man's love.

She kissed his warm forehead and, carefully disentangling herself from his arms and legs, silently crawled from the bed. Quickly, she donned her chemise and robe. She did not want the servants to find them in "twisted sheets", as he had once said.

No one was in the corridor as she slipped into her bedchamber and brushed the tangles from her hair.

When Gabrielle entered, along with the morning sun, Joanna called for a bath.

Soaking in the hot water, she wondered where this new path would take her and whether she would have any regrets.

Chapter 19

Jean left his chamber, slightly annoyed the vixen had deserted his bed without waking him for a last kiss or more. Images of her willowy body and beautiful breasts flitted through his mind. He had made her his, and he was almost certain she had reciprocated by claiming him.

At the foot of the stairs, Lefèvre waited wearing another shockingly bright suit. Before it had been bright orange; this one was the color of immature grapes. Jean tried not to cringe. Only his softhearted brother Henri could have retained such a one.

"Bonjour," he said to the butler and strode into the small dining room where his family had always eaten their morning meal.

He thanked Sophie for the coffee she handed him and took his seat at the head of the table, adding the cream that made the drink *café au lait*.

Feeling sated from the night before, but bleary-eyed for lack of sleep, he drank half the cup before turning to the only other person at the table.

His niece sat watching his every move as she quietly ate her eggs and brioche and sipped her chocolate. "I always waited for Papa to drink his coffee before I spoke."

"Wise child," he muttered, turning his attention to his brioche and berries.

A tear rolled down her cheek. To speak of her papa must be

painful. Reaching across the corner of the table, he took her hand. "I know you miss your papa, Zoé. I miss him, too." In truth, Jean had missed Henri for a very long time.

She nodded and wiped away the tear. "'Tis not so bad since you came, *mon oncle*. 'Tis almost like having him here again. He was in Paris much of the time before the accident. I was so happy to have him back." She looked down at her plate. "I kept pretending he was away again on one of his trips, even though I knew he was gone and not coming back."

Jean squeezed her hand. "Perhaps one day I will take you to England. Would you like that?"

"Oh, yes! When I grow up I want to travel on a ship like you!"

He laughed. "Well, maybe not exactly like me." He popped some of the ripe strawberries into his mouth, thinking they tasted like Joanna.

He rather enjoyed his niece's company. She reminded him of Claire at that age. He would gladly act as Zoé's guardian. Holding his grandson Jean Nicholas and his lovemaking with Joanna raised the possibility of fathering another child. Until now, he had not considered it. What would he do if their lovemaking produced a child?

"What did you want to be when you were my age, *Oncle* Jean?"

Roused from his musings, he thought for a moment, remembering the long days of summer when he and Henri walked together among the vines, planning their lives. "I wanted to grow the best grapes in Saintonge and to make the finest cognac in all of France." Winking at his niece, he added, "For a short time, I even entertained the possibility of becoming a violin virtuoso."

She gave him a look of pity. "You didn't get to do those things, did you?"

"*Non*. But sometimes, Zoé, when one dream dies, another is born. My new dream was to become a ship's captain and master the sea. Eventually, I discovered I love the sea more than I do the land."

"I cannot wait to sail on your ship!" she exclaimed.

He patted her hand. "You will and soon." He downed the rest of his coffee and finished his meal, then rose from the table. "I don't suppose you know where I can find M'sieur Bequel."

"When I came in, he was speaking with Monsieur Giroud, who wants to take you into the vineyard today to show you something."

Amazed at all the girl gleaned from keeping her ears open, Jean made to leave.

Zoé said, "If you agree, *Oncle* Jean, I was hoping Lady Joanna and I could go to Saint Jean d'Angély. I want to show her the abbey church and the market."

"I would like that," said Lady Joanna from the doorway where she appeared, looking beautifully poised in a sky blue gown. Her cheeks were slightly flushed.

No one would guess she had spent the night in his bed where there had been very little sleeping. He desperately wanted to take her upstairs and make love to her again. Instead, he said, "Good morning, Lady Joanna." He could not very well call her "Joanna" in front of his niece.

He pulled out a chair for her, catching a whiff of her floral scent. Was he imagining things or did she ease herself into the chair more carefully than usual? Now that he thought of it, she might need a few days to recover from their night together. And then what would he do? They could never go back to the way things had been, but how would they go forward?

"Good morning to you, M'sieur." She took her seat and smiled at Zoé. "We can take Gabrielle with us."

"And M'sieur Bequel," Jean insisted, as he resumed his seat. "I will not have you roaming around the town without a guard. Giroud and I will be taking horses to the vineyard so you can have the carriage."

"There is the Saintonge carriage," offered Zoé.

He glanced at Joanna, hoping she saw his concern for their using any vehicle that announced a member of the Saintonge family was within. "For the time being, I'd prefer you take the one I brought from Lorient."

Zoé didn't seem to mind what vehicle they took. With eager anticipation, she turned to Joanna. "I have much to show you, my lady."

The coachman snapped the whip and Joanna and her companions were off, taking the road that led through the vineyards. Zoé had told her the town of Saint Jean d'Angély lay only a few miles away. The sky had clouded over, portending rain, and, while not terribly cold, she and her two traveling companions had worn hooded cloaks.

M'sieur Bequel, who had bowed to his captain's orders and agreed to escort them, rode on top.

Zoé, sitting next to her, pointed out the sights: a mill, a small church, some new vines and, when they had gone some distance, another nobleman's château and vineyards.

Sitting across from Joanna, Gabrielle gazed out the window, wide-eyed.

"Have you never been here before, Gabrielle?" Joanna asked.

"*Non*. I am grateful to you for bringing me." The young maid was a pleasure to be around. Perhaps the quality Joanna most valued at the moment was the maid's discretion. She had asked no questions when she had arranged for the bathwater to be brought in that morning. Her gaze had taken in the unrumpled bed before looking away, making Joanna realize her mistake. She had sat upon the bed cover that Gabrielle had pulled down for the night, but it did not look slept in and the pillows lacked even a dent. What must Gabrielle think of her?

Many noblemen had mistresses. Very likely, her maid assumed Joanna was Donet's *chère amie*, a label she never thought to bear. But it had been her choice to go to him, even knowing it might lead to this.

As they left the vineyards behind, Joanna glimpsed thatched cottages along each side of the road. Unlike those in Chichester, they were made of mud, not whitewashed. And they had no windows. In front of them, children played in the dirt in threadbare clothing and bare feet. The women standing nearby stared at their coach with hostile eyes.

"Those cottages are nothing but miserable heaps of dirt," observed Joanna, sitting back, her voice laced with pity. "Whose are they?"

"Peasants," said Zoé. "Some are vineyard workers, some farmers."

"Their cottages have earthen chimneys," remarked Joanna, "but few have windows. 'Tis worse than the homes of the poor families where I come from in England."

Zoé's face remained placid. "It has always been that way, my lady. Papa wanted to help them but Grand-père said not to. They fought over it."

"When I was still in England," said Joanna, "I was told the French people are unhappy. Now I see it for myself. If they pay taxes to live in such hovels, I can understand their discontent."

The carriage moved on, but the somber scene she had witnessed remained with her. She would speak to Donet about what could be done. Perhaps for his own workers, he could at least provide new cottages.

Before they reached the town, Joanna heard a loud bell and turned to Zoé for an explanation.

"That's the bell in the clock tower. 'Tis very old."

The carriage slowed as it entered the small town. The narrow, cobblestone streets reminded Joanna of Chichester, except this town had more of a medieval feel with its gray stone buildings. And, instead of a great cathedral, it possessed the tall clock tower Zoé had spoken of and an old abbey church with two very impressive towers.

Zoé gazed out the window as they passed the huge edifice. "The abbey is not finished. The monks have been building it for a very long time."

"Where are we going?" asked Joanna.

"*Oncle* Jean asked the driver to stop near the market. It's in the center of town."

"Your uncle thinks of everything."

With her eyes reflecting her sorrow, Zoé said, "Just like Papa."

Joanna put her arm around the girl's shoulder. "I know what it is to lose both parents. It will get easier over time and you have your uncle who will be like a father to you." She only hoped it would be true.

Once they alighted from the carriage, Zoé's spirits picked up as she headed down one of the streets with Joanna and Gabrielle in tow and M'sieur Bequel following closely behind with sword and pistol at the ready. Joanna assumed the weapons were per Donet's instructions, such precautions due to the carriage accident that hadn't been an accident at all. He might be worried about his niece. But what kind of a monster would want to harm a child?

The people of the town were a mixture of the very poor and those who were more richly dressed and had money to spend or business to transact. Soot-faced children ran through the streets. An occasional beggar sat against a building, sheltered under an eave. Every place had its desperately poor and Joanna always noticed them.

Zoé led them to a cluster of stands and stalls where farmers and merchants sold a variety of things from bread and cheese to oysters and fish. Summer fruits were available in abundance.

Cloth, too, was displayed, mostly the plain muslin and wool worn by the working class. Occasionally, she glimpsed a seller of lace.

Mingled among the people standing around and shopping were small groups of soldiers, their cream-colored uniforms trimmed in dark green so different from those worn by British soldiers.

Zoé noticed her watching them. "The soldiers you are looking at are from the *Régiment de Saintonge* that has returned from the American War. My papa told me they served under the comte de Rochambeau who helped the Americans win a battle at a place called Yorktown."

"Yorktown was a great victory for the Americans and a great loss for the British," Joanna said.

"Do you mind so much?" asked Zoé.

"I am glad 'tis over, but it cost me my father." In truth, Joanna had mixed feelings about the war, unpopular as it was in England. France had helped America win her independence, but the war had taken the lives of many of her countrymen. Her father had been killed early in the war at the Battle of Saratoga. Polly Ackerman lost her husband much later but in the same war.

"I am sorry," said Zoé.

"Let's just hope there will not be another."

"Ye have spoken well," said M'sieur Bequel, standing nearby. "I lost my brother in the war. I wish for no more, but I fear my hope may be baseless."

"I am sorry," she told the quartermaster who, for a moment, looked very sad. "I, too, lost a brother who was a soldier." Lord Hugh's words came back to her. Would there be another war between England and France? And, if there were, would she be caught between her family in England and Donet in France? She thought of his exchange of fire with Commander Ellis off the coast of Bognor and shuddered. She couldn't bear to think of Donet fighting against England.

Until he had taken to the sea, Jean had loved walking through the vines with his father. He and Henri would go with him, checking on each stage of the ripening grapes. As Jean walked among the vines with his estate manager, he thought of those earlier days. He had loved the familiar smell of the grapes, harvested in the winter, being pressed and then made into white wine, acidic and undrinkable, but perfect for distillation. Afterward, the distilled spirits, or *eau de vie*, would be aged in oak casks until the brandy became fine cognac.

That had been a lifetime ago. Today the sun was hidden behind gray clouds, the unripened green grapes long on the vines. In the time he'd been gone, his knowledge had not faded. He found it easy to fall back into the role of the master's son asking questions of Giroud about the soil and condition of the vines. Only now he was the master.

As Jean thought of it, he preferred the merchant's role to that of the grower and brandy maker. Transporting the casks from the estate and sailing them to England and other parts of Europe was more to his liking. For that, he wouldn't have to live in Saintonge. He could retain Giroud and others to handle this end of things. It would be enough if he came several times a year, allowing him to live in Lorient. He would still keep his warehouse on Guernsey and, perhaps, his townhouse in Paris.

"The grapes are doing well," he remarked.

Giroud, his wiry gray hair hanging in waves to his nape and his scant, short beard adorning his chin, stood next to Jean surveying the vines. "*Oui*, Monsieur, the grapes they are fine. For the time being, we have enough peasants to tend them. But I must speak to you of another matter, something that has concerned me in the last few years."

Jean looked into the man's ageless gray eyes. "What would that be?"

"I can show you as easily as I can explain it."

Jean swept his arm away from the vines. "Lead on."

Remounting their horses, they rode to the large warehouse next to the distillery where the brandy was stored and allowed to age. By now, this year's *eau de vie* would be in the casks and the three prior years' yield would be there as well, nearing the time they would sell it.

As they entered the warehouse, Jean looked around seeing the dusty oak casks. He blinked, unsure of what he was seeing. In the dim light from the windows, there appeared to be twice as many casks as he expected. "Why so many?" he asked Giroud. "Did *mon père* somehow increase production?"

"*Non*, Monsieur. While you have been gone, the taxes charged on Cognac's brandy have trebled. Two years ago, they were raised again so that the growers pay double the amount levied on the vineyards near La Rochelle. Your father stopped shipping in protest even though the demand from Ireland and Holland had grown."

"*Et alors*, he was a stubborn man. We will sell the extra stock. Aged longer, it will be more valuable. You have buyers, I assume?"

"*Oui*, many. Edinburgh, London and Ireland among them. The estate's cognac is a fine one."

"*Très bien*. Join me at dinner and we can discuss it. My initial thought is to change the shipping port from La Rochelle to Tonnay-Charente. 'Tis closer and, since it's within Saintonge, we'll pay fewer duties. You can use the existing shippers for now, but eventually I will keep at least one of my ships at the ready."

Giroud grinned and dipped his head. "It will be done as you say, Monsieur le comte."

He gave the *maître du château* a kindly look. "I have been Jean Donet for a very long time, old friend. M'sieur Donet will do. Oh, and tonight you can meet my guest from England, Lady Joanna West."

Giroud nodded. Jean thought the man would walk away, but he hesitated as if not knowing how to broach whatever was on his mind. "There is something else I must tell you."

Jean lifted his gaze expectantly. "*Oui*?"

His expression grave, Giroud said, "Shortly after the carriage accident, I found the body of the driver behind the warehouse. His throat had been slit. I buried him, but I have told no one. I can show you the grave if you would like."

Jean let out a breath. "It is enough to know he was murdered. I do not need to see the grave. You should be aware, he is not the only one deliberately killed. In examining the carriage involved in the accident, I discovered it had been tampered with."

The estate manager furrowed his brow. "*Mon Dieu*. Do you mean—"

"*Exactement*. Do you know anyone who would want to kill my father?"

Giroud shook his head. "*Non*. He was ever at odds with the other vineyard owners, of course, but then you would know that. The peasants are not happy, but that is due to more than your father. 'Tis possible someone meant the comte ill for his noble status, but I know of nothing specific."

Jean thanked him and turned toward his horse. "Take care, Giroud. I will see you at supper."

"'Twill be an honor, M'sieur."

Jean rode back to the château thinking of the carriage driver. Why had he been killed? The most obvious answer, of course, was that he had been complicit in the crime and his partners, worried he might talk, did away with him.

Jean thought of Joanna and Zoé, wondering about their day. If someone had meant to kill the comte, would they next seek to kill his granddaughter? She could not inherit, of course, but vengeance would not consider that. And if Zoé was in danger, then Joanna might be as well.

And suddenly he had to know she was safe.

Joanna's feet hurt and she stopped to rest on a stone bench in the gardens in front of the abbey. Overhead, the clouds had darkened to the same color as the stone towers of the church.

Several feet away, Zoé spoke in animated fashion to M'sieur Bequel about the monks and their slow work on the church. The quartermaster patiently listened, seemingly entertained.

Gabrielle joined Joanna on the bench.

"A remarkable little town," observed Joanna.

"'Tis very different from Lorient," said her maid.

"Are you missing your home, Gabrielle?"

"I think of it, Mademoiselle, but miss it? *Non*, I don't think so. I am enjoying myself too much. What about you, mistress? Do you miss England?"

"Sometimes, but like you, I am glad to see more of France. I never thought I would have the chance."

M'sieur Bequel came toward them, Zoé at his side. "I think we should go," he said. "The *capitaine* will be wanting to know what I've done with ye."

Joanna grinned. "Or what we have done with his quartermaster."

Zoé did not protest, but docilely went with Bequel as he turned to go. The two made an odd pair, but she could tell they liked each other's company.

Joanna got to her feet and, together with Gabrielle, followed Jean's niece and his quartermaster as they retraced their steps back to the carriage.

Soon, they were on the same road they had taken from the château.

About halfway there, the road narrowed as they entered a dense stand of oak. Joanna was thinking of Donet and their night together when, all of a sudden, two men on horseback, their faces masked in black, rode out of the forest, brandishing pistols.

Gabrielle screamed. Zoé's face was frozen in terror.

Joanna's heart was in her throat as she ordered Zoé and the

maid to the floor of the carriage. "Stay down!"

There must have been a third man for Joanna heard a voice in front of the carriage commanding the driver to halt. At the same time, one of the two she could see shouted to his companion, "No shots into the carriage! He wants the girl."

Suddenly, the air erupted in pistol shots. For a moment, smoke blocked her view. When it cleared, the two riders lay on the ground, blood seeping from their chests.

The sound of clashing steel sliced through the air. Bequel swore and hoof beats sounded as a rider galloped away.

Silence reigned until the quartermaster shouted, *"Allons-y!"* Presumably the coachman was still alive because she heard the lash of the whip and they took off, speeding down the road.

Gabrielle and Zoé resumed their seats, shaken but unharmed.

As the carriage raced ahead, the three of them were jostled about so badly they had to grab the strap and grip the windowsills to keep from being thrown together.

Heart pounding, Joanna peered out the window, wondering where the third brigand had gone.

Before they reached the château, the driver brought the carriage to a sudden stop. The horses snorted, restless in their traces. Joanna braced for another attack.

Unexpectedly, Donet appeared at the window astride a horse. He jumped down, yanked open the door and pulled Joanna into his arms, crushing her to his chest.

He pulled back, his forehead creased in an expression of concern. "You are all right?"

"Yes, all of us," she said.

In the carriage window, Zoé nodded. "*Bien*. I must help Émile and the driver. They are wounded."

Zoé leaned out of the window, watching anxiously as Joanna followed Donet. At the front of the carriage, he climbed on top. A ball had pierced the coachman's calf and blood coated his stockings.

Joanna was sickened by the sight. Donet acted as if it were an everyday occurrence. Perhaps, for him, it was.

M'sieur Bequel was slumped over, blood oozing from his shoulder.

"I am fine, *Capitaine*," he said. "Just a prick to my shoulder."

"I'll be making my own assessment, *mon ami*." Donet took off his cravat and tied it around the driver's wound. Then he helped the quartermaster down.

"You will ride with the ladies," said Donet, helping Bequel into the passenger compartment.

The quartermaster bristled. "Really, *Capitaine*, this is unnecessary."

Donet ignored him and, once the quartermaster had taken a seat, handed Joanna into the carriage. As he closed the door, through the open window, he offered her a pistol. "Do you know how to use one of these?"

"I do," she said, taking it from him. "My brother Wills taught me when he was on leave from the Coldstream Guards."

"Keep it ready should you need it on the way back."

He led his horse toward the back of the carriage. As he returned to the front, he passed by her window.

She heard the whip crack and the carriage lurched forward.

Inside, Gabrielle tended M'sieur Bequel as best she could, pressing her handkerchief and the one Joanna offered into the wound to try and stop the bleeding.

Joanna kept the pistol close, unsure of what to expect.

Zoé looked on anxiously, but she did not cry. A brave little girl, thought Joanna.

Wondering what had prompted Donet to set out to find them, she looked at the quartermaster, who gritted his teeth with every movement of the carriage. "How did he know?"

"I could tell ye stories, Mademoiselle. 'Twould make yer hair stand on end. The *capitaine* has instincts that often baffle the crew. When the war raged on the Channel, more times than I can remember, with not a sail in sight, he would suddenly order Lucien to change course. Only later would we learn an English frigate had been heading for our ship."

"You think he sensed there would be trouble?"

"*Oui*. I expect so. He gets a feeling something's not right. At such times, I have learned not to question him."

Joanna heard the pride in his voice and the affection for the man to whom Bequel gave his loyalty, the one he called "*Capitaine*".

"You and Donet have been friends for a long time, no?"

The quartermaster's breathing was labored. The ball in his shoulder had to be causing him great pain. Still, he managed to say, "Many years. And I hope for many more."

A man who could engender such loyalty and unfettered obedience from a crew of cutthroats was not a man to be ignored. "I, too, hope you and he will have many years together, Monsieur. And I am glad his instincts told him to come after us. I feel safer for knowing he is with us."

Bequel smiled and shut his eyes.

Gabrielle said, "I believe the bleeding is slowing."

"We should be to the château soon," Zoé encouraged.

The carriage was just rolling to a stop when Jean jumped down, shouting for the butler and a footman. Together with Lefèvre, Jean got the protesting quartermaster into the château. The footman helped the driver into one of the available chambers, while Donet returned M'sieur Bequel to the bedchamber he had been occupying.

Joanna and Gabrielle had followed the three men, while Zoé went in search of Marguerite.

Émile grumbled as Jean helped his quartermaster onto the bed. Out of the corner of his eye, Jean saw Joanna standing in the doorway.

"Find Giroud and bring him to me," Jean ordered the butler.

Lefèvre skittered out of the room. "*Oui*, Monsieur."

At Joanna's urging, Gabrielle removed the quartermaster's shirt, just as Marguerite came hurrying into the room, the maid Sophie following on her heels.

She rushed to Émile's bedside, her lined face expressing her anxiety. "What has happened now?"

"A scratch, no more," said the quartermaster.

Donet and the housekeeper shared a glance and Marguerite went to work.

"The driver has been shot as well," Jean informed the housekeeper.

At the open door, Zoé joined Joanna. "Will he be all right?" asked Jean's niece.

Joanna put her arm over the girl's shoulder. "He will be, you'll see."

The housekeeper set about cleaning the wound, fussing over Bequel and shouting instructions to Sophie to bring hot water, bandages and brandy. "When you are done with that," she told the maid, "see if you can help the coachman."

Sophie nodded and scurried to find what was needed. Gabrielle went with her, offering to help.

Donet pulled up a chair in front of the bed. "What happened?"

"The trip to town went well," said M'sieur Bequel. "We were on the way back when three brigands on horseback attacked us with pistols and swords. I got two before the third came at me with his blade. Ye know the sword's not my weapon, *Capitaine*, and both my pistols had fired." With a sheepish grin, he said, "That third one got away. In the future, I'm thinking we need to give the driver a pistol."

Donet patted Bequel's leg. "You did fine, *mon ami*, and I will see to arming the driver. I should have thought of that before. Now, get some rest."

"He'll not be getting any rest till I'm finished with him," said Marguerite.

Donet shifted his gaze to the door. "No more trips to town," he fired at Joanna.

She nodded. "What's going on?"

"I do not know, but I intend to find out."

Joanna took Zoé's hand. "Let's go have some tea, shall we?"

The two disappeared and Giroud took their place at the door. "M'sieur?"

"The carriage was attacked returning from Saint Jean d'Angély. Send some men to retrieve the two bodies left by M'sieur Bequel."

"Immediately, M'sieur." The estate manager quickly departed.

Jean stayed with Émile until the ball was out to offer his support and to keep his quartermaster supplied with brandy. Several times, a dig to hunt for the ball had the quartermaster cursing loudly.

When Jean opened his mouth to apologize, Marguerite said, "No need, Monsieur. I have heard men curse before. 'Tis expected in such circumstances."

Émile took a large swallow of the brandy Jean handed him and smiled at the housekeeper. *"S'il vous plaît, pardonnez-moi."*

With Émile's apology, Jean left the bedchamber. "I'll look in on you later. I must check on the driver."

Jean was descending the stairs when Giroud stepped into the entry hall.

Worrying his hat in his hand, the estate manager looked up at him. "The bodies are gone, M'sieur, their horses, too."

Jean frowned and stepped down to the tile floor. "I half-expected it. Whoever they were working for would not want to leave bodies behind that might reveal his identity."

Joanna walked in from the parlor, a worried look on her face. He wanted to take her in his arms and comfort her, but the presence of the others stayed his hand.

"Lady Joanna," he said, "I don't believe you have met my estate manager, M'sieur Giroud."

Joanna acknowledged Giroud with a smile and he dipped his head.

"We are discussing the men who attacked the carriage, my lady." He couldn't bring himself to think of it as an attack on her or Zoé. "Did you happen to see them?"

"I did, but only the two M'sieur Bequel shot. The other one must have been in the front. They were rough men. On their faces, they wore black masks. Their hair was long and unkempt. Were they hired ruffians, do you think?"

"Possibly. But who would have hired them? Did they say anything?"

"Yes, one shouted a demand for the driver to stop, but I could not see him. One of the two close to me ordered his comrade not to fire into the carriage, that 'he' wanted '*la fille*'."

"Zoé?"

"I thought so at the time. Wouldn't he have said "*la femme*" if he meant me or Gabrielle?"

He was tempted to tell her with her hair worn long and tied back, she could pass for a girl, but he didn't want to scare her. "Probably, but the more intriguing question is to whom was the man referring when he said 'he'?"

Neither Giroud nor Joanna had any idea. Why would someone want to capture his niece? She was not the heir after all, could never be. And a ten-year-old girl could have no enemies. Was it to hold her for ransom for something they wanted from Jean? Money? An exchange of her life for his? If the vengeance against the Saintonges ran deep, the perpetrators might want to kill the new heir. They couldn't know there was still another, his grandson, the babe Jean Nicholas.

Zoé came into the entry hall from the kitchens. "How is Monsieur Bequel?" she asked.

"Marguerite is stitching his wound and then she will give him something to make him sleep."

Flashing her cognac-colored eyes, Joanna said, "I hear laudanum works well."

At least the vixen still had her sense of humor. He remembered her rising from a laudanum-induced sleep to fire questions at him, as spirited as ever. What a wild one she must have been as a child.

Jean suggested they go in to dinner and led his small party into the dining room. They took their seats at the long table, sitting clustered together at one end. The meal that followed was a somber affair, which Jean regretted, but he and Giroud accomplished what they needed to regarding the large number of stored casks of cognac.

As the supper drew to a close, he turned to Joanna. "I want you and Zoé to stay close to the château for the time we are here."

She nodded. "Of course, I understand."

"Are we going somewhere, *Oncle* Jean?"

"Eventually, *oui*. I cannot leave you in Saintonge, Zoé. 'Tis not safe for anyone named Donet at the moment." Casting a glance at Joanna, he added, "Or anyone close to us. Besides," he said looking at his *maître du château*, "M'sieur Giroud is well able to handle the estate in my absence."

Giroud appeared pleased for the trust placed in him, which made Jean wonder at the relationship the man must have had with the former comte. It could not have been a good one.

Chapter 20

The summons from the king came the next morning. Jean was not sorry for it. Given recent events, he was only too glad to leave Saintonge. Had he not been concerned for Joanna and his niece, he might have wanted to stay and solve the mystery of the attack on the carriage and the deaths of his father and brother, but that could wait.

As one new to his title, he would be expected to make an appearance before Louis. With Jean's sojourn in England, his sovereign must have grown impatient. Then, too, he still had Vergennes to see. *Oui*, it was past time for him to return to Paris.

He found Marguerite in the kitchens. "Can our patients be moved?"

She nodded. "But I would not ask Monsieur Bequel to lift anything heavy for a while. And the coachman will not be much use till his wound is healed."

"I will assure Bequel lifts nothing save a pistol. Meanwhile, we will be leaving tomorrow. The king requires my presence in Paris, so I will need another driver. Might one of the servants be fit for the job?"

"One of the footmen has driven carriages before."

"*Parfait*. We will take the Saintonge carriage so the wounded driver will have his to return to La Rochelle when he is recovered. Will you be all right in my absence?"

"Of course." Wiping errant gray hairs off her forehead with the back of her hand, she cast him an anxious glance. "Will you take your niece, Monsieur?"

"With her having the last name Donet, I would not leave her here with the current threat." The housekeeper appeared to relax. "She has never been to Paris?"

Marguerite put one hand on her hip. "Monsieur, she has never been far from Saintonge."

"Well then, she will enjoy seeing Paris."

"There can be no doubt of it. And, given all she has lost, she would not want you to leave her behind. You have taken the place of her papa."

As he climbed the stairs to check on Émile and the coachman, he thought of his ward. Should he place her in the care of the Ursuline Sisters of Saint-Denis? They had been good to Claire. Many daughters of the aristocracy were sent there for their education prior to marriage. Zoé was the right age. But she was all he had of his brother. And she had no father.

Putting that decision aside for the moment, he considered his options for getting to Paris. The roads in France had improved substantially since he'd lived in Saintonge, making the carriage trip to Paris bearable, but he preferred to travel by ship. With all the stops the carriage would make, it would take no longer sailing from La Rochelle to Le Havre and then a day's ride to Paris. He would have to make a brief stop in Lorient to change ships to his sloop.

If, notwithstanding the night in his bed, Joanna insisted on being returned to England, he would need that ship. The modifications he'd made would serve well if she were to remain with him. He did not want her to go. But could she be persuaded to stay?

Émile had just finished his breakfast when Jean walked through the open bedchamber door. Sophie picked up the tray and, bobbing a curtsy, carried it from the room.

"You are well?" he asked. "No fever?"

"I am fine and tired of lying abed. Marguerite objects, of course, but I am getting up. Unlike ye, *Capitaine*, I do not carry books about. Staring at the walls and worrying about the ship are driving me mad."

Jean laughed. "You will be pleased to learn we depart tomorrow."

"We do?" His quartermaster's face brightened. "And where are we going? To return the English lady to her home?"

"Only if she insists. My preference is not to return to England just now. The king has summoned me to Paris."

"Why?"

"Louis rarely gives reasons, *mon ami*, but I assume 'tis the customary appearance for one newly titled. He will want to be assured of the comte de Saintonge's continued loyalty."

"Ah." Émile let out a breath and ran his hand through his thick russet hair loose on his shoulders. "Then I must again dress as a gentleman, *non*?"

"*Oui*, but consider this, my townhouse in Paris has fine beds and a good cook."

"And the nearest tavern has pretty wenches. *Oui*, I recall it well." His quartermaster sat up and slid his legs off the edge of the bed, wincing as he put weight on his arm. "*Très bien*, we go. Do ye expect to persuade Lady Joanna to accompanying ye to Paris?"

"I hope for that result." His quartermaster did not need to know Joanna was now his lover.

Émile gave him a smug smile. "Ah...'tis as I expected. Ye're caught as sure as a cod in a net."

Jean shrugged, not wishing to admit the truth growing inside him. What he felt for Joanna scared him to death. "Since you are rejoining the living, *mon ami*, ask my garishly attired butler, Lefèvre, to send a messenger to La Rochelle. Have M'sieur Ricard recall the crew and ready the sloop." He pulled an envelope from his pocket, a letter he had prepared for the modiste. "And see that

Madame Provot gets this. Lady Joanna will need additional gowns if she's to accompany me to Paris."

"*Oui, Capitaine.*" Émile slid his feet to the floor. "It will be done as ye say."

Jean squared his shoulders. "While you are doing that, I will see if I can convince the redhead to come with me."

Joanna enjoyed walking in the estate's gardens. This morning she and Zoé decided to pick wildflowers for the breakfast room. As they passed through the manicured gardens to the field of flowers beyond, Joanna shared stories of her childhood in West Sussex.

When she spoke of her sister and brothers, she could see the envy in Zoé's eyes. Joanna wanted to tell the girl that she would be pleased to act the part of an older sister. Having been that for Tillie, it would be easy to adopt the same role for this motherless child, but how could she say that when she had no idea of her permanence in Donet's life?

Zoé ran ahead and Joanna followed with the basket as they wandered away from the château. A gentle breeze stirred the tall grass as they walked along, Zoé bringing her flowers to contribute to the basket slung over Joanna's arm.

Joanna paused to gaze back at the château. Smaller turrets decorating the roof pointed to the sky, making the whole affair appear more like a castle than she had thought when she had seen only the front. She had difficulty imagining the pirate captain as lord of this grand estate. He seemed more at home on the deck of his ship. Raised the son of a comte, educated in the manner of French nobility, he could well do both. Donet was no ordinary smuggler, but then, neither was she.

"Lady Joanna, won't you marry soon?"

The question seemed to come out of nowhere, but then children often asked questions Joanna found startling. "Why do you ask?"

"You should have a husband and *mon oncle* needs a wife. We could be a family."

She smiled down at the girl. "I am honored you would consider me, Zoé, but your uncle may not want another wife. From what I hear, he loved his first wife very much."

"'Tis true," she said with downcast eyes. "I once heard Papa and Grand-père arguing about her."

"None of that matters now, Zoé. You have no need to fear being alone. Your uncle loves you and will take care of you." She hoped he would keep the child with him, but his life didn't seem to have room for Zoé, any more than it did for her. And then she remembered that Donet's daughter had been educated in a convent near Paris. Did he mean to do the same with his niece?

They walked on through the long grass. Red, lavender and yellow flowers bobbed in the breeze amid the green blades. Zoé bent her head to pick more flowers.

Joanna drank up the summer sun, tilting her hat back to feel the warmth on her face. It was late June and the thought came to her that time was slipping away. She ignored it. If she had spent the summer at The Harrows, she would have missed the only man she might ever love.

"Look!" Zoé pointed toward the château. "It's *Oncle* Jean."

Joanna lifted her eyes to see Donet striding toward them with an easy grace, as smoothly as he crossed the deck of his ship. He wore no coat. In his black waistcoat and breeches, he appeared the smuggler she had first glimpsed in Bognor, except for his white shirt.

"What can he want?" He would not come looking for them unless the matter was of some importance.

Her heart overflowed with love, watching him draw close. She blushed, remembering what he looked like when he wore nothing. She had touched his lean muscled body and knew its scars as well as her own. The words of his surgeon came back to her: *He bears wounds only seen with the heart, and the scars that have formed over the years still pain him.* Would she ever see those wounds, touch those deeper scars?

As he reached her, an easy smile crossed his face. "Here you are!" he exclaimed. "Lost among the flowers."

"Did you come to pick flowers with us, *mon oncle*?" asked Zoé with a hopeful expression.

The look in his dark eyes told Joanna he hadn't come to pick flowers. His purpose was more serious.

"*Non*." He picked up one of his niece's long curls, the color so like his own. "I must speak to Lady Joanna alone for a moment. Do you think you could carry the flowers back to Marguerite? I promise to join you shortly."

"All right." Zoé glanced at the two of them and reluctantly accepted the basket Joanna handed her. "But don't be long. We are to have tea on the terrace."

The girl skipped away, swinging her basket, the blue ribbons from her straw hat flying behind her in the breeze.

Donet watched her for a moment, then turned back to Joanna. "She is becoming quite attached to you."

"I like her, too." She was afraid to say more, afraid to confide her thought that she would love to be a sister to his niece, even a mother if the girl would allow it. "What is it you wish to discuss with me?"

He took her hand and led her to one side of the field where a copse of oak trees provided shelter from the sun and, she thought, from prying eyes.

"I have been summoned to Paris by the king. We are leaving Saintonge tomorrow." At her raised brows, he added, "'Tis probably only the usual requirement for one new to a title to pay homage to his sovereign."

"Oh." She looked down at the ground, remembering Richard had done the same when he became the Earl of Torrington. She had a sinking feeling her time in France, her time with him, was about to end.

His thumb rubbed the top of her hand, making sensual circles over her skin. She grew warm at his nearness, at the memory of their night together. At the desire that flooded her senses.

"I know you have wanted to return to England," he began in his French-accented voice, "but I would prefer you go with me to Paris."

Go with him to Paris? She looked up, losing herself for a moment in his obsidian eyes. "As what, M'sieur?"

He pulled her close, their bodies touching. His lips were so close. Their eyes met and neither looked away. "As my guest, if you like. More, if you would have it. I have made a few changes on my sloop so that you will have your own cabin. In Paris, you would have your own rooms, though I would welcome you in mine."

His gaze remained intense, his eyes so dark and heated she could fall into their depths. "I would like to see Paris."

He touched her cheek with his fingers. She shivered at his touch, at the prospect of staying with him.

His hands went to her waist and he bent his head to brush his lips over hers, once, twice. "I want you in my bed, Joanna." He kissed her, sliding his tongue into her mouth, possessing, plundering. Like a pirate claiming his gold.

She gave in to the wanting of him, raising her hands to his nape, and welcomed the kiss. Her breasts pressed against his hard chest and she felt her body yearning to be joined with his again. She had never realized a woman could feel such hunger for a man.

When he broke the kiss, she opened her eyes, feeling slightly dazed. His kisses always left her witless.

He touched his forehead to hers. "Will you go?"

"You knew I would say 'yes', didn't you?"

"I had hoped. I don't wish to go without you, and I must take Zoé for her safety. She would want you to go, too." Joanna did not tell him that if Zoé had her way, they would be wed. Her instincts told her doing so might frighten him away.

He took her hand and they walked back to the château. "I have ordered gowns for you for Paris. You will need them for Versailles."

"Versailles. I thought never to see it."

"Now you will," he said, squeezing her hand.

She glanced at him, unsure how to broach the next subject. "Before you leave Saintonge, I wanted to ask you about your tenants and the workers in the vineyards."

"Yes?"

"The cottages I saw on our way to Saint Jean d'Angély were miserable heaps of mud, without even windows. Is that where your workers and tenants live?"

"It might be. I'd have to ask Giroud. It has been many years since I lived here, you may recall. At that time, they lived close."

"Is there nothing you can do for them? The children looked so miserably poor."

"I see you are still the lady who smuggles French goods into Sussex to feed the English poor. And now you would have me taking on the woes of the French."

Her forehead creased with concern. "The children were barefoot and in rags. As the women watched our carriage, some looked angry. I couldn't blame them. You have spoken of the egregious taxes they pay. If the comte de Saintonge is wealthy, might you pay them? Or give them new cottages?"

He took a deep breath and let it out, as if to think. Finally, he said, "I can and because you ask, I will. M'sieur Giroud can be put to the task of reducing the rents they pay. And we can increase their wages. 'Twill be the same result in the end. I do not wish to become one of those aristocrats who expects to be carried on the backs of the poor."

"Thank you," she said. "It means much to me that you would do something for them."

He brought her hand to his lips and pressed a kiss to her skin.

"I do it for you, Joanna."

Her emotions were mixed as they returned to the château. Already, her awkward position was making her feel uncomfortable. A female "guest" traveling with an unmarried aristocrat would be thought his mistress. And if she returned to his bed that is precisely what she would be. Here on his estate, she did not worry for her reputation, but how would they treat her in Paris?

Early the next morning, the carriage loaded, Jean said his goodbyes to the servants lined up in front of the château. The parting was vastly different from his stormy exit a score of years before when they had stared openmouthed at the shouting match between him and his father.

Tears flowed down Marguerite's cheeks as she hugged his niece to her bosom. Zoé, too excited to be sad, told her not to worry. The girl's only thought was for what lay ahead, sailing on his ship and seeing Paris for the first time.

He had spoken with Giroud about doing something to lighten the burden on his tenants. With the money from the stored casks they would sell, the estate would be flush with coin. Jean did not need to dip into his own considerable wealth to help his tenants, though he would have done so if need be to make Joanna happy.

The estate manager seemed relieved to hear of his plans. "Take care, M'sieur. I will send word should I hear of anything." Jean nodded, knowing he referred to the murders and the carriage attack.

When Marguerite finally let go of Zoé, Émile gave the housekeeper a kiss on both cheeks.

Marguerite blushed.

"I'm in yer debt for sewing up the gash in my shoulder."

"'Twas nothing, Monsieur."

When all the goodbyes were said, they climbed into the carriage. The new driver was one of his footmen, pressed into service as his coachman. Inside, Joanna and Zoé took the forward-facing seat while Émile and Gabrielle took the other.

His quartermaster had wanted to ride on top with the driver, now armed, but Jean would not hear of it. With both his pistols poised and ready, he took Émile's place, climbing on top and ordering the driver to depart.

As the carriage hurtled down the road, Jean scanned the long rows of vines and the ripening grapes, wondering when he might return. It would not be soon. Perhaps in winter when the grapes were harvested.

Since Joanna and Zoé were with him, he had all he wanted from Saintonge.

Chapter 21

Lorient, France

It took Jean and his crew a day to sail from La Rochelle to Lorient. They arrived midday to find his three-masted sloop waiting for him.

The figurehead on the prow, a woman in a flowing gown, had a new coat of paint on her long hair, rendering it the color of a red fox. On the stern, the new name, *la Renarde*, in gold script spoke of the auburn-haired beauty for whom it was named.

The ship's rigging had been changed to square sails for the Channel instead of fore and aft for the Atlantic crossing. And some cargo space had been sacrificed to add two more cabins and a temporary bulkhead separating the stern cabins from his crew's quarters in the forecastle.

He'd had his cat, Franklin, transferred from *la Reine Noire* to the sloop, but given the way he followed Joanna about, the cat might have managed the transfer on his own.

Jean escorted Joanna, Zoé and Gabrielle up the gangplank to the deck of the sloop where his cabin boy waited. "Gabe can show you to your cabins. Instead of crowding into mine, you will have two, smaller but yours alone. I suggest you take one of them, Lady Joanna, and your maid and my niece the other, but if you prefer a different arrangement, that is fine."

Joanna met his gaze. She had to know there was a purpose in the new arrangement that was different from that on *la Reine Noire*. Hoping the vixen would join him, he'd also had a larger shelf bed installed in the captain's cabin. Since they had left Saintonge, he'd not had a moment alone with her and the thought of their being together brought his body alive.

"How long will it take to get to Le Havre?" asked Zoé, her gray eyes alight with interest as she watched the crew making ready to set sail. His niece had enjoyed their journey north and never once became seasick even though they'd had rough seas for part of the time.

"A day and a half with favorable winds. We will sail tomorrow with the evening tide and should arrive in Le Havre in time for supper the next day. Then on to Paris."

Then to Joanna, "While there is still time today, you must visit Madame Provot. She has some new gowns for you and my niece."

Zoé beamed her happiness and followed Joanna and her maid as they went below.

He shouted after them, "M'sieur Bequel will take you to Madame Provot's and return you to the ship for supper!"

Madame Provot welcomed Joanna and Zoé as they entered her shop, ushering them into the inner room where her assistants bustled around, hanging gowns on the pegs. These gowns were more ornate, more elaborately decorated than the other ones the modiste had made for Joanna.

"*Capitaine* Donet was most specific in his instructions," she said as she fidgeted with the gowns. "As if I do not know what is required for Paris. I was trained there!"

Flavie helped Joanna to undress and Madame Provot slipped a gown over her head. Another assistant was helping Zoé who appeared delighted to be receiving the attention paid a young woman.

"I am sorry to be so much trouble," said Joanna in an effort to soothe the modiste's temper.

"You are no trouble but the *capitaine*, impatient as always, insists on haste. How am I to create a masterpiece in haste?"

Joanna smiled encouragingly at the petite woman. "Oh, but you have."

Madame Provot laced her tight, more from her mood than Joanna's need. At least her wound no longer pained her. The gown's ivory silk, embroidered with flowers, was beautiful.

"The gown is lovely," Joanna remarked.

In a calmer voice than before, the modiste said, "*Oui*, the *capitaine* has excellent taste. And with you, Mademoiselle, he is most particular."

Joanna wasn't certain how to take that. Was it for his own sake and the reception she might receive at the French Court that he cared so much about her gowns? Or, did his feelings run deeper?

They were with the modiste for some time before she and Zoé dressed and returned to the antechamber where M'sieur Bequel waited, no more patiently than had his captain.

"Ye are done?" he inquired, his heavy brows raised in hope.

The modiste answered for Joanna. "*Oui, nous avons terminé.* The gowns shall be delivered to the ship tomorrow afternoon."

"*Bien*, but do not be late, Madame. Tomorrow, we sail on the evening tide."

Jean had invited Joanna and Zoé to dine with him and Émile in his cabin. Gabe left with Joanna's maid to escort her to the galley where they would eat together as they had the night before. When they'd gone, Joanna asked, "Will Gabrielle be all right with your men?"

"No one will bother her in the galley," he replied. "My crew knows she is your maid and you are my guest." He gave her a look meant to convey he had communicated to his men she belonged to him. "Definitely out of bounds."

While his niece conversed with Émile, the two having become fast friends, Jean handed Joanna a glass of sherry and picked up his brandy, beckoning her to join him at the stern windows. From here, they could glimpse the lights on shore from the taverns and hillside homes.

"Did you enjoy your time with Madame Provot?"

"'Tis much easier to be fitted for breeches," she said, a mischievous grin lighting her face. "And you might want to know that Madame Provot would appreciate having more time for her creations."

He laughed. "Ah, *oui*. She has made her feelings known before."

Some of his men entered, carrying trays with their supper. He and Joanna joined the others at the table.

The meal was simple by a nobleman's standards but elaborate for seafaring men. For all the time he spent on his ships, Jean insisted on decent food. Perhaps it was the memory of those first years with Ariane when he'd been poor and their food was often a simple fish stew. Ariane never complained and he had loved her all the more for it. Once he had been able to afford better fare and a cook, he made sure his small family ate well.

Jean liked his food French and cooked with skill. The white fish served them tonight, cooked in wine and butter with fennel, was among his favorites.

"In France, it's called *'le loup'*," Zoé explained to Joanna, showing her pride at knowing something an English earl's sister might not.

Joanna screwed up her face. "The wolf?"

"'Tis an aggressive fish," teased Émile in serious fashion.

They all laughed at Joanna's reaction, looking at them askance as if she did not believe his quartermaster.

"But it is an aggressive fish," Jean insisted.

In addition to the fish, they also had fowl wings *en hâtelets*, cooked on skewers, cauliflower with Parmesan and a salad. He made sure all his ships carried fine Bordeaux wine as well as cognac, which they drank this evening.

He watched Joanna sip the dark red wine, her cheeks flushed and her laughter ringing out at Zoé's chatter. He loved watching the candlelight flicker across her face and causing the copper strands in her auburn hair to glisten. She was a woman any man would be proud of.

It frightened him to think he could lose her to England, or worse, to illness or some attack by brigands. He was beginning to think it mattered not if she were mistress or wife. The pain of losing her would be just as great. Hadn't Louis XV mourned the death of his mistress, Madame de Pompadour? Jean had refused to consider marrying again, thinking he could protect his heart from the pain of loss and avoid the plunge into darkness that had followed Ariane's death. Now, he had to wonder if it were even possible to protect his heart from Joanna.

Paris became the topic of their conversation since neither Joanna nor Zoé had been there. His niece asked Joanna her opinion about the gowns Madame Provot had made for them. Joanna expressed her pleasure at the vermilion silk robe *à la française*. "I shall save it for something special. And the gown with the green satin underskirt is lovely."

It should not have surprised him that his niece looked to Joanna for a woman's advice. Zoé needed more than a father; she needed a mother. He had raised Claire alone with the help of the Ursuline Sisters of Saint-Denis. But even they could not take the place of a mother.

At the end of the meal, they climbed to the weather deck to enjoy the balmy evening. Franklin, who'd likely been hunting for his own dinner, sauntered up to Joanna and rubbed against the foot of her gown, his long black tail raised high. Holding on to the rail, she reached down to scratch his ears. "Funny cat," she said to the animal.

Jean came up behind her and whispered in her ear, "You have claimed my cat, Mademoiselle."

She laughed. "So I have. Do you mind terribly?" She looked at him in all innocence.

"Not as long as I have you both," he teased.

A short distance away, Zoé tagged after Émile as he inspected the deck. Though rough in appearance and voice, his quartermaster showed great patience with the child, just as he had with Claire at that same age. It made Jean wonder why Émile had never married. He had nieces and nephews he cared for—his brother's children—but none of his own.

"Those are deck prisms, little one," Émile explained to Zoé when she asked about the glass set into the weather deck. "They bring light into the deck below but without allowing water to leak downward. The glass is flat here, but the prism hangs below the overhead and sends the light sideways. A very clever invention."

"Most clever," said Zoé, staring down at the glass under her feet.

"Your niece has an intelligent and curious mind," said Joanna.

He slowly let out a breath. "She does, and I must decide what to do with her." He turned to gaze over the rail at the sun, now lower in the sky and reflecting off the blue waters. "Should I send her to the Sisters of Saint-Denis for her education? Or should I keep her with me? My life is not exactly one in which a child, particularly a girl, fits easily."

Joanna turned to place her palms on the rail's brightwork. "Given all she has suffered and her great attachment to you, I would keep her with you. She needn't go on all your voyages, but when you come home, she would be there."

"True. She could live in Lorient or even Saintonge."

"Must you sail so much?"

He jerked his head around to catch the serious look on her face. Whatever her thoughts, she cared deeply about his answer. Was she asking for Zoé or for herself? "*Non*. I have men to manage my affairs and worthy seamen to sail my ships. 'Tis just that I love the sea. But now I have more to be concerned with: the estate in Saintonge, my ships in Lorient, the king's demands—which will no doubt take me more often to Paris—and you."

"Me? Do you think to find room for me in all of that?"

He chuckled, lifting one of her curls from her shoulder and rubbing it between his fingers. "I do not worry about you, Joanna, at least not about finding room for you in my life." He did not think he could live without her.

She pressed her lips together as if holding back words she wanted to speak.

"Come to me tonight," he whispered in her ear. "I will send Gabe away as soon as I return to my cabin."

She did not reply but continued to stare out to sea.

Would she come?

Alone in her small cabin, Joanna watched the flame flicker in the lantern, thinking about the last few days and the comte. He had teased her about his cat becoming hers. She had wondered, at the time, if he meant what he said about not minding as long as he could have both the cat and her.

If she returned to England, the cat might mourn her loss, but would he? How did she fit into his life? He had said he did not worry about including her. Did that mean he was confident she would stay with him? Follow him around like the cat followed her? Ironically, just when she'd found a man she wanted, he seemed in no hurry to make their relationship more than it was. Perhaps the lusty comte considered her a mere convenience, a woman to be enjoyed for a time and then cast aside.

She had grown close to his niece, tucking her in each night and hearing her prayers. It would be hard on both of them if Joanna were to return to England.

She wished she had her friend Cornelia to talk to. She had left her home in America to marry a British nobleman and remained by his side even when England declared war with her country. Of all women, surely Cornelia would understand Joanna's love for a Frenchman. And she would understand Joanna's choice of Donet, who Cornelia once described as a hero decorated by both America and France. But would she agree with Joanna's decision to become Donet's mistress?

Running her brush through her hair, she felt suspended between the inner voice that told her to stay in her cabin and her longing to go to his. Would she go to him tonight? Donet's arrangement of the cabins provided a way for her to go to his cabin without others knowing. Surely he had planned it just for that reason.

She had gone to him once. How much easier to go to him now when she knew the passion that awaited her? Perhaps, that is how a woman raised to be a lady became a man's mistress. The first time would be difficult, even a bit frightening. But the remembered passion would make the next time easier. After all, such a woman would already be ruined in the eyes of all. Once compromised, the path ahead would be clear. And if she loved the man, she would willingly go to him.

As if a tether connected them, she felt the pull of his dark beauty, his man's body, lithe and muscled. She wanted to be with him, had longed for his touch. And she wanted to feel him moving against her, kissing her, making love to her.

They had not come together since that night in Saintonge, but she had glimpsed the desire in his eyes. Perhaps others had seen it, too. She was certain Gabrielle had guessed what lay between them after she had glimpsed Joanna's bed, turned down but unused.

Having made up her mind, Joanna realized she would have to move as silently as the cat curled up on her bed so as not to draw the attention of one of his crew or her maid.

What did one wear to a tryst aboard a ship? She still had on her gown of cinnamon patterned cotton with a bit of lace around the bodice. Perhaps she should not change into her nighttime attire. He would only remove it anyway. Better to be discovered wearing a gown than a chemise and a robe.

Heart racing, she quietly slipped into the passageway and took the few steps to his cabin. She didn't knock but slowly opened the cabin door, careful to make no sound as she entered.

He stood with his back to her, staring out the windows at the moonlight dancing on the waters. His midnight hair hung loose over his black velvet robe. When he turned, she saw beneath it he wore a white shirt, open at the neck, and black breeches. He was barefoot.

"You came," he said in his richly accented voice.

"Did you know I would?" Sometimes she hated that he read her so well.

"One can never be certain with a vixen." He walked to the pedestal table in the center of the cabin. "Would you like something to drink?"

She shook her head. "*La Renarde*... the name on the ship?"

He lifted the crystal decanter from the fenced tray and poured himself a brandy. "*Oui*, 'tis named for you, Joanna. I trust it meets with your approval?"

"'Tis embarrassing," she scolded, twisting her hands at her waist. "What will people think?"

He took a drink and set the glass down, coming closer. Lifting her hand to his mouth, he placed a warm kiss on her knuckles. Behind him, the light of the lantern cast his face in shadows. "My crew, no doubt, wonders at your continued presence. If they make the connection between the ship's new name and the red-haired beauty who travels with me, they will only smile at the change in their *capitaine*. But no one will speak a word of it."

Raised to be a proper lady, Joanna was feeling uncomfortable in her new role as his mistress. She had thought she could go along with it being as she was in France, away from her family and those who knew her well, but her mind was plagued with second thoughts.

He pulled her into his arms and kissed her. Like a brimstone match set to dry timber, she caught fire, opening her mouth to him, drinking deeply of his brandy-tinged kiss.

Her second thoughts flew away.

She raised her arms to his shoulders, threaded her fingers through his long hair and returned his kiss with all the love she possessed. His mouth blazed a trail of heated kisses down the side of her throat to the tender place at the base of her neck. "Jean," she rasped as an ache grew between her thighs.

He raised his head. "You have never spoken my Christian name before."

She lifted her eyes to his. "Would you prefer I call you Donet? I often think of you by that name. But it seems rather formal given where we are and what we are doing."

He chuckled. "I like that you call me Jean when we are alone. No one else does." He pressed his warm lips to her forehead and captured one breast in his hand, his rough palm sending shivers up her spine and causing her nipple to harden. "Let me undress you. I want to feel your skin next to mine. I want to touch your soft rounded places."

Swiftly, he rid her of her gown, petticoats and stays and then shed his robe and breeches. He backed her to the bed and they tumbled onto the blue cover.

He gazed into her eyes. "Do you like my new bed?"

"'Tis nearly the size of the one in Saintonge." She nuzzled his stubbled cheek and inhaled his scent that always reminded her of the sea. "Did you have us in mind?"

"How did you guess?" In a swift movement that spoke his impatience, he lifted her chemise to her waist and then above her head. "I only left this strip of silk for your modesty. I can see 'twas a mistake."

She slipped her hands free of the chemise and tugged up his shirt. She wanted nothing between them. He pulled the shirt over his head and tossed it to the floor. Then he set about kissing her mouth, her breasts, her belly, all the while moving his hands over her.

Her skin burned with heat under his deft touch.

"You're like satin, Joanna, softer than a baby's skin. And so warm. You are not afraid this time, are you?"

"No, not afraid." She was hungry for him. She opened her thighs to welcome him and he slipped his hands beneath her thighs, lifting them, separating them to rub his hard flesh against her womb, wet from want of him. "Now, Jean, oh now."

He eased himself into her, filling her. "Joanna," he murmured against her neck. "You are like silk inside."

It felt glorious to be one with him again. She gripped his shoulders and raised her hips to meet his slow thrusts, panting out her breath as their bodies grew slick moving together.

With every thrust, his furred chest met her breasts, the sensation lifting her higher and higher.

The first tremor came, causing her to try and hold him inside her. He wouldn't allow it, becoming fierce as he took her. The tremors increased, becoming a spasm of intense pleasure, sending her into a sublime ecstasy.

As Donet neared the end, he shook with the violence of his passion. His heart pounded so hard, she could feel it against her chest.

Breathing heavy, he sank against her, his mouth against her neck. "Joanna," he whispered, "making love to you is like riding a storm to a haven I never want to leave."

What could she say to that? Like a storm, he had taken over

her life. So she spoke the words in her heart in the way she knew best, kissing him and holding him as his heart calmed, loving the feel of him still inside her. Loving the man who had taken her.

Beyond all else, she wanted Jean Donet for her own.

Jean came awake to Joanna's soft breathing against his neck. They lay entwined, one of her legs captured between his and her breasts softly pressing into his chest. He savored the moment, for he knew it would soon end.

Dawn crept into his cabin as the ship's bell sounded the beginning of the morning watch. Soon there would be many feet scurrying to and from the weather deck. He'd wait till they quieted before scouting the passageway to let her slip back into her cabin. He had time to make love to her one last time.

He pulled his head back on the pillow to look at her. Auburn hair cascaded over her ivory shoulder. Her hand, flat on his chest, was the color of fresh cream on his olive skin.

Unable to resist her, he had taken her innocence. Yet he believed she had more of him than he had intended to give.

In sleep, she appeared very young. Was he too old for her? Perhaps she should have a younger man, someone closer to her own age. And yet the thought of another man having her was unthinkable. When it came to Joanna, his thoughts were all selfish. She would belong to no one but him.

He kissed the top of her head. When she titled her head up, eyes still closed, he pressed a kiss to her lips and drew her into his arms, letting her feel how she affected him.

"You're awake," she muttered, drowsy but stirring.

"I am, sleepyhead. And I want you."

She opened her eyes, mischief in their cognac depths. "Who am I to deny a pirate?"

He chuckled. "Wise woman."

Exhausted from the night before, Joanna went back to her cabin and promptly fell asleep. By the time she awoke, it was late morning. After she'd washed, Gabrielle helped her to dress in the green day gown.

She enjoyed a late breakfast with Zoé, who had been up for hours. After breakfast, the two of them climbed the companionway to the main deck, bustling with activity. The air was cool and the sky blue and clear, making her glad for her straw hat, but she had no need for a cloak. Donet was huddled with his quartermaster in the prow. Not wishing to disturb him, she went to the rail and Zoé followed.

In the harbor, gulls shrieked, vying for scraps. Men shouted to each other as they loaded ships tied up at the quay.

He had said they would sail tonight for Le Havre. The first time he had kissed her it had been on the terrace of his home here in Lorient. She couldn't help but wonder if she would ever return. After Paris, would he sail to England to keep his promise to take her home? It was what she had wanted, after all.

Chapter 22

Le Havre

The ship arrived at Le Havre the next afternoon. Joanna and Zoé were on deck to glimpse the harbor bustling with activity.

"Does it remind you of London?" said a familiar voice as Donet came up behind them. Joanna turned to see him in his familiar black coat, white shirt with lace at his throat and black breeches tucked into polished boots. On his head was a fancier tricorne than the one he'd worn that first night in Bognor.

Zoé grinned up at him. "*Bonjour, mon oncle.*"

He mussed her hair. "Where's your hat, *ma petite*?"

"In my cabin," she said and dashed away to where M'sieur Bequel stood near the helm.

Joanna met Donet's gaze, her body thrumming with his nearness. She had slept alone in her cabin last night and missed him. He had not asked her to come.

She wanted to lean back against his chest and savor his familiar scent, but to do so would announce to all their intimate relationship. Even a wife might not do so. Instead, she grasped the rail with both hands and faced the harbor, letting the wood anchor her to the deck.

"No, it doesn't remind me of London," she said. "There are many ships, of course, but the buildings are much taller than the warehouses on the Thames. Some are five stories high. Many look like homes."

"Le Havre has become a favored place for the aristocracy to build homes. When Louis XV's mistress, Madame de Pompadour, wanted to visit the sea, he brought her here."

"But that must have been long ago. Yet you remember her?"

"All of France remembers her, my lady. She was well educated, smart and gave the king wise advice, even in foreign affairs. She was only three and forty when she died, the year I left Saintonge. I still remember it. Even Voltaire mourned her death."

Joanna didn't know how she felt about Donet admiring a king's mistress, but perhaps that contributed to his being content with her own status. The French would likely think little of a nobleman taking a mistress.

Zoé and M'sieur Bequel came to join them at the rail. The girl motioned to a distant point in the harbor and asked the quartermaster, "What is that round fortress over there with the building on top?"

Joanna remarked to Donet, "You'd never see *that* on London's quay. It looks positively medieval."

"Nearly so." He stepped to the rail. His arm touched hers, lighting a fire in her breast. "That's *la citadelle du Havre de Grâce*. It has guarded the harbor since the sixteenth century."

"'Tis very old, little one," M'sieur Bequel explained to Zoé.

"London's port is on the Thames," said Joanna, thinking of another difference, "while Le Havre is a seaport, open to the Channel."

"I can see you are in fine form today," said Donet. "'Tis true that London's port has its differences, but Le Havre lies at the mouth of the Seine, the river that runs through Paris."

"Paris!" piped up Zoé, who was petting the black cat that had slinked up to them. "When will we be there, *Oncle* Jean?"

"If we leave today, our carriage should get us there by tomorrow evening."

Zoé beamed her happiness. "Will I get to see Versailles?"

"There aren't many children at Versailles, *ma petite*, but you will see Notre Dame and all of Paris. My townhouse is well situated. Perhaps M'sieur Bequel can take you and Lady Joanna for a day's trip around the city."

"Oh, yes!" exclaimed Zoé.

"A day in Paris would be a welcome change," said the quartermaster. "We might even see more of those air balloons floating over the Tuileries."

"I would like to see them," said Zoé excitedly, her eyes full of wonder.

One of Donet's crew stepped forward and thrust a paper into his hand. "*Capitaine*, this was waiting for you. 'Tis from our contact in London."

Joanna hoped it might be a letter from Freddie, but he would have sent his letter to Lorient. Sadly, no reply from him waited for her when they had arrived there. At the moment, Freddie would have no idea where she was.

Donet read the message and looked up at her, a smile forming on his face. "What?" she asked. He took her elbow and led her a short distance away, leaving M'sieur Bequel with Zoé and the cat.

On the quay, a fishmonger cried of his fresh catch as gulls circled above him.

"It appears your Prime Minister Pitt has taken action to end smuggling as he said he would. He has slashed the duty on tea and spirits."

So they had done it. "The night of the concert in the Pantheon," she told Donet, "I heard my brother and Lord Danvers speak of a bill Pitt had just proposed. But there are other goods. The smuggling will continue."

"Not for you, Joanna. I won't let you risk yourself again like that. Besides, 'tis unseemly for an earl's sister."

Laughter erupted from her throat. "*This* from the smuggler himself?"

He frowned. "That is different. You are a woman."

She gave him an exasperated look.

"What's more," he said, rather sternly she thought, "you are not just any woman." His voice had been low, only a whisper. "I will not have it."

Joanna was tempted to stomp off in a fit of pique but the look on his face spoke of concern, not a disdain of women.

"Very well," she said. "I will find some other way to help the poor in Chichester. But if I am to give up free trade, then you, too, must cease smuggling."

The look on his face was one of incredulity. This time, she did turn and stride off, pleased with herself at the condition she would exact for her compliance.

Paris

As the carriage drove through the arched *porte-cochère* of his townhouse in Paris, Jean looked up to admire the fawn-colored stone, tall paned glass windows and scrolling wrought iron balconies.

He had acquired the three-story home two years before when he'd thought he would be coming to Paris more often to see his daughter. Her marriage to the English captain made that unnecessary but, now that he had acquired the Saintonge title, Jean supposed it would be convenient to keep a *pied-à-terre* in the city.

Built in a rectangle with an inner stone courtyard decorated with potted topiary, it was the most elegant of his three homes, though the château in Saintonge was much larger.

Once the carriage passed through the arched entrance, it stopped in the courtyard in front of the glass doors. Jean climbed down and greeted his butler. After serving for years as a crew-member on *la Reine Noire,* when Jean bought the townhouse,

Flèche had asked to move to Paris to help his widowed sister and her children. The *majordome* excelled at managing the household and his skill with a blade added to the security about the place.

"Welcome back, *Capitaine*," said Flèche. Taking Jean's hat and sword, he passed them to a waiting footman. Determined to look the part of a proper butler, Flèche had insisted on wearing a wig and elaborately embroidered waistcoats, this one of bronze brocade. With the new clothes came a greatly improved speech. Few would recognize the former gunner who once wore gritty seaman's clothes and spoke with rough speech.

Jean assisted Joanna, her maid and his niece down from the carriage. For the sake of Émile's pride, Jean allowed his quartermaster to exit the vehicle on his own. They'd arrived in the early afternoon, but he could see the carriage ride had left them weary.

"Glad I am that ride's over," muttered Émile, as his feet touched the stone. He handed his hat and sword to the footman. "*Bonjour*, Flèche," he said, shaking the butler's hand.

Jean introduced Flèche to Joanna, Zoé and Gabrielle, and they walked into the townhouse. Flèche asked, "How long might you be in Paris, *Capitaine*?"

"That is unclear," Jean replied. "I am here to see the king. You are aware I now have the title?"

"*Oui*. Bequel sent word from England of the title and your preference not to use it. Allow me to congratulate you, *Capitaine*, on your new grandson."

"Thank you. 'Tis yet another reminder I grow older." Glancing at Joanna, who was speaking in a low voice to his niece, he wondered again if she shouldn't be with a younger man. He had left her alone that last night in Le Havre, thinking perhaps he should give her a choice.

"I think tea might be in order, Flèche. In the salon, if you will. And see that chambers for my guests are made ready."

"Of course, *Capitaine*." Flèche snapped his fingers and the footman hurried toward the kitchens. "I will personally see the maid about the rooms."

"Will you also help Lady Joanna's maid get settled?

"Oui, certainement."

Jean escorted Joanna and his niece into the salon, the room where he entertained dignitaries as well as friends. Gabrielle went with Flèche.

Unusual for his taste, Jean had retained the existing décor, mostly shades of red, including the ceiling, the curtains and a red Aubusson carpet with ivory flowers. The walls were paneled in bird's-eye maple inlaid with cream-colored marble. Gilded red velvet chairs and a pale salmon-colored sofa formed the main pieces of furniture clustered around the fireplace. An ebony desk, set against the back of the sofa, had been a favorite acquisition of his and a useful place to write letters.

As tea was served, Jean watched Joanna. She appeared exhausted from the long carriage ride. Even his niece was flagging.

Once she finished her tea, Joanna expressed a desire to retire to her bedchamber. "You don't mind, do you?"

"Of course not." He considered escorting her there, but thought better of it. Determined not to take her to his bed again until he had sorted out what to do with her, he would not allow himself to be tempted beyond his ability to resist.

Zoé trailed behind Joanna, following the footman up the stairs.

Émile took the seat across from Jean on the sofa. "Are ye off to Versailles, then?"

"I wasn't planning to call upon the king until tomorrow."

Flèche stepped into the salon and handed Jean a sealed missive on a silver tray. "The comte de Vergennes' man brought this yesterday."

Jean recognized the familiar seal of the Foreign Minister, Louis XVI's own choice for the post. Vergennes and Benjamin Franklin had been Jean's partners in his privateering during the American War.

He tore open the letter. *M. le comte, see me before you go to Versailles.*

"It seems Vergennes requires my presence. Do you wish to come or would you stay and tend your shoulder?"

Émile gently rolled his wounded shoulder, wincing only slightly, and got to his feet. "I have been sitting long enough. 'Sides, I'd like to hear what the Foreign Minister has to say."

They set off on horseback toward Passy, just west of Paris, and pulled rein in front of a gray stone château where Vergennes kept apartments when not at Versailles. It was here Jean and Émile had met with the Foreign Minister many times during the war to discuss the ships Jean had seized.

In the antechamber, one of the minions who worked for Vergennes approached. "The minister will see you now."

Vergennes had not changed. Now in his sixth decade, surprisingly, his face bore few wrinkles. He looked more the country gentleman, retired to hunting and books, save for his blue eyes that sparkled with the energy of one consumed by the intrigues of state. Always bewigged, his temples were graced with silver curls. Ever loyal to the king, Vergennes backed those causes that diminished England's power and made France more secure.

"Monsieur," said Jean, "I came as soon as I got your message. As you see, M'sieur Bequel is with me."

"Come, *mes amis*," said Vergennes, gesturing them to two sofas on either side of a small table. The minister sat on one and Jean and Émile on the other. The minion who'd escorted them inside walked to Vergennes, who turned to Jean and Émile. "Something to drink?"

"Brandy, *s'il vous plaît*," said Jean.

Émile nodded his agreement.

"*Brandy pour trois*," Vergennes instructed the footman.

Once the servant had gone, the minister turned to Jean. "I must convey my sympathy on the deaths of your father and brother. I know the king has summoned you, but I wanted to see you first. There are things you need to know and, right now, I need you in your elevated status."

"Before you begin," Jean said, "I assume you know of the carriage incident."

"*Oui*. A great tragedy."

Jean trusted Vergennes to hold the truth close. "I doubt you are aware their deaths were not an accident."

A furrow developed between Vergennes' brows.

"When I arrived at Saintonge, I discovered the carriage had been tampered with, the axle partly severed. And later, my estate manager told me he had found the driver's body behind a building with his throat cut."

The conversation abruptly ceased as the footman entered and set a decanter of brandy and three glasses on the small table. When he left, the minister said, "I had no idea. Still, I am not altogether surprised."

Jean looked at Vergennes, perplexed. "Why are you unsurprised? I can think of no one, save his tenants, who might want my father dead and even they might not be so bold as to kill him."

Vergennes poured the brandy and sat back. He turned his glass in his hand, his steady gaze meeting Jean's. "As irascible as your father could be, I am quite certain the target was not him, but your brother."

"Henri? How can that be?" In his mind he saw his brother as he remembered him, young and full of life. "He only made friends."

"In the past, that might have been true. But for some time, Henri had been making enemies on my behalf. You were not the only one working for me. He, too, offered his services."

Jean could hardly believe what he was hearing. "Henri?" He recalled Zoé telling him her papa had been away much of the time. "When?"

"It began when you were off capturing English ships. I had

enough problems with the Dutch and other matters of foreign affairs, but then the king made me chief of the Council of Finance and domestic matters also became my concern. Your brother helped me expose Jacques Necker, the Director of Finance, for the dangerous man he is. His criticism of the king and spread of false information concerning our credit have weakened the French citizens' confidence in the monarchy."

"Exactly what did Henri do for you?" Jean asked, sharing a look with Émile, who sat stone-faced before the minister.

"Henri was my agent, moving among the nobility, secretly gathering information on Necker's misdeeds, which I then brought to the attention of the king. *Eh bien*, following this, Necker was removed. Last November, with my support, Charles Alexandre, vicomte de Calonne, became the Controller General of Finances. He is working on a plan to help France out of its dire financial situation."

"I fear the hour is late for that," Jean said. He felt the coming storm all too keenly and knew its cause. France's support of America had cost the country much, leaving it deeply in debt. The peasants distrusted their king, who continued to spend. It was only a matter of time before they rose up in a violent temper. Jean only hoped at the end of it, France would retain what was good while throwing out the bad.

Vergennes nodded. "True, but we must try. Necker did not help us. And among his Swiss friends, there is much bitterness for his being sent from Versailles in disgrace."

"You believe Necker's friends wanted to kill my brother?"

The minister sipped his brandy. "I fear it is so. And now they may seek your life believing you are your brother. After all, you and your brother are near twins." His gaze darted to Jean's hand. "I see you now wear the Saintonge ring. The first news we had from Saintonge spoke only of your father's death and Henri's injuries. Your brother would have been the comte, at least for the short time he lived. It may be that Necker's friends see your return as Henri's recovery."

Jean sat back, looking at the brandy he held in his hand, seeing Joanna's eyes. "My carriage was attacked near Saintonge. I was not in it, but one of the men spoke of capturing my niece, Henri's daughter, who is now my ward."

"Be prudent, *mon ami*. The wolves circle. They do not realize it is the privateer Jean Donet they hunt."

"I would have justice."

Vergennes shrugged. "*Oui,* and no one will fault you if you get it."

Reminded of the king's request, he asked, "Do you know why Louis wants to see me?"

"I told the king you survived Henri, so he knows you are now the comte de Saintonge. When we spoke of you, he recalled with amusement your efforts for his good friend, Monsieur Franklin. I think the young king is rather charmed by your life at sea, as was his grand-père when Monsieur Franklin bragged to him of the many ships you seized. He merely wants to be assured of your loyalty."

Jean set down his glass and got to his feet. "I thank you for the brandy and the warning, Monsieur."

Vergennes and Émile stood.

"The king is giving a fete tonight at Versailles," said Vergennes. "It would be a good time to visit him. Watch carefully the faces in the crowd and you may detect which are your enemies."

Chapter 23

Versailles

Joanna slipped her arm through Donet's as they entered the crowd of elegantly attired men and women in the *galerie des Glaces*, the great hall of mirrors at Versailles. Intimidated by a sight so far removed from her experience, she drew comfort from knowing the man beside her had been invited by the king and could well navigate these waters.

Tall arched windows overlooking the gardens faced a long row of mirrors, equally tall, that reflected the subtle light of a midsummer's eve.

It seemed to her a magical place, the courtiers in their silks, satins and brocades with white wigs and powdered hair moving about like sugar sculptures on an iced cake. Even the men had rouged cheeks and lips, a scandalous sight if it were in London.

Donet cut a very different figure here than he did on his ship. Though his black velvet coat, richly embroidered in gold thread, and his gold satin waistcoat spoke of his noble beginnings, his unpowdered ebony hair with its silver streaks hinted of a very different life. He had a masculine aura very unlike the dandies floating about the hall.

Many women turned to admire him, leaving Joanna torn between pride and a rising jealousy.

He placed his hand over hers as his gaze flitted about the room full of mirrors, gilded surfaces and crystal chandeliers. "A bit ostentatious, *non*?"

"I have never seen anything so grand," she answered truthfully. "The golden glitter dazzles the eye."

Beside her, Jean chortled. "I'll not comment on the pale faces and rouged lips, but that display of gold, light and crystal you call dazzling is what Louis XIV thought necessary to convey the majesty of France." Donet tilted his head back, gazing up at the barrel-vaulted ceiling. "The paintings above us speak of the Sun King's victories over the foreign powers that dared to oppose France." Lowering his head, he gave her a teasing smile. "The hundreds of gilded mirrors tell of his wealth and majesty. He had the building specially positioned to capture the rising and setting of the sun."

"He compared himself to Apollo?"

"Just so," Donet said in clipped fashion.

Joanna experienced an overwhelming feeling of awe as her gaze roved about the long mirrored hall. Above and to the side of her were crystal chandeliers with hundreds of candles, their flickering light reflected in the mirrors and the polished parquet floors.

Through the tall arched windows, she glimpsed the sky, which had become a muted canvas of blue, lavender and pink.

Donet led her forward, examining the faces in the crowd as he spoke. "Two hundred years ago when the hall was finished, such a display would have been a rare luxury. Even today, Versailles is extraordinary in its splendor."

"And the courtiers who gather here are painted with the same elaborate brush," Joanna remarked. Having worn one of the gowns Madame Provot had made for her in Lorient, Joanna did not feel inappropriately dressed.

Fashioned from cream silk decorated with pale clusters of grapes, yellow flowers and leaves, it was lovely with its underskirt of verdigris green satin. Edged all around in the same green satin with bows at the waist and elbows, the effect was quite flattering against her auburn hair, unpowdered but piled high with curls. As she watched the other ladies, however, she could see no others whose hair was worn in its natural state. "Perhaps I should have powdered my hair?"

"Nonsense. Your hair is one of the things I love about you, Joanna. Even the queen, known for her beauty, could not be more beautiful than you this night, though I am rather fond of you in breeches."

She gave him a sidelong glance at the reminder of her smuggler's clothing. "Something tells me I'll not be wearing breeches anytime soon."

"Never again in view of others, if I have my way."

She stiffened at his proprietary remark. "You have become quite domineering, M'sieur."

"Yes, I daresay I have, particularly when it comes to you." And then, with a smirk, "Or, perhaps, you are just now seeing the real pirate."

She bit back a snort as men and women in their finery passed them by, giving them curious looks. None bothered to greet Donet. "Don't they know you?"

"Why ever should they? They are always here while I have only visited the king a few times and then surreptitiously. Most of these people have never seen me. Saintonge to them would be my father. I do not look like him. Henri and I favored our mother."

A man came toward them out of the crowd but then veered off at the last moment. His expression was one of shock. "That man must know you from your pirate days," she said. "He appeared dismayed to see you here."

"*En effet*, he did." Donet glanced over his shoulder, his gaze following the man as he strode away. An obvious aristocrat, the man's clothing was not unlike that of the others, but his great height and very slender form distinguished him.

"Do you think these people know anything of the peasants' great unhappiness? I have often wondered the same thing when I have attended elaborate balls in England."

"From what I have observed, the nobility in Paris remains blithely ignorant of the mounting danger. Instead, they take secret pleasure in attacking the *Ancien Régime* they consider antiquated and ridiculous, yet at the same time, you see how willingly they enjoy its pleasures." He glanced ahead as they approached the end of the hall. "Louis is just ahead."

The king stood surrounded by a crowd of people. Behind him were watchful servants in blue livery decorated with red and white braid.

As she and Donet drew near, the king looked over the shoulders of those speaking to him and smiled. "Ah, the comte de Saintonge finally comes."

Joanna would have guessed him to be the king even if Donet had not pointed him out. Louis had to be six feet tall. Where Donet was muscled and lithe, the king was slightly plump and his face round, even though he had to be a decade younger. Louis wore a red velvet coat and breeches, the shoulders embroidered in gold. His waistcoat, stretched over his belly, was ivory silk embellished in gold. He wore a white wig but his eyebrows were a light brown, making her think he might have fair hair.

The king had a benevolent look about him that immediately put Joanna at ease. In his eyes, which were a brilliant blue, she glimpsed amusement as he gazed at Donet. The king beckoned Donet to him. The men speaking with the king stepped aside.

Joanna gripped Donet's arm and walked forward.

He bowed before the king. "Your Majesty, I come to assure you of my continued loyalty."

The king smiled. "I would expect no less from one who has served me for many years."

Rising, Donet said, "May I introduce Lady Joanna West, sister of the Earl of Torrington?"

Joanna sank into a deep curtsy. "My Lord." She could not very well call him her king.

"An Englishwoman?" Louis asked, his brows lifting toward the ceiling.

Joanna blanched. Many French disliked the English. After all, they were ever enemies.

"Oui," said Donet, helping her to rise. "I met Lady Joanna at a reception for Mr. Pitt, England's Prime Minister, who spoke well of his time in France and of his meeting you and the queen."

Joanna recalled Wilberforce's comment about the king. *A clumsy figure in immense boots.* He did not appear clumsy tonight but, for a king, his demeanor was certainly unassuming. Not that of a haughty monarch. She had heard he liked to dabble in matters of science, which might explain his great friendship with Benjamin Franklin.

With Donet's words, the king's face resumed a placid expression. "You must meet the queen, my lady," Louis said to her. "I believe she is entertaining her ladies at the Petit Trianon tomorrow. I know she would want you to attend. It seems you and she have something in common."

"I would be honored," said Joanna, trying to fathom what she and the French queen might possibly have in common. To meet Marie Antoinette, about whom she had heard much, would be a great treat.

The man standing beside the king suddenly spoke. "I will be in attendance, my lady, and would be pleased to introduce you."

Donet's hand tightened over hers in a gesture she took as possessive. Joanna had been so focused on the king she had not noticed the bewigged nobleman until he spoke. Turning her attention to him, she saw he was almost as tall as the king but, unlike Louis, he was slender of form and strikingly handsome. His features were refined and his eyes brown.

"My younger brother, Charles Philippe, comte d'Artois," said the king. "He is ever beside my queen as her chevalier."

The comte's smile, directed at Joanna, made her uncomfortable for it seemed to her almost predatory. Still, she would not be ungracious to the king's brother. "Thank you, Monsieur. I would be most grateful."

Joanna turned her attention back to the king. He asked Donet, "Have you met with my Foreign Minister?"

"I have." Donet and the king exchanged a look that spoke of an understanding between them not voiced. Whatever had transpired between Donet and the Foreign Minister had been something of which the king was also aware. A matter of importance that concerned them both.

"Will you be here for a while, Lady Joanna?" asked d'Artois.

"My stay in France is of uncertain duration."

"*Eh bien*, I shall look for you tomorrow, say about noon?"

Joanna glanced at Donet. He nodded, reluctantly she thought. With Donet's approval, she turned to the comte d'Artois. "That would be fine."

"Come," said the king, walking away, "there is a magnificent repast to be enjoyed."

She and Donet followed the king but trailed behind him and the others.

"Beware the comte d'Artois, Joanna. He may be the queen's loyal champion, but his *liaisons amoureuses* outside his marriage are many. He enjoys beautiful women."

"Such men are not unfamiliar to me, M'sieur. There are many among England's aristocracy. 'Tis one reason I have never married."

"So that is it," he muttered. "I have wondered."

"And you? Surely it is not for a woman's infidelity that you remain unwed."

"*Non*, nothing like that."

He inclined his head, looking at her, but said nothing more. Joanna did not ask. She was quite certain she knew the reason. His dead wife still held his heart.

The next morning, Joanna dressed in her gown of vermilion silk, nervous for the meeting with the queen. On top of her auburn curls, she fixed her straw hat. Circling the hat was a wide silk ribbon. Soaring from it were plumes of white and green. Madame Provot had insisted she wear the feathers if she met with the queen. "All her ladies wear plumes."

Émile and Zoé had left earlier in a carriage bound for the sights of Paris and the lemonade the quartermaster said they sold on the streets of Paris. She would have gone with them for they were to see Notre Dame, the Louvre and the Tuileries, but how could she turn down an invitation to meet the Queen of France?

Joanna only had time for a brief breakfast of coffee, brioche and fruit with Donet. He seemed preoccupied, saying little of his own destination, only that he'd be riding and would find her later.

She believed his business involved the deaths of his father and brother. Dangerous business, most likely. She desperately wanted to ask, but doubted it would do any good. He seemed disinclined to converse about anything, save the pleasant summer weather.

Being so close to him, as she had been the night before at Versailles and then again this morning, was difficult for her. She wanted to touch him, to kiss him, to make love with him, but she had the distinct impression he was distancing himself from her.

Since their time on his ship in Le Havre, he had left her to sleep alone. Had he suddenly developed a conscience toward her? A disinterest? Or, might it be his preoccupation with his other affairs? She was fretting over the possibilities when his disquieting gaze captured hers across the table. His dark eyes sizzled with desire. The contradiction was driving her mad.

When they were finished, he walked her to the courtyard and the waiting carriage, warning her again of the comte d'Artois. "He is not to be trusted."

She had listened, glad that he cared enough to be concerned, though she thought his warning overdone. She was not his young niece, after all. What harm could come to her surrounded by the queen and her ladies?

He helped her into the carriage and shut the door. Reaching for her hand through the open window, he pressed a kiss to her gloved knuckles. A slight frown clouded his darkly handsome face. "Come back to me, *ma chérie*."

He stepped back and the vehicle rolled through the archway into the street, the horses' hooves clambering over the cobblestones as they took off across Paris.

Still wondering what he had meant by his parting comment, she gazed out the window, seeing in the daylight what she had missed the night before. In some places, waste ran down the middle of the street as it did in London, the stench rising to her open window. The carriage wheels splattered mud everywhere. She would have to remind Donet their large cities were not so dissimilar.

But she did notice one difference.

In London, everyone walked, but in Paris the carriage seemed to be the preferred means of getting around, at least for those who could afford it. The conveyances, both large and small, were everywhere, crowding the streets as they struggled to pass each other.

Once outside the city, they sped down dirt roads that meandered through dense stands of oaks. The sun filtering through the green leaves made for a beautiful canopy above them. Gratefully, she inhaled deeply of the country air, a delightful change from the smell of the city. The carriages were fewer here, as well.

The two-hour journey gave her much time to reflect on the path she had taken since leaving England. She had chosen to become the mistress of the man she loved, hoping for more, but he had not spoken of a future together. She feared broaching the subject because it would dig up the ghosts of his past and touch his hidden scars.

He had come to Paris to see the king, but she was certain he had other business to attend to. The matter of what happened in Saintonge remained to be solved. And after that, what would he do?

This morning, he had asked her to come back to him as if he thought she might not. What could he mean?

Her position as his mistress was not a comfortable one but, thus far, it had not caused her to be shunned in Polite Society. In England, however, the downfall of an earl's sister would be on every tongue. There were no secrets in *le bon ton*. She would not be able to move among the *ton* as before and Richard would never forgive her. Too, it might ruin Tillie's chances for a good match.

A sigh escaped her lips as she remembered he had made it her choice. She had let go of the life she once had to embrace another. Now she must wait to see what that new life held for her.

Jean had an idea of the identity of the man who had been horrified by his appearance at Versailles. Among Necker's friends were a few unsavory characters that might hire brigands to carry out vengeance. A sword and pistol would be their usual methods. Arranging a carriage accident was a subtler weapon, though no less effective than a knife slitting a throat, the body left in a dark alley.

The man he intended to call upon could help him.

He ducked into a narrow street not far from the Seine and knocked on the first door.

A dark head of curls framed the ruddy face of the brawny man that appeared. "*Ah ça alors*, it is the *capitaine*!"

"*Bonjour*, Gaspar. May I come in?"

"*Oui*, of course. Come, come!" Jean's former carpenter led the way into his apartments. "My wife is shopping with the children so we have the place to ourselves. I was just about to have some *déjeuner*. Would you join me?"

"Coffee only."

Gaspar said a few words to the gaping servant girl who disappeared into the kitchen. He walked to a room facing a small inner courtyard. The bricked yard contained pots of various sizes overflowing with plants. All the pots were set on neat wooden benches and shelves.

Gaspar offered Jean a seat on one of the well-crafted chairs at the polished table.

"I see your woodworking skills are as fine as ever," noted Jean.

Gaspar gestured to the courtyard. "My wife likes to grow things and I must accommodate her with places to put the pots."

"Is the new business keeping you in coin?"

Gaspar smiled. "I have not lacked for *livres* since turning my skills to the Paris trade. But you have not come for a new chair or a cabinet, *n'est-ce pas*?"

"*Non*. I come for information. My father and my brother were murdered in Saintonge in an arranged carriage accident."

"I am sorry for your loss, *Capitaine*. What bastard did it? What information do you seek so that we might end his days?"

"What I say next must remain between us."

"*Bien entendu*," Gaspar graciously agreed.

The excitement in Gaspar's eyes bespoke his longing for their days as privateers. But Jean would not ask his friend to partake in the vengeance he had in mind. "I don't know who did it, but perhaps you can help me find out. I understand my brother Henri had been working for our old friend the comte de Vergennes, gathering evidence against Jacques Necker."

"Ah. A very powerful enemy, that one. *Mon Dieu*, until a few years ago, Necker controlled all the wealth of France."

"He did, but he made enemies of the king and queen with lies about the state of France's finances he fed to the people. That is why Calonne is now Finance Minister. Vergennes believes Henri was murdered—and my father along with him—for his work against Necker. I need to know who is behind the killings, be he noble or peasant."

Gaspar nodded. "That can be learned. Such things are never held secret for long."

"One would have to know something about a carriage axle to have cut the wood in just the right place, but such talent can be bought." Jean leaned forward. "The arranged accident is not all, *mon ami*. While I was in Saintonge, brigands attacked the carriage in which my niece, a lady friend and Bequel were riding. Bequel was wounded."

"*Sacrebleu!*" Gaspar ran his hand through his head of curls. "Why would they want your niece or a lady of yours?"

"Leverage, I suspect. Vergennes believes Necker's friends might not know that my brother succumbed to his injuries. They may believe I am Henri recovered. Do you still have your network in Paris we made use of in the past?"

"*Certainement*. It has not been so long as that. I will do what I can and send word the moment I learn anything. Are you at your townhouse?"

"*Oui*. Bequel is with me along with my niece and my lady friend. Come by if you've a mind to do so. Émile has recovered and would like to see you."

"It would be good to see my old friend." Gaspar smiled, a teasing twinkle in his eyes. "And if the *capitaine* has taken a lady, I would very much like to meet her."

The servant girl returned with a tray of eggs, ham and brioche. Another servant brought them coffee. The fragrance of the dark brew wafted through the room. Jean watched as the servant poured it into cups.

Gaspar waited until the servants departed. "Now, about that coffee."

The carriage rolled to a stop. A liveried servant opened the door and helped Joanna to the ground. She noticed immediately he did not wear the king's livery of the night before. Instead of a dark blue coat with red and white braid, this one wore the reverse in colors: red wool with blue and white braid.

"Welcome to the Petit Trianon, Mademoiselle. The queen is expecting you. For your visit, she and her guests are having a picnic in the *Jardin anglais*."

The English garden? "How very thoughtful."

"This way, *s'il vous plaît*," he said, gesturing her forward.

She followed him down a stone path that wound its way through shaded gardens. Birds tweeted in the surrounding trees. Eventually, they came to a large expanse of lawn surrounded by hedges intermingled with irises and rose bushes. At one end sat a group of ladies and a few gentlemen. She could hear their laughter.

One of the gentlemen stood, a tall man, bewigged and dressed in blue and silver, a plumed tricorne hat above his finery. Gazing her way, he smiled broadly, then set off across the lawn toward her.

Arriving in front of her, the comte d'Artois bowed. "Mademoiselle, I am delighted." He offered his arm and she laid her gloved hand on the sleeve of his elaborately embroidered silk coat.

"You are as beautiful as I remember. Most delectable."

His hungry gaze had the look of a man eyeing his dinner. "Thank you, Monsieur."

He guided her to the ladies and, when he reached the one sitting in the center of a semi-circle of chairs, bowed. "Madame, may I introduce to you Lady Joanna West, recently arrived from England."

Joanna subsided into a deep curtsy. "*Votre Majesté*."

"Welcome to Versailles, Lady Joanna," said the queen in a light, lilting voice. "My husband spoke of meeting you. He told me you are a guest of that handsome devil Jean Donet, now the comte de Saintonge."

Rising, Joanna thought she might as well own up to it now. "I am." A glint of interest appeared in Marie Antoinette's blue eyes and a subtle smile crossed her face. Joanna did not doubt the conclusion the French queen had drawn.

Marie Antoinette was, indeed, a beauty. Her perfect face was appropriately pale, her cheeks and lips slightly rouged and her hair powdered white and piled high with several plumes in her straw hat. In her pale blue silk gown, she reminded Joanna of a confection on an elaborate marchpane dessert.

"Won't you join us?" invited the queen. "We are having a small repast, and my ladies and gentlemen drink champagne from the vineyards east of Paris."

The queen beckoned Joanna to sit in the empty chair next to her. The comte d'Artois waved away another man to take the seat next to Joanna.

D'Artois hailed a waiting servant holding a tray of champagne, who hurried toward them. The comte lifted two glasses from the tray and handed one to Joanna. Raising his glass in toast, he said, "Voltaire claims 'this fresh wine sparkling foam is the living image of us French.'"

The queen laughed. "Charles, you would quote Voltaire?"

"Only when it suits, Madame."

"Rascal!" the queen said, but Joanna could see by her manner, Marie Antoinette and d'Artois were friends.

Joanna took a sip of her drink. It was very good champagne. "Did you know that Voltaire lived in England for a time?"

"I did," said the comte, "and he admired many things about your government."

"True," she admitted, "but he also returned to Paris."

"As any good Frenchman would," said d'Artois. Then leaning in close, he whispered, "Repartee with you, my lady, stirs my blood."

Joanna's cheeks heated. She had no desire to stir the blood of the king's handsome brother. So instead, she exchanged pleasantries with the queen and drank more champagne.

When a footman in red livery passed around a silver tray of canapés, Joanna looked over the small pieces of bread holding tidbits of various foods and took a small onion *omelette* atop a round bit of toast.

"The tiny *omelettes* are *très bonnes*," quipped d'Artois, taking one from the tray and popping it into his mouth. He downed his champagne and asked for another. It was immediately supplied.

Joanna ate her canapé at a more leisurely pace, watching the queen and her guests. Most of them were ladies who, like their queen, wore elaborate gowns and powdered hair under their plumed hats.

Only one other woman wore her hair unpowdered and Joanna was anxious to meet her.

The queen ate sparingly and drank not at all. To Joanna, she said, "We have been discussing Beaumarchais' play, *Le Mariage de Figaro*. The king initially opposed a public appearance in Paris and for good reason." When Joanna looked at her with raised brows, the queen added, "The play is a comedy that subjects the nobility to ridicule."

"But it is highly amusing," put in the comte.

"Yes, and we enjoyed it." Then to Joanna, the queen said, "After it became very popular at Court, I thought it should be shown in Paris. Louis allowed it to go forward and the first performance at the end of April in the *théâtre de l'Odéon* was a grand success. But now I wonder if my request was wise."

D'Artois filled Joanna's glass from a bottle he had sitting on the grass by his feet and looked toward the queen. "Louis can deny Madame nothing."

The queen's only answer was a frown that marred her beautiful face as if still concerned she had wrongly argued for the play to be shown to public audiences.

"A speech in the fifth act particularly troubled the king," said d'Artois. "I memorized it. Would you like to hear me recite from it, Lady Joanna?"

"Only if Her Majesty is comfortable with that."

"Oh, do tell her, Charles. By now it is all over Paris."

The comte began to recite. "Nobility, fortune, rank, position! How proud they make a man feel! What have *you* done to deserve such advantages? Put yourself to the trouble of being born—nothing more."

"Oh my," said Joanna. She looked at the queen. "I do see what you mean." Joanna felt sympathy for the queen whose age had to be near her own. Marie Antoinette had been very young when she assumed the French throne. How difficult it must have been to be married by proxy at fourteen to a young man she had yet to meet and then summarily packed off to a foreign country, the enemy of her own. What did such a girl know of being Queen of France?

"I admire your lovely hair, Lady Joanna," said the queen. Joanna thought she was searching for a more pleasant subject. "My husband spoke of it."

Joanna met the young queen's brilliant blue gaze. "I must confess, Madame, when I saw you and your ladies today, my first thought was that I should have powdered it."

Marie Antoinette shook her head. Her powdered hair, fixed in place, did not move. "Oh, no, I am glad you did not. You see, you and I both have red hair."

Joanna was surprised but then she remembered what the king had said. "I did not know."

"Mine is a lighter shade," said the queen. "Few at Court have seen it *au naturel*."

D'Artois leaned over Joanna to speak to the queen. "I think your hair is lovely." Joanna was certain his arm pressing into her breast had been intentional. Relief flooded her when he sat back.

Joanna sipped her champagne thinking she might ask for another canapé to go with it. Above her, birds sang in the trees. A breeze wafted through the air. "The gardens are so lovely." She spoke her thought aloud.

The queen leaned forward to speak to d'Artois. "Charles, you must introduce Lady Joanna to my ladies and show her around the gardens. The flowers are splendid this time of year."

"As you wish, Madame." To Joanna, he said, "Drink up, Mademoiselle. We must not disappoint Her Majesty."

Joanna smiled at the queen and downed what was left of her champagne. A footman immediately collected her glass.

She rose and curtsied to the queen. "Thank you, Madame. I have so enjoyed meeting you."

Chapter 24

The comte d'Artois introduced Joanna to the queen's ladies and the few gentlemen who had been invited to the queen's picnic. For the most part, the dozen men and women were all young. Only a few looked to be over thirty. Two of those, the duchesse de Polignac and the princesse de Lamballe, the comte introduced as the queen's closest friends.

All the others were similarly of the nobility save one, who Joanna quite enjoyed. Madame Lebrun was the queen's portraitist and, except for her unpowdered brown hair and eyes, she could have been the queen's sister in appearance and age.

Joanna would have liked to get to know her better, but it was not to be.

She was still speaking with the artist when the comte took her arm and pulled her away. "I must show you the gardens of the Petit Trianon."

Having consumed two glasses of champagne, Joanna was feeling lightheaded and wished she had managed to eat another canapé, but she went with him. She did want to see the gardens.

They took the path that ran by a stream leading them toward a white folly shining in the distance. In the trees, she recognized the pleasant song of the goldfinch.

The folly stood on an island, its domed roof set upon Corinthian columns circling a statue.

"What is that structure?"

"*Le temple de l'Amour*, so appropriate for what I have in mind."

"And what is that, Monsieur?"

He answered with a question. "How long have you known Saintonge, my lady?"

"Several months, why?"

"Ah, yes. I recall now he told my brother he met you at a reception for Pitt." D'Artois took her hand and pressed it to his lips. "I find you not only beautiful, Lady Joanna, but sensual and with a keen wit. Your aristocratic birth gives you the speech of a lady and the graceful carriage of a queen. Above all that, you speak *français* remarkably well. To the point, a perfect mistress."

Joanna quickly retrieved her hand as her anger rose. Of course he, like the queen, would assume that she was Donet's mistress, but should he be so cavalier as to speak of it? "What business is it of yours, Monsieur, if I choose to become a man's mistress?"

"None at all," he answered blithely, "unless, of course, I want you to be mine. Which I do." His manner was easy, even gay, but behind it she sensed a serious intent.

Joanna coughed and pressed her hand to her chest. "Surely you jest! I hardly know you. We only met last night." She would have been righteously offended for her virtue had she not given herself to Donet but, since she was his mistress in truth, she could only despise the man who would try and take her from him.

"I know all I need to," d'Artois replied indolently. He steered her into the woods that lay next to the folly and pressed her up against the wide trunk of an oak tree. "You obviously have an affinity for Frenchmen, Mademoiselle. But why would you want to be the mistress of Saintonge, a man with a dubious past, when you could be the mistress of a prince of royal blood?"

Before she could respond, he grabbed her upper arms, pressed his body into hers and kissed her. Not a gentle kiss but a demanding possessive one. She turned her head to the side to avoid his lips and they slid to her throat. "Ah, Lady Joanna, I think I have only to make love to you and you will be mine." Raising his head, he gazed lustily into her eyes. She burned with anger. "You need not be shy. I can feel your rising passion. I can see it in your eyes."

She pushed at his chest with both hands, but it did little good. He was stronger and very determined. "That is not passion, sir, that is anger!"

"We will see if you feel the same once I have made love to you. There are rooms in the queen's house in the Petit Trianon that would avail." He tried to kiss her again, but even with her mind fogged with champagne, she was very clear about the man she loved.

She fought harder, twisting in his arms. "Let go of me! The only man I want is Jean Donet. I care not for royal blood!"

The sound of a sword sliding from a scabbard caused d'Artois to freeze. A blade touched his chin, the metal reflecting the sunlight filtering through the trees.

"Let the lady go, d'Artois, or I will be forced to speak to the king about your lack of manners for a guest of the queen."

Donet. D'Artois blocked Joanna's view but she thrilled at the sound of his voice. He had come!

The comte slowly lifted his chest from her and, with the point of the sword still touching his chin, turned to face a scowling Donet.

"We could duel for her, Saintonge," said d'Artois. "You might lose. I was trained in the fencing salle of the master, Monsieur Donnatieu."

Donet lowered his sword from d'Artois' chin but held it ready. "I, too, was trained by Donnatieu, but since then I've had much practice killing men. If I were to fight you, d'Artois, it would be to the death. Alas, as you are the king's brother, I cannot kill you. Louis might not appreciate me spilling your royal blood."

Freed from d'Artois, Joanna ran to Donet. He wrapped his free arm around her, drawing her close. She wept into his shoulder. "I don't think I make a very good mistress."

"I, for one," said d'Artois, not in the least subdued, "think you would make *me* a fine mistress."

"We are leaving," said Donet in a voice as hard as the steel in his sword. "I trust you will not again bother my lady, Monsieur."

She raised her head and glanced at d'Artois.

"Very well." Artois brushed his coat sleeve as if removing dust. "If that is how you feel. However, the invitation shall remain open, Lady Joanna, should you change your mind."

She was tempted to spit at the arrogant prince but, reminded he was the king's brother and a favorite of the queen, she glared. "Never!"

"Ah, the lady's spirit draws me," said d'Artois.

Donet clenched his jaw and returned his sword to its sheath, never taking his eyes off d'Artois as he led her away.

Jean held Joanna as the carriage made its way back to Paris. She had fallen asleep, presumably from the champagne, the excitement at fighting off d'Artois' ravishment and the long ride. If any man, save the king's brother, had tried to force her, Jean would have happily run him through.

He gazed down at her, nestled against him like a bird with a broken wing. Her wounded spirit called to his better nature. He was certain now that he had one. For many years, he had thought it gone forever.

The years following Ariane's death had been bleak, lost to the drunken haze in which he had existed. He'd been reckless in his adventuring then, risking his life as a pirate, uncaring if he survived. Hoping he would not. Bouchet had patched him up many times, testing the miracle working power of the good surgeon. What finally brought him back to life was his friend Émile, sent by the crew to see if he could pull their *capitaine* back from Hell's door.

Once out of the stupor, Jean had resumed his life as a privateer. He remembered well those exciting days, seizing ships for bounty. Before he gained his letter of marque, he preyed on merchantmen with allegiances other than France. His prizes had gained him much wealth.

With the American War, his fortunes had turned. His battles on the Channel and his spying became legitimate efforts to win America her freedom and weaken the British threat to France. He'd accepted the praise that came after, knowing his men were proud of their service.

But now, because of this English vixen, he wanted more. He could not imagine his world without her. And letting her go or watching her live with a shame she could not accept were not acceptable. She had the right of it. She was not a very good mistress—because she was a lady born.

The remedy was clearly before him. He must make her his wife. He could no longer deny the truth. He loved her. Hadn't he known it when he'd first invited her to his bed? Like an echo in the wind, love had come to him a second time and he was more than grateful it had. It meant risking again the loss of the woman he loved, but there was no help for it. He could not live without her.

Would she marry a Frenchman? A Catholic? He would not give her a choice. She would simply accept his decision. He would remain in Paris only to see them wed and dispose of the ones who threatened his very existence.

Joanna woke as the carriage entered Paris, rolling over the cobblestone streets. She regretted that she had not been able to say goodbye to the queen, but Donet had insisted, telling her he would send the queen a note saying they would be available should their presence be required again.

"You're awake. *Parfait*. I have something to say to you."

Joanna feared what might come. With his recent indifference and the embarrassing episode with the comte d'Artois, perhaps Donet would be returning her to England when he sailed. She sat up and faced him, ready for the blow that was coming.

"You will become my wife."

Shocked, Joanna blurted out, "Your wife? Why?"

He shrugged. "I have decided it must be."

"Am I to take this as a proposal?"

"More like a demand," he said without humor.

"Because of what happened with d'Artois? I am sorry I was not more careful." She did feel guilty for not paying proper attention to his warning.

"*Non*. It is merely something I have come to."

"But you don't want to marry! You have never before mentioned it."

"I have changed my mind."

Joanna wondered at this sudden change, from indifference to a desire to marry, with no mention of love. "I will think on it," she said shortly.

"Do not think overlong, Joanna."

She stared out the window as they crossed Paris. All she had wanted was to be his wife, but his jealousy and abrupt demand for her to become his wife seemed insincere.

"By the way," she said, "I have seen enough of the streets of Paris to know they compete well with London for mud, filth and sludge."

"*Oui, peut-être*." His manner was curt. She could see he would not give her an inch in which to move. She needed some insight into what had happened to bring about this change. As she thought on it, she knew just the one to ask. His closest friend, the man who was ever at his side.

At the townhouse, Zoé ran to greet them, telling them about her day. "'Twas so exciting, the grand cathedral, the colored windows, the gardens and the paintings. I have never seen so many in one place. Paris is wonderful! And Monsieur Bequel bought us lemonades."

Donet patted his niece on the head. "I must see M'sieur Bequel. Where is he?"

"Just here, *Capitaine*," said the quartermaster in his gruff voice.

"Let us retire to my study," said Donet. The two men walked off together, leaving Joanna to wonder what Donet might say to his quartermaster about what had happened at Versailles.

Zoé took Joanna's hand and pulled her toward the glass doors. "Come, I want to show you the doll Monsieur Bequel bought me!"

Joanna and Zoé shared a cup of chocolate in the parlor and Donet's niece told her of all she saw. Joanna listened, regretting she had not gone with them. When she heard the men leaving the study, she went to the doorway and watched Donet climbing the stairs.

Excusing herself, she went in search of the quartermaster.

He was just coming from the kitchen when she stopped him. "Might I speak with you for a moment, M'sieur?"

"Of course. In the *capitaine*'s study?"

"That would be fine." She followed him into the same room he and Donet had left earlier. It was not unlike the study in Lorient with cases of books lining the walls and a desk in one corner, more elaborate than the writing desk in the parlor. The room's windows looked out on the inner courtyard.

He closed the door and turned to face her. "How may I help ye, Mademoiselle?"

"Did Donet mention that he intends to marry me?"

"*Oui*. He spoke of it briefly. 'Tis a good thing, no?"

"I cannot help but wonder why he insists upon this after so much time. He gave me no reason. Perhaps it is only because of the comte d'Artois' actions today. Did he tell you of that?"

"He mentioned it. D'Artois has long had a reputation. I expect the *capitaine* went to find ye, suspecting the comte might try something like that."

"But don't you see, M'sieur? I don't want him to marry me out of jealousy. I know Donet is still in love with his wife."

Bequel shook his head. "Not as ye think, my lady. He loves her as ye do the memory of one lost forever. Ye must remember when he married Ariane, he was passionately in love as only a young man can be. She was the woman he needed then. Ye are the woman he needs now."

"But surely, I am nothing like her!"

"*Dieu merci* for that," he said, beckoning her to take one of the chairs flanking the fireplace. He took the other.

"Ariane was fragile and fearful. She begged him not to take up smuggling. Always, she felt guilty for what he gave up to have her. He regretted naught, such was his love for her. Ariane gave him the strength to do what he must to keep her and the little one fed. After she died, he would sometimes drink a bit too much brandy and then he would speak of those early days."

Joanna listened as he described Donet's life as a smuggler.

"They were hard times, but he was clever. Smuggling was his daily pursuit and he was good at it. Very good. Brandy, lace and tea passed through his fingers on their way to England's aristocrats, often them none the wiser."

"My own family—" She had suspected they had been customers of the Bognor smugglers long before she became involved.

"Aye, I do not doubt it, living so close to the coast. The goods passed right through Sussex. Did ye ever wonder why the brandy came to ye at so reasonable a cost? Or why yer vicar never lacked for tea?"

Joanna felt a pang of guilt. "Nay, I never asked, not until I joined the smugglers." She could hardly criticize Donet without finding fault in herself.

"He doesn't like that ye risk yer neck that way."

"I know. In his demanding way, he has told me it must end."

"Only because he cares for ye." The quartermaster leaned his elbow on one arm of the chair, looking toward the window but seeing, she thought, the distant past. "The *capitaine* served the poor of both England and France, helping them to feed their families as he fed his own. He never asked more than a fair price but, in time, his wealth grew. When Vergennes suggested to Monsieur Franklin, who was then in Paris, that the *capitaine* could outrun the English frigates plying the Channel, the two met. And the *capitaine* accepted America's letter of marque."

Turning to face her, his dark eyes gleaming in his swarthy face, he said, "He will never tell ye this, but he is respected by King Louis, who personally thanked him."

"You make Donet out to be an heroic figure."

"To me and his crew, he is. And I daresay to ye, as well."

The light in the study was dim, giving her hope Bequel could not see her flush at the truth of his words. "But why was he indifferent to me before this demand we marry? I fear he will regret his hasty decision."

The quartermaster let out a huff. "*Peut-être* only I have seen it. The *capitaine* has been like a wild animal caught in a trap, fighting to be free, thinking he should drive ye away but hoping ye'd not go. He thinks ye young and he fears loving again."

"He is afraid? But that is absurd."

"It only seems so to ye, my lady. There is one thing the *capitaine* fears more than war, more than another man's sword, even more than a storm threatening his ship: a bond of love that can be severed by death."

"Because of Ariane."

The quartermaster folded his arms over his broad chest. "I saw it when the English captain abducted his daughter, Claire. And sometimes, I see it when he looks at ye."

Joanna let out a sigh. It was so hard to believe Jean Donet feared anything at all.

Bequel continued. "The *capitaine* loves in a way few men do. When Ariane died, it nearly destroyed him. His recent indifference, as ye call it, is only the death throes of a losing fight."

She recalled the words of the surgeon in Lorient... *the scars that have formed over the years still pain him*. "He loves me?"

"*Oui*. And he knows it. I have been with him a long time, Mademoiselle. I know him well. There have been few women since Ariane and only the kind who satisfy a man's baser needs. None of them affected him like ye. At two score, he has lived much, but his soul is much older than his years."

"What must I do?"

"Challenge him with something he cannot accept and ye will see his true heart."

Joanna pondered what Donet might consider a challenge as applied to her. An idea came to her. If he truly loved her, he would not want her to go on as his mistress, would he?

It was late afternoon when she found Donet in his bedchamber, donning a fresh coat. "I have thought about your demand we marry," she said, standing very straight as she made her announcement. "I know you do not really wish to marry. You have only spoken of it now because of d'Artois." She did not look at him as she spoke these next words but kept her eyes on the carpet. "I have decided to remain your mistress." Pressing her point, she added, "I shall content myself to live in sin."

She looked up and encountered his piercing look, the same look he must give men who defied him. It would have frightened her to death had she not understood him as well as she did.

He stalked toward her and took her arms in a vise-like grip. "No woman of mine will live in sin, Mademoiselle! Do you understand?"

She might have pointed out that she had been doing precisely that, but realization suddenly dawned. "What makes you think I am *your* woman?"

"This." His mouth came down on hers in a crushing kiss as he wrapped one arm around her waist and used the other to hold the back of her head. She did not resist, but reveled in his fierce reaction, for it did not just say she was his, but he was hers.

He lifted her into his arms and carried her to the bed. His black eyes flinty with shards of silver, he threw her down on the cover and shrugged out of his jacket. With his gaze fixed on her, he began to unbutton his waistcoat. "Before I am finished," he snarled, "you will know whose woman you are, Joanna, and whose wife you will be."

She laid her head on the pillow, her eyes following his every move. Her heart pounded in her chest as he slowly shed the rest of his clothes. When he was naked, he came to the edge of the bed and loomed over her, his beautiful scarred body stark before her.

"It shall be as you wish," she said as meekly as she could manage with outrageous joy filling her heart.

Now that Jean had made love to Joanna in a way that left her in no doubt that she was *his* woman, his mind spun with plans. She lay complaisant in his arms, but her fingers playing with the hair on his chest told him she was not asleep.

"You are not fearful of this marriage, are you, my love?" Her words came out in tentative fashion as if the question itself frightened her.

"Terrified," he frankly admitted. "I might lose you to disease, childbirth or… *Mon Dieu*, England."

"Then why—"

"Because I love you, Joanna. It would kill me to lose you, but since I am unwilling to live without you, I must do the honorable thing and make you my wife. Did it never occur to you that I, too, found your role as my mistress unacceptable?"

"No. I thought, 'Well, he's French'. It seemed to explain all."

He laughed. "It explains much but not all."

"You needn't laugh," she said, tugging on the hair on his chest. "I have loved you for a long while, Jean Donet." She pressed kisses into his shoulder. He inhaled deeply, finding it hard to think with her soft lips on his skin.

"And I have known for a long while. I tried not to love you, Joanna, for fear of losing you, but I had no success in that."

"None of us knows how many years we have, but however many we are given, I want to spend them with you." She looked up at him. "And what of you, Sir Pirate? You sail a ship into storms; you battle revenue cutters and the Royal Navy on the Channel; you draw your sword on brigands. What if I lost *you*?"

"I think you far more resilient than I, *chérie*. You would survive." He thought of something that had long bothered him. "Do you think I am too old for you?

She laughed. "I think you may not be old enough!"

"I shall take that as a sign I am still gaining wisdom. So be it. Since it is agreed we will wed, let us speak of plans. I thought we might marry here in Paris before a priest and then again before one of your Anglican clergy, perhaps on Guernsey. What say you?"

Her hand began moving in slow circles on his belly. "Yes, 'tis best. Though I am certain God would not care, in England, we must be wed by an Anglican clergyman for our marriage to be valid. And I would like to see Guernsey."

"Since I am a Catholic, we must also be wed by a priest. By the bye, should you want to know the name of the man you will marry, I was born Jean-Philippe Donet. But when I went to sea, I dropped all but Jean."

Her hand paused a few inches short of his groin. "Shall I call you Jean-Philippe?"

"*Non*. I am used to the name Jean Donet." He kissed her

forehead. "But I would like it if you called me Jean when we are alone."

"I would like that, too." Her palm circled just above his groin. "There will be a dowry, you know. Richard will insist."

"I will not insult him by refusing." He placed his hand over hers so he could think. What might they do with the dowry? He had no need of money. "Perhaps, if you like Guernsey, we can use your dowry to build a home there." He lifted his hand and stroked her hair.

"Another home?" she asked, her fingers playing with the thatch of black hair at his groin. "Are three not enough?"

"More than we need, certainly, but it occurs to me that it would be good to have a place on what is considered English soil. If violent times are ahead for France, as I fear they are, you and my niece would be safe there." He kissed the top of her head, smoothed her auburn hair over her shoulders and caressed one of her breasts. "An excellent place for a honeymoon, *mon amour*."

"What about Zoé?" she asked, bringing her palm back to his chest and laying her chin on it to look up at him. "Can she live with us?"

"My niece is so attached to you, I rather think she will insist."

"I was hoping you would agree. It will make her very happy." She stroked his belly and his imagination followed the direction of her fingers. "At some point, we must return to England," she said in a husky voice, "if only to see my family and share the news. Richard will be pleased I have wed, I think." She laid her cheek on his chest and trailed her fingers to his groin.

His body responded to her increasingly provocative touches. "If my business in Paris can be soon concluded, we can be married and back in Sussex by the end of August. Would that please you, *ma chérie*?"

Her breathing began to speed and her heart pounded against his chest. "Oh, yes. Richard and Tillie will be home from London by then. Perhaps once we are wed, I might send a letter from Paris so they will not worry overmuch if they return and find me gone. I can tell them you took me from The Harrows, a willing bride."

Her hand grasped his hardened flesh sending a shudder through him. The blood in his veins boiled. Unable to stand another minute of her ministrations, Jean rolled her beneath him.

She parted her thighs, her soft body welcoming him.

"*Oui*," he whispered in her ear, "a most willing bride."

Chapter 25

After supper, Jean retired to the salon with Joanna, Émile and Zoé. Joanna had just poured tea and he and Émile were sipping their cognac when Flèche appeared at the door.

"Gaspar is here to see you, *Capitaine*."

Jean looked up, his eyes meeting Émile's sitting across from him. "We will see him in the study." Rising, he kissed Joanna on the cheek.

Once the three of them were ensconced in the study, Jean poured each of them a glass of cognac and, leaning against his desk, watched his quartermaster and former carpenter get reacquainted. "Ye old dog, Gaspar, how many children do ye have now?"

"Three, but a fourth is on the way. What about you, Émile?"

"Too many ladies to satisfy to settle with one."

"Enough, you two," said Jean. He met Gaspar's steady gaze. "You have information for me?"

Gaspar reached into the pocket of his waistcoat and pulled out a piece of paper. "The man who did the dirty work is Joseph Frey, a Swiss mercenary working for one of Necker's Swiss friends, a Joseph de Vogelsang."

"Whose address is this?"

"Vogelsang's. 'Tis near the Seine. I do not have one for Frey, but you might find him at one of the taverns the mercenaries frequent."

"Is there any reason to believe Necker himself is involved? I'd rather not kill one of the king's former ministers even if he is now disfavored."

"Nay, 'tis thought Necker may know nothing of it. The word is he accepted his change in station, but those who benefitted from his high position did not. They sought to send a message to Vergennes by killing his spy."

"Thank you, Gaspar. You have served me well." Jean went to his desk and took a bag of coins from the bottom drawer. "You earned this and I am grateful."

"*Merci.*" Gaspar bowed and accepted the coins. "For the little ones. Now, can I meet this new lady of yours?"

"But of course," said Jean. "And, by the way, that lady will soon be my wife."

The next day, Jean and Émile set off on horseback to find Vogelsang. The streets of Paris were wet with the rain from the night before. A carriage would have had to fight its way across town, while horses could better maneuver and afforded them a quick escape if need be.

The directions Gaspar had provided Jean led them to the fashionable area of *faubourg Saint-Germain* near the Seine River. This morning, the river was crowded with small boats. Voices rose from the quay where people, engaged in business of one sort or another, shouted to passersby. Adding to the cacophony of sounds were seagulls shrieking above the banks. A duel amid all of this would not suit.

A short distance away, they dismounted in front of the townhouse, modest for the area, but no less well built. Jean lifted the knocker and dropped it a few times while Émile secured the horses to a post. No groom or footman had appeared.

The door opened and a young maid in mobcap and apron gave them a blank look. Clearly she had expected no visitors. "Messieurs?"

"We are here to see Monsieur Vogelsang. You may tell him Monsieur Donet has come to call."

She invited them into the entry, a rather dim place with a stone floor and scant windows, then disappeared through a corridor.

Jean checked his pistol and put his hand on the hilt of his sword when the maid returned.

"The master will see you. Please follow me."

The large room they entered appeared to be a combination of parlor and study. Jean recognized the tall thin man who rose from behind the ornate desk though the wig he wore today was a darker gray and his face not the powdered white it had been at Versailles.

Behind the desk stood two burly henchmen like a pair of andirons flanking a cold fireplace.

"So, 'tis true," said Vogelsang in a high voice that grated on Jean's nerves, "there are two of you. I can see now you are not Henri Donet. A brother, *peut-être*? A twin?" Carefully, he appraised Jean. "So very alike, so easy to kill." His voice echoed his arrogance for what he obviously considered a trivial matter soon dispensed with.

Jean spoke in a voice his men would have taken as a warning. "You will find, Monsieur Vogelsang, I am nothing like my brother. Henri was the more refined of the comte de Saintonge's sons. The kinder one. I, on the other hand, have a darker side and a much blacker past."

Émile smirked at Vogelsang. "Have ye never heard of the pirate Jean Donet?"

The Swiss man narrowed his gaze on Jean. From his expression, Vogelsang clearly knew the name and he feared the man behind it. "You are he?" When Jean nodded, Vogelsang shouted to his henchmen, "Seize him!"

The two andirons lunged forward. Jean and Émile drew their pistols, causing the andirons to pause mid-stride.

"Which one of you guard dogs is Joseph Frey?" Jean asked, his voice edged with loathing.

One of the andirons grimaced and Jean returned him a harsh glower. "You arranged for my brother's *accident*?"

"What if I did?" he spit out arrogantly.

Jean didn't hesitate. He fired his pistol and the man dropped to the ground, a ball through the center of his forehead. Facing Vogelsang, Jean said, "So, now there are two. Not so very many."

Vogelsang began to shake.

"Did you think we came only to talk?" asked Jean.

"The *capitaine* is short on patience today," chimed in Émile.

Vogelsang held out his hand, palm facing Jean, as if to hold back his fury. "*Non*," he whimpered. Jean hated cowards who hid behind swaggering bullies.

The other guard drew his sword and stalked toward Jean with a stiff stride.

"Watch the master, Émile, while I deal with the servant."

His quartermaster smiled and pointed his pistol at the tall man. "*Avec plaisir, Capitaine*."

Jean had previously assessed the andirons as opponents. They were not well matched, as the ensuing swordfight made clear. This lumbering mercenary had strength on his side and, from his initial parries, some expertise. However, he lacked the *finesse d'esprit* Jean had been taught long ago as one of Pierre Donnatieu's most avid pupils.

After a preliminary exchange, the guard lunged.

Jean parried and then backed away only to push in, slicing across the man's cheek.

"Damn Frog!" the man bellowed, touching his face. His fingers came away covered in blood.

"Does the Swiss cow bellow?" Jean asked mockingly.

The mercenary raged and, with less precision than before, lunged.

Jean parried the thrust using his left hand to block the man's arm and brought his own blade around his back and turned to sink his sword into the man's belly. The guard had not expected the move, one Jean's fencing master had taught him long ago.

The mercenary grabbed his belly, staggered to the wall and slid to the carpet. He would die but not soon. In some small measure, it compensated for what Henri must have suffered.

Jean wiped the sweat from his forehead with his lace cuff and faced the only miscreant left standing.

Vogelsang's thin face already appeared like a death mask. He sank into his chair behind the desk.

"You directed the so-called accident that killed my father and brother? And the murder of the driver?"

The truth of it spoke loudly from Vogelsang's guilty expression. He did not even cast blame on another as Jean had expected.

"And you arranged for the attack on my carriage near Saint Jean d'Angély?"

His nose in the air, Vogelsang replied, "I have no knowledge of these trivial country villages."

"It was not trivial to my niece and my lady, nor to my quartermaster and driver both of whom were wounded in the attack. I can assure you, they will forever remember the name."

"Let me have this one, *Capitaine*," drawled Émile. "I am owed a blood debt and seek vengeance of my own."

"If you wish, *mon ami*. I know you enjoy firing that pistol and I can think of no target more worthy."

"No!" shouted Vogelsang "I have money. I can make you rich!"

"You do not have enough of France's money to make up for the lives you have taken from me!" Jean threw back.

Vogelsang yanked open his desk drawer and pulled a pistol from its depths.

The shot rang loud in the room as Émile fired first. Vogelsang slumped in his chair and fell to the floor, joining his guard.

The maid came to the doorway, glanced at the bodies and screamed. Covering her mouth, she turned to stare in horror at Jean.

"Do not be concerned, Mademoiselle." Jean spoke in a gentle voice. "I will send someone to remove the bodies. But lest you think we are brigands of the worst sort, know what has been done here is justice for the murder of my father, a nobleman, and my brother. There will be no inquiries."

That night, Jean would arrange for the bodies to be dumped in the Seine. In the morning, they would be found along with others. All knew Paris could be a dangerous place.

Joanna heard the horses' hooves in the courtyard and rushed from the parlor. Flèche opened the glass doors and Donet stepped inside, handing his hat, pistol and sword to the butler.

She went to him, looked into his eyes and wrapped her arms around him, hugging him tightly. The tension in his body told her the task had been difficult, but the relief she had glimpsed in his eyes told her it was finished. She had feared for him, but she had not tried to persuade him to stay. She never would.

Jean Donet had carved a life of danger for himself, winning the respect of his men and his country. More than one man looked up to him. More than one country had depended upon him. If she were to become his wife, she must let him face the danger and trust him to return. If the day ever came he did not, she would count herself lucky to have had the years with him she did.

She let go of him to search for wounds and found none. "You and M'sieur Bequel are well?" she asked, her gaze shifting from Donet to his quartermaster standing just behind him.

"We are fine, *chérie*. Rest assured, there will be no attacks on my carriage in the future. The deaths of my father and brother have been avenged, sending a message that will deter any others."

"You killed the bad man who killed my papa?" asked Zoé from behind Joanna. "Tell me you did, *mon oncle*. I want him to be dead." The child's bold manner did not surprise Joanna. Zoé was a lot like her uncle.

Donet leaned down to give his niece a hug. "The bad men are gone, *ma petite*. Now we must look to the future. Has Lady Joanna told you she is to become my wife?"

"*Oui*! I am so happy. She says I'm to live with you always."

Joanna reached down to take Zoé's hand, and the girl smiled up at her.

Donet gave them each a kiss. "*Mes amours*."

M'sieur Bequel stepped close and, in his rough voice, said, "I don't suppose any of ye are hungry? A good fight always gives me *un appétit*."

Zoé laughed. "You are *always* hungry, Monsieur Bequel!" Then to Joanna she said, "When we went to Paris to see the sights, he stopped often to eat at the *cafés*. And he drank two lemonades!"

The quartermaster smiled sheepishly and turned his eyes on the floor. A lock of russet hair fell onto his forehead. "'Twas a warm day."

The wedding took place two days later. The king gave Jean permission for them to marry in the lower chapel of the magnificent *Sainte-Chapelle*, the place of worship for the king's household.

He'd had just enough time to secure the ring, a gold band with stars etched all around. Engraved inside in English were the words, "Many are the stars I see, but in my eyes no star like thee." When he'd seen it in the goldsmith's shop, he knew it would remind them of the night sky and perhaps also the planetarium clock they had argued about in London, a memory that always brought a smile to his face.

Joanna loved the ring. He promised to buy her a sapphire the color of the sky on the night they met when they arrived on Guernsey where his whole crew and many merchants would attend the Anglican ceremony.

The small ceremony in the *Sainte-Chapelle* was attended by a few of Jean's friends, including Vergennes, the American statesman Benjamin Franklin, and Gaspar, Flèche and Gabrielle.

In the front of the chapel, his niece stood with Joanna, each holding a small bouquet of roses, and Émile stood next to Jean.

When the short ceremony was concluded, they all retired to Jean's townhouse for a wedding breakfast.

He and Joanna had a most delicious night in his bed as man and wife. The next day they left for Le Havre and Guernsey.

Joanna loved the island, as he knew she would. Not being precisely England or France, the independently minded island would make them a fine home when they weren't in Saintonge, Lorient or Paris.

He would take Joanna to England to visit her family, but he had no desire to live there.

Chapter 26

The Harrows, near Chichester, West Sussex, England

Joanna sat on the terrace that graced the side of the house, enjoying the quiet morning and the peace that had always been a part of The Harrows. Her new husband and Zoé were still upstairs, sleeping after their late night celebrating with Freddie.

Nora, who was up before Joanna, was showing Gabrielle the kitchens.

Joanna's time to herself did not last long. She heard a carriage arrive and, moments later, Richard stepped onto the terrace. Realizing he might not know she'd been gone, as quickly as she could, she explained she was now a married woman.

"Married! What do you mean you are *married*? When did this happen?" Richard's face turned red beneath his neatly queued auburn hair.

"Richard, you knew nothing of my letter?"

"May I remind you, Sister, I have only just arrived. What letter?"

She let out a sigh. "Oh, very well." Her younger brother strode through the doors to join them. "Here is Freddie." Looking at her younger brother, she said, "Freddie, do you have the letter I sent?"

"Hello, Richard," he said. "Welcome home." Reaching into

the pocket of his jacket, Freddie handed Richard the letter she had sent from Paris. "Joanna informs us she has wed the comte de Saintonge, twice as a matter of fact. You remember he is that friend of Lady Danvers. We met him at the reception for Mr. Pitt."

"I remember," said Richard, ripping the letter from Freddie's fingers. "But I recall no request for your hand, Sister."

"I am of age, Brother," she reminded him.

"Given all your protestations about the leg-shackled state, I thought you were loath to wed."

"M'sieur Donet changed my mind. He can be very persuasive." She winked at Freddie.

"Women!" Richard opened the letter and began to read.

Tillie took that opportunity to slip onto the terrace. She ran to Joanna. "Oh Joanna, it is so good to see you. The Season was amazing. I have much to tell you. I am in love!"

"That would make two of us," said Joanna, hugging her sister. "You look happy, Tillie. We must have tea, so you can tell me all about the Season and I can tell you something of my summer." She would never tell Tillie all, but perhaps enough to let her know to be happy for her older sister.

Richard looked up from reading the letter. "Your sister is married, Matilda."

Tillie turned to Joanna, startled. "You are? To whom?"

"Jean Donet, the comte de Saintonge."

Much to Joanna's relief, Tillie didn't appear at all disappointed that Joanna had managed to snag the man Tillie had adored. "The French comte? But how? When?"

"It's a very long story, Tillie. He and his young niece, Zoé, who is now our ward, will be down momentarily."

"The comte is upstairs? In your bedchamber?"

"Well, yes." Joanna felt rather proud of the fact now that they were wed.

"Enough of that, Matilda," chided Richard.

Joanna met her sister's startled gaze. "I also acquired a French maid in France. Gabrielle is a sweet girl of an age with you, Tillie. She is with Nora meeting Cook and the kitchen servants.

"What will happen to Nora?" asked Tillie.

"She will have a choice, to come with me or to stay, as she likes."

"This is all so sudden," remarked Tillie.

A dark figure appeared at the door to the terrace, the look on his face telling her he was uncertain if joining them would be wise. Joanna's heart leapt at seeing him. It reminded her of all those months ago when she had first glimpsed him at the door to their parlor.

"Jean, come greet the family."

He walked straight to Joanna and kissed her, his midnight eyes glistening with mirth. "*Bonjour, ma chérie*. Are you surviving the onslaught?"

"Barely, but reinforcements are welcome." She turned to her brothers and sister. "Dearest siblings, say hello to my husband, M'sieur Donet."

"Good morning, Brother-in-law," said Tillie, her eyes sparkling.

Donet dipped his head to Joanna's sister. Then he reached out his hand to greet her eldest brother.

Reluctantly, Richard took it. "We have much to discuss, Monsieur."

"*Oui*, whenever it pleases you. I am at your service."

Richard gave Donet a stern look. "Now would be good. I will have coffee and some rolls served in the study."

Joanna caught the flicker of amusement in her husband's eyes. He despaired of English breakfasts. To Richard, he said, "As you wish, Lord Torrington."

After the two men left the terrace, Freddie suggested Joanna and Tillie retire with him to the dining room where a breakfast had been laid. "We might as well eat."

In the dining room, Joanna accepted a cup of chocolate from the servant and took her place at the table. "I want to go into Chichester today. I must look in on Polly Ackerman. How is she doing, Freddie?"

Freddie piled a plate high with food from the sideboard and joined her. "Oh, you don't have to worry about Polly anymore."

Tillie brought her eggs and ham to the table. The footman poured her a cup of tea.

"And why is that?" Joanna inquired, concerned. "She is well, isn't she?" Joanna had visions of her friend having suffered a relapse.

"Very well," said Freddie, biting into a piece of bacon. "She is happily married."

"It must be contagious," said Tillie, lifting a fork full of egg to her mouth.

"Whom did she marry?" asked Joanna. "He must be someone who will care for her and the children. I couldn't bear it otherwise."

Freddie's mouth twitched up in a grin. "I think you will approve. Remember when you asked Zack to watch over her?"

"Yes."

"Well, he took your charge seriously. Zack is her new husband. She is now Mrs. Barlow."

Joanna beamed. "Oh, that *is* good news. Zack will treat her well and she will make him a good wife. 'Tis a splendid result."

Freddie returned her smile. "Yes, and he loves the boys and little Briney. And they him. Brilliant of you to think of it."

"That was Providence, Brother, not my matchmaking. But I am pleased. We must visit them."

Freddie gave Joanna a side glance. "I think Zack will be most interested to hear of your choice for a husband."

"What would Zack have to do with the French comte?" asked Tillie.

"Oh, nothing," said Joanna. "But since Zack and I are good

friends, he will want to know the man I have married." She kicked Freddie under the table. He fought a grin.

"Where is Aunt Hetty?" asked Joanna. "I have not sneezed once since I returned." When she and Donet returned to his sloop in Le Havre, Franklin, the black cat, sauntered up to her and meowed loudly, rubbing his sleek black fur against her gown. She would have to tell Freddie about the marvelous cat.

Tillie said, "She went upstairs immediately upon our return, cat in hand, begging leave to rest. I think my Season quite wore her out." Between sips of tea, she asked, "How long are you here for?"

"For a few days," said Joanna. "My husband has three homes and three ships. For a while, I think he means to go between them."

Freddie raised his brows. "Three?"

"I know it seems like a lot, but each has its purpose. He keeps a townhouse in Paris for his business with the government. Lorient is the home port for his ships. Saintonge is the site of his family estate where the vineyards are."

"Vineyards?" asked Freddie with raised brows.

"He grows grapes for cognac," said Joanna with a smirk.

Freddie choked on his bacon and grabbed for his tea. "Oh, that is rich."

Joanna shot him a speaking glance. "For now, I think we are to make our home in Lorient. But we will come to The Harrows for Christmas, I promise."

Donet appeared at the door. "I wondered where you'd gotten to, *chérie*." He strode to Joanna. "I do not like to let you out of my sight for long."

Tillie gazed at him admiringly and sighed. "I should like to have a husband like that."

Donet kissed the top of Joanna's head and asked the servant for coffee before taking a seat next to her.

"Is it all worked out?" she asked him, anxious to know. "Richard can be difficult."

"I am never difficult," said Richard, stepping into the room. "I am pleased you have been wed by an Anglican minister. As for the rest, the comte and I have settled things rather well."

Donet accepted the cup of coffee and asked Joanna, "What would you like to do today?"

"I would like to walk the streets of Chichester with you, my love. And then I must have tea with Tillie to catch up on her news. Zoé might like to go riding then."

"*Eh bien*, we will do as you wish. Our days here are few so you will decide what we do."

Richard buttered his roll and asked Donet, "Will you stay long enough for me to give you both a reception? Our friends in London would look forward to a few days in the country."

Joanna met Jean's eyes and, in them, she saw a reluctance to accept Richard's invitation. "I think the party may have to wait until Christmas, Brother."

"Very well, Christmas it is," said Richard.

Carter, their butler, brought Zoé to the dining room. Donet's niece cast her gaze about the room. Spotting her uncle and Joanna, she moved to them.

"Zoé," said Joanna. "You must meet my family." After introductions were made, Freddie offered to show Donet's niece around The Harrows.

"Is it much like our château at Saintonge?" she asked Donet.

"Smaller, *ma petite*."

Zoé seemed to consider the invitation and smiled coyly at Freddie. "*Peut-être* after some chocolate."

"I love chocolate, too," said Tillie, pouring the girl a cup.

Zoé sipped her chocolate, looking around the table. "Is this my new family?" she asked Joanna.

In uncharacteristic fashion, Richard smiled at Donet's niece. "It is if you want it to be."

"I would like that," said Zoé.

A feeling of joy filled Joanna's heart as her husband reached for her hand.

"While Frederick is showing my niece around, let us ride into Chichester and take that walk you wanted. I hear they have good brandy in the town and I mean to try some."

Joanna chuckled and placed her hand in his. "I think you should. And I want you to meet my friend Zack and his wife Polly."

With a wry smile, he leaned in and whispered, "*Oui*, it is time I met your accomplice."

They took their leave amidst the smiles of his niece and her family and headed for the carriage. A feeling of contentment settled within Joanna. She would happily go with him wherever he led and for the rest of her life.

Author's Note

If you love the dashing Jean Donet, comte de Saintonge, you are not alone. How could you not love a man who gave up all for the woman he loved? With his aristocratic manners, handsome dark looks and bold privateer ways, he might be my favorite of all my heroes. When he first appeared on the deck of *la Reine Noire* in *To Tame the Wind*, shouting orders to his men as guns blazed all around him, he quite stole my heart. I knew then he had to have his own story. And I knew it would take an unusual woman for Jean Donet to consider loving again. I believe I found her in Lady Joanna West.

By the end of the eighteenth century, smuggling on the south coast of England had escalated to alarming rates. From the prosecutions at the Old Bailey during the 1780s, most of which did not result in a conviction, it appears many communities were more frequently the smugglers' willing accomplices than their terrorized victims.

By 1784, the large organized smuggling gangs of the mid-century were a thing of the past. However, smuggling remained a widespread business. Out of a population of eight million, it is estimated that as many as twenty thousand people were full-time smugglers with twenty-one million pounds of tea smuggled into Britain each year.

Smuggling was not confined to the poor. Robert Walpole, the country's first prime minister, used the Admiralty barge to smuggle in wine, lace and other goods. As mentioned in my story, Lady Holderness, whose husband was Lord Warden of the Cinque Ports from 1765 to 1778, used Walmer Castle as a base for her smuggling more than one hundred French silk gowns and fine French furniture.

Even during periods of war, English smugglers brazenly traded with France. Between 1763 and 1783, the number of customs vessels patrolling the coast increased from twenty-two to forty-two. But when one considers the miles of coastline these forty-two boats had to patrol, it is clear that the odds vastly favored the smugglers. Commander James Ellis, a character in my story, was a real historic figure. Just as I portrayed him, he captained the HMS *Orestes* hunting smugglers off the Sussex coast.

Women might be involved in smuggling, but it was always from the land side. If they did not sell, transport or hide the smuggled goods, they provided protection, alibis and assistance to those who did. Thus, it is not out of the realm of possibility that Joanna could be "master of the beach" for the smugglers in Bognor (today called Bognor Regis).

While the public condoned smuggling, they did not sanction violence by smugglers. During the period 1780 to 1800, smugglers tried at the Old Bailey were frequently charged with assaulting officers, punishable by imprisonment, rather than assembling or transporting smuggled goods, punishable by death. However, as in the case of John Shelley in my story, it was possible to be executed for beating a revenue officer. (The trial in my story is taken from an actual record of a trial at the Old Bailey.)

In 1784, firing on a customs vessel after it had identified itself became a felony. However, as a French citizen, Jean Donet would not have been subject to being dragged back to England for trial. England was the only country that did not have an agreement with France to trade criminals (what we would call today an extradition treaty). But Jean had cause to worry about Joanna, who was subject to English justice.

Among the most coveted of the smuggled goods was French brandy, cognac even more so. By the 1770s, London, home to the great connoisseurs, had become the largest consumer of the best brandy.

In the Cognac region of France, then located in the Province of Saintonge, grapes were the most valuable crop. The clay soil was too impoverished for any other. As a result, the clergy and the nobility farmed the land themselves and did not lease it to others. In the 1780s, cognac became a profitable and prestigious product in demand throughout France and across Western Europe. Even though this was a good time for the region, the peasants still grumbled about tithes paid to priests and taxes to landlords. Their complaints were not without reason given the humble state of their living conditions.

We often think of the French Revolution as beginning in 1789 with the storming of the Bastille, but the winds of revolution were stirring long before that. Writers like Voltaire raised people's consciousness. When the food shortages arrived, bread riots occurred in various places. Then, too, the American Revolution made French citizens long for what they did not have. The money to support America's troops came from France and left that country bankrupt at a time when the French king and queen spent lavishly. The desire for freedom, like that won by America, was not limited to the French. Even in England, the government feared the common people would rise up. (That story is told in *Against the Wind*, book 2 in the Agents of the Crown series.)

The comments that William Wilberforce and William Pitt made at the reception Joanna's brother gave for the Prime Minister are accurate. Wilberforce, recording his thoughts of their trip to France, did, indeed, find the young Marie Antoinette charming and the king a bit of an oaf. Louis and Marie Antoinette had come to the throne very young. One might forgive them, save for the result.

Because I know many of you will ask, all the taverns and restaurants referred to by name existed at the time. The Angel Posting House in Surrey, Lidstone's and the Crown & Anchor on Guernsey and The Devil's Tavern on the London quay were all real establishments. The Devil's Tavern did, in fact, have a dubious reputation as a favorite of smugglers and pirates. As I have portrayed it, the tavern had a flagstone floor and the bar was pewter-topped. (The tavern, rebuilt after a later fire, exists today under another name.) And, of course, Twinings Tea Room had opened in 1706 and was in business when Joanna and Cornelia stopped in for tea.

The food, drink and dress of the time are all authentic. Breakfast in France at the time was called *"déjeuner"*, not *"petit-déjeuner"*, as we might refer to it today.

The clothing was in transition from the mid-eighteenth century to the Regency era, and Marie Antoinette greatly influenced the fashion of her day. The chemise dress or gown Joanna wore was a style pioneered by the French queen amid much controversy for its rather flimsy appearance. Should you be wondering, Marie Antoinette was a redhead, a strawberry blonde to be precise.

In the late eighteenth century, the men still wore their hair long and queued at their nape, unless shaved for the wearing of a wig. And powdered hair was in vogue.

The ships and the ports of Guernsey, Lorient, La Rochelle and Le Havre are portrayed as accurately as research allows. Guernsey is today part of the Channel Islands, but at the time they were called "the French Isles". Versailles, of course, had been a lavish place since Louis XIV and the Hall of Mirrors breathtaking.

It is my hope you will feel as if you traveled back in time and experienced late eighteenth century England and France.

One thing not in my story is the French slave trade, which was booming in this period. (The French were the third largest slave traders.) The ports of Lorient and Le Havre were busy with slavers. Le Havre was the major slave-trading port. From there, African captives were delivered to French colonies in the Caribbean. (While William Wilberforce became an Evangelical Christian in the summer of 1784, he did not begin to oppose slavery for several years after my story.) I did not include the slave trade issue because I feared it would swamp the story. Neither Jean nor Joanna would have approved, of course, but to get into that would have added many pages. Who knows? It might pop up in the next book in the trilogy.

I invite you to visit my Pinterest board for *Echo in the Wind*: There you can view maps and pictures of the ports and significant places, items unique to the era and the characters as I see them. It's my research in pictures!

I love to hear from readers. Contact me via my website, and I promise to answer: www.reganwalkerauthor.com. There, you can also sign up for my newsletter. Each quarter, I give away one of my books to a lucky reader who signs up.

If you want to read Claire Donet's story, it's in *To Tame the Wind*. And if you want to read about her eldest son, Jean Donet's grandson, Jean Nicholas Powell, it's in *Wind Raven*.

Coming next in 2017: *A Secret Scottish Christmas*, book 4 in my Regency series, the Agents of the Crown. This is the story of the Powell twin brothers who vie for the love of Miss Aileen Stephen, sister of William Stephen, the handsome Scottish shipbuilder who is the hero in *The Holly & The Thistle*.

What was at first to be the Donet Duology is now going to be the Donet Trilogy. In 2018, I'll be writing Zoé Donet's story, *A Fierce Wind*, set in France and England during the time of the French Revolution.

Author's Bio

Regan Walker is an award-winning, Amazon #1 bestselling author of Regency, Georgian and Medieval romances. A lawyer turned full-time writer, she has six times been featured on USA TODAY's HEA blog and nominated six times for the prestigious RONE award (her novel, *The Red Wolf's Prize* won Best Historical Novel for 2015 in the Medieval category). Her novel *The Refuge: An Inspirational Novel of Scotland* won the Gold Medal in the Illumination Awards in 2017.

Years of serving clients in private practice and several stints in high levels of government have given Regan a love of international travel and a feel for the demands of the "Crown". Hence her romance novels often involve a demanding sovereign who taps his subjects for special assignments. Each of her novels features real history and real historical figures. And, of course, adventure and love.

Keep in touch with Regan on Facebook, and join Regan Walker's Readers.

facebook.com/regan.walker.104

facebook.com/groups/ReganWalkersReaders

You can sign up for her newsletter on her website.

www.reganwalkerauthor.com

Books by Regan Walker

The Agents of the Crown series:

To Tame the Wind (prequel)

Racing with the Wind

Against the Wind

Wind Raven

A Secret Scottish Christmas (coming in 2017)

The Donet Trilogy:

To Tame the Wind

Echo in the Wind

A Fierce Wind (coming in 2018)

Holiday Novellas (related to the Agents of the Crown):

The Shamrock & The Rose

The Twelfth Night Wager

The Holly & The Thistle

The Medieval Warriors series:

The Red Wolf's Prize

Rogue Knight

Rebel Warrior

King's Knight

www.ReganWalkerAuthor.com

Printed in Great Britain
by Amazon

Bouddha Bol

L'équilibre est dans le bol !

Jean-Michel Cohen

Thomas Clouet

Flammarion

Photographies de Laurent Rouvrais
Stylisme : Sarah Vasseghi
Conception graphique : Justeciel
Fabrication : Louisa Hanifi
Photogravure : IGS-CP à Angoulême (16)

ISBN : 978-2-0814-0855-5
N° d'édition : L.01EPMN000918. A004
Dépôt légal : avril 2017
www.editions.flammarion.fr

Sommaire

Introduction

Dr Jean-Michel Cohen

Souvenir de restaurant

J'aime assez écrire des livres de cuisine, surtout avec la collaboration d'un cuisinier, afin de commenter les recettes et d'en découvrir les secrets. En effet, dans notre assiette, ou plutôt dans notre bol en l'occurrence, se cachent souvent de nombreux avantages santé. À la façon d'un détective, je m'amuse à décrypter les vertus nutritionnelles de ces compositions afin que notre repas soit un élément de bonne santé. J'ajoute que je méprise, en général, tous les gadgets, les artifices, les outils marketing, et Dieu sait s'il y en a !

Lorsque l'on m'a proposé de travailler sur ces fameux B*uddha bowls*, j'ai commencé par être sceptique, par peur de tomber dans le travers que je redoute. Mais un événement m'a fait changer d'avis...

Je passais une semaine à Manhattan avec mon épouse, invité par une société de nutritionnistes pour laquelle je devais donner une conférence sur la qualité et les propriétés diététiques de la cuisine française. L'un d'eux, extrêmement aimable et parlant couramment le français, nous invita à dîner un soir au restaurant *Le Botaniste*, sur Lexington Avenue. On y servait entre autres des plats végétariens. Je suis toujours avide de découvertes et prêt à goûter différents types de nourriture. À ma grande surprise, une fois la commande passée, je découvris que les plats étaient servis dans des bols.

Hors-d'œuvre ou plat, le menu donnait le détail exact de ce que nous allions trouver dans ce bol. Les aliments étaient disposés de façon assez gracieuse et leur répartition était très probablement réfléchie. De surcroît, chacun était prédécoupé. Nous ne mangions pas avec des baguettes mais bien avec un couteau, une fourchette et une cuillère. J'ai à la fois passé un délicieux moment et fait une expérience culinaire remarquable, car je me suis fait à cette occasion un certain nombre de réflexions que je tiens à partager avec vous.

Les arts de la table

L'art de la table, la présentation des mets, nous préoccupe généralement moins que ce que nous mangeons, et pourtant nous savons que la disposition des assiettes, la présentation des mets, leurs couleurs et tous les éléments « artistiques » liés à la cuisine font partie intégrante de la dégustation. Sans oublier que, sur le plan physiologique, la vision et l'odorat stimulent la digestion et déclenchent, avant la mastication, le processus qui nous permet d'intégrer les aliments et d'en apprécier la saveur.

Certains scientifiques expliquent, de façon parfaitement rigoureuse, que les neurones de notre cerveau, par l'intermédiaire de stimulations électriques, peuvent activer la notion de plaisir, sous l'effet de la simple découverte d'un aliment par nos yeux. C'est un principe largement connu en marketing alimentaire : chaque jour, la publicité sur vos écrans, dans les magazines ou dans la rue vous en donne des exemples. Chacun de nous a déjà salivé en contemplant un aliment, un plat.

Pour compléter ce propos, rappelons que le service de repas à la française, à la façon des rois de France, consiste à présenter l'ensemble des plats sur une table. Or, au XIXe siècle, nous avons modifié cette habitude en adoptant le service à la russe, où chaque plat est délivré l'un après l'autre.

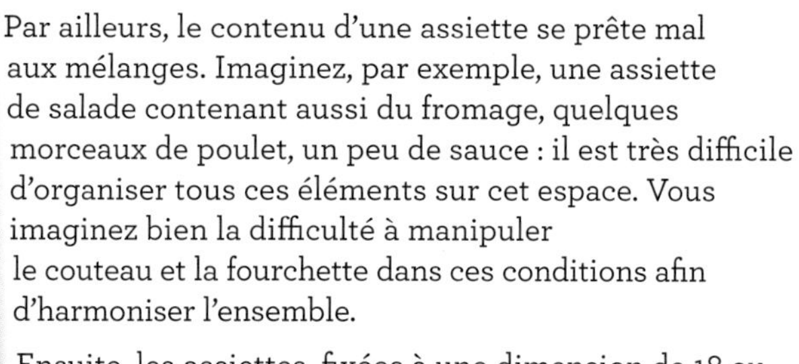

Par ailleurs, le contenu d'une assiette se prête mal aux mélanges. Imaginez, par exemple, une assiette de salade contenant aussi du fromage, quelques morceaux de poulet, un peu de sauce : il est très difficile d'organiser tous ces éléments sur cet espace. Vous imaginez bien la difficulté à manipuler le couteau et la fourchette dans ces conditions afin d'harmoniser l'ensemble.

Ensuite, les assiettes, fixées à une dimension de 18 ou 21 centimètres, circonscrivent nos portions de façon définitive et, bien entendu, ne peuvent être remplies qu'à l'horizontale. C'est justement tout le contraire du bol, qui permet de superposer la nourriture en couches et de jouer sur la notion de volume global. J'ai donc découvert, à l'occasion de ce repas, que le bol offrait une vision complète de la recette, pouvait être rempli d'une grande variété d'ingrédients et permettait de moduler la quantité souhaitée tout en proposant la totalité des aliments en une seule fois.

La valeur nutritionnelle

Lorsqu'on veut organiser un repas — pourvu que l'on décide de manger sain et équilibré —, il faut normalement disposer de plusieurs végétaux, d'un produit céréalier tels que les pâtes, le riz, le quinoa (ou de pommes de terre), d'une source de protéines (viande, œuf, poisson, fromage, produits laitiers, légumineuses pour les végétariens), d'un produit laitier (fromage) et d'un fruit. Tout cela reste compliqué dans la mesure où les économies de temps sont désormais une priorité pour la plupart d'entre nous. De même, si nous savons que les herbes et les épices sont un élément fondamental de la qualité nutritionnelle et gustative, il nous est difficile d'en utiliser suffisamment au cours d'un même repas sans que cela devienne un casse-tête.

Or, au fond de ce *Buddha bowl* que j'avais commandé se trouvait une sauce qui contenait probablement un peu de coriandre, recouverte d'une couche de quinoa, elle-même nappée de fines tranches de fromage grec. Au-dessus, un lit de salade mélangée (roquette, mâche, cresson, quelques tomates cerises finement tranchées) servait de « repose-plat » à des petits morceaux de poulet recouverts de curcuma, à côté desquels se trouvaient des œufs brouillés avec un peu de ciboulette. Enfin, le plat était complété par des lanières de saumon nappées d'une petite sauce à la crème fouettée et à la menthe. Des quartiers de pomme, dont je me servais parfois pour pousser les aliments comme avec du pain, entouraient l'ensemble.

J'avais dans un seul bol la totalité d'un repas intelligemment composé et nutritionnellement parfait.

Je commençais à être convaincu de l'intérêt de cette pratique comparée au fait de servir une assiette de salade, puis une autre de saumon ou de poulet accompagné de féculents, puis une autre de fromage, puis une autre de fruits. Tout cela nécessitant, d'ailleurs, des assaisonnements différents. Jolie découverte !

Facilité de préparation

Je demandai à mon hôte ce qu'il en pensait, tout en lui livrant mes propres réflexions. Il évoqua combien ce type de plat était facile à préparer, ajoutant qu'il permettait aussi d'éviter le gaspillage en utilisant des restes. D'ailleurs, dans ce restaurant, les *Buddha bowls* étaient composés à partir de plusieurs grands saladiers posés sur un établi. Le serveur y piochait pour assembler le plat dont il connaissait la définition exacte. Certains étaient froids, d'autres chauds.

La notion de découpe

Je fus aussi très sensible à la notion de découpe préalable. En effet, pour composer ces bols, on ne se contente pas de déposer un blanc de poulet, une poignée de quinoa, de la salade et un morceau de fromage : il faut les découper, ce qui d'une part met les saveurs en valeur et d'autre part nous permet d'organiser le plat comme nous le souhaitons. Autre avantage : la sauce est définie une bonne fois pour toutes pour l'ensemble du plat, ce qui empêche d'en consommer en excès et entraîne aussi une mixité des goûts.

J'avais oublié de préciser que ce plat comportait des noix, que je découvrais par moments, car elles étaient placées de façon aléatoire à l'intérieur du bol. Pour ma part, je me suis souvent essayé à introduire des oléagineux (noix, noisettes, noix de cajou, cacahuète, amandes, pistaches) dans mes recettes, sans réussir à les disposer correctement dans l'assiette.

Cette notion de *bowl* permet donc de réunir dans un même récipient de nombreux ingrédients, sans trop de complications, à la recherche à la fois du goût parfait et de l'équilibre idéal, avec une pratique de découpe préalable qui limite les manipulations et les gestes au moment du repas. Ma cuillère servait d'ailleurs à créer des mini-plats à partir du bol. En effet, lors de la dégustation il m'arrivait parfois de mélanger le poulet avec le fromage et une noix, ou encore de prendre un peu de sauce avec le quinoa et le cresson. Cette recette pouvait être consommée de multiples manières.

La valeur gustative

Trouver du plaisir au cours d'un repas est une des questions fondamentales de l'alimentation et de la nutrition, au-delà des préoccupations de santé.

Il y a d'abord le choix des aliments. Certains préfèrent le poisson à la viande, les légumes aux féculents, ou l'inverse. D'autres veulent bien consommer le fromage mais n'aiment pas les autres produits laitiers... Bref, le produit a son importance !

La qualité de la cuisine française réside dans l'assemblage des aliments. Ce qui fait la qualité du cassoulet, c'est l'association des haricots et de la viande. L'assaisonnement contribue aussi à donner sa spécificité au plat. Mais tout cela relève d'un principe assez rigide que nous appelons la recette. Le restaurant traditionnel à la française est noyé désormais sous le flot des restaurants japonisants, américains, mexicains, thaïs, espagnols... car nous cherchons de plus en plus la variété, l'originalité et l'exotisme. Nous avons développé une appétence particulière pour les saveurs, notamment pour les épices et les herbes que nous découvrons chaque jour en provenance du monde entier.

Or, toujours dans ce bol, je réalisais des mélanges originaux, j'éprouvais des sensations variées que je suscitais moi-même en organisant chaque bouchée à ma façon. Tout cela donnait à ce repas une valeur ajoutée très différente de celle que j'aurais pu trouver dans un autre restaurant.

Encore une fois, j'insiste sur la valeur gustative d'un repas, car il existe un élément que les gens mésestiment en permanence et que j'appelle « le rassasiement psychologique ». Je m'explique : j'ai expliqué plus haut que la digestion s'opère par la vision de ce que nous allons manger, par l'intermédiaire d'une stimulation électrique qui agit sur nos neurones cérébraux en déclenchant l'ensemble des signaux nécessaires à la sécrétion de tout ce qui va former le principe de digestion – enzymes, hormones, sels biliaires... De même, la satiété ne résulte pas simplement d'une sensation de distension de l'estomac, d'un pic de sécrétion d'insuline ou de tout autre élément physique ou chimique, mais également d'une réflexion intellectuelle. C'est la certitude d'avoir acquis une dose suffisante de plaisir qui ralentit la sensation de faim, puisqu'il y a rassasiement intellectuel. Rappelons la théorie de Claude Lévi-Strauss : l'aliment n'est pas seulement bon à manger mais également bon à penser. C'est le cas de ces bols qui démultiplient la variété des plaisirs, l'organisation des saveurs... bref, permettent d'atteindre une plénitude complète au cours du repas.

Spiritualité

Le repas traditionnel manque un peu de sérénité et de convivialité, notamment à cause de ses aspects techniques et du service. La succession des plats, la gestion de l'aspect matériel du repas pendant que l'on mange avec sa famille ou ses amis, m'ont semblé, après cette soirée, une inutile perte de temps. Mais pour évoquer à la fois la nutrition, le côté pratique et le côté spirituel, j'aimerais que le repas soit un moment d'échange et de plaisir. Il est donc nécessaire de conserver à la fois le plaisir de la consommation et le plaisir de l'échange et de l'instant — donc, selon moi, de profiter de tout ce qui peut simplifier les tâches matérielles. Et pour être un peu ésotérique, cette notion de bol, forme arrondie parfaitement adaptée à un contenu et à un brassage, me semble contribuer à ce moment de rassemblement. C'est toute l'atmosphère d'un repas que j'évoque ici en substance : elle va bien au-delà de ce que j'appelle, un peu brutalement, le nourrissage !

Voilà comment, revenant d'un pays célèbre pour ses hamburgers, ses repas sur le pouce et ses énormes portions, je suis devenu adepte de cette façon de manger qui peut faire de nos repas une forme de jeu subtile, goûteuse, diététique, à travers ce nouveau récipient qui s'adapte à de nouveaux ingrédients. Mon ami Thomas Clouet a composé pour vous, à partir de ses connaissances professionnelles, un ensemble de recettes à partir d'ingrédients relativement faciles à trouver partout, dans le respect des goûts et des habitudes de chacun : végétarien, végétaliens, omnivores...

Laissez votre imagination se lancer à la recherche de nouvelles recettes. C'est ce que je vous souhaite ! Bon appétit !

Jean-Michel Cohen

Introduction

Thomas Clouet

Buddha bowl... Que vient faire ce maître spirituel au fond de nos bols ? Le *Buddha bowl* s'inscrit dans le cadre de la *healthy food* (manger-sain), un des résultats de l'évolution récente de nos façons de manger, traduisant un désir de consommer non plus seulement pour se nourrir et prendre du plaisir mais aussi pour obtenir un « plus ». Le problème est néanmoins de définir ce « plus », car les attentes sont multiples selon les personnes. Il peut s'agir d'un désir de manger sainement, d'être un « consom'acteur », de militer pour la protection et la défense des animaux, de rechercher une élévation spirituelle... Toutes ces voies trouvent leur expression dans la *healthy food*, la *fit food*, l'antigaspi, la consommation durable, le locavorisme, le végétarisme, le végétalisme, le veganisme, la *raw food* (crudivorisme), et enfin les *Buddha bowls*.

Les origines du *Buddha bowl* sont assez mystérieuses. La forme du bol ferait penser au ventre généreux de certaines représentations du Bouddha ; le terme peut également se référer au bol qui sert aux moines bouddhistes errants à collecter l'aumône pour leur repas et qui est leur dernière possession matérielle. Ce qui est certain, c'est qu'il est apparu il y a deux ou trois ans aux États-Unis et qu'il répond à une tendance de fond. La référence au Bouddha ne concerne pas une religion mais une philosophie de vie. Le bouddhisme prône la non-violence, la gentillesse, le respect de tout être vivant ; il ne s'agit en aucun cas d'un commandement mais d'une recommandation. L'important, dans cette philosophie, est d'être en accord avec soi-même. Sans tous devenir végétariens, végétaliens ou véganes, nous avons conscience qu'il est aujourd'hui important, voire essentiel, de réduire notre consommation de protéines animales tout en améliorant notre équilibre alimentaire (moins de gras, moins de sel, une palette de fruits et de légumes variée...). Les sources alternatives sont nombreuses. Cette voie incarne un certain bon sens, et certains peuvent considérer le *Buddha bowl* comme la plus parfaite expression du flexitarisme.

Je ne suis ni végétarien, ni végétalien, ni végan, mais je me définis comme un « consom'acteur » soucieux d'acheter mes produits dans le respect des saisons. Je fais attention à mon poids et à ma forme sans en faire une contrainte ou une obsession ; je suis un père qui souhaite que ses enfants profitent de l'ensemble des ressources alimentaires dont j'ai pu profiter ; je suis aussi un chef pour qui la cuisine est une passion et le goût une recherche constante.

Pour toutes ces raisons, mais aussi pour m'adresser au plus grand nombre, j'ai choisi de proposer quelques recettes 100 % végétales, mais la plupart comportent des protéines animales (œuf, fromages, viandes, poissons) sélectionnées parmi les plus courantes, en diminuant leurs quantités. Ces recettes peuvent facilement être adaptées pour les végétariens, les végétaliens et les véganes : le « truc en plus » en fin de recette les y aidera.

Toujours selon cette démarche, j'ai donné la préférence à des ingrédients à l'indice glycémique bas, c'est-à-dire exerçant un impact plus faible sur notre taux de glycémie sanguin. De plus en plus d'études semblent confirmer que les régimes alimentaires à indice glycémique bas* aident à prévenir le diabète tardif et les maladies coronariennes. Ils favoriseraient également la perte de poids en augmentant la sensation de satiété. Mais je laisse le Dr Cohen vous expliquer tout cela d'une recette à l'autre. D'une manière générale, ce choix me semblait en pleine cohérence avec la composition des *Buddha bowls*, dont les légumineuses, les choux sous toutes leurs formes, l'avocat, les fruits secs, entre autres, sont les produits stars.

Composition

Maintenant que nous avons posé les bases, plongeons-nous dans l'univers des *Buddha bowls*. Le concept repose sur le fait de proposer dans un bol tous les éléments nutritionnels dont on a idéalement besoin dans un repas. Il doit regrouper six éléments essentiels :

1. Les protéines

Elles doivent représenter 25 % du total. Il peut s'agir :

• De protéines végétales

- Tofu : 12 g de protéines pour 100 g
- Fèves, haricots et autres légumineuses : en moyenne 10 g pour 100 g
- Céréales : en moyenne 10 g pour 100 g
- Graines oléagineuses (noix, noisettes, amandes...) : en moyenne 17 g pour 100 g
- Graines de courge, de citrouille, de tournesol... : 24 g pour 100 g

Remarques :
La germination des légumineuses, des céréales et des graines augmente très fortement la proportion de protéines de l'aliment concerné.
En cas de composition d'un bowl *purement végétal, il est important de mixer les sources de protéines végétales afin de couvrir l'ensemble de nos besoins en acides aminés*.*

• De protéines animales

- Poissons et crustacés : en moyenne 16 g pour 100 g
- Laitages (fromages, yaourt...) : en moyenne 25 g pour 100 g
- Viande en moyenne : 20 g pour 100 g
- Œuf : 13 g pour 100 g

*Vous trouverez à la fin de cette introduction un tableau indiquant les indices glycémiques de nombreux produits (source Internet). Je suis certain que vous aurez quelques surprises : par exemple, la carotte, crue ou cuite, ne possède pas les mêmes qualités.

2. Légumes et fruits

Légumes-racines, légumes-tiges, pousses telles que les asperges et les endives, légumes-fruits et fruits doivent représenter au moins 40 % de votre bol et, idéalement, être pour partie crus et pour partie cuits. Les algues sont incluses dans cette catégorie.

3. Légumes-feuilles

Sont inclus dans cette catégorie différentes formes de chou, toutes les salades, les épinards, les herbes aromatiques et les fanes de légumes (carottes, navets, radis...), et la liste n'est pas close.

4. Glucides complexes

Les glucides complexes sont assimilés par le corps plus lentement que les glucides simples. Ils libèrent graduellement leurs micronutriments nécessaires à la production d'énergie afin de couvrir nos besoins sur une longue période.

On les trouve dans l'orge, le son, le germe de blé, le sarrasin, la semoule, l'avoine, le riz complet, les pâtes complètes, les légumes-racines, les pois, les haricots, les lentilles, le quinoa, l'épeautre, le riz rouge, le millet, le boulgour, le riz complet...

5. Du « bon gras »

Ce bon gras a la particularité de réduire notre mauvais cholestérol, d'être anti-inflammatoire et de stimuler l'activité de notre cerveau. Dans cette classe, on peut citer l'avocat, l'huile de coco, l'huile d'olive extra-vierge ; les poissons gras tels que le saumon, le thon, le maquereau ; les olives, les graines telles que les noisettes, les noix de pécan, les amandes ; les huiles de noix et de graines ; les graines telles que le sésame, les graines de courge, les graines de tournesol...

6. Un assaisonnement pêchu

Une bonne sauce ou vinaigrette fera le lien entre tous les éléments de votre *bowl* : elle est donc essentielle. Certains ingrédients stars sont issus de la cuisine végétarienne comme la purée de sésame ou la purée de cacahuète, mais la base reste un élément acide, du sel et de l'huile. En ce qui concerne l'élément acide, le vinaigre vient en tête ; mais j'aime, pour ma part, utiliser les jus d'agrumes (citron, orange, pamplemousse...). Le sel peut aussi être apporté par la sauce de soja ou le nuoc-mâm. Pour encore plus de peps, n'hésitez pas à ajouter des condiments et des épices à vos vinaigrettes et à vos sauces.

Pensez au topping, la petite touche en plus qui peut faire toute la différence. Il peut s'agir d'herbes fraîches, de noix, de noisettes ou d'amandes grossièrement hachées, grillées ou non ; de graines diverses, mais également de paillettes d'algues de nori. Ces éléments augmenteront l'attrait visuel de votre bol mais surtout apporteront du goût et des textures supplémentaires.

En conclusion

Les *Buddha bowls* sont, par leur nature, une nourriture du quotidien, mais leur réalisation demande un peu d'organisation. Pensez à anticiper les temps de trempage et les temps de cuisson des légumineuses, des céréales et des pâtes, qui peuvent être un peu longs. Ce temps n'est pas perdu, car il ne demande aucune surveillance particulière et vous pouvez vaquer à d'autres occupations. Munissez-vous enfin d'une balance électronique qui vous sera très utile pour obtenir la portion adéquate et éviter tout gaspillage alimentaire.

Avec ces *bowls*, vous vous apprêtez à modifier vos habitudes alimentaires pour manger mieux : cela vaut bien le coup de modifier légèrement votre manière de cuisiner.

Écrire ces recettes fut pour moi un véritable parcours initiatique, un chemin culinaire exaltant, car riche en découvertes. Quel goût pouvaient bien avoir le sarrasin ou le riz *Venere* (riz noir) ? Avec quels autres aliments avais-je instinctivement envie de les associer ? Quelle sauce ou vinaigrette pour les lier ? Et les textures dans tout cela ? Autant de questions qui ne cessaient de tourner dans ma tête avec le goût comme seule obsession. Mon *bowl* de crème de butternut, crabe, olives, physalis, quinoa et emmental (page 13) en est le parfait exemple. L'association peut sembler improbable sur le papier, mais goûtez, et vous comprendrez que les recettes de ce livre sont celles d'un cuisinier.

Voilà : au fil des pages de cet ouvrage, j'espère de tout cœur vous apporter du plaisir et ce « plus » que vous recherchez, car moi je me suis éclaté à l'écrire !

Tableau des indices glycémiques

Classés par niveaux, du plus faible au plus fort

De 0 à 10

Aliment	IG
Avocat	10
Bœuf (steak, pavé, filet, entrecôte...)	0
Café, thé, tisanes	0
Charcuterie et salaisons (saucisson, jambon, salami, coppa...)	0
Crème fraîche	0
Crustacés (homard, crabe, langouste...)	5
Épices (poivre, persil, basilic, cannelle...)	5
Foie gras	0
Fromages (gruyère, camembert, mozzarella, edam...)	0
Fruits de mer (crevettes, moules, huîtres...)	0
Graisse d'oie, graisse végétale, margarine	0
Huile d'olive, de tournesol...	0
Mayonnaise naturelle	0
Œufs	0
Poissons (saumon, thon, sardines, anchois...)	0
Sauce de soja (sans sucre ni édulcorants)	0
Viandes (bœuf, porc, volaille, veau, agneau, mouton...)	0
Vin rouge, vin blanc, champagne	0
Vinaigre	5
Volaille (poulet, dinde...)	0

De 15 à 25

Aliment	IG
Airelles, myrtilles	25
Amandes	15
Artichaut	20
Asperge	15
Aubergine	20
Baies de goji	25
Blette	15
Brocoli	15
Cacahuètes, arachides	15
Cacao en poudre sans sucre	20
Cassis	15
Céleri branche	15
Céréales germées	15
Cerises	25
Cerises des Antilles, acérola	20
Champignon	15
Chocolat noir à plus de 70 % de cacao	25
Chocolat noir à plus de 85 % de cacao	20
Chou-fleur	15
Choucroute	15
Choux de toute variété	15
Choux de Bruxelles	15
Citron	20
Cœur de palmier	20
Concombre	15
Cornichons	15
Courgette	15
Échalote	15
Endive, chicorée	15
Épinard	15
Farine d'amande	20
Farine de noisette	20
Farine de soja	25
Fenouil	15
Flageolets	25
Fraises	25
Framboises	25
Germe de blé	15
Gingembre	15
Graines de courge	25
Graines de soja	15
Graines germées	15
Groseilles	25
Groseilles à maquereau	25
Haricots coco, haricots mange-tout	15
Haricots mung	25
Hoummous	25
Jus de citron sans sucre	20
Lentilles vertes	25
Lupin (graines)	15
Mûres	25
Noisettes	15
Noix	15
Noix de cajou	15
Oignons	15
Olives	15
Orge mondé	25
Oseilles	15
Pesto	15
Physalis	15
Pignons de pin	15
Piments	15
Pistaches	15
Poireau	15
Pois cassés	25
Pois mange-tout	15
Poivron	15
Poudre de caroube	15
Pousses de bambou	20
Purée d'amandes complètes sans sucre	25
Purée de cacahuètes sans sucre	25
Purée de noisettes entières sans sucre	25
Radis	15
Ratatouille	20
Rhubarbe	15
Salades diverses	15
Sirop d'agave	15
Soja (crème pour la cuisine)	20
Son de blé ou d'avoine	15
Tamari sans sucre	20
Tempeh	15
Tofu	15
Yaourt nature au soja	20

De 30 à 50

Aliment	IG
Abricots frais	30
Abricots secs	35
Ail	30
Airelle rouge, canneberge	45
All-Bran® (céréales)	50
Amarante	35
Ananas	45
Avoine	40
Banane plantain crue	45
Banane verte	45
Barre chocolatée diététique sans sucre	35
Barre de céréales énergétique sans sucre	50
Betterave crue	30
Beurre de cacahuète sans sucre ajouté	40
Biscuits à la farine complète sans sucre	50
Blé Ebly® (blé légume)	45
Boulgour cuit	45
Brugnons, nectarines	35
Capellini (pâtes très fines à la farine de blé)	45
Carottes crues	30
Cassoulet	35
Céleri-rave cru	35
Céréales complètes sans sucre	45
Chayote en purée	50
Chirimoya (anone, pomme cannelle, corossol)	35
Chicorée en boisson	40
Cidre brut	40
Coing	35
Confiture ou marmelade sans sucre	45
Couscous intégral, semoule intégrale	45
Couscous de semoule complète	50
Crème glacée au fructose	35
Épeautre à la farine intégrale	45
Falafel	35
Farine de coco	35
Farine de pois chiches	35
Farine de quinoa	40
Farine intégrale de grand épeautre (farro)	45
Farine intégrale de kamut	45
Farro (grand épeautre)	40
Fèves crues	40
Figues fraîches	35
Figues sèches	40
Flocons d'avoine crus	40
Fromage blanc non égoutté	30
Fruits de la Passion	30
Gelée de coing sans sucre	40
Graines de lin, de sésame, de pavot	35
Graines de tournesol	35
Grenade	35
Haricots borlotti	35
Haricots azuki	35
Haricots blancs	35
Haricots noirs	35
Haricots rouges	35
Haricots rouges en boîte	40
Haricots verts	30
Jus d'airelle rouge ou de canneberge sans sucre	50
Jus d'ananas sans sucre	50
Jus d'orange sans sucre et pressé	45
Jus de carottes sans sucre	40
Jus de pamplemousse sans sucre	45
Jus de pomme sans sucre	50
Jus de tomate	35
Kaki	50
Kamut intégral	40

Kiwi 50
Lactose 40
Lait d'amande 30
Lait d'avoine crue 30
Lait de coco 40
Lait de soja 30
Lait écrémé ou entier 30
Lait frais ou en poudre 30
Lentilles jaunes ou brunes 30
Levure 35
Levure de bière 35
Litchi 50
Macaroni au blé dur 50
Maïs ancestral indien 35
Mandarines, clémentines 30
Mangue 50
Marmelade sans sucre 30
Moutarde 35
Müesli sans sucre 50
Navet cru 30
Noix de coco 35
Orange 35
Pain 100 % intégral au levain pur 40
Pain au quinoa (à 65 %) 50
Pain à la farine intégrale 45
Pain azyme à la farine intégrale 40
Pain croquant suédois Wasa®, 24 % de fibres 35
Pain croquant Wasa léger® 50
Pain de céréales germées 35
Pain d'épeautre intégral 45
Pain de kamut 45
Pain grillé (farine intégrale sans sucre) 45
Pain ou farine de seigle intégrale 45
Pamplemousse 30
Patate douce 50
Pâtes complètes au blé entier 50
Pâtes intégrales cuites al dente 40
Pêches 35
Pepino, poire-melon 40
Petits pois 35
Petits pois en boîte 45
Pilpil (blé biologique complet, précuit et concassé) 45
Poire 30
Pois chiches 30
Pois chiches en boîte 35
Pomme en compote 35
Pomme 35
Pommes séchées 35
Pruneaux 40
Prune 35
Pumpernickel standard (pain noir de seigle) 45
Purée d'amandes blanches sans sucre 35
Quinoa 35
Raisin 45
Riz basmati complet 45
Riz basmati long 50
Riz complet 50
Riz sauvage 35
Sablé à la farine intégrale sans sucre 40
Salsifis 30
Sarrasin, blé noir (intégral, farine ou pain) 40
Sauce tomate avec sucre 45
Sauce tomate sans sucre 35
Sorbet sans sucre 40
Spaghetti cuits al dente pendant 5 minutes 40
Surimi 50
Tahini (purée de sésame) 40
Tomate 30
Tomates séchées 35
Topinambour 50
Vermicelles de blé dur 35
Vermicelles de soja 30
Yaourt au soja aromatisé 35
Yaourt nature 35

De 50 à 75

Abricots au sirop en boîte 60
Amarante soufflée 70
Ananas en boîte 65
Bagels 70
Baguette, pain blanc 70
Banane plantain cuite 70
Banane mûre 60
Barres chocolatées Mars®, Snickers®... 65
Barres chocolatées sucrées 70
Betterave cuite 65
Biscottes 70
Biscuits 70
Biscuits sablés (avec farine, beurre, sucre) 55
Boissons gazeuses, sodas 70
Bouillie de farine de maïs 70
Boulgour cuit 55
Brioche 70
Céréales raffinées sucrées 70
Céréales Special K® 70
Châtaigne, marron 60
Chips 70
Confiture standard sucrée 65
Courges 75
Couscous, semoule 65
Crème glacée classique sucrée 60
Croissant 70
Dattes 70
Doughnuts 75
Épeautre (farine raffinée) 65
Farine complète 60
Farine de châtaigne 65
Farine de maïs 70
Farine de riz complète 75
Farine semi-complète 65
Fèves cuites 65
Fruit à pain 65
Gaufre au sucre 75
Gelée de coing sucrée 65
Gnocchi 70
Igname 65
Jus de canne à sucre 65
Jus de canne à sucre séché (sucre intégral) 65
Jus de mangue sans sucre ajouté 55
Jus de raisin sans sucre ajouté 55
Ketchup 55
Lasagnes au blé dur 60
Lasagnes au blé tendre 75
Maïs courant en grains 65
Manioc doux ou amer 55
Marmelade sucrée 65
Mayonnaise industrielle sucrée 60
Mélasse 70
Melon 60
Miel 60
Mil, millet, sorgho 70
Moutarde avec sucre ajouté 55
Müesli avec sucre ou miel 65
Nèfles 55
Nouilles au blé tendre 70
Nutella® 55
Orge perlé 60
Ovomaltine® 60
Pain au chocolat 65
Pain au lait 60
Pain au seigle à 30 % 65
Pain azyme de farine blanche 70
Pain bis au levain 65
Pain complet 65
Pain de riz 70
Papaye 55
Pastèque 75
Pâtes de riz intégrales 65
Pêches au sirop 55
Pizza 60
Polenta, semoule de maïs 70
Pomme de terre cuite dans sa peau à l'eau ou à la vapeur 65
Pommes de terre bouillies sans la peau 70
Porridge (bouillie de flocons d'avoine) 60
Potiron 75
Poudre chocolatée sucrée 60
Raisins secs 65
Raviolis au blé dur 60
Raviolis au blé tendre 70
Risotto 70
Riz au lait sucré 75
Riz blanc standard 70
Riz de Camargue 60
Riz long 60
Riz parfumé (riz jasmin par exemple) 60
Riz rouge 55
Rutabaga, chou-navet 70
Semoule de blé dur 60
Sirop d'érable 65
Sirop de chicorée 55
Sorbet sucré 65
Spaghetti de farine blanche bien cuits 55
Sucre blanc (saccharose) 70
Sucre roux, complet ou intégral 70
Sushi 55
Tacos 70
Tagliatelle bien cuites 55
Tamarin doux 65
Vermicelles de riz 65

De 75 à 115

Amidons modifiés 100
Arrow-root (farine de dictame) 85
Bière 110
Carottes cuites 85
Céleri-rave cuit 85
Pétales de maïs (corn flakes) 85
Farine de blé blanche 85
Farine de riz 95
Fécule de pomme de terre 95
Gâteau de riz 85
Glucose 100
Lait de riz 85
Maïzena® (amidon de maïs) 85
Maltodextrine 95
Navet cuit 85
Pain blanc sans gluten 90
Pain blanc sans gluten 90
Pain pour hamburger 85
Pain très blanc, pain de mie 85
Panais 85
Pomme de terre en flocons (purée instantanée) 90
Pomme de terre en purée 80
Pommes de terre au four 95
Pommes de terre frites 95
Pop-corn sans sucre 85
Riz à cuisson rapide (précuit) 85
Riz soufflé, galettes de riz 85
Sirop de blé, sirop de riz 100
Sirop de glucose 100
Sirop de maïs 115
Tapioca 85

Conseils pratiques
pour bien composer son bowl

Le poids des aliments

Composer un *bowl*, c'est respecter des proportions. Toutes les recettes de ce livre ont été réalisées à l'aide d'une balance électronique afin que chaque bol salé fasse un peu plus de 300 g. Vous trouverez donc des grammages précis pour chaque ingrédient d'une recette, mais si vous souhaitez vous lancer dans la réalisation de vos propres *bowls*, et pour vous simplifier les courses, nous avons mis à votre disposition divers tableaux vous indiquant les poids moyens des fruits et des légumes.

Poids moyens des fruits

Fruits	Poids en grammes
Abricot	55 g à 70 g
Ananas avion	1 200 à 2 000 g
Ananas Victoria	1 000 g
Citron	120 g
Citron vert	100 g
Clémentine	70 g à 100 g
Figue	50 g à 70 g
Fraise	12 à 15 g
Fruit de la Passion	70 à 80 g
Grenade	500 à 600 g
Kiwi	100 g à 140 g
Litchi	15 à 20 g
Mangue	400 g à 600 g
Melon (gros)	800 à 1000 g
Melon (portion)	500 g
Nectarine	120 g
Orange	220 g à 300 g
Pamplemousse	360 à 460 g
Papaye	500 à 800 g
Pêche	120 à 150 g
Poire conférence	200 g à 260 g
Poire comice	250 à 350 g
Pomme gala	190 g
Pomme golden	210 g
Pomme Granny Smith	180 g à 220 g
Pomme Pink Lady	180 g à 220 g

Poids moyens des légumes

Légumes	Poids en grammes
Artichauts poivrades (botte de 5 environ)	500 à 600 g
Asperge verte	45 g
Aubergine moyenne	300 à 500 g
Avocat	220 g à 280 g
Botte d'asperges vertes (environ 9 asperges)	420 g
Botte de radis longs (environ 36 radis)	400 à 500 g
Botte de radis ronds (environ 25 radis)	300 à 400 g
Carotte de conservation	120 à 130 g
Carotte primeur en botte	80 g
Branche de céleri	30 g
Céleri-rave	800 à 1 500 g
Champignon de Paris	15 à 30 g
Chou blanc	2 000 g
Chou de Bruxelles	15 à 25 g
Chou-fleur	1 500 g
Chou rouge	1 500 g à 1 700 g
Chou vert	2 000 g
Concombre	300 g à 500 g
Courgette	100 à 250 g
Échalote	20 à 25 g
Endive	140 à 150 g
Fenouil	300 à 500 g
Girolle	10 g
Haricot coco plat	20 g
Laitue	250 à 300 g
Navet	120 g
Navet boule-d'or	120 à 140 g
Oignon	100 g à 200 g
Oignons nouveaux (botte)	250 à 350 g
Oignon rouge	120 à 160 g
Patate douce	500 à 700 g
Poireau	150 g à 180 g soit 70 g de blanc
Poivron	160 g à 260 g
Radis long	5 à 10 g
Radis noir	300 à 400 g
Radis rond	10 à 15 g
Shiitake	5 à 15 g
Tomate moyenne	90 à 140 g
Tomate cerise	12 g

Les fruits et les légumes ont parfois besoin d'être préparés avant d'être cuisinés, ce qui modifie leur grammage. Les tableaux qui suivent vous permettront de composer vos bowls plus précisément. N'hésitez pas à compléter ces tableaux avec vos propres observations, car ils sont loin d'être exhaustifs.

Comparaisons de poids brut/épluché

légumes

Légume	Brut sur base 100 g	Préparé	Perte ou gain en %
Algue haricot de mer	100 g	125 g dessalés et égouttés	+25 %
Algue wakamé	100 g		
Asperges vertes entières	100 g	55 g pelées, bases ligneuses éliminées	– 45 %
Avocat	100 g	72 g sans peau ni noyau	– 28 %
Carotte entière	100 g	90 g pelée, extrémités éliminées	– 10 %
Céleri-rave	100 g	75 g pelé	– 25 %
Champignons de Paris	100 g	85 g bases des pieds coupées	– 15 %
Choux de Bruxelles	100 g	80 g bases coupées, premières feuilles éliminées	– 20 %, – 35 % effeuillés
Chou-rave	100 g	86 g sans peau	– 14 %
Concombre	100 g	45 g dégorgé au sel puis pressé	– 55 %
Épinards, grandes feuilles	100 g	80 g sans les côtes des feuilles	– 20 %
Fèves avec peau	100 g avec peau	71 g sans peau	– 29 %
Poivron	100 g	60 g sans peau, pédoncule ni veines	– 40 %

Fruits

Fruit	Brut sur base de 100 g	Préparé	Perte en %
Ananas	100 g	50 g sans peau, ni yeux, ni partie centrale ligneuse	– 50 %
Fruit de la Passion	100 g de fruits	40 g de graines uniquement	– 60 %
Grenade	100 g	53 g de graines sans peau	– 47 %
Litchi	100 g de fruits	75 g de fruits sans peau ni noyau	– 25 %
Mangue	100 g	75 g de chair sans peau ni noyau	– 25 %
Papaye	100 g	69 g sans peau ni graines	– 31 %
Physalis	100 g de fruits	92 g sans membranes entourant les fruits	– 8 %
Pomme	100 g	95 g sans trognon, 80 g sans trognon ni peau	– 5 % sans trognon, – 20 % sans trognon ni peau

Graines oléagineuses

Graines	Brut	Préparé	Perte en %
Noisettes	100 g en coques	50 g sans coques	– 50 %
Noix	100 g en coques	50 g sans coques	– 50 %
Pistaches	100 g en coques	60 g sans coques	– 40 %

La cuisson

La cuisson a, elle aussi, une incidence sur le poids final des ingrédients. Là encore, n'hésitez pas à compléter ce tableau en fonction de vos observations et mesures.

Ingrédient	Préparé sur une base de 100 g	Cuit	Perte ou gain de poids en %
Bœuf (steak)	100 g	84 g cuit à la poêle, saignant	– 16 %
Brocoli	100 g	83 g cuit à la poêle	– 17 %
Champignons de Paris	100 g	77 g cuits à la poêle	– 23 %
Chanterelles	100 g	40 g cuits à la poêle	– 60 %
Chou-rave	100 g	78 g cuits à la poêle	– 22 %
Courge butternut	100 g de cubes avec peau	50 g cuits à la vapeur	– 50 %
Courgette	100 g de rondelles	60 g cuit à la poêle	– 40 %
Épinards	100 g	89 g cuits à la poêle	– 11 %
Pieds-de-mouton	100 g	44 g cuits à la poêle	– 66 %
Pleurotes	100 g	75 g cuits à la poêle	– 25 %
Trompettes-des-morts	100 g	48 g cuits à la poêle	– 52 %

Céréales et pâtes

Comme indiqué dans l'introduction, j'ai sélectionné pour mes recettes des céréales et des pâtes dotées d'un indice glycémique bas.

Il est intéressant de toaster légèrement à la poêle certaines céréales comme le sarrasin avant de les cuire à l'eau. Cela développe leurs arômes. Veillez, cependant, à remuer constamment lors de cette opération pour éviter de les brûler ce qui donnerait une amertume très désagréable en bouche.

Vous pouvez aromatiser l'eau de cuisson de vos céréales et pâtes avec du bouillon (volaille, légumes...), des épices (cardamome, anis étoilé, cannelle...), de la citronnelle, du gingembre, des zestes d'agrumes, des herbes fraîches ou séchées...

Vous pouvez également cuire vos céréales, y compris le riz, à la vapeur.

- Mises en garde -

Les soba (« sarrasin » en japonais) sont, comme leur nom japonais l'indique, des pâtes de sarrasin de couleur beige que vous trouverez en magasin bios et dans toute épicerie spécialisée dans les produits asiatiques. Elles sont très populaires au Japon, au même titre que les ramen et les udon. On les sert aussi bien froides que chaudes. Attention pour les intolérants au gluten : choisissez des soba 100 % sarrasin, car certaines pâtes vendues sous l'appellation soba contiennent aussi de la farine de blé.

Attention, certaines marques vendent sous l'appellation « vermicelles de soja » un produit composé de soja et d'amidon de pomme de terre. Cette version possède un indice glycémique plus élevé que celui des véritables vermicelles de soja, composés à 100 % de soja. Vérifiez bien la composition.

Type	Sec	Cuit	Temps de cuisson	Eau	Sans gluten
Riz basmati complet	100 g	200 g	25 minutes	1 volume de riz pour 2 volumes d'eau	Oui
Spaghetti intégrales	100 g	300 g	8 minutes	Grand volume d'eau	Non
Quinoa	100 g	300 g	10 minutes	1 volume de quinoa pour 2 volumes d'eau	Oui
Avoine	100 g	200 g	40 minutes	1 volume d'avoine pour 2 volumes d'eau	Non
Sarrasin	100 g	275 à 300 g	20 minutes	Grand volume d'eau	Oui
Riz complet	100 g	250 g	20 minutes	Grand volume d'eau	Oui
Pâte de type torsades intégrales	100 g	220 g	6 minutes	Grand volume d'eau	Non
Soba 100 % sarrasin	100 g	260 g	4 minutes	Grand volume d'eau	Oui
Riz noir (ou riz Venere ou riz Nérone)	100 g	220 g	45 minutes	1 volume de riz pour 2 volumes d'eau à couvert	Oui
Vermicelles de soja	100 g	500 g	4 minutes	Recouverts d'eau bouillante	Oui
Boulgour	100 g	250 g	10 minutes	Dans 2 fois le volume d'eau bouillante salée	Non
Orge	100 g	300 g	12 heures de trempage, 45 minutes de cuisson à partir de l'ébullition	4 fois le volume d'eau froide	Non

Légumineuses

- Il est important de tremper certaines légumineuses afin de les rendre plus digestes. Comptez au minimum 3 volumes d'eau pour 1 volume de légumineuses. Une fois cette opération effectuée, il faut toujours jeter l'eau de trempage et bien les rincer.
- Si vous manquez de temps pour le trempage, mettez vos légumineuses dans une grande casserole, couvrez largement d'eau, portez à ébullition, couvrez puis laissez reposer une heure hors du feu. Égouttez-les, rincez-les et faites-les cuire normalement. Elles seront, cependant, un peu moins digestes qu'après un trempage classique.
- Il faut toujours rincer abondamment les légumineuses en conserve avant de les utiliser.
- Le temps de cuisson des légumineuses peut varier en fonction de la teneur en calcaire de votre eau. Pour contourner ce problème, n'hésitez pas à utiliser de l'eau filtrée, mais en aucun cas l'eau que vous aurez utilisée pour la phase de trempage.
- La fraîcheur de vos légumineuses a aussi un impact sur le temps de cuisson. S'ils ont été stockés longuement dans votre placard, le temps de cuisson en sera sensiblement augmenté.

- Évitez de mettre du bicarbonate de sodium dans l'eau de cuisson, car il détruit la vitamine B1.
- Ne salez l'eau qu'en toute fin de cuisson.
- Vous pouvez, en revanche, aromatiser l'eau de cuisson avec un oignon, un bouquet garni, du vert de poireau, des gousses d'ail… Évitez tout ingrédient acide (tomate, vinaigre) qui allongerait le temps de cuisson. Vous pouvez les ajouter en fin de cuisson, tout comme le sel.
- Les légumineuses peuvent être cuites plus rapidement à l'autocuiseur. Dans ce cas, suivez les instructions de la notice ou du cahier de recettes de votre modèle.
- Une fois cuites et revenues à température ambiante, les légumineuses se conservent de 1 à 3 jours au réfrigérateur et plusieurs mois au congélateur.
- Notez qu'il est possible de faire germer vos légumineuses. La germination augmente fortement leurs valeurs nutritives en vitamines, minéraux et permet de les rendre plus facile à digérer.

Type	Sec	Cuit	Temps de trempage	Temps de cuisson	Sans gluten
Lentilles vertes, petites	100 g	220 g	0	Départ eau froide, 25 minutes à partir de la reprise de l'ébullition	Oui
Lentilles corail	100 g		0	Départ eau froide, 15 minutes à partir de la reprise de l'ébullition	Oui
Pois chiches	100 g	250 g	12 heures	1 h 30	Oui
Pois cassés	100 g		0	1 heure	Oui
Haricots azukis			0	1 heure	Oui
Flageolets			0	1 h 30	Oui
Haricots mungo			0	30 minutes	Oui
Lentilles beluga			0	20 minutes	Oui
Lentilles brunes			0	Départ eau froide, 15 minutes à partir de la reprise de l'ébullition	Oui
Haricots blancs			12 heures	1 h 30	Oui
Soja jaune			12 heures	1 heure	Oui
Haricots noirs			12 heures	1 h 30	Oui
Haricots rouges			12 heures	1 h 30	Oui
Pois secs jaunes ou verts			12 heures	2 heures	Oui
Flageolets			4 heures	1 h 30	Oui

Les mots suivis d'un astérisque (*) sont définis en page 192.

Légumes

VÉGÉTALIEN

Algues, riz complet, tomate, concombre, edamame, poivron

Préparation
15 minutes

Cuisson
25 minutes

Pour 2 bowls
50 g de riz long complet
90 g de haricots de mer conservés au sel
160 g d'edamame surgelés (Picard®)
1 poivron vert
120 g de tomates cerises
80 g de concombre
Quelques branches de persil plat
20 g de cacahuètes

La sauce cacahuète
1 cuillerée à soupe de sauce de soja
1 cuillerée à soupe de vinaigre de riz
1 cuillerée à café de purée de cacahuète
3 cuillerées à soupe d'huile d'olive
Poivre du moulin

1 Rincez le riz et faites-le cuire environ 20 minutes à l'eau bouillante salée. Égouttez-le.

2 Plongez les haricots de mer dans un grand saladier d'eau froide pendant une quinzaine de minutes. Égouttez-les et rincez-les pendant 3 minutes sous un filet d'eau claire. Laissez-les légèrement sécher à l'air libre.

3 Décongelez les edamame au four à micro-ondes avec un peu d'eau.

4 Lavez le poivron vert. Ôtez le pédoncule, les côtes et les graines, puis coupez la chair en bâtonnets. Enrobez-les d'une cuillerée à soupe d'huile d'olive et d'un peu de sel. Marquez-les 2 minutes sur un gril en fonte (ou dans une poêle en fonte) sur feu vif.

5 Lavez les tomates cerises. Coupez-les en deux ou en quartiers selon leur taille. Lavez le concombre. Coupez-le en petits cubes.

6 Dans un bol, préparez la sauce cacahuète : mélangez la sauce de soja, le vinaigre de riz, la purée de cacahuète, 2 cuillerées à soupe d'huile d'olive et un peu de poivre.

7 Dans un bol, enrobez les edamame avec un tiers de la sauce cacahuète.

8 Dans un autre bol, mélangez les tomates cerises, les cubes de concombre et un tiers de la sauce cacahuète.

9 Lavez et effeuillez le persil. Hachez grossièrement les cacahuètes.

10 Garnissez deux bols d'edamame, de mélange tomates-concombre, de haricots de mer, de riz complet et de bâtonnets de poivron grillés. Arrosez les algues avec le reste de sauce. Agrémentez de persil et de cacahuètes. Servez.

Trucs Santé

Le haricot de mer est l'algue bretonne la plus consommée en France. Crue ou cuite, elle apporte une saveur iodée. Elle est également remarquable d'un point de vue nutritionnel pour sa richesse en fibres, en antioxydants (fucoxanthine), en calcium, en magnésium, en iode, en sodium, en oméga 3, en vitamines A et C.

Trucs de Chef

Vous trouverez les haricots de mer au sel en vitrine réfrigérée dans les magasins bios, plus particulièrement ceux de la chaîne Naturalia. La purée de cacahuète s'achète également dans les magasins bios. Il ne faut pas la confondre avec le beurre de cacahuète qui est parfois sucré.

Edamame, shiitaké, pousses d'épinard, riz basmati, sauce coco

VÉGÉTALIEN

Préparation
10 minutes

Cuisson
25 minutes

Pour 2 bowls
50 g de riz basmati complet
1/2 bâton de cannelle
1 gousse de cardamome
200 g d'edamame (Picard®)
280 g de shiitakés
1 gousse d'ail
2 cuillerées à soupe d'huile d'olive
20 g de noisettes
1 échalote
1/4 de bouquet de coriandre fraîche
4 cuillerées à soupe de lait de coco
2 cuillerées à soupe de jus de citron
1 cuillerée à soupe de sauce de soja
80 g de pousses d'épinard
1/2 piment vert doux
Sel, poivre du moulin

1 Rincez et égouttez le riz basmati complet. Couvrez-le avec deux fois son volume d'eau dans une casserole, ajoutez la cannelle et la cardamome, portez à ébullition, couvrez et baissez le feu. Faites cuire sur feu doux jusqu'à absorption totale du liquide. Égouttez le riz, retirez la cannelle et la cardamome.

2 Faites décongeler les edamame au four à micro-ondes avec un peu d'eau. Lavez les shiitakés. Coupez la base des pieds. Coupez les champignons en tranches épaisses. Fendez la gousse d'ail au couteau.

3 Faites chauffer une grande poêle sur feu vif avec une cuillerée à soupe d'huile d'olive et la gousse d'ail. Faites-y revenir les shiitakés avec un peu de sel pendant 7 minutes en remuant régulièrement. Ôtez la gousse d'ail.

4 Hachez grossièrement les noisettes. Faites-les dorer dans une poêle antiadhésive sans matière grasse en remuant constamment.

5 Pelez et émincez l'échalote. Lavez et hachez la coriandre.

6 Dans un bol, mélangez le lait de coco, le jus de citron, la sauce de soja, l'huile d'olive, l'échalote et la coriandre. Poivrez, versez la moitié de la vinaigrette sur les edamame et mélangez afin de les enrober.

7 Lavez et essorez les pousses d'épinard. Assaisonnez-les avec le reste de la vinaigrette. Coupez le piment doux en fines rondelles.

8 Garnissez deux bols d'edamame, de shiitakés, de riz basmati complet et de pousses d'épinard. Agrémentez de noisettes et de piment. Servez immédiatement.

Trucs Santé

Le shiitaké ou lentin de chêne est le champignon le plus cultivé au monde après le champignon de Paris. Outre sa saveur douce, il est réputé pour ses propriétés médicinales : grâce à sa teneur en lentinane (principe actif), il est fortement conseillé aux personnes immunodéprimées.
C'est aussi un hypocholestérolémiant et un hypolipidémiant. Enfin, ses apports en cuivre, sélénium, zinc, phosphore, magnésium et surtout en vitamine D sont remarquables.

Trucs de Chef

On peut remplacer les edamame par des fèves fraîches en saison. Dans ce cas, écossez puis ébouillantez les fèves quelques secondes avant de les rafraîchir rapidement dans de l'eau glacée. Pelez ensuite les fèves en les incisant légèrement avec les ongles et en pressant.
Dans une version qui ne serait plus que pesco-végétariste ou dans le cas d'un régime sans gluten, vous pouvez remplacer la sauce de soja par du nuoc-mâm.

Figues, sarrasin au nori, brocoli, tomates

VÉGÉTALIEN

SANS GLUTEN

Préparation
10 minutes

Cuisson
20 minutes

Pour 2 bowls
4 figues fraîches
75 g de sarrasin décortiqué
1 feuille d'algue nori
100 g de tomates cerises
150 g de brocoli
10 g de noisettes décortiquées
4 cuillerées à soupe de jus de citron
2 cuillerées à café de câpres
3 cuillerées à soupe d'huile d'olive
1 cuillerée à café de sirop d'érable
20 feuilles de menthe fraîche
1 petit bouquet de coriandre
Sel, poivre du moulin

1 Faites cuire le sarrasin 20 minutes à l'eau bouillante salée. Égouttez-le. Roulez la feuille de nori bien serré, puis coupez-la en fines lanières. Hachez-les. Mélangez le sarrasin avec les paillettes d'algue nori.

2 Lavez le brocoli. Coupez les têtes en tranches épaisses. Faites-les colorer sur feu vif sur leurs deux faces dans une grande poêle avec 1 cuillerée à soupe d'huile.

3 Préchauffez le four à 180 °C.

4 Lavez les tomates cerises, coupez-les en quartiers ou en deux en fonction de leur taille. Lavez les herbes. Conservez quelques petites feuilles de menthe et quelques brins de coriandre pour la décoration. Hachez le reste. Rincez les câpres et hachez-les grossièrement.

5 Dans un bol, mélangez le jus de citron, le sirop d'érable, les herbes, les câpres, du poivre et 2 cuillerées à soupe d'huile d'olive. Salez.

6 Dans un petit saladier, mélangez le brocoli, les tomates et la moitié de la vinaigrette.

7 Lavez les figues et incisez-les en croix. Déposez-les sur une plaque de cuisson puis faites-les cuire 5 minutes au four.

8 Hachez grossièrement les noisettes. Faites-les colorer sur feu vif dans une poêle antiadhésive sans matière grasse en remuant constamment.

9 Garnissez chaque bol de 2 figues, de sarrasin au nori et du mélange brocoli-tomates. Assaisonnez avec le reste de vinaigrette. Agrémentez de noisettes et de quelques feuilles de coriandre et de menthe. Servez immédiatement.

Trucs Santé

Contrairement aux autres céréales, les protéines du sarrasin contiennent tous les acides aminés essentiels et possèdent ainsi une haute valeur biologique.*
Sa teneur en fibres est équivalente à celle des autres céréales, mais le sarrasin contient une proportion plus élevée de fibres solubles, qui contribuent à normaliser les taux sanguins de cholestérol, de glucose et d'insuline, ce qui peut aider au traitement des maladies cardiovasculaires et du diabète de type 2.

Trucs de Chef

Pour une version non végétalienne, vous pouvez remplacer le sirop d'érable par du miel.
On trouve le sarrasin décortiqué au rayon céréales des magasins bios.

Purée de pois cassés, carotte, riz complet, œuf, cheddar

VÉGÉTARIEN

Préparation
10 minutes

Cuisson
1 heure

Pour 2 bowls
120 g de pois cassés
55 g de riz complet
3 carottes
2 oignons nouveaux
20 g de cacahuètes
40 g de cheddar
2 œufs
1 cuillerée à soupe de crème fraîche
Une dizaine de feuilles de menthe fraîche
Huile d'olive, sel, poivre du moulin

La vinaigrette
1 cuillerée à soupe de jus de citron
1 cuillerée à soupe de sauce Worcestershire
2 cuillerées à soupe d'huile d'olive

1 Rincez les pois cassés. Faites-les cuire dans une casserole, largement recouverts d'eau, pendant 1 heure sur feu moyen jusqu'à ce qu'ils soient tendres.

2 Faites cuire le riz complet dans une casserole d'eau salée. Égouttez-le.

3 Dans un bol, mélangez les ingrédients de la vinaigrette. Salez et poivrez.

4 Épluchez les carottes puis coupez-les en rondelles. Pelez les oignons nouveaux puis émincez-les finement. Dans un petit saladier, mélangez les carottes et les oignons avec la vinaigrette.

5 Hachez grossièrement les cacahuètes. Coupez le cheddar en tranches puis en bâtonnets.

6 Faites cuire les œufs 5 minutes dans une casserole d'eau bouillante. Rafraîchissez-les immédiatement à l'eau froide pour stopper la cuisson. Écalez-les avec soin.

7 Égouttez les pois cassés puis mixez-les au blender avec 1 cuillerée à soupe de crème fraîche, du sel et du poivre du moulin. Faites chauffer la crème de pois cassés dans une casserole sur feu doux.

8 Garnissez deux bols de crème de pois cassés, de riz complet, de carottes et d'un œuf coupé en deux. Agrémentez de lamelles de cheddar, de cacahuètes, de quelques feuilles de menthe fraîche, de fleur de sel, de poivre du moulin et d'un filet d'huile d'olive. Servez immédiatement.

Trucs Santé

Zoomons sur le cheddar, encore peu utilisé en France. C'est pourtant le fromage le plus vendu au monde et la star des hamburgers, reconnaissable à sa pâte jaune. Il est riche en calcium avec 720 mg pour 100 g et possède une intéressante teneur en vitamine B12 (1,1 µg/100 g). Cette dernière est très importante dans le cadre d'une alimentation végétarienne puisqu'elle est, d'ordinaire, apportée essentiellement par les produits carnés, d'autant plus qu'il semble que la biodisponibilité de la vitamine B12 d'origine laitière soit supérieure à celle des œufs.

Trucs de Chef

Pour obtenir une recette végétarienne ou dans le cas d'un régime sans gluten, supprimez la sauce Worcestershire de la vinaigrette.

Purée de potimarron au curry, haricots verts, emmental

SANS GLUTEN

VÉGÉTARIEN

Préparation
20 minutes

Cuisson
20 minutes

Pour 3 bowls
La moitié d'un petit potimarron, soit environ 400-450 g
1 petit pâtisson, soit environ 200 g
30 g de riz complet
420 g de haricots verts
30 g de noisettes séchées (ou 75 g de noisettes fraîches en saison)
3 oignons nouveaux
6 tomates cerises
2 cuillerées à soupe de crème fraîche épaisse
1/2 cuillerée à café de poudre de curry doux
30 g d'emmental
Huile d'olive, sel, poivre du moulin

1 À l'aide d'une cuillère à soupe, ôtez les graines du potimarron. Coupez la chair (avec la peau) en cubes réguliers. Faites-les cuire à la vapeur pendant une vingtaine de minutes ; ils doivent être tendres.

2 Coupez le pâtisson en deux. À l'aide d'une petite cuillère, ôtez les graines. Coupez-le en 12 quartiers, mettez-les dans un bol ; frottez-les de sel et d'une cuillerée à soupe d'huile d'olive.

3 Faites cuire le riz complet à l'eau salée. Égouttez-le.

4 Équeutez les haricots verts puis faites-les cuire à l'eau bouillante salée. Après cuisson, plongez-les dans un saladier d'eau et de glaçons. Égouttez-les puis hachez-les grossièrement.

5 Faites chauffer une poêle ou un grill en fonte sur feu moyen à vif. Déposez-y les quartiers de potimarron et marquez-les sur toutes leurs faces pendant une dizaine de minutes.

6 Décortiquez les noisettes. Hachez-les grossièrement. Faites-les dorer dans une poêle antiadhésive sans matière grasse en remuant constamment.

7 Pelez et émincez les oignons nouveaux. Lavez les tomates cerises puis coupez-les en quartiers.

8 Dans un saladier, mélangez les haricots verts, les oignons nouveaux, le riz, les quartiers de tomates et 2 cuillerées à soupe d'huile d'olive. Rectifiez l'assaisonnement.

9 Mixez dans un blender le potimarron cuit avec la crème fraîche, un peu de sel, le curry et quelques cuillerées à soupe d'eau de cuisson selon la consistance souhaitée (entre 2 et 4 cuillerées).

10 Râpez l'emmental à la râpe Microplane.

11 Déposez au fond de chaque bol environ 100 g de crème de potimarron. Répartissez les haricots verts. Agrémentez chaque plat de 10 g de noisettes, 10 g d'emmental et 4 quartiers de pâtisson. Servez immédiatement.

Trucs Santé

Avec une base de potimarron et une belle portion d'emmental, cette recette se démarque par sa richesse en provitamine A qui contribue à la qualité de la peau et des muqueuses, à la vision nocturne mais également au fonctionnement du système immunitaire.*

Vous pouvez remplacer l'oignon nouveau par de l'échalote. Dans ce cas, hachez-la le plus finement possible.

Riz noir, edamame, endive rouge, avocat, concombre

VÉGÉTALIEN

Préparation
10 minutes

Cuisson
45 minutes

Pour 2 bowls

75 g de riz noir (appelé aussi riz Venere ou riz Nérone)
200 g d'edamame (Picard®)
1 pamplemousse
100 g de concombre
1 endive rouge (ou blanche si vous n'en trouvez pas)
Quelques brins de coriandre fraîche
1 avocat
2 cuillerées à café de graines de sésame

La vinaigrette

1 cuillerée à soupe de sauce de soja
1 cuillerée à café de sirop d'érable
1 cuillerée à soupe d'huile de sésame
2 cuillerées à soupe d'huile d'olive
Poivre du moulin

1 Rincez le riz noir, couvrez-le de deux fois son volume d'eau dans une casserole, puis faites-le cuire sur feu doux pendant 45 minutes à couvert.

2 Faites décongeler les edamame au four à micro-ondes avec un peu d'eau.

3 Coupez la base et le sommet du pamplemousse. Ôtez la peau au couteau en suivant la courbure de l'agrume et en prenant soin de ne pas laisser de partie blanche. Faites des incisions en V en lisière des membranes qui séparent chaque quartier pour prélever les suprêmes. Coupez-les en petits morceaux. Pressez le restant du pamplemousse pour récupérer le jus.

4 Dans un bol, préparez la vinaigrette : mélangez 4 cuillerées à soupe de jus de pamplemousse, la sauce de soja, le sirop d'érable, l'huile de sésame, l'huile d'olive et du poivre du moulin.

5 Dans un petit saladier, mélangez les edamame, les suprêmes de pamplemousse et une partie de la vinaigrette.

6 Lavez le concombre. Coupez-le en deux puis en tranches. Dans un bol, enrobez-le d'un peu de vinaigrette.

7 Égouttez et rincez le riz noir. Lavez et effeuillez l'endive rouge. Lavez la coriandre et effeuillez-la grossièrement.

8 Coupez l'avocat en deux. Ôtez le noyau. À l'aide d'une cuillère à soupe, récupérez la chair. Coupez chaque moitié d'avocat en tranches.

9 Garnissez deux bols de riz noir, d'une moitié d'avocat, d'edamame au pamplemousse, de feuilles d'endive rouge et de concombre. Assaisonnez l'avocat, l'endive et le riz avec le reste de la vinaigrette. Agrémentez d'un peu de coriandre et d'une cuillerée à café de graines de sésame. Servez immédiatement.

Trucs Santé

L'association de l'avocat, de l'huile et des graines de sésame offre un profil lipidique remarquable avec une grande quantité vitamine E mais aussi en acides gras polyinsaturés ; dont principalement l'acide linoléique, favorable au bon fonctionnement du système cardiovasculaire. S'ajoutent à cela des apports en phytostérols (lipides végétaux) intéressants. Une recette idéale en cas d'hypercholestérolémie*.*

Trucs de Chef

Le riz noir peut être remplacé par du riz noir de Camargue. Vous en trouverez dans les magasins bios et en grandes surface sous la marque Riso Gallo®. Attention : cette marque met en garde contre des traces possibles de gluten dans son produit. En saison, vous pouvez remplacer les edamame par des fèves fraîches. Écossez-les puis ébouillantez-les quelques secondes avant de les rafraîchir rapidement dans de l'eau glacée. Pelez ensuite les fèves en les incisant légèrement avec les ongles.

VÉGÉTARIEN

Asperges, flocons d'avoine, tomates, pesto déstructuré, épinards

Préparation
10 minutes

Cuisson
5 minutes

Pour 2 bowls
6 belles asperges vertes
20 g de pignons de pin
100 g de gros flocons d'avoine
100 g de sauce tomate
200 g de tomates cerises
20 g de parmesan
15 g de feuilles de basilic
15 g de pousses d'épinard
2 cuillerées à soupe d'huile d'olive
2 cuillerées à soupe de vinaigre balsamique
Fleur de sel, poivre du moulin

1 Pelez les asperges vertes. Cassez la base de la tige afin d'éliminer la partie ligneuse. Faites cuire les asperges à l'eau bouillante salée en les gardant croquantes, puis rafraîchissez-les immédiatement dans de l'eau glacée. Égouttez-les et séchez-les avec du papier absorbant.

2 Faites dorer les pignons de pin dans une poêle antiadhésive sans matière grasse sur feu vif en remuant sans cesse. Laissez-les refroidir.

3 Dans un bol, mélangez les flocons d'avoine avec la sauce tomate.

4 Lavez les tomates cerises puis coupez-les en quatre.

5 Taillez le parmesan en copeaux. Lavez et essorez les feuilles de basilic ainsi que les pousses d'épinard. Dans un saladier, mélangez le basilic, les épinards, les pignons et le parmesan.

6 Garnissez deux bols d'asperges, de tomates, de flocons d'avoine à la sauce tomate et de salade d'herbes. Assaisonnez les tomates et la salade d'herbes d'huile d'olive, de vinaigre balsamique, de fleur de sel et de poivre du moulin. Servez.

Trucs Santé

Les flocons d'avoine, base de cette recette, sont riches en glucides complexes et en fibres. De plus, les bêta-glucanes qu'ils contiennent ralentissent l'absorption du glucose et des graisses, favorisant la réduction du taux de cholestérol sanguin et, par là même, des besoins en insuline.

Trucs de Chef

Vous pouvez ajouter quelques feuilles de menthe fraîche à votre salade d'herbes.

Aubergine, feta, pomme, sauce tomate

SANS GLUTEN

VÉGÉTARIEN

Préparation
10 minutes

Cuisson
30 minutes

Pour 2 bowls

30 g de riz complet
4 tomates cerises, lavées
1 belle aubergine ou 2 petites
1/2 oignon
1 gousse d'ail non pelée
1/2 cuillerée à café de graines de cumin
30 g de pignons de pin
1/2 pomme non pelée, épépinée
6 olives noires
100 g de feta, coupée en cubes
Quelques sommités de thym frais
40 g de sauce tomate
Quelques feuilles de roquette
3 cuillerées à soupe d'huile d'olive
Sel, poivre du moulin, noix de muscade râpée

1 Faites cuire le riz dans une casserole d'eau salée. Égouttez-le. Réservez.

2 Coupez les tomates cerises en quartiers. Réservez.

3 Coupez l'aubergine en cubes d'environ 1 cm de côté. Pelez et ciselez l'oignon. Incisez légèrement la gousse d'ail. Écrasez le cumin dans un mortier.

4 Faites chauffer une grande poêle sur feu moyen avec 2 cuillerées à soupe d'huile d'olive. Faites-y revenir l'oignon et l'ail avec un peu de sel pendant 3 minutes en remuant régulièrement pour éviter toute coloration. Ajoutez les cubes d'aubergine, le cumin, un peu de noix de muscade râpée. Salez et poursuivez la cuisson 25 minutes en mélangeant de temps en temps.

5 Faites colorer les pignons de pin sur feu vif dans une poêle antiadhésive sans matière grasse, sans cesser de remuer. Réservez.

6 Coupez la pomme en petits dés. Dénoyautez les olives. Ajoutez ces ingrédients à l'aubergine ainsi que le riz et les pignons. Poursuivez la cuisson 5 minutes en mélangeant.

7 Hors du feu, ajoutez la feta et le thym. Mélangez, poivrez et rectifiez l'assaisonnement.

8 Versez la sauce tomate au fond de deux bols. Ajoutez la préparation à base d'aubergine. Agrémentez chaque bol de quartiers de tomate cerise et de quelques feuilles de roquette. Arrosez d'un filet d'huile d'olive.

9 Servez immédiatement.

Il est rare que des aliments végétaux apportent tous les acides aminés que contiennent les protéines d'origine animale. Cette recette vous propose une association originale de feta et de riz complet — un produit laitier et une céréale — dont les protéines sont complémentaires, pour une recette végétarienne rassasiante et complète.*

Choisissez de préférence des aubergines de petite taille, elles contiendront moins de graines.
Pour une recette végétalienne et végane, remplacez les cubes de feta par des cubes de tofu.

VÉGÉTARIEN

Avoine, œuf, kale, champignons, pistaches

Préparation
10 minutes
(Trempage de l'avoine 12 heures)

Cuisson
40 minutes

Pour 2 bowls
200 g d'avoine décortiquée
240 g de champignons de Paris
120 g de kale (chou frisé non pommé)
1 cuillerée à soupe d'huile d'olive
2 gros œufs
20 g de pistaches décortiquées ou environ 35 g de pistaches entières (à décortiquer)
Sel, poivre du moulin

La vinaigrette
1 échalote
1 cuillerée à café de moutarde de Dijon
1 cuillerée à soupe de vinaigre de vin rouge
1 cuillerée à soupe de sauce Worcestershire
2 cuillerées à soupe d'huile d'olive
Sel, poivre du moulin

1 Faites tremper l'avoine dans de l'eau froide pendant 12 heures. Ce temps écoulé, rincez-la sous l'eau courante à travers une passoire fine. Faites-la cuire sur feu doux avec 2 fois son volume d'eau pendant une quarantaine de minutes. Égouttez-la.

2 Pour la vinaigrette, pelez et émincez l'échalote. Dans un bol, mélangez-la avec la moutarde, le vinaigre de vin rouge, la sauce Worcestershire, l'huile d'olive, du sel et du poivre du moulin.

3 Coupez la partie terreuse du pied des champignons. Lavez-les soigneusement sous un filet d'eau. Séchez-les et coupez-les en tranches. Dans un saladier, mélangez-les avec la vinaigrette.

4 À l'aide d'un couteau, retirez les côtes des feuilles de kale. Lavez les feuilles puis plongez-les pendant une trentaine de secondes dans une casserole d'eau bouillante salée. Rafraîchissez-les immédiatement dans de l'eau glacée. Égouttez-les, pressez-les entre vos mains pour les essorer, puis hachez-les grossièrement. Faites-les revenir 5 minutes dans une poêle sur feu vif avec l'huile d'olive. Salez et poivrez en cours de cuisson.

5 Faites cuire les œufs 6 minutes à l'eau bouillante salée. Rafraîchissez-les dans de l'eau froide, puis écalez-les.

6 Décortiquez les pistaches (si nécessaire) et hachez-les grossièrement.

7 Garnissez chaque bol d'un œuf coupé en deux, d'avoine assaisonnée, de kale et de champignons. Agrémentez de pistaches. Servez immédiatement.

Trucs Santé

Le kale est présenté comme le nouveau légume phare de la nutrition. Riche en magnésium, en potassium, en fibres et en vitamines B9 principalement, il est pauvre en calories et regorge d'antioxydants dont la lutéine qui prévient la dégénérescence maculaire et la cataracte. Comme tous les caroténoïdes, la lutéine est mieux absorbée en présence de matière grasse : ainsi, la présence de pistache et d'huile d'olive est idéale dans cette recette.*

Trucs de Chef

Pour que cette recette convienne aux végétariens, il suffit de remplacer la sauce Worcestershire par une cuillerée supplémentaire de vinaigre de vin rouge. L'avoine décortiquée et le kale se trouvent dans les magasins bios. Il est préférable de faire tremper l'avoine 12 heures pour réduire son temps de cuisson.

Brocoli, chou-fleur, boulgour, poivron, cacahuètes

VÉGÉTALIEN

Préparation
10 minutes

Cuisson
10 minutes

Pour 2 bowls
70 g de boulgour
160 g de brocoli
160 g de chou-fleur
1 poivron vert
20 g de cacahuètes
Sel, poivre du moulin

La vinaigrette
Quelques brins de coriandre fraîche
4 cuillerées à soupe de jus de citron
2 cuillerées à soupe d'huile d'olive
Sel, poivre du moulin

1 Faites cuire le boulgour sur feu moyen dans deux fois son volume d'eau bouillante salée pendant 10 minutes ou jusqu'à totale absorption du liquide.

2 Lavez le brocoli et le chou-fleur. Détachez les sommités des deux légumes et faites-les cuire à la vapeur pendant 5 minutes.

3 Pelez le poivron vert avec un économe. Coupez-le en deux, ôtez le pédoncule, les graines et les côtes. Émincez-le en fines lanières.

4 Préparez la vinaigrette : lavez, effeuillez la coriandre et hachez-la finement. Dans un bol, fouettez le jus de citron avec du sel et du poivre, puis ajoutez l'huile d'olive et la coriandre.

5 Hachez grossièrement les cacahuètes.

6 Garnissez deux bols de boulgour, de brocoli, de chou-fleur et de lanières de poivron. Assaisonnez de vinaigrette tous les éléments, sauf le boulgour. Agrémentez de cacahuètes. Servez.

Trucs Santé

Très peu énergétique (25 kcal pour 100 g), le brocoli est une remarquable source de vitamines C et K, B9, B2, B5, B6, ainsi que de calcium et vitamine E. Côté minéraux, le magnésium et le fer sont bien représentés. Enfin, cette recette est particulièrement riche en fibres, et le boulgour y contribue.

Trucs de Chef

Si vous ne possédez pas de cuit-vapeur, utilisez une simple passoire en métal posée sur une casserole et couverte d'une assiette. Il existe aussi des paniers à vapeur pliants en acier inoxydable que vous pouvez poser dans une casserole pour cuire à la vapeur Vous pouvez remplacer le boulgour par du sarrasin.
Pelé, le poivron est plus digeste.

Taboulé de brocoli, concombre, radis, raisins secs

SANS GLUTEN

VÉGÉTALIEN

Préparation
15 minutes

Cuisson
20 minutes

Pour 2 bowls
30 g de sarrasin décortiqué
200 g de brocoli
150 g de concombre
100 g de radis roses
20 g de pignons de pin
1/2 bouquet de persil plat
Une trentaine de feuilles de menthe fraîche
60 g de raisins secs
Sel

La vinaigrette
4 cuillerées à soupe de jus de citron
2 cuillerées à soupe d'huile d'olive
1 cuillerée à café de ras-el-hanout
Sel, poivre du moulin

1 Faites cuire le sarrasin 20 minutes à l'eau bouillante salée. Égouttez-le.

2 Lavez les légumes et les herbes. Hachez grossièrement le brocoli. Mixez-le jusqu'à l'obtention d'une grosse semoule. Lavez le concombre. Taillez-le en tranches dans l'axe du légume, autour des graines. Taillez ces tranches en bâtonnets puis en petits cubes. Parez les radis puis coupez-les en fines rondelles.

3 Faites dorer les pignons de pin dans une poêle antiadhésive très chaude sans matière grasse en remuant constamment.

4 Hachez grossièrement le persil et la menthe fraîche.

5 Préparez la vinaigrette : dans un bol, mélangez le jus de citron, l'huile d'olive et le ras-el-hanout. Salez et poivrez.

6 Dans un saladier, mélangez la semoule de brocoli, les radis, le concombre, les raisins secs, les pignons de pin et les herbes. Assaisonnez de vinaigrette au ras-el-hanout.

7 Répartissez la préparation dans deux bols. Servez.

Trucs Santé

C'est une très belle idée de proposer une base de brocolis crus finement râpés ! Ils permettent de bénéficier pleinement de la vitamine C que ce légume contient en bonne quantité, car la cuisson la réduit de moitié.

Trucs de Chef

Vous trouverez le sarrasin décortiqué au rayon céréales des magasins bios. N'hésitez pas à préparer ce taboulé de brocoli quelques heures à l'avance et à le conserver au réfrigérateur. L'osmose des goûts aura le temps de se réaliser, et il n'en sera que meilleur.

Tofu, boulgour, brocoli, kale

Préparation
10 minutes

Cuisson
10 minutes

Pour 2 bowls
45 g de boulgour
140 g de choux de Bruxelles
5 cuillerées à soupe d'huile d'olive
140 g de kale
1 cuillerée à café de poivre en grains
180 g de tofu
120 g de brocoli
Sel, fleur de sel, poivre du moulin

La vinaigrette
2 cuillerées à soupe de jus de citron
2 cuillerées à soupe de nuoc-mâm
2 cuillerées à soupe d'huile de sésame
2 cuillerées à café de miel
2 cuillerées à soupe de graines de sésame
Poivre du moulin

1 Faites cuire le boulgour sur feu doux dans deux fois son volume d'eau salée pendant environ 10 minutes, jusqu'à totale absorption du liquide.

2 Éliminez le trognon et les premières feuilles des choux de Bruxelles. Coupez ceux-ci en deux et faites-les revenir à la poêle sur feu moyen à vif avec 1 cuillerée à soupe d'huile d'olive pendant 6 à 7 minutes. Ajoutez un peu d'eau ; salez et poivrez en cours de cuisson.

3 Ôtez les côtes des feuilles de kale à l'aide d'un couteau. Lavez les feuilles puis plongez-les 30 secondes dans de l'eau bouillante salée. Rafraîchissez-les immédiatement dans de l'eau glacée. Égouttez et essorez les feuilles de kale, hachez-les grossièrement. Poêlez-les 5 minutes sur feu vif avec 1 cuillerée à café d'huile d'olive. Salez et poivrez en cours de cuisson.

4 Concassez les grains de poivre dans un mortier pour obtenir un poivre mignonnette. Mélangez-le avec un peu de fleur de sel dans une assiette.

5 Égouttez le tofu puis séchez-le dans du papier absorbant. Coupez le bloc en gros cubes. Faites-les colorer à la poêle sur toutes leurs faces pendant 5 minutes sur feu vif avec 1 cuillerée à soupe d'huile d'olive. Égouttez-les sur du papier absorbant puis enrobez-les d'un peu de mélange poivre-fleur de sel.

6 Lavez le brocoli et prélevez-en les sommités.

7 Préparez la vinaigrette : dans un petit bol, mélangez le jus de citron, le nuoc-mâm, l'huile de sésame, le miel, les graines de sésame et un peu de poivre du moulin.

8 Garnissez deux bols de tofu, de choux de Bruxelles, de boulgour et de kale. Assaisonnez les 3 derniers éléments de vinaigrette. Servez immédiatement.

Trucs Santé

Le tofu offre un apport en protéines végétales d'excellente qualité. On lui reproche parfois sa saveur trop neutre. Il est ici doré et pané dans le poivre concassé et la fleur de sel, ce qui lui donne du croustillant en nous faisant bénéficier de tous ses intérêts nutritionnels.

Trucs de Chef

Pour obtenir une recette végétalienne, remplacez le nuoc-mâm par de la sauce de soja et le miel par du sirop d'érable. Vous trouverez le kale sur les marchés, chez quelques primeurs ou dans les magasins bios.
Le tofu est disponible dans tous les magasins bios ainsi que dans les épiceries asiatiques.

Chou rouge, riz noir, brocoli, laitue, orange

VÉGÉTALIEN

SANS GLUTEN

Préparation
15 minutes

Cuisson
45 minutes

Pour 2 bowls
70 g de riz noir (appelé aussi riz Venere ou riz Nérone)
160 g de brocoli
1 orange
40 g de baies de cassis
40 g de feuilles de laitue
120 g de chou rouge
20 g de noix de macadamia

La sauce au yaourt
Le jus de l'orange (voir la recette)
1 yaourt
1 cuillerée à café de moutarde de Dijon
1 cuillerée à café de sirop d'érable
Sel

1 Rincez le riz noir, couvrez-le dans une casserole de deux fois son volume d'eau et faites-le cuire à couvert 45 minutes sur feu doux. Égouttez-le.

2 Lavez le brocoli. Détachez-en les sommités et faites-les cuire 5 minutes à la vapeur.

3 Coupez la base et le sommet de l'orange. Ôtez la peau et la partie blanche à l'aide d'un couteau tranchant en suivant la courbure du fruit afin de n'avoir plus que la chair à vif. Faites des incisions en V en lisière des membranes qui séparent chaque quartier pour prélever les suprêmes.

4 Pour la sauce au yaourt, pressez le reste de l'orange au-dessus d'un bol afin de récupérer le maximum de jus. Ajoutez le yaourt, la moutarde de Dijon et le sirop d'érable. Salez et mélangez.

5 Lavez les baies de cassis. Dans un saladier, mélangez la laitue, les suprêmes d'orange, les baies de cassis et un peu de sauce au yaourt.

6 Émincez le chou rouge. Dans un saladier, mélangez-le avec un peu de sauce au yaourt.

7 Hachez grossièrement les noix de macadamia.

8 Garnissez deux bols de laitue aux suprêmes d'orange et au cassis, de chou rouge, de brocoli et de riz noir. Déposez un peu de sauce au yaourt sur les sommités de brocoli. Agrémentez de noix de macadamia. Servez.

Trucs Santé

Chou rouge et brocoli sont associés dans cette recette. Les choux sont particulièrement bien pourvus en vitamine C, tonifiante et anti-infectieuse, et contiennent des substances telles que les indoles, les isothiocyanates et les dithiolthiones qui semblent avoir des effets anticancéreux. Le chou rouge se distingue des autres par son contenu plus élevé en flavonoïdes aux propriétés antioxydantes.

Trucs de Chef

Pour une version non végétalienne et non végétarienne, ou pour un régime sans gluten, vous pouvez remplacer le sirop d'érable par du miel et la sauce de soja par du sel ou du nuoc-mâm.

Chou, aubergine, pomme, framboises, emmental, riz complet

SANS GLUTEN

VÉGÉTARIEN

Préparation
20 minutes

Cuisson
30 minutes

Pour 2 bowls
50 g de riz long complet
La moitié d'une grosse aubergine
La moitié d'une pomme Pink Lady
130 g de chou de Savoie (ou chou de Milan)
120 g de framboises
80 g d'emmental
1 cuillerée à café de graines de sésame

La vinaigrette
1/2 cuillerée à café de graines de carvi
2 cuillerées à café de vinaigre de vin rouge
3 cuillerées à soupe d'huile d'olive
Sel, poivre du moulin

1 Faites cuire le riz à l'eau salée pendant une vingtaine de minutes. Égouttez-le.

2 Lavez l'aubergine et la pomme. Coupez la pomme en deux quartiers, retirez le cœur puis coupez la chair en gros morceaux.

3 Coupez l'aubergine en tranches épaisses puis en gros cubes. Faites-les revenir à la poêle avec une cuillerée à soupe d'huile d'olive et un peu de sel sur feu moyen pendant 20 minutes en remuant régulièrement. Au bout de ce temps, ajoutez les morceaux de pomme et poursuivez la cuisson 10 minutes.

4 Éliminez la côte centrale des feuilles de chou. Plongez les feuilles dans une grande casserole d'eau bouillante salée et faites-les cuire 5 minutes. Rafraîchissez-les immédiatement dans de l'eau glacée pour préserver leur vert éclatant. Égouttez les feuilles puis coupez-les en lanières.

5 Lavez les framboises. Coupez l'emmental en bâtonnets.

6 Préparez la vinaigrette : écrasez les graines de carvi dans un mortier. Dans un petit bol, mélangez le vinaigre de vin rouge, du sel, du poivre, le carvi puis l'huile d'olive.

7 Garnissez deux bols de riz complet, du mélange aubergine-pomme, de framboises, de chou et d'emmental. Assaisonnez le chou et l'emmental avec la vinaigrette. Agrémentez de graines de sésame. Servez immédiatement.

Trucs Santé

Une recette sucrée-salée qui utilise la framboise. Ce petit fruit rouge peu sucré est connu pour être le plus riche en acide ellagique, un polyphénol aux propriétés antioxydantes. Ses petites graines caractéristiques sont également riches en cellulose, qui aide à accélérer le transit.*

Trucs de Chef

Le chou de Savoie ou chou de Milan est une variété de chou pommé aux feuilles finement cloquées. On l'appelle parfois, à tort, « chou frisé », ce nom étant en réalité l'appellation française du kale.

Falafel

VÉGÉTARIEN

SANS GLUTEN

Préparation
20 minutes
(Réhydratation 12 heures)

Cuisson
1 heure

Pour 4 bowls
60 g de pois chiches secs
1/2 oignon jaune
1 cuillerée à soupe d'huile d'olive
170 g de fèves surgelées avec leur peau
1 cuillerée à café de graines de coriandre, 1 de graines de cumin
1 gousse d'ail
1 cuillerée à soupe de graines de sésame
1/2 cuillerée à café de bicarbonate de sodium, 1/2 de piment d'Espelette
1/4 de bouquet de coriandre fraîche
1/4 de bouquet de persil plat
Huile pour friture
200 g de batavia
Sel, poivre du moulin
200 g de concombre
320 g de tomates cerises
1 oignon rouge
1 pain pita
40 g de pistaches décortiquées ou environ 70 g de pistaches entières
Sel, poivre du moulin

La sauce
2 cuillerées à soupe de tahini (crème de sésame)
12 cuillerées à soupe de crème liquide
Le jus de 1/2 citron

1 Faites tremper les pois chiches 12 heures dans un grand volume d'eau. Égouttez-les et faites-les cuire 1 heure à l'eau bouillante salée. Égouttez-les et rincez-les.

2 Pelez et ciselez l'oignon jaune. Faites-le revenir pendant 3 minutes à la poêle avec l'huile d'olive et un peu de sel en remuant constamment pour éviter toute coloration.

3 Ébouillantez les fèves. À la reprise de l'ébullition, égouttez-les, rafraîchissez-les dans de l'eau glacée puis pelez-les.

4 Écrasez les graines de coriandre et de cumin dans un mortier.

5 Pelez la gousse d'ail, coupez-la en deux, retirez le germe puis écrasez la pulpe à l'aide d'un presse-ail.

6 Mixez les pois chiches avec les fèves, l'ail, l'oignon, le cumin, la coriandre, les graines de sésame, le bicarbonate, le piment d'Espelette et du sel afin d'obtenir une pâte homogène. Ajoutez un peu d'eau si elle est trop dense.

7 Lavez et essorez le persil et la coriandre. Hachez finement les feuilles et les tiges. Dans un grand saladier, mélangez la pâte à falafel avec les herbes fraîches. Rectifiez l'assaisonnement si nécessaire. Façonnez à la main une vingtaine de boulettes.

8 Versez l'huile de friture dans une casserole à mi-hauteur, faites-la chauffer à 180 °C (aidez-vous d'un thermomètre de cuisson si possible). Faites frire les falafels par petites quantités, sur les deux faces. Lorsqu'ils sont bien dorés, égouttez-les sur du papier absorbant.

9 Préparez la sauce : mélangez dans un bol la crème de sésame, la crème liquide et le jus de citron. Salez et poivrez.

10 Lavez et essorez la batavia. Hachez grossièrement les feuilles. Coupez le concombre en quartiers, puis en tranches. Dans un saladier, mélangez la batavia, le concombre et la sauce à la crème de sésame.

11 Lavez les tomates cerises et coupez-les en quartiers. Pelez et émincez l'oignon rouge. Toastez le pain pita et coupez-le en gros morceaux. Décortiquez les pistaches, si nécessaire, et hachez-les grossièrement.

12 Garnissez quatre bols de salade au concombre, de falafels, d'oignon rouge et de tomates. Agrémentez de morceaux de pita et de pistaches. Servez.

Trucs Santé

Avec les pistaches, les graines de sésame et le tahini, cette recette apporte une bonne quantité d'acides gras insaturés et plus particulièrement d'acide oléique, dont les effets sur le cholestérol sanguin sont bénéfiques. Elle est également riche en fibres que procurent ces graines, mais aussi les fèves et les pois chiches.*

Trucs de Chef

On peut aussi faire les falafels avec des pois chiches juste réhydratés, non cuits.

Pour transformer cette recette en recette végétalienne, il suffit de remplacer la crème liquide par de la crème de soja, que vous trouverez en magasin bio et même en grande distribution.

Hoummous aux petits légumes façon jardinière

VÉGÉTARIEN

Préparation

15 minutes

(Réhydratation 12 heures)

Cuisson

2 heures

Pour 4 bowls

Le tahini

125 g de pois chiches secs
1 cuillerée à café de graines de cumin
1 gousse d'ail
150 g de cream cheese (Philadelphia® ou Kiri®)
50 g de tahini (crème de sésame)
1/2 yaourt brassé
Le jus de 1/2 citron jaune
1 cuillerée à soupe d'huile d'olive
Sel, poivre du moulin

La garniture

12 asperges vertes
200 g de brocoli
200 g d'endives
440 g de petites carottes
100 g de petites branches de céleri
4 tranches de pain croquant suédois au seigle (Wasa® léger)
40 g de baies de grenade
Sel

1 Faites tremper les pois chiches 12 heures dans un grand volume d'eau. Égouttez-les et faites-les cuire 2 heures à l'eau bouillante salée. Égouttez-les et rincez-les.

2 Écrasez le cumin dans un mortier. Pelez, dégermez la gousse d'ail puis écrasez-la dans un presse-ail.

3 Mixez les pois chiches avec le cream cheese, le cumin, le tahini, l'ail, le yaourt, le jus de citron, l'huile d'olive, du sel et du poivre du moulin. Laissez durcir cette crème au réfrigérateur.

4 Éliminez la base fibreuse des asperges vertes. Faites-les cuire de 4 à 5 minutes à l'eau bouillante salée, plongez-les immédiatement dans de l'eau glacée, égouttez-les sur du papier absorbant puis coupez-les en deux.

5 Lavez le brocoli et coupez-le en petites sommités. Effeuillez les endives et coupez en deux les feuilles les plus grosses. Pelez et lavez les carottes. Lavez les branches de céleri.

6 Cassez grossièrement les pains croquants au seigle.

7 Répartissez la crème de hoummous dans quatre bols. Garnissez de branches de céleri, de brocoli, de carottes, d'asperges, de feuilles d'endive et de morceaux de pain croquant. Agrémentez de baies de grenade. Servez.

Trucs Santé

Le pois chiche, comme toutes les légumineuses, est naturellement riche en protéines végétales (8,9 g pour 100 g de pois chiches cuits). Ces dernières étant déficientes en un acide aminé, la méthionine, il faudra les compléter par une céréale, ce qui est le cas dans cette recette avec les pains croquants au seigle, qui apportent une qualité protéique intéressante à ce plat végétarien.*

Trucs de Chef

Cette recette peut être proposée à l'apéritif. Dans ce cas, comptez un bol pour 3 ou 4 personnes.

Jardinière de légumes, sauce dip au gorgonzola

SANS GLUTEN

VÉGÉTARIEN

Préparation
10 minutes

Cuisson
5 minutes

Pour 2 bowls
Quelques brins de ciboulette
150 g de cream cheese (Philadelphia®, Kiri®...)
1/2 yaourt
125 g de gorgonzola
6 asperges vertes
100 g de haricots verts
1 courgette
2 cuillerées à soupe d'huile d'olive
120 g de champignons de Paris
Sel, poivre du moulin

1 Émincez la ciboulette. Conservez-en une petite partie pour la décoration.

2 Dans un petit saladier, mélangez à la fourchette le cream cheese, le yaourt, le gorgonzola et la ciboulette. Goûtez, salez et poivrez selon nécessité. Gardez la sauce au réfrigérateur afin qu'elle reprenne de la consistance.

3 Éliminez la base fibreuse des asperges vertes. Faites-les cuire de 4 à 5 minutes à l'eau bouillante salée, plongez-les immédiatement dans de l'eau glacée, égouttez-les sur du papier absorbant puis coupez-les en deux.

4 Équeutez et lavez les haricots verts. Faites-les cuire à l'eau bouillante salée puis rafraîchissez-les immédiatement dans de l'eau avec des glaçons pour conserver leur couleur. Égouttez-les et coupez-les en deux.

5 Lavez et parez la courgette. Coupez-la en tranches épaisses dans le sens de la longueur autour des graines centrales. Taillez ces tranches en bâtonnets. Saisissez-les très rapidement dans une poêle sur feu vif avec 1 cuillerée à soupe d'huile d'olive et un peu de sel.

6 Coupez la base du pied des champignons. Lavez ceux-ci sous un filet d'eau, puis coupez-les en quartiers.

7 Répartissez la crème au gorgonzola dans deux bols. Garnissez harmonieusement de haricots verts, d'asperges, de champignons et de bâtonnets de courgette. Arrosez du reste d'huile d'olive et agrémentez de ciboulette réservée. Servez.

Trucs Santé

Une recette riche en protéines d'origine laitière ! On pensera, pour compléter l'apport en acides aminés, à ajouter par exemple une portion de pain. Les légumes, peu cuits, restent croquants dans cette recette, ce qui favorise le rassasiement.*

Trucs de Chef

Cette recette peut être servie à l'apéritif. Dans ce cas, comptez un bol pour 3 ou 4 personnes.
Vous pouvez remplacer la ciboulette par de la sauge.
En saison, profitez des asperges blanches, que vous ajouterez à cette recette.

Jardinière de légumes, sauce dip au parmesan

SANS GLUTEN

VÉGÉTARIEN

Préparation

15 minutes

Pour 2 bowls

75 g de parmesan
10 belles feuilles de basilic
150 g de cream cheese (Philadelphia®, Kiri®...)
1/2 yaourt
1 cuillerée à café de moutarde de Dijon
1 cuillerée à soupe d'huile d'olive
60 g de brocoli
1 endive
120 g de petites carottes
120 g de tomates cerises
60 g de radis roses
Sel, poivre du moulin

1 Râpez le parmesan à la râpe Microplane®.

2 Superposez les feuilles de basilic et roulez-les très serré tel un cigare. Coupez-les en fines lanières.

3 Dans un petit saladier, mélangez le cream cheese, le yaourt, la moutarde, le parmesan, l'huile d'olive et le basilic. Goûtez, salez et poivrez selon nécessité.

4 Lavez tous les légumes. Coupez le brocoli en petites sommités. Effeuillez l'endive et coupez en deux les feuilles les plus grosses. Pelez les carottes.

5 Répartissez la crème de parmesan dans deux bols. Garnissez de tomates cerises, de radis roses, de brocoli, de carottes et feuilles d'endive. Servez.

Trucs Santé

Vous pouvez être généreux sur la quantité de basilic : ses feuilles possèdent d'importantes propriétés antioxydantes, avec une quantité non négligeable de vitamine C, mais surtout un taux record de bêtacarotène (provitamine A). Il contribue également à couvrir vos besoins en vitamine B9.*

Trucs de Chef

Cette recette peut être servie à l'apéritif. Dans ce cas, comptez un bol pour 3 ou 4 personnes.
Vous pouvez également garnir cette jardinière de quelques morceaux de chou-rave poêlé et de bâtonnets de poivron cru. Pelez le poivron avant de le découper.

Jardinière de pomme, poire, champignons, sauce dip au roquefort

VÉGÉTARIEN

SANS GLUTEN

Préparation
15 minutes

Cuisson
2 heures 30

Pour 2 bowls
150 g de cream cheese (Philadelphia® ou Kiri®)
1 yaourt brassé
125 g de roquefort, émietté
2 petites poires de type conférence
1 petite pomme de type Pink Lady
Le jus de 1/2 citron
140 g de champignons de Paris
20 g de noix de pécan
Sel, poivre du moulin

1 Dans un petit saladier, mélangez à la fourchette le cream cheese, le yaourt et le roquefort émietté. Rectifiez l'assaisonnement avec du sel et du poivre du moulin. Gardez la sauce au réfrigérateur afin qu'elle prenne de la consistance.

2 Préchauffez le four à 90 °C (th. 3). Lavez les poires. À l'aide d'une mandoline, taillez-en une en tranches régulières d'environ 1 mm d'épaisseur. Déposez-les sur une plaque garnie d'un tapis en silicone (Silpat®) ou d'une feuille de papier sulfurisé et faites sécher au four pendant 2 heures 30 en retournant les tranches à mi-cuisson. Laissez refroidir les chips de poire sur une grille.

3 Coupez la poire restante et la pomme en quartiers. Ôtez le cœur puis coupez chaque quartier en fines tranches. Citronnez-les légèrement.

4 Coupez le pied sableux des champignons. Lavez-les sous un filet d'eau. Coupez-les en deux ou en quartiers selon leur taille. Hachez grossièrement les noix de pécan.

5 Répartissez la crème de roquefort dans deux bols. Garnissez harmonieusement de tranches de pomme et de poire, de champignons et de chips de poire. Agrémentez de noix de pécan. Servez.

Trucs Santé

Une recette sucrée-salée à consommer sans couverts, en prenant son temps. Les fruits crus associés aux noix de pécan ajoutent de la consistance et favorisent la mastication, donc la satiété.

Trucs de Chef

Cette recette peut être servie à l'apéritif. Dans ce cas, comptez un bol pour 3 ou 4 personnes.

Taboulé bowl

VÉGÉTALIEN

Préparation
15 minutes

Cuisson
10 minutes

Pour 2 bowls
85 g de boulgour
2 gros bouquets de persil, soit environ 350 g
1 gros bouquet de menthe
Le jus de 1 citron
3 cuillerées à soupe d'huile d'olive
60 g de baies de grenade
80 g de tomates cerises
80 g de concombre
20 g d'oignon rouge
Sel, poivre du moulin

1 Faites cuire le boulgour sur feu doux dans deux fois son volume d'eau salée pendant environ 10 minutes, jusqu'à totale absorption du liquide.

2 Coupez la base des tiges des deux bouquets de persil à hauteur des premières feuilles. Pesez le persil afin d'en obtenir 150 g. Effeuillez la menthe et pesez-la afin d'obtenir 50 g de feuilles. Lavez et essorez le persil et la menthe, hachez-les au couteau.

3 Dans un saladier, mélangez les herbes, le jus de citron, l'huile d'olive, les baies de grenade, du sel et du poivre du moulin. Réservez au réfrigérateur.

4 Lavez les tomates cerises, coupez-les en quartiers. Émincez l'oignon rouge. Lavez le concombre et coupez-le en petits cubes. Dans un petit saladier, mélangez les tomates, l'oignon et le concombre.

5 Garnissez deux bols de salade d'herbes à la grenade, de salade tomates-oignon-concombre et de boulgour. Servez.

Trucs Santé

Un taboulé revisité, bien plus riche en fines herbes et en légumes que la recette classique. On améliore ainsi les apports en fibres et on booste les apports en vitamines et en minéraux !

Trucs de Chef

Vous pouvez remplacer le boulgour par de la semoule, sans oublier que l'indice glycémique de cette dernière est plus élevé (65 contre 55).
N'hésitez pas à préparer votre salade d'herbes un peu à l'avance et à la garder au moins 1 heure au réfrigérateur : elle n'en sera que meilleure.

Soba, butternut au paprika, œufs brouillés, persil, amandes

VÉGÉTARIEN

Préparation
10 minutes

Cuisson
20 minutes

Pour 2 bowls

La moitié d'un butternut d'environ 400 g
1 cuillerée à café de paprika
4 gros œufs
2 cuillerées à soupe de crème fraîche
10 g de beurre
75 g de nouilles soba
1 bouquet de persil plat
1 cuillerée à soupe de jus de citron
20 g d'amandes grillées
Huile d'olive, sel, poivre du moulin

1 À l'aide d'une cuillère à soupe, retirez les graines du butternut. Pelez-le et coupez la chair en cubes de taille régulière.

2 Faites chauffer sur feu vif une poêle antiadhésive avec une cuillerée à soupe d'huile d'olive. Faites-y revenir les cubes de butternut avec du sel et le paprika pendant une vingtaine de minutes en remuant fréquemment. Poivrez en fin de cuisson.

3 Cassez les œufs dans une casserole et faites-les cuire au bain-marie en les brouillant à l'aide d'une fourchette. Quand ils forment une masse onctueuse et homogène, ajoutez la crème fraîche et le beurre. Salez et poivrez. Retirez du feu et mélangez une dernière fois.

4 Faites cuire les soba dans un grand volume d'eau bouillante salée. Égouttez-les, ajoutez 1 cuillerée à soupe d'huile d'olive. Salez, poivrez et mélangez.

5 Lavez et égouttez le persil plat. Effeuillez-le grossièrement. Dans un petit saladier, assaisonnez le persil d'une cuillerée à soupe d'huile d'olive, du jus de citron, de sel et de poivre du moulin.

6 Hachez grossièrement les amandes grillées.

7 Garnissez deux bols de cubes de butternut, de soba, d'œufs brouillés et de salade de persil. Agrémentez d'amandes. Servez immédiatement.

Trucs Santé

Les soba auraient été créées au Japon afin de pallier une déficience en vitamine B1 dans l'organisme de populations qui consomment essentiellement du riz blanc, pauvre en vitamine B1, et qui s'alimentent fréquemment de poissons crus, dont certains contiennent de la thiaminase, une enzyme qui détruit la vitamine B1.

Trucs de Chef

Les soba (« sarrasin » en japonais) sont, comme leur nom japonais l'indique, des pâtes de sarrasin de couleur beige que vous trouverez en magasin bio et dans toute épicerie spécialisée dans les produits asiatiques. Elles sont très populaires au Japon, au même titre que les ramen et les udon. On les sert aussi bien froides que chaudes. Attention pour les intolérants au gluten : choisissez des soba 100 % sarrasin, car certaines pâtes vendues sous l'appellation soba contiennent aussi de la farine de blé.

Bouillon de légumes, tofu, soba, champignons, courgette

VÉGÉTALIEN

Préparation
10 minutes

Cuisson
5 minutes

Pour 2 bowls
40 g de nouilles soba
320 g de champignons de Paris
2 cuillerées à soupe d'huile d'olive
2 petites courgettes
1 petit bouquet de coriandre fraîche
2 oignons nouveaux
20 g de cacahuètes
70 cl de bouillon de légumes
1 cuillerée à soupe de sauce de soja
120 g de tofu
Sel, poivre du moulin

1 Faites cuire les soba dans un grand volume d'eau bouillante salée. Égouttez-les et rincez-les.

2 Coupez la base du pied des champignons, lavez-les en les passant rapidement sous un filet d'eau. Coupez-en les deux tiers en quartiers. Poêlez ceux-ci avec une cuillerée à soupe d'huile d'olive et un peu de sel sur feu vif afin de les colorer sur toutes leurs faces.

3 Lavez, parez les courgettes puis coupez-les en rondelles épaisses. Faites-les colorer à la poêle sur feu vif avec une cuillerée à soupe d'huile d'olive et un peu de sel.

4 Lavez la coriandre, hachez grossièrement les tiges et les feuilles. Pelez et émincez les oignons nouveaux. Hachez grossièrement les cacahuètes. Dans un petit saladier, mélangez ces trois ingrédients.

5 Portez le bouillon de légumes à ébullition, ajoutez la sauce de soja, poivrez et mélangez.

6 Rincez et égouttez le tofu, puis coupez-le en cubes. Coupez le dernier tiers des champignons en lamelles.

7 Garnissez deux bols de soba, de champignons de Paris cuits et crus, de tofu, de courgettes et de salade de coriandre. Arrosez le tout de bouillon de légumes. Servez immédiatement.

Trucs Santé

Le tofu est riche en protéines végétales (14,6 %) d'excellente qualité. Le soja, son ingrédient de base, est en effet une des seules protéines du monde végétal qui contienne tous les acides aminés essentiels. Il est également une source intéressante d'acides gras oméga 3, de calcium et de magnésium.*

Trucs de Chef

Comme les soba, le tofu est disponible sous diverses formes dans les magasins bios et les épiceries asiatiques.

VÉGÉTALIEN

Vermicelles de soja, carotte, concombre, pomme, salade d'herbes

Préparation
10 minutes

Cuisson
3 minutes

Pour 2 bowls
45 g de vermicelles de soja
2 carottes, soit environ 200 g
230 g de concombre
1/2 pomme Granny Smith
Le jus de 1/2 citron
2 oignons nouveaux
1/2 bouquet de coriandre fraîche
20 g de cacahuètes
Une vingtaine de feuilles de menthe fraîche

La sauce
4 cuillerées à soupe de sauce pour rouleaux de printemps (marque Ayam® en grande distribution)
2 cuillerées à soupe de sauce de soja
Le jus de 1/2 citron

1 Faites bouillir de l'eau, retirez-la du feu et plongez-y les vermicelles de soja. Au bout de 3 minutes, égouttez-les puis coupez-les grossièrement avec des ciseaux de cuisine.

2 Pelez et parez les carottes, râpez-les à la râpe à gros trous.

3 Lavez le concombre. Coupez-le en tranches fines dans le sens de la longueur, autour des graines. Coupez ces tranches en fins bâtonnets.

4 Coupez la demi-pomme en deux. Retirez le cœur et coupez chaque quartier en fines tranches, puis en triangles. Citronnez-les légèrement pour éviter l'oxydation.

5 Pelez et émincez les oignons nouveaux. Lavez la coriandre ; hachez grossièrement les feuilles et les tiges. Hachez grossièrement les cacahuètes.

6 Dans un petit saladier, mélangez les herbes, les oignons nouveaux et les cacahuètes.

7 Préparez la sauce : dans un bol, mélangez la sauce pour rouleaux de printemps, la sauce de soja et le jus de citron.

8 Garnissez deux bols de vermicelles de soja, de pomme, de carottes, de concombre et de salade d'herbes. Assaisonnez l'ensemble avec la sauce. Agrémentez de graines de sésame. Servez.

Trucs Santé

Cette recette est riche en herbes fraîches, avec l'association de la menthe et de la coriandre. La coriandre se démarque par sa teneur en vitamine K, indispensable à la coagulation sanguine, et sa richesse en potassium associée un faible apport en sodium, produisant un effet diurétique. Enfin, les feuilles de coriandre et de menthe fraîches contiennent des caroténoïdes, dont le bêtacarotène.

Trucs de Chef

La sauce pour rouleaux de printemps s'achète en grande distribution sous la marque Ayam®.

Vermicelles de soja, radis noir, courgette, cocos plats, tofu

SANS GLUTEN

Préparation
10 minutes

Cuisson
5 minutes

Pour 2 bowls
130 g de cocos plats
120 g de tofu
1 cuillerée à soupe d'huile d'olive
50 g de vermicelles de soja
65 g de radis noir
130 g de courgette
1 petit bouquet de coriandre fraîche
Sel, poivre du moulin

La sauce
4 cuillerées à soupe de sauce pour nems (nuóc-cham, ou marque Ayam®, en grande surface)
1 cuillerée à soupe de sauce de soja
2 cuillerées à soupe de jus de citron
1 cuillerée à soupe d'huile de sésame
1 cuillerée à soupe d'huile d'olive
2 cuillerées à soupe de graines de sésame
Poivre du moulin

1 Coupez les cocos plats en morceaux d'environ 1,5 cm de largeur. Faites-les cuire 5 minutes dans un grand volume d'eau bouillante salée. Égouttez-les et rafraîchissez-les immédiatement dans de l'eau glacée. Égouttez-les de nouveau.

2 Égouttez le tofu, séchez-le avec du papier absorbant. Coupez-le en gros cubes. Faites-les colorer 5 minutes sur toutes leurs faces dans une poêle sur feu vif avec l'huile d'olive. Salez et poivrez en cours de cuisson.

3 Faites bouillir de l'eau, retirez-la du feu et plongez-y les vermicelles de soja. Au bout de 3 minutes, égouttez-les puis coupez-les grossièrement avec des ciseaux de cuisine.

4 Préparez la sauce : dans un petit bol, mélangez la sauce pour nems, la sauce de soja, le jus de citron, l'huile de sésame, l'huile d'olive et les graines de sésame. Poivrez.

5 Pelez le radis noir. Râpez-le à l'aide d'une râpe à gros trous. Lavez et parez la courgette. Râpez-la à l'aide d'une râpe à gros trous. Lavez la coriandre et effeuillez-la grossièrement.

6 Garnissez deux bols de vermicelles de soja, de courgette et de radis noir râpés, de haricots plats et de tofu. Arrosez l'ensemble de vinaigrette. Agrémentez de coriandre. Servez immédiatement.

Trucs Santé

Le radis noir est moins souvent consommé que le radis rose. Pourtant, tout en étant plus riche en glucides que ce dernier, il est aussi mieux pourvu en potassium et en calcium. Sa teneur en vitamine C (100 mg pour 100 g) est d'autant plus remarquable qu'il conserve bien mieux cette vitamine que ne le font les légumes feuilles. Comme les choux, il renferme des composés appelés indols qui suscitent beaucoup d'intérêt en vue de la recherche contre le cancer.

Trucs de Chef

Selon votre préférence, vous pouvez servir tous les ingrédients séparés ou mélangés dans les bols.
Pour une version végétalienne de cette recette, vous pouvez remplacer la sauce pour nems par un mélange de 4 cuillerées à soupe de jus d'orange et 1 cuillerée à soupe de sirop d'érable.

Patate douce, lentilles corail, jeunes pousses, carottes

Préparation
25 minutes

Cuisson
25 minutes

Pour 4 bowls
- 100 g de lentilles corail
- 10 g de gingembre frais
- 1/4 de gousse d'ail
- 1 cuillerée à soupe de crème fraîche épaisse
- 2 cuillerées à soupe de jus de citron
- 1 cuillerée à soupe de tahini ou de purée de sésame blanc
- 2 patates douces, soit environ 1 kg
- 2 cuillerées à soupe d'huile d'olive
- 4 carottes de taille moyenne
- 100 g de jeunes pousses
- 30 g de pistaches en coques
- 40 g de graines de courge
- Sel

La vinaigrette
- Quelques branches d'estragon
- 4 cuillerées à soupe d'huile d'olive
- 2 cuillerées à soupe de jus de citron
- 2 cuillerées à soupe de sauce Worcestershire
- Sel, poivre du moulin

1 Rincez les lentilles corail. Faites-les cuire dans 3 fois leur volume d'eau salée pendant 15 à 20 minutes. Égouttez-les et rincez-les.

2 Pelez le gingembre et râpez-le à la râpe Microplane. Écrasez l'ail dans un presse-ail.

3 Mixez les lentilles corail avec la crème fraîche, le jus de citron, le tahini et la pulpe d'ail. Salez et poivrez. Versez la préparation dans une casserole et faites-la chauffer sur feu doux, en mélangeant régulièrement, pendant une dizaine de minutes afin de l'épaissir légèrement. Laissez refroidir.

4 Préchauffez le four à 210 °C. Pelez les patates douces. Coupez la chair en gros cubes. Déposez-les sur une plaque allant au four et enrobez-les d'huile d'olive. Salez et faites cuire de 25 à 30 minutes au four. Remuez les patates douces à mi-cuisson.

5 Préparez la vinaigrette : effeuillez et émincez l'estragon. Dans un bol, mélangez la sauce Worcestershire, le jus de citron, 4 cuillerées à soupe d'huile d'olive et l'estragon. Salez et poivrez.

6 Parez et pelez les carottes. Râpez-les à la râpe à gros trous. Mélangez les carottes râpées avec la moitié de la vinaigrette.

7 Lavez et essorez les jeunes pousses. Assaisonnez-les avec le reste de vinaigrette.

8 Décoquillez les pistaches et hachez-les grossièrement.

9 À l'aide de deux cuillères à soupe, réalisez des quenelles de lentilles corail.

10 Garnissez quatre bols de patates douces rôties, de jeunes pousses, d'une quenelle de lentilles corail et de carottes râpées. Agrémentez de pistaches et de graines de courge. Servez.

Trucs Santé

La patate douce est riche en glucides complexes et en fibres (2,9 g/100 g), ce qui lui permet de bénéficier d'un index glycémique bas. Plus sa chair est colorée, puis elle apporte de provitamine A, qui a des effets bénéfiques sur le système immunitaire et qui permet également la synthèse des pigments de l'œil, prévenant ainsi divers troubles de la vue.*

Trucs de Chef

Vous pouvez utiliser la crème de lentilles corail juste mixée. Dans ce cas, faites-la chauffer, déposez-en un peu au fond de chaque bol et ajoutez le reste des ingrédients. Le tahini, ou purée de sésame blanc, s'achète en magasin bio ou dans les épiceries orientales.

Semoule de chou, riz noir, piment, endive

VÉGÉTALIEN

SANS GLUTEN

Préparation
10 minutes

Cuisson
45 minutes

Pour 2 bowls

55 g de riz noir (appelé aussi riz Venere ou riz Nérone)
200 g de chou-fleur
200 g de piments doux
1 cuillerée à soupe d'huile d'olive
1 endive
10 g de graines de courge
10 g de graines de tournesol
Sel

La vinaigrette

2 cuillerées à café de vinaigre de vin rouge
1 cuillerée à café de moutarde de Dijon
2 cuillerées à soupe d'huile d'olive
Sel

1 Rincez le riz noir, couvrez-le de deux fois son volume d'eau dans une casserole, puis faites-le cuire sur feu doux pendant 45 minutes à couvert.

2 Préparez la vinaigrette : dans un bol, mélangez le vinaigre avec du sel, puis ajoutez la moutarde de Dijon et l'huile d'olive.

3 Lavez le chou-fleur. Mixez-le jusqu'à obtenir une texture semblable à une semoule. Mélangez celle-ci avec la moitié de la vinaigrette.

4 Lavez les piments. Enrobez-les d'huile d'olive et salez-les. Saisissez-les sur feu très vif au gril ou dans une poêle-gril en fonte.

5 Ôtez les premières feuilles de l'endive et coupez celle-ci en quatre dans le sens de la longueur.

6 Garnissez deux bols de riz noir, de piments, d'endive et de semoule de chou-fleur. Assaisonnez l'endive avec le reste de vinaigrette. Agrémentez de graines de courge et de graines de tournesol. Servez.

Trucs Santé

Voici une recette généreuse en piment. Le principal atout des piments est leur teneur en vitamine C, laquelle, entre autres, favorise l'absorption du fer et accélère la cicatrisation ; et également en vitamine A. Enfin, ils contiennent de la capsaïcine, un alcaloïde extrêmement puissant qui fait saliver, active la digestion et aiderait à faire baisser le taux de cholestérol.*

Trucs de Chef

Le riz noir peut être remplacé par du riz noir de Camargue. Vous en trouverez dans les magasins bios et en grande surface sous la marque Riso Gallo®. Vérifiez toujours la force d'un piment en goûtant un petit morceau avant de l'incorporer à une recette, afin de bien le doser et d'éviter toute mauvaise surprise.

SANS GLUTEN

Pois chiches, grenade, fenouil, céleri, orange, carotte

VÉGÉTALIEN

Préparation
15 minutes
(Réhydratation 12 heures)

Cuisson
1 heure

Pour 2 bowls
80 g de pois chiches secs
80 g de baies de grenade
2 belles carottes
1 petit bulbe de fenouil
60 g de petites feuilles de céleri branche
1 orange
Une dizaine de feuilles d'estragon
2 cuillerées à soupe d'huile d'olive
Sel, poivre du moulin

1 Faites tremper les pois chiches pendant 12 heures. Égouttez-les et faites-les cuire 1 heure à l'eau bouillante salée. Égouttez-les et rincez-les. Dans un bol, mélangez-les avec les baies de grenade.

2 Pelez et parez les carottes, puis râpez-les à la râpe à gros trous. Coupez la base du bulbe de fenouil. Lavez-le puis émincez-le. Lavez et essorez les feuilles de céleri branche. Hachez-les grossièrement.

3 Coupez la base et le sommet de l'orange. Ôtez la peau et la partie blanche à l'aide d'un couteau tranchant en suivant la courbure du fruit afin de n'avoir plus que la chair à vif. Faites des incisions en V en lisière des membranes qui séparent chaque quartier pour prélever les suprêmes.

4 Pour la vinaigrette, pressez le reste de l'orange au-dessus d'un bol afin de récupérer le maximum de jus. Hachez les feuilles d'estragon et ajoutez-les. Ajoutez l'huile d'olive, salez, poivrez et mélangez.

5 Garnissez deux bols de pois chiches à la grenade, de salade de feuilles de céleri, de fenouil et de carottes râpées. Assaisonnez de vinaigrette à l'orange et à l'estragon. Servez.

Trucs Santé

La grenade est riche en fibres (3,5 %) essentiellement insolubles qui stimulent le transit, surtout quand elle est associée aux pois chiches. Ce fruit est aussi une bonne source de vitamine B6, laquelle intervient dans la régulation de l'influx nerveux. Enfin, avec la grenade et l'orange, la vitamine C est bien représentée dans la recette.

Trucs de Chef

N'hésitez pas à aromatiser l'eau de cuisson des pois chiches avec une carotte pelée, un oignon coupé en deux et une feuille de laurier. Vous pouvez utiliser une orange sanguine si vous en trouvez : le résultat n'en sera que meilleur.

Pois chiches, mâche, roquette, avocat, pomme, concombre

SANS GLUTEN

Préparation

10 minutes

(Réhydratation 12 heures)

Cuisson

1 heure 30

Pour 2 bowls

75 g de pois chiches secs
80 g de concombre
50 g de roquette
50 g de mâche
1/2 pomme de type Pink Lady
Le jus de 1/2 citron
1 avocat
2 cuillerées à café
de graines de sésame
Sel

La vinaigrette

2 cuillerées à soupe
de vinaigre de cidre
4 cuillerées à soupe d'huile d'olive
1 cuillerée à café de miel
Sel, poivre du moulin

1 Faites tremper les pois chiches pendant 12 heures. Égouttez-les et faites-les cuire 1 heure 30 à l'eau bouillante salée. Égouttez-les et rincez-les. Dans un bol, mélangez-les avec les baies de grenade.

2 Préparez la vinaigrette : dans un petit bol, mélangez le vinaigre de cidre, l'huile d'olive et le miel. Salez et poivrez.

3 Coupez le concombre en quartiers, puis en tranches afin d'obtenir de petits triangles. Lavez et essorez la roquette et la mâche.

4 Coupez la demi-pomme en deux, retirez le cœur et coupez chaque quartier en tranches fines. Citronnez légèrement la chair afin d'éviter qu'elle ne s'oxyde.

5 Coupez l'avocat en deux et dénoyautez-le. Récupérez la chair à l'aide d'une cuillère à soupe en rasant l'écorce pour détacher les deux moitiés. Coupez chacune en tranches épaisses. Citronnez légèrement la chair pour éviter qu'elle ne s'oxyde.

6 Garnissez deux bols de pois chiches, de mâche, de roquette, d'avocat, de concombre et de pomme. Assaisonnez le tout avec la vinaigrette. Agrémentez de graines de sésame. Servez.

Trucs Santé

Les pois chiches, dans cette recette, fournissent l'essentiel des protéines. Pour optimiser la qualité protéique de l'ensemble, on ajoutera un morceau de pain en accompagnement. On apprécie par ailleurs le profil lipidique grâce à l'avocat, aux graines de sésame et à l'huile d'olive.

Trucs de Chef

Pour un résultat encore plus explosif en bouche, vous pouvez remplacer la pomme Pink Lady par une pomme Granny Smith.

Pour une recette végétalienne, remplacez le miel par du sirop d'érable.

Pois chiches, pamplemousse, carotte, mâche, verveine, noisettes

SANS GLUTEN

VÉGÉTALIEN

Préparation
10 minutes
(Réhydratation 12 heures)

Cuisson
1 heure 30

Pour 2 bowls
- 80 g de pois chiches secs
- 2 pamplemousses
- 20 g de noisettes
- 2 belles carottes
- 40 g de mâche

La vinaigrette
- Le jus du pamplemousse (voir recette)
- 2 cuillerées à soupe d'huile d'olive
- Le jus de 1/2 citron
- 1 cuillerée à soupe de verveine séchée
- Sel, poivre du moulin

1 Faites tremper les pois chiches 12 heures dans un grand volume d'eau. Égouttez-les et faites-les cuire 1 heure 30 à l'eau bouillante salée. Égouttez-les et rincez-les.

2 Coupez la base et le sommet des pamplemousses. Ôtez la peau au couteau en suivant la courbure de l'agrume et en prenant soin de ne pas laisser de partie blanche. Faites des incisions en V en lisière des membranes qui séparent chaque quartier pour prélever les suprêmes.

3 Pour obtenir la vinaigrette, pressez le restant des pamplemousses au-dessus d'un bol afin de récupérer le jus. Ajoutez l'huile d'olive, le jus de citron et la verveine émiettée. Salez, poivrez et mélangez.

4 Coupez les noisettes en tranches. Faites-les dorer dans une poêle antiadhésive sans matière grasse sur feu vif.

5 Pelez et parez les carottes, puis coupez-les en fines rondelles. Lavez et essorez la mâche.

6 Garnissez deux bols de pois chiches, de mâche, de suprêmes de pamplemousse et de rondelles de carotte. Assaisonnez le tout de vinaigrette à la verveine. Agrémentez de noisettes grillées. Servez.

Trucs Santé

Le pomelo est un fruit peu sucré et peu calorique, mais sa saveur acidulée et sa petite amertume stimulent les sécrétions digestives. Il est également une source de vitamine P, exerçant une action favorable sur la résistance des petits vaisseaux sanguins.

Trucs de Chef

N'hésitez pas à aromatiser l'eau de cuisson des pois chiches avec une carotte pelée, un oignon coupé en deux et une feuille de laurier. En saison, profitez de la verveine fraîche. Coupez alors les feuilles en petits morceaux.

Quinoa, endive, radis, avocat, courgette

SANS GLUTEN

VÉGÉTALIEN

Préparation
10 minutes

Cuisson
20 minutes

Pour 2 bowls
55 g de quinoa
2 courgettes
1 cuillerée à soupe d'huile d'olive
12 radis roses
1 belle endive
1 avocat
Le jus de 1/2 citron
2 cuillerées à café
de graines de pavot
Sel

La vinaigrette
10 feuilles d'estragon
2 cuillerées à soupe
de vinaigre de xérès
2 cuillerées à soupe d'huile d'olive
1 cuillerée à café de miel
1 cuillerée à café
de moutarde de Dijon
Sel

1 Couvrez le quinoa d'eau dans une casserole. Salez, portez à ébullition et faites cuire de 10 à 15 minutes sur feu moyen. Égouttez et rincez le quinoa.

2 Lavez et parez les courgettes ; coupez-les en rondelles épaisses. Poêlez-les avec l'huile d'olive et un peu de sel sur feu vif en les colorant sur leurs deux faces.

3 Lavez les radis. Coupez-les en fines rondelles. Coupez la base de l'endive puis effeuillez celle-ci.

4 Coupez l'avocat en deux et dénoyautez-le. Récupérez la chair à l'aide d'une cuillère à soupe en rasant l'écorce pour détacher les deux moitiés. Coupez chacune en tranches épaisses. Citronnez légèrement la chair pour éviter qu'elle ne s'oxyde.

5 Préparez la vinaigrette : émincez les feuilles d'estragon. Dans un bol, mélangez le vinaigre, l'huile d'olive, le miel, la moutarde et l'estragon. Salez.

6 Garnissez deux bols de quinoa, d'avocat, de radis, d'endive et de courgettes. Assaisonnez de vinaigrette le quinoa, les radis, l'endive et l'avocat. Agrémentez de graines de pavot. Servez.

Trucs Santé

Les graines de pavot, avec leur petit goût de noisette, sont une source intéressante d'oméga 3, lesquels manquent à l'huile d'olive utilisée pour l'assaisonnement de cette recette. Le pavot contient également de l'iode, du magnésium, du manganèse, du cuivre et du zinc.

Trucs de Chef

Pour obtenir une recette végane, il suffit de remplacer le miel par du sirop d'érable.

Champignons crus et cuits, courgette, tomate, riz complet au nori

Préparation
15 minutes

Cuisson
35 minutes

Pour 2 bowls
55 g de riz complet
300 g de champignons de Paris
1 gousse d'ail entière, fendue
2 courgettes, soit environ 275 g
1 feuille d'algue nori
100 g de tomates cerises
20 g de noix de cajou
1 petit bouquet de coriandre fraîche
1/2 piment vert
Huile d'olive, sel, poivre du moulin

La vinaigrette
1 échalote, pelée (retirez aussi la première couche)
1 cuillerée à café de moutarde de Dijon
2 cuillerées à café de nuoc-mâm
4 cuillerées à café de sauce de soja
2 cuillerées à café de vinaigre de riz
2 cuillerées à café d'huile de sésame
4 cuillerées à soupe d'huile d'olive

1 Faites cuire le riz complet à l'eau salée pendant environ 20 minutes ou jusqu'à ce qu'il soit tendre. Égouttez-le.

2 Préparez la vinaigrette : pelez l'échalote, retirez-en la première couche. Émincez l'échalote. Dans un petit bol, mélangez la moutarde, le nuoc-mâm, la sauce de soja, le vinaigre de riz, l'huile de sésame, l'huile d'olive et l'échalote. Réservez.

3 Coupez la partie terreuse du pied des champignons, lavez ceux-ci. Coupez-en la moitié en tranches épaisses. Dans un saladier, mélangez-les soigneusement avec la moitié de la vinaigrette.

4 Coupez l'autre moitié des champignons en quartiers et faites-les colorer 5 minutes sur feu vif dans une poêle chaude avec 1 cuillerée à soupe d'huile d'olive et la gousse d'ail. Salez en cours de cuisson. Réservez (récupérez la gousse d'ail).

5 Lavez les courgettes. Coupez-les en rondelles. Faites-les colorer sur leurs deux faces 10 minutes dans une poêle chaude avec 1 cuillerée à soupe d'huile d'olive et la gousse d'ail sur feu vif. Salez en cours de cuisson. Réservez.

6 Roulez la feuille de nori bien serré, puis coupez-la en fines lanières. Hachez-les. Ajoutez-les au riz.

7 Lavez les tomates cerises puis coupez-les en quartiers. Hachez grossièrement les noix de cajou. Lavez la coriandre. Coupez le piment vert en fines rondelles.

8 Garnissez deux bols de champignons marinés et cuits, de tomates cerises, de riz à l'algue nori et de courgettes. Agrémentez de coriandre, de noix de cajou et de piment. Assaisonnez avec le reste de la vinaigrette. Servez immédiatement.

Trucs Santé

Le terme nori désigne plusieurs variétés d'algues rouges aux reflets pourpres. Séchées, ces algues prennent une couleur vert sombre. La teneur en protéines du nori est exceptionnelle : environ 27 %, avec les dix acides aminés essentiels en bon équilibre. Elle apporte également des quantités intéressantes de vitamine A (carotène), B12, de fer et de zinc. Elle confère à cette recette sa saveur douce de thé fumé.*

Trucs de Chef

Choisissez de préférence des courgettes de petite taille et fermes, qui auront moins de graines. J'aime particulièrement les courgettes blanches qui ont la particularité de cuire plus rapidement que les vertes Dans une version qui ne serait plus que pesco-végétarienne ou dans le cas d'un régime sans gluten, vous pouvez remplacer la sauce de soja par du nuoc-mâm.

Champignons, avoine, œuf au plat

VÉGÉTARIEN

Préparation
25 minutes
(Réhydratation 12 heures)

Cuisson
40 minutes

Pour 2 bowls
50 g d'avoine décortiquée
150 g de pleurotes
210 g de trompettes-des-morts
230 g de pieds-de-mouton
250 g de chanterelles
150 g de champignons de Paris
30 g de beurre
1 œuf
1 branche de romarin
Sel, poivre du moulin

1 Faites tremper l'avoine dans de l'eau pendant 12 heures. Ce temps écoulé, rincez-la sous l'eau courante dans une passoire fine. Faites-la cuire sur feu doux avec 2 fois son volume d'eau pendant une quarantaine de minutes. Égouttez-la et rincez-la.

2 Lavez soigneusement les champignons et séchez-les avec du papier absorbant. Coupez les bases des pieds. Faites revenir chaque variété de champignon séparément, selon son temps de cuisson, dans une grande poêle sur feu vif avec, pour chacune, 5 g de beurre et un peu de sel.

3 Faites cuire l'œuf au plat dans une poêle avec 5 g de beurre sur feu moyen. Salez en fin de cuisson. À l'aide d'un emporte-pièce rond de 8,5 cm de diamètre, parez le blanc de l'œuf.

4 Prélevez les feuilles de la branche de romarin et hachez-les finement.

5 Garnissez les deux bols des différentes variétés de champignon, assaisonnées de romarin et de poivre selon votre goût, et d'avoine. Déposez un œuf au plat au centre de chaque bol. Servez immédiatement.

Trucs Santé

Les champignons, peu caloriques, figurent au centre de cette recette. Leur fraction lipidique est composée en partie de stérols végétaux qui ont une action bénéfique sur l'absorption du taux de cholestérol sanguin, d'autant plus intéressante associée à la consommation d'un œuf. On note également la présence d'ergostérol, qui agit comme précurseur de la vitamine D, faisant des champignons une source indirecte de cette vitamine.

Trucs de Chef

L'avoine décortiquée se trouve dans les magasins bios. Il est préférable de la faire tremper 12 heures pour réduire son temps de cuisson. Vous pouvez réaliser cette recette avec d'autres types de champignons en fonction de la saison et des arrivages chez votre primeur : cèpes, morilles, girolles...

Crème de butternut au carvi, œufs brouillés au riz complet, pomme Pink Lady

VÉGÉTARIEN

SANS GLUTEN

Préparation
10 minutes

Cuisson
25 minutes

Pour 2 bowls
La moitié de 1 butternut d'environ 350-400 g
1/2 cuillerée à café de graines de carvi
4 cuillerées à soupe de crème fraîche
4 gros œufs
10 g de beurre
1/2 pomme de type Pink Lady
37 g de riz complet
20 g de cacahuètes
Quelques brins de ciboulette
Un filet de jus de citron
Sel, poivre du moulin

1 Écrasez le carvi dans un mortier.

2 Lavez le butternut. À l'aide d'une cuillère à soupe, ôtez les graines. Coupez la chair en cubes de taille régulière. Faites-les cuire 25 minutes à la vapeur : la chair et la peau doivent être tendres. Mixez le tout avec 2 cuillerées à soupe de crème fraîche et le carvi ; salez et poivrez. Versez la crème dans une casserole et gardez-la au chaud sur feu très doux.

3 Faites cuire le riz complet à l'eau salée pendant environ 20 minutes ou jusqu'à ce qu'il soit tendre. Égouttez-le.

4 Cassez les œufs, faites-les cuire au bain-marie en mélangeant sans cesse à la fourchette. Lorsqu'ils deviennent des œufs brouillés homogènes, ajoutez le riz, 2 cuillerées à soupe de crème fraîche, le beurre, du sel et du poivre. Retirez du feu et mélangez une dernière fois.

5 Coupez la pomme en quartiers. Ôtez le trognon puis coupez chaque quartier en 4 tranches égales. Hachez grossièrement les cacahuètes. Ciselez finement la ciboulette.

6 Garnissez deux bols de crème de butternut au carvi, répartissez les œufs brouillés dessus. Ajoutez 4 morceaux de pomme par plat. Agrémentez de cacahuètes et de ciboulette. Servez immédiatement.

Trucs Santé

Cette recette est un concentré de protéines : les œufs ont longtemps été la protéine de référence, contenant les acides aminés indispensables en proportions idéales. Les céréales (riz) et les cacahuètes constituent une association complémentaire. Le butternut, le riz complet, les cacahuètes et la pomme fraîche vous assurent aussi près de 10 g de fibres, soit 40 % de vos besoins quotidiens.*

Trucs de Chef

Vous pouvez peler le butternut avant de le faire cuire à la vapeur. La cuisson sera un peu plus courte, mais je trouve que la peau apporte un goût plus marqué à cette crème.

Œuf, edamame, mâche, asperges, champignons

VÉGÉTARIEN

Préparation
10 minutes

Cuisson
5 minutes

Pour 2 bowls
6 belles asperges vertes
160 g d'edamame surgelés (Picard®)
50 g de mâche
20 g de cacahuètes
130 g de champignons de Paris
2 gros œufs extra frais
Sel

La sauce
Le jus de 1/2 petit citron
2 cuillerées à café de purée de cacahuète
1 cuillerée à soupe de sauce de soja
2 cuillerées à soupe d'huile d'olive
Poivre du moulin

1 Cassez la base de la tige des asperges afin d'éliminer la partie ligneuse. Faites cuire les asperges à l'eau bouillante salée en les gardant croquantes, puis rafraîchissez-les immédiatement dans de l'eau glacée. Égouttez-les et séchez-les avec du papier absorbant.

2 Faites décongeler les edamame au four à micro-ondes avec un peu d'eau. Lavez et essorez la mâche. Hachez grossièrement les cacahuètes.

3 Préparez la sauce : dans un bol, mélangez le jus de citron, la purée de cacahuète, la sauce de soja, l'huile d'olive. Poivrez.

4 Coupez le pied terreux des champignons. Lavez-les rapidement sous un filet d'eau froide. Coupez-les en tranches.

5 Faites bouillir de l'eau dans une casserole. Baissez le feu. Cassez 1 œuf dans un petit bol. À l'aide d'une cuillère à soupe, agitez l'eau de la casserole d'un mouvement circulaire afin de créer un tourbillon central. Versez l'œuf au centre et laissez cuire 3 minutes. Récupérez l'œuf avec une écumoire et déposez-le sur du papier absorbant. Parez-le si nécessaire. Recommencez avec l'autre œuf.

6 Garnissez deux bols d'asperges vertes, d'edamame, de champignons de Paris et de mâche. Arrosez le tout de sauce. Déposez 1 œuf au centre de chaque bol. Agrémentez de cacahuètes. Servez.

Trucs Santé

La cacahuète, également appelée arachide, a mauvaise réputation. Pourtant, c'est une source de graisses insaturées et de protéines de qualité intéressante. À condition de la choisir non salée, il est intéressant de l'intégrer dans une recette.

Trucs de Chef

En saison, vous pouvez remplacer les edamame par des fèves fraîches. Écossez-les puis ébouillantez-les quelques secondes avant de les rafraîchir rapidement dans de l'eau glacée. Pelez ensuite les fèves en les incisant légèrement avec les ongles.
La purée de cacahuète s'achète également dans les magasins bios. Il ne faut pas la confondre avec le beurre de cacahuète qui est parfois sucré.

Œuf, avoine, aubergine, laitue, tomate, parmesan

VÉGÉTARIEN

Préparation
10 minutes
(Réhydratation 12 heures)

Cuisson
40 minutes

Pour 2 bowls
90 g d'avoine décortiquée
1/2 aubergine, soit environ 200 g
1 gousse d'ail
1 cuillerée à soupe d'huile d'olive
2 gros œufs
1/2 oignon rouge
50 g de feuilles de laitue
20 g de parmesan
120 g de tomates cerises
Sel

La vinaigrette
2 cuillerées à café de vinaigre de cidre
3 cuillerées à soupe d'huile d'olive
Sel, poivre du moulin

1 Faites tremper l'avoine pendant 12 heures (toute une nuit par exemple), puis rincez-la dans une passoire fine. Faites-la cuire sur feu doux dans 2 fois son volume d'eau pendant environ 40 minutes. Égouttez-la et rincez-la.

2 Lavez et parez l'aubergine, coupez-la en gros cubes. Fendez la gousse d'ail sans la peler.

3 Faites chauffer une grande poêle sur feu moyen avec l'huile d'olive et la gousse d'ail. Faites-y revenir les cubes d'aubergine pendant 25 minutes en mélangeant de temps en temps et en salant en cours de cuisson.

4 Faites cuire les œufs durs (environ 10 minutes). Écalez-les et coupez-les en deux.

5 Préparez la vinaigrette : dans un bol, mélangez le vinaigre de cidre et l'huile d'olive ; salez et poivrez.

6 Pelez et émincez l'oignon rouge. Lavez et essorez la laitue. Ajoutez l'oignon, puis la vinaigrette.

7 Taillez le parmesan en copeaux.

8 Garnissez chaque bol d'un œuf dur, d'avoine, de tomates cerises, de cubes d'aubergine et de laitue à l'oignon rouge. Agrémentez de copeaux de parmesan.

Trucs Santé

Les œufs bénéficient de protéines d'excellente qualité, complétées ici par les protéines du parmesan. Cette recette est parfaite dans un menu végétarien.

Trucs de Chef

L'avoine décortiquée se trouve en magasin bio. Il est préférable de la faire tremper pour réduire son temps de cuisson.

Œuf, pleurotes, riz noir, parmesan, roquette

SANS GLUTEN

VÉGÉTARIEN

Préparation
20 minutes

Cuisson
45 minutes

Pour 2 bowls
90 g de riz noir (appelé aussi riz Venere ou riz Nérone)
1 échalote
240 g de pleurotes
20 g de beurre
40 g de noisettes en coques
50 g de roquette
50 g de parmesan
2 gros œufs extra-frais
Sel

La vinaigrette
2 cuillerées à soupe de vinaigre balsamique
2 cuillerées à soupe d'huile d'olive
Sel, poivre du moulin

1 Rincez le riz noir, couvrez-le de deux fois son volume d'eau dans une casserole, puis faites-le cuire sur feu doux pendant 45 minutes à couvert. Salez l'eau en fin de cuisson. Égouttez le riz.

2 Pelez et émincez l'échalote. Lavez rapidement les pleurotes et coupez la base des pieds. Fendez les pleurotes afin d'obtenir des morceaux de taille régulière. Faites fondre le beurre dans une grande poêle jusqu'à ce qu'il prenne une couleur noisette. Faites-y revenir les pleurotes sur feu vif pendant 2 minutes. Ajoutez l'échalote, un peu de sel, et poursuivez la cuisson 2 minutes.

3 Préparez la vinaigrette : mélangez le vinaigre balsamique et l'huile d'olive ; salez et poivrez.

4 Décortiquez les noisettes. Hachez-les grossièrement et faites-les dorer dans une poêle antiadhésive sans matière grasse en remuant très régulièrement.

5 Lavez et essorez la roquette. Taillez le parmesan en copeaux. Dans un saladier, mélangez la roquette, les noisettes et le parmesan.

6 Faites bouillir de l'eau dans une casserole. Baissez le feu. Cassez 1 œuf dans un petit bol. À l'aide d'une cuillère à soupe, agitez l'eau de la casserole d'un mouvement circulaire afin de créer un tourbillon central. Versez l'œuf au centre et laissez cuire 3 minutes. Récupérez l'œuf avec une écumoire et déposez-le sur du papier absorbant. Parez-le si nécessaire. Recommencez avec l'autre œuf.

7 Garnissez deux bols de salade de roquette, de riz noir et de pleurotes. Placez un œuf poché au centre de ces éléments. Servez immédiatement.

Trucs Santé

Les pleurotes n'apportent que 25 kcal aux 100 g, principalement sous forme de protéines. Elles sont bien pourvues en potassium et faibles en sodium, ce qui leur confère des propriétés diurétiques. Associées à la roquette et au riz noir, elles donnent une préparation riche en fibres.

Trucs de Chef

Le riz noir peut être remplacé par du riz noir de Camargue. Vous en trouverez dans les magasins bios et en grande surface sous la marque Riso Gallo®. Attention : cette marque mentionne la possibilité de traces de gluten dans son produit.
Afin que le blanc de l'œuf coagule plus vite et plus facilement, ajoutez un peu de vinaigre blanc dans l'eau de pochage. Cela simplifie l'opération mais modifie le goût de l'œuf : à vous de choisir.

Œuf, avoine, épinards, chou-fleur, gruyère, noisettes

VÉGÉTARIEN

Préparation
20 minutes
(Réhydratation 12 heures)

Cuisson
40 minutes

Pour 2 bowls
65 g d'avoine décortiquée
280 g de feuilles d'épinard
10 g de beurre
1 cuillerée à soupe de crème fraîche
2 gros œufs
20 g de noisettes
120 g de chou-fleur
60 g de gruyère suisse
Sel

La vinaigrette
1 cuillerée à soupe d'huile d'olive
1 cuillerée à café de vinaigre de cidre
Sel, poivre du moulin

1 Faites tremper l'avoine pendant 12 heures (toute une nuit par exemple), puis rincez-la dans une passoire fine. Faites-la cuire sur feu doux dans 2 fois son volume d'eau pendant environ 40 minutes. Égouttez-la et rincez-la.

2 Ôtez les côtes centrales des feuilles d'épinard. Lavez et essorez celles-ci, puis faites-les fondre pendant 5 minutes dans une grande poêle avec le beurre. Salez ; ajoutez la crème fraîche en fin de cuisson.

3 Faites cuire les œufs durs (environ 10 minutes). Écalez-les et coupez-les en deux.

4 Hachez grossièrement les noisettes. Faites-les dorer dans une poêle antiadhésive sans matière grasse sur feu vif.

5 Préparez la vinaigrette : dans un bol, mélangez le vinaigre de cidre et l'huile d'olive ; salez et poivrez.

6 Lavez le chou-fleur, coupez-le en petites sommités. Coupez le gruyère en fines tranches.

7 Garnissez deux bols d'un œuf dur chacun, d'avoine, d'épinards, de chou-fleur et de tranches de gruyère. Assaisonnez le chou-fleur de vinaigrette. Agrémentez de noisettes. Servez.

Trucs Santé

En associant œuf, épinards, gruyère et beurre, cette recette vous aidera à compléter fortement vos apports en vitamine A, tant directement sous forme de rétinol que sous forme de bêtacarotènes, leurs précurseurs végétaux.

Trucs de Chef

L'avoine décortiquée se trouve en magasin bio. Il est préférable de la faire tremper pour réduire son temps de cuisson.

Œufs, tomate, fèves, piment, quinoa, noisettes

SANS GLUTEN

VÉGÉTARIEN

Préparation
10 minutes

Cuisson
20 minutes

Pour 2 bowls
- 50 g de quinoa
- 4 gros œufs
- 2 cuillerées à soupe de crème fraîche
- 10 g de beurre
- 115 g de fèves surgelées avec leur peau (Picard®)
- 120 g de tomates cerises
- 1 piment vert doux
- 20 g de noisettes
- 2 cuillerées à café d'huile d'olive
- Une dizaine de feuilles de menthe fraîche
- Sel, fleur de sel et poivre du moulin

1 Couvrez le quinoa d'eau dans une casserole. Salez, portez à ébullition et faites cuire de 10 à 15 minutes sur feu moyen. Égouttez et rincez le quinoa.

2 Cassez les œufs, faites-les cuire au bain-marie en mélangeant sans cesse à la fourchette. Lorsqu'ils deviennent des œufs brouillés homogènes, ajoutez la crème fraîche et le beurre. Salez et poivrez. Retirez du feu et mélangez une dernière fois.

3 Plongez les fèves dans une casserole d'eau bouillante. À la reprise de l'ébullition, égouttez-les, plongez-les dans de l'eau glacée, puis pelez-les en les pinçant entre le pouce et l'index.

4 Lavez les tomates cerises et coupez-les en deux ou en quatre selon leur taille. Lavez le piment doux et coupez-le en fines rondelles. Dans un bol, mélangez les tomates et les rondelles de piment.

5 Hachez grossièrement les noisettes. Faites-les dorer dans une poêle antiadhésive sans matière grasse sur feu vif.

6 Garnissez deux bols d'œufs brouillés, de fèves, du mélange tomate-piment et de quinoa. Assaisonnez les fèves et les tomates d'huile d'olive, de sel et de poivre du moulin. Agrémentez de noisettes et de quelques feuilles de menthe fraîche. Servez immédiatement.

Trucs Santé

Le beurre et les œufs sont de bonnes sources de vitamine D. Cette vitamine D joue un rôle très important dans notre organisme : elle facilite l'absorption du calcium et du phosphore, favorisant ainsi la minéralisation des os et des dents.

Trucs de Chef

Vérifiez toujours la force d'un piment en le goûtant avant de l'incorporer à une recette, afin de bien le doser et d'éviter toute mauvaise surprise.

Poissons

Saumon aux flocons d'avoine, jeunes pousses, aubergine au poivron et aux noisettes

Préparation
10 minutes

Cuisson
25 minutes

Pour 2 bowls
1 petite aubergine d'environ 280 g
1 gousse d'ail en chemise
1/2 poivron vert
20 g de noisettes
1 dizaine de grandes feuilles de basilic et quelques petites feuilles pour la décoration
320 g de saumon
50 g de gros flocons d'avoine
70 g de jeunes pousses de salade et d'herbes
1 cuillerée à soupe de vinaigre balsamique
80 g de sauce tomate
Huile d'olive, sel, poivre du moulin

1 Lavez l'aubergine et coupez la chair en cubes d'environ 1 cm. Incisez légèrement la gousse d'ail.

2 Faites chauffer une grande poêle sur feu moyen avec 1 cuillerée à soupe d'huile d'olive et la gousse d'ail. Faites-y revenir les cubes d'aubergine avec un peu de sel pendant 25 minutes en mélangeant de temps en temps à l'aide d'une spatule.

3 Pelez le demi-poivron à l'aide d'un économe. Éliminez les renflements et les graines. Coupez la chair en lanières puis en petits dés.

4 Hachez grossièrement les noisettes. Faites-les dorer dans une poêle antiadhésive sans matière grasse en remuant constamment.

5 Posez les grandes feuilles de basilic l'une sur l'autre. Roulez-les serré, comme un cigare, puis émincez-les.

6 Dans un petit saladier, mélangez l'aubergine avec le poivron, les noisettes, le basilic, 1 cuillerée à soupe d'huile d'olive, du sel et du poivre du moulin.

7 Coupez le saumon en deux pavés de 160 g chacun. Versez les flocons d'avoine dans une assiette plate, ajoutez un peu de sel. Enrobez-en soigneusement toutes les faces des pavés de saumon.

8 Faites chauffer une poêle antiadhésive sur feu vif avec une cuillerée à soupe d'huile d'olive. Déposez-y les pavés de saumon et saisissez-les 1 minute par face. Coupez-les ensuite en tranches épaisses.

9 Dans un saladier, assaisonnez les pousses d'une cuillerée à soupe d'huile d'olive, une cuillerée à soupe de vinaigre balsamique, de sel et de poivre du moulin.

10 Versez la sauce tomate au fond de deux bols. Garnissez de tranches de saumon panées aux flocons d'avoine, de jeunes pousses et d'aubergine au poivron. Décorez de quelques petites feuilles de basilic. Servez immédiatement.

Trucs Santé

L'association du saumon, qui contient en moyenne 20 % de protéines d'excellente qualité, et des flocons d'avoine, qui contiennent 11 % de protéines et dont l'index glycémique est particulièrement bas, donne à cette recette un fort pouvoir rassasiant.

Trucs de Chef

Choisissez de préférence des aubergines de petite taille, elles contiendront moins de graines. Préférez aussi le saumon sauvage au saumon d'élevage : il sera moins gras. Je préfère ôter la peau du poivron, car celle-ci est difficile à digérer et apporte une amertume assez désagréable.

Saumon, riz basmati complet au nori, concombre, mayonnaise light au wasabi

Préparation
40 minutes

Cuisson
25 minutes

Pour 2 bowls
70 g de riz basmati complet
1 feuille d'algue nori
200 g de concombre
20 g d'oignon nouveau
30 g de cornichons
Quelques brins d'aneth
320 g de saumon
Sel

La mayonnaise sans huile
1 jaune d'œuf
Un peu de wasabi
1 cuillerée à soupe de sauce de soja
1 cuillerée à café de jus de citron
2 cuillerées à soupe de cream cheese (Philadelphia®, Kiri®, Saint-Môret®...)
2 cuillerées à soupe de yaourt

1 Dans un bol, confectionnez la mayonnaise sans huile en fouettant le jaune d'œuf, le wasabi, la sauce de soja, le jus de citron, le *cream cheese* et le yaourt jusqu'à obtenir une texture lisse. Gardez la préparation 30 minutes au réfrigérateur afin qu'elle se raffermisse.

2 Rincez le riz, égouttez-le et faites-le cuire sur feu doux avec deux fois son volume d'eau et un peu de sel jusqu'à absorption totale du liquide.

3 Roulez la feuille de nori très serré, coupez-la en fines lanières puis hachez-la. Dans un saladier, mélangez le riz basmati et les paillettes de nori.

4 Coupez le concombre en fines tranches. Mettez-les dans une passoire, salez-les abondamment et laissez-les dégorger 30 minutes. Rincez-les soigneusement pour éliminer le sel. Pressez le concombre entre vos mains pour évacuer le maximum d'humidité.

5 Pelez l'oignon nouveau et émincez-le finement. Coupez les cornichons en rondelles. Hachez l'aneth ; gardez quelques pluches pour la décoration.

6 Dans un petit saladier, mélangez le concombre, les oignons nouveaux et les cornichons.

7 Coupez le saumon en tranches épaisses comme un sashimi.

8 Garnissez deux bols de saumon, de riz basmati au nori et de concombre. Placez au centre la mayonnaise sans huile. Agrémentez de quelques pluches d'aneth. Servez immédiatement.

Trucs Santé

Le jaune d'œuf qui sert de base à la mayonnaise apporte une quantité appréciable de vitamine D, tout comme le saumon qui en contient 10 µg pour 100 g. La vitamine D joue des rôles très importants dans l'organisme : elle facilite l'absorption du calcium et du phosphore, favorisant la minéralisation des os et des dents, et garantissant ainsi leur solidité.

Trucs de Chef

Préférez du saumon sauvage au saumon d'élevage, il sera moins gras.
Vous pouvez remplacer le wasabi par de la crème de raifort.
Dans le cas d'un régime sans gluten, remplacez la sauce de soja par du sel.

Saumon fumé, pomme, riz basmati, asperges grillées et crues

SANS GLUTEN

Préparation
10 minutes

Cuisson
20 minutes

Pour 2 bowls
12 asperges vertes
1 cuillerée à soupe d'huile d'olive
1/2 pomme Pink Lady
Un peu de jus de citron
40 g de riz basmati complet
20 g de noisettes décortiquées
20 feuilles de menthe fraîche
Quelques pluches d'aneth
4 tranches de saumon fumé, soit environ 160 g
Sel

La vinaigrette
Le jus de 1/2 citron
2 cuillerées à soupe d'huile d'olive
Sel, poivre du moulin

1 Cassez la base ligneuse des asperges vertes. Coupez-en huit en deux dans le sens de la longueur. Enrobez-les d'huile d'olive et salez-les légèrement. Saisissez-les pendant 3 minutes sur un gril ou dans une poêle-gril en fonte sur feu vif. Coupez les quatre asperges restantes en très fines tranches, légèrement de biais.

2 Rincez le riz, égouttez-le et faites-le cuire sur feu doux avec deux fois son volume d'eau et un peu de sel jusqu'à absorption totale du liquide.

3 Coupez la demi-pomme en quartiers. Ôtez le cœur et coupez chaque quartier en fines tranches, puis en deux. Citronnez-les légèrement.

4 Coupez les noisettes en deux. Faites-les griller dans une poêle antiadhésive sans matière grasse sur feu vif en remuant constamment.

5 Préparez la vinaigrette : dans un petit bol, mélangez le jus de citron et l'huile d'olive. Salez légèrement et poivrez.

6 Mélangez les feuilles de menthe et les pluches d'aneth.

7 Garnissez deux bols de saumon fumé, de riz basmati complet, de pomme et d'asperges grillées et crues. Assaisonnez la pomme et les asperges de vinaigrette au jus de citron. Agrémentez d'herbes et de noisettes grillées. Servez.

Trucs Santé

La fabrication du saumon fumé nécessite une étape de salage, au cours de laquelle les filets sont disposés en couches successives avec du gros sel marin. Cette technique permet de limiter le dessèchement du poisson et assure une meilleure conservation. Choisissez de préférence un saumon fumé de qualité, non congelé au préalable, et évitez l'ajout de sel.

Trucs de Chef

Préférez le saumon fumé sauvage au saumon d'élevage. Son prix est un peu plus élevé, mais il est beaucoup moins gras.

Saumon, choux de Bruxelles, avoine, chou chinois, shiitake, orange

Préparation
25 minutes
(Réhydratation 12 heures)

Cuisson
40 minutes

Pour 2 bowls
1 pavé de saumon de 160 g, avec la peau
1/4 de chou chinois
2 cuillerées à soupe d'huile d'olive
200 g de shiitaké
150 g de choux de Bruxelles
60 g d'avoine décortiquée
1 orange
2 oignons nouveaux
20 g de noix de macadamia
Sel

La vinaigrette
Le jus de l'orange (voir recette)
2 cuillerées à soupe de nuoc-mâm
2 cuillerées à soupe d'huile d'olive
1 cuillerée à café de miel
Poivre du moulin

1 Faites tremper l'avoine dans de l'eau pendant 12 heures. Ce temps écoulé, rincez-la sous l'eau courante dans une passoire fine. Faites-la cuire sur feu doux avec 2 fois son volume d'eau pendant une quarantaine de minutes. Égouttez-la et rincez-la.

2 Coupez le chou chinois en lanières en partant du sommet jusqu'à la base ; éliminez celle-ci. Poêlez les lanières de chou pendant 4 à 5 minutes sur feu moyen avec une cuillerée à soupe d'huile d'olive et un peu de sel.

3 Coupez le pied des shiitake. Lavez-les soigneusement et séchez-les dans du papier absorbant. Coupez-les en deux ou en quatre. Faites-les revenir pendant 5 minutes dans une grande poêle antiadhésive sur feu vif avec une cuillerée à soupe d'huile d'olive et du sel en remuant régulièrement.

4 Coupez la base des choux de Bruxelles puis effeuillez-les. Faites blanchir les feuilles 2 minutes à l'eau bouillante salée, plongez-les immédiatement dans de l'eau glacée, puis égouttez-les.

5 Coupez le pavé de saumon en deux. Salez-les. Déposez-les côté peau vers le bas dans une poêle antiadhésive sans matière grasse et commencez la cuisson sur feu moyen à vif, jusqu'à ce que le tiers inférieur de la chair ait blanchi. Retournez-les et poursuivez la cuisson jusqu'à ce que le tiers inférieur ait blanchi et le tiers central paraisse cru.

6 Ôtez la peau et la partie blanche de l'orange à l'aide d'un couteau tranchant en suivant la courbure du fruit afin de n'avoir plus que la chair à vif. Prélevez les suprêmes. Pour la vinaigrette, pressez le reste de l'orange au-dessus d'un bol pour récupérer le jus. Ajoutez le nuoc-mâm, l'huile d'olive et le miel. Poivrez, mélangez.

7 Dans un saladier, mélangez les feuilles de chou de Bruxelles, les suprêmes d'orange, l'oignon nouveau émincé et une partie de la vinaigrette.

8 Garnissez deux bols de ces ingrédients. Assaisonnez le chou chinois et les morceaux de saumon avec le reste de vinaigrette. Agrémentez de noix de macadamia grossièrement hachées. Servez immédiatement.

Trucs Santé

Les choux de Bruxelles sont source de fibres, mais surtout de vitamines C et B9 qui participent toutes les deux au bon fonctionnement du système immunitaire et aident à réduire la fatigue.

Trucs de Chef

L'avoine décortiquée se trouve dans les magasins bios.
Préférez le saumon sauvage au saumon d'élevage, il sera moins gras.

Saumon, chou rouge, pomme, quinoa, laitue

SANS GLUTEN

Préparation
10 minutes

Cuisson
15 minutes

Pour 2 bowls
40 g de quinoa
120 g de chou rouge
1/4 de pomme Pink Lady
50 g de feuilles de laitue
1 pavé de saumon de 240 g, avec la peau
20 g de noix de macadamia
Sel

La sauce au yaourt
2 petites échalotes
1 branche de persil plat
1 yaourt brassé
1 pointe de wasabi
2 cuillerées à soupe de jus de citron
Sel, poivre du moulin

1 Couvrez le quinoa d'eau dans une casserole. Salez, portez à ébullition et faites cuire de 10 à 15 minutes sur feu moyen. Égouttez et rincez le quinoa.

2 Préparez la sauce : pelez et émincez les échalotes. Rincez la branche de persil plat ; hachez finement les feuilles et les rameaux les plus fins. Dans un bol, mélangez le yaourt, le wasabi, les échalotes, le jus de citron et le persil. Salez et poivrez.

3 Émincez le chou rouge. Retirez le cœur du morceau de pomme et râpez celui-ci à la râpe à gros trous. Dans un saladier, mélangez le chou et la pomme avec une partie de la sauce au yaourt.

4 Lavez et essorez les feuilles de laitue. Dans un saladier, mélangez-les avec le reste de la sauce au yaourt.

5 Passez légèrement le doigt sur le filet de saumon pour vérifier qu'il ne reste plus d'arête. S'il en reste, ôtez-les à l'aide d'une pince à arêtes. Coupez le pavé de saumon en deux moitiés égales. Salez-les. Déposez-les côté peau vers le bas dans une poêle antiadhésive sans matière grasse et commencez la cuisson sur feu moyen à vif, jusqu'à ce que le tiers inférieur de la chair ait blanchi. Retournez les pavés et poursuivez la cuisson jusqu'à ce que le tiers inférieur ait blanchi. Pour une parfaite cuisson, le tiers central doit paraître cru.

6 Hachez grossièrement les noix de macadamia.

7 Garnissez deux bols d'un morceau de pavé de saumon chacun, de quinoa, de chou rouge et de laitue. Agrémentez de noix de macadamia. Servez.

Trucs Santé

Sans ajout de matières grasses, cette recette contient essentiellement les graisses du saumon et des noix de macadamia, c'est-à-dire des graisses essentiellement polyinsaturées intéressantes pour le système cardio-vasculaire et un apport en acides gras essentiels sous forme d'EPA et DHA directement utilisables par l'organisme.

Trucs de Chef

Vous pouvez remplacer les feuilles de laitue par de jeunes pousses de betterave. Préférez le persil plat au persil frisé, car il est bien plus aromatique.

Saumon, courgette, épinards, spaghettis, tomate

Préparation
20 minutes

Cuisson
10 minutes

Pour 2 bowls

35 g de spaghettis à la farine intégrale
1 pavé de saumon d'environ 300 g, avec la peau
1 courgette
1 cuillerée à soupe d'huile d'olive + 2 cuillerées à soupe pour les pâtes
50 g de tomates cerises
280 g de feuilles d'épinard
10 g de beurre
1 cuillerée à soupe de crème fraîche épaisse
Sel, poivre du moulin

1 Faites cuire les spaghettis dans un grand volume d'eau bouillante salée. Rincez-les et égouttez-les.

2 Passez légèrement le doigt sur le pavé de saumon afin de vérifier qu'il ne reste plus d'arête. S'il en reste, ôtez-les à l'aide d'une pince à arêtes. Entaillez la chair à l'extrémité la plus fine du pavé, puis passez la lame d'un couteau bien aiguisé entre la peau et la chair en maintenant bien la peau contre le plan de travail. Faites glisser la lame jusqu'au bout du pavé pour retirer la peau. Coupez la chair en gros cubes et salez-les. Colorez-les sur feu vif dans une poêle antiadhésive sans matière grasse, entre 30 et 40 secondes par face (le cœur doit rester cru).

3 Lavez et parez la courgette. Coupez-la en tranches épaisses. Faites-les colorer 5 minutes à la poêle avec 1 cuillerée à soupe d'huile d'olive sur feu moyen à vif.

4 Lavez les tomates cerises, coupez-les en deux ou en quatre selon leur taille.

5 Ôtez la côte centrale de chaque feuille d'épinard. Lavez et essorez les feuilles, et faites-les fondre 5 minutes dans une grande poêle avec le beurre et un peu de sel. Ajoutez la crème fraîche en fin de cuisson.

6 Garnissez deux bols de cubes de saumon, de spaghettis, d'épinards, de rondelles de courgette et de tomates cerises. Arrosez les pâtes d'huile d'olive. Poivrez selon votre goût. Servez.

Trucs Santé

L'utilisation de pâtes intégrales dans cette recette stimule l'apport en fibres, ce qui ralentit la digestion et la vidange gastrique, favorisant une sensation durable de satiété. C'est d'autant plus le cas si les pâtes sont cuites al dente. Veillez à bien mastiquer.

Trucs de Chef

Plusieurs marques proposent une gamme de pâtes intégrales ou complètes en grande distribution. Vous en trouverez à coup sûr en magasin bio.
Vous pouvez ajouter quelques feuilles de basilic à la garniture finale de cette recette.

Saumon, mangue, fruit de la passion, concombre, avocat, riz basmati

Préparation
20 minutes

Pour 2 bowls
30 g de riz basmati complet
1 pavé de saumon d'environ 300 g, avec la peau
1/2 mangue
1 fruit de la passion
1/2 avocat
Un peu de jus de citron
50 g de concombre
2 oignons nouveaux
1 petit bouquet de coriandre fraîche
2 cuillerées à café de graines de sésame
Poivre du moulin

La vinaigrette
2 cuillerées à soupe de sauce de soja
2 cuillerées à soupe de jus de citron
2 cuillerées à soupe d'huile d'olive
Poivre du moulin

1 Rincez le riz, égouttez-le et faites-le cuire sur feu doux avec deux fois son volume d'eau et un peu de sel jusqu'à absorption totale du liquide.

2 Passez légèrement le doigt sur le pavé de saumon afin de vérifier qu'il ne reste plus d'arête. S'il en reste, ôtez-les à l'aide d'une pince à arêtes. Entaillez la chair à l'extrémité la plus fine du pavé, puis passez la lame d'un couteau bien aiguisé entre la peau et la chair en maintenant bien la peau contre le plan de travail. Faites glisser la lame jusqu'au bout du pavé pour retirer la peau. Coupez la chair en tranches épaisses, puis en lanières, puis en cubes réguliers.

3 Coupez en deux la demi-mangue, pelez-la, coupez la chair en tranches, celles-ci en lanières puis en cubes de taille régulière. Récupérez les graines du fruit de la passion à l'aide d'une petite cuillère. Mélangez les deux ingrédients.

4 Dénoyautez l'avocat. Récupérez la chair à l'aide d'une cuillère à soupe en rasant l'écorce. Coupez-la en tranches, puis en lanières, puis en cubes de taille régulière. Citronnez légèrement la chair pour éviter qu'elle ne s'oxyde.

5 Lavez le concombre. Coupez-le en tranches dans le sens de la longueur, autour des graines. Coupez les tranches en lanières puis en cubes de taille régulière.

6 Préparez la vinaigrette : dans un bol, mélangez la sauce de soja, le jus de citron et l'huile d'olive. Poivrez.

7 Pelez et émincez les oignons nouveaux. Lavez la coriandre, hachez grossièrement les feuilles et les tiges. Mélangez la coriandre et les oignons nouveaux.

8 Garnissez les deux bols de tartare de saumon, de concombre, d'avocat, de mélange mangue-passion, de riz basmati complet et de salade de coriandre. Assaisonnez le tout de la vinaigrette à la sauce de soja. Agrémentez de graines de sésame. Servez immédiatement.

Trucs Santé

La note sucrée apportée par le fruit de la passion et la mangue offre un bon apport en provitamine A antioxydante. L'avocat, l'huile d'olive et les graines de sésame fournissent quant à eux une belle quantité de vitamine E. Un joli cocktail antioxydant !*

Trucs de Chef

Ce bol peut être présenté avec les ingrédients séparés ou mélangés. Pour encore plus de fraîcheur, vous pouvez remplacer le riz basmati complet par de petits dés de pomme Granny Smith. Le riz basmati complet se trouve dans les magasins bios et en grande surface sous la marque Taureau Ailé®.

Lentilles, saumon fumé, canneberges, concombre, oignon rouge

Préparation
30 minutes

Cuisson
20 minutes

Pour 2 bowls
90 g de lentilles vertes du Puy
300 g de concombre
1 feuille d'algue nori
1 oignon rouge
2 tranches de saumon fumé, soit 80 g
80 g de canneberges séchées
1 cuillerée à soupe de graines de sésame
Sel

La vinaigrette
1 cuillerée à soupe de vinaigre de riz
1 cuillerée à soupe de sauce de soja
2 cuillerées à soupe d'huile d'olive
Poivre du moulin

1 Mettez les lentilles dans une casserole et couvrez largement d'eau. Portez à ébullition, couvrez et comptez 25 minutes de cuisson sur feu doux. Égouttez les lentilles.

2 Coupez le concombre en très fines tranches. Recueillez-les dans une passoire, salez-les abondamment puis laissez-les dégorger une demi-heure. Rincez-les abondamment et pressez-les entre vos mains pour éliminer le maximum d'humidité.

3 Enroulez la feuille de nori, coupez-la en fins filaments puis hachez ceux-ci. Dans un bol, mélangez le concombre et les paillettes d'algue.

4 Pelez et émincez l'oignon rouge.

5 Dans un bol, préparez la vinaigrette : mélangez le vinaigre de riz, la sauce de soja et l'huile d'olive. Poivrez.

6 Garnissez deux bols de lentilles, de saumon, de concombre au nori et de canneberges séchées. Arrosez les lentilles, les oignons et le concombre de vinaigrette. Agrémentez de graines de sésame. Servez.

Trucs Santé

Cette recette utilise les protéines des lentilles pour compléter l'apport du saumon et assurer, par la même occasion, un complément en fer et magnésium. De plus, avec le concombre et sa peau ainsi que des canneberges séchées, elle ne manque pas de fibres !

Trucs de Chef

Préférez le saumon fumé sauvage au saumon d'élevage. Son prix est un peu plus élevé, mais il est moins gras.
N'hésitez pas à aromatiser l'eau de cuisson des lentilles avec une carotte pelée, un oignon coupé en deux et une feuille de laurier, mais ne salez surtout pas l'eau : le sel a tendance à durcir les lentilles.

Cabillaud au sésame et au nori, riz basmati, edamame, brocoli

Préparation
10 minutes

Cuisson
20 minutes

Pour 2 bowls
120 g de riz basmati complet
1 feuille d'algue nori
6 cuillerées à soupe de graines de sésame
1 blanc d'œuf
300 g de dos de cabillaud
120 g de brocoli
2 cuillerées à soupe d'huile d'olive
160 g d'edamame surgelés (Picard®)
20 g de cacahuètes
Sel, poivre du moulin

La vinaigrette
2 cuillerées à soupe de sauce de soja
2 cuillerées à soupe de jus de citron
1 cuillerée à café de moutarde de Dijon
2 cuillerées à soupe d'huile d'olive

1 Rincez le riz et faites-le cuire sur feu doux dans deux fois son volume d'eau salée jusqu'à absorption totale du liquide. Rincez-le et égouttez-le.

2 Préchauffez le four à 180 °C.

3 Mixez la feuille de nori afin d'obtenir des paillettes. Sur une assiette plate, mélangez-les avec les graines de sésame. Dans un bol, fouettez légèrement le blanc d'œuf à la fourchette.

4 Coupez le cabillaud en deux pavés. Salez-les légèrement, enrobez-les de blanc d'œuf, puis panez-les dans le mélange nori-sésame. Déposez-les sur une plaque de cuisson couverte de papier sulfurisé. Faites cuire 15 minutes au four.

5 Lavez le brocoli. Coupez les sommités en tranches épaisses. Enrobez-les d'huile d'olive et salez-les. Saisissez-les pendant 3 minutes sur un gril ou une poêle-gril en fonte à feu vif.

6 Faites décongeler les edamame au four à micro-ondes avec un peu d'eau.

7 Pour obtenir la vinaigrette, mélangez dans un bol la sauce de soja, le jus de citron, la moutarde, le reste de panure nori-sésame, l'huile d'olive et du poivre du moulin.

8 Hachez grossièrement les cacahuètes.

9 Garnissez deux bols d'un pavé de cabillaud, d'edamame, de brocoli et de riz basmati complet. Assaisonnez de vinaigrette les edamame, le riz et le brocoli. Agrémentez de cacahuètes. Servez immédiatement.

Trucs Santé

Le dos de cabillaud est au cœur de cette recette. Ce poisson à la chair fondante est une source de protéines intéressante (plus de 20 %), tout en étant particulièrement maigre avec moins de 1 % de lipides. Il permet également de compléter les apports en iode, en sélénium et en vitamine B12.

Trucs de Chef

Le riz basmati complet se trouve dans les magasins bios et en grande surface sous la marque Taureau Ailé®.

Cabillaud, flocons d'avoine à la vanille, tomates, parmesan, asperges, fèves

Préparation
15 minutes

Cuisson
10 minutes

Pour 2 bowls

240 g de dos de cabillaud
4 belles asperges vertes
3 cuillerées à soupe d'huile d'olive
85 g de fèves congelées, avec leur peau (Picard®)
60 g de tomates cerises
20 g de parmesan
1 petite branche de romarin
1/2 gousse de vanille
100 g de gros flocons d'avoine
10 cl de lait demi-écrémé
Sel, fleur de sel, poivre du moulin

1 Coupez le cabillaud en deux pavés. Salez-les et faites-les cuire à la vapeur une petite dizaine de minutes. Poivrez selon votre goût.

2 Coupez les asperges vertes en deux dans le sens de la longueur. Enrobez-les d'une cuillerée à soupe d'huile d'olive et salez-les. Faites-les colorer pendant 3 minutes sur un gril ou une poêle-gril en fonte sur feu vif.

3 Plongez les fèves dans une casserole d'eau bouillante. À la reprise de l'ébullition, égouttez-les, plongez-les dans de l'eau glacée, puis pelez-les en les pinçant entre le pouce et l'index.

4 Lavez les tomates cerises et coupez-les en deux ou en quatre selon leur taille. Taillez le parmesan en copeaux. Effeuillez le romarin et hachez-le. Fendez la vanille et grattez-la avec le dos d'un couteau sur une planche afin de récupérer les graines.

5 Dans un bol, mélangez les flocons d'avoine, le lait et les graines de vanille. Salez et poivrez.

6 Garnissez deux bols d'un pavé de cabillaud, de flocons d'avoine à la vanille, de tomates cerises, d'asperges et de fèves. Assaisonnez les tomates et les fèves d'huile d'olive, de fleur de sel et de poivre du moulin. Agrémentez de copeaux de parmesan et de romarin haché. Servez.

Trucs Santé

Bien que riche en calories, le parmesan est un fromage intéressant par sa densité nutritionnelle. Il est en effet riche en vitamines A, B2, B3 et B12. Côté minéraux, il est extrêmement bien pourvu en phosphore et en calcium. La bonne portion est de 20 g par personne.

Trucs de Chef

Pour que votre cabillaud garde toute sa blancheur une fois cuit, poivrez-le au poivre blanc.

Cabillaud, orange, concombre, riz basmati, carotte, cassis

SANS GLUTEN

Préparation
15 minutes

Cuisson
20 minutes

Pour 2 bowls
100 g de riz basmati complet
240 g de dos de cabillaud
20 g de beurre
2 cuillerées à soupe d'huile neutre (par exemple de pépins de raisin)
1 orange
1 belle carotte
100 g de concombre
20 g de baies de cassis
20 g de noix de cajou
Sel, poivre du moulin

La vinaigrette
2 cuillerées à soupe d'huile d'olive
2 cuillerées à soupe de jus de citron
Quelques brins d'aneth, hachés
Sel, poivre du moulin

1 Rincez le riz et faites-le cuire sur feu doux dans deux fois son volume d'eau salée jusqu'à absorption totale du liquide. Rincez-le et égouttez-le.

2 Coupez le cabillaud en deux pavés. Salez-les sur les deux faces. Faites chauffer une poêle sur feu moyen à fort avec le beurre et l'huile neutre. Faites-y colorer les pavés de cabillaud sur les deux faces en les arrosant régulièrement de leur matière grasse à l'aide d'une cuillère.

3 Coupez la base et le sommet de l'orange. Ôtez la peau et la partie blanche à l'aide d'un couteau tranchant en suivant la courbure du fruit afin de n'avoir plus que la chair à vif. Faites des incisions en V en lisière des membranes qui séparent chaque quartier pour prélever les suprêmes.

4 Pour la vinaigrette, pressez le reste de l'orange au-dessus d'un bol afin de récupérer le maximum de jus. Ajoutez l'huile d'olive, le jus de citron et l'aneth haché. Salez, poivrez et mélangez bien.

5 Lavez le concombre et coupez-le en fines tranches. Pelez et parez les carottes, puis râpez-les à l'aide d'une râpe à gros trous. Lavez les baies de cassis. Hachez grossièrement les noix de cajou.

6 Garnissez les deux bols d'un pavé de cabillaud, de carotte râpée, de rondelles de concombre, de suprêmes d'orange et de riz basmati complet. Assaisonnez la carotte et le concombre avec la vinaigrette au jus d'orange. Agrémentez de baies de cassis et de noix de cajou. Servez.

Trucs Santé

Avec des crudités, de l'orange, du cassis et du jus de citron, cette recette apporte une bonne quantité de vitamine C. Celle-ci favorisera l'absorption du fer apporté par le cabillaud. Une bonne alliance !

Trucs de Chef

Le riz basmati complet se trouve dans les magasins bios et en grande surface sous la marque Taureau Ailé®.

Cabillaud, saumon, pois chiches, algues, concombre, salade

Préparation
15 minutes
(Réhydratation 12 heures)

Cuisson
1 heure

Pour 2 bowls
55 g de pois chiches secs
40 g d'algues wakamé au sel
250 g de concombre
70 g de jeunes pousses de salade et d'herbes
120 g de dos de cabillaud
120 g de saumon frais
Sel

La sauce
1 tige de citronnelle
4 cuillerées à soupe de jus de citron
1 cuillerée à soupe de sauce de soja
1 cuillerée à café de miel liquide
1 cuillerée à soupe d'huile de sésame
1 cuillerée à soupe d'huile d'olive
1 cuillerée à soupe de graines de sésame

1 Faites tremper les pois chiches 12 heures dans un grand volume d'eau. Égouttez-les et faites-les cuire 1 heure à l'eau bouillante salée. Égouttez-les et rincez-les.

2 Préparez la sauce : coupez la base de la tige de citronnelle et ne conservez que le tiers inférieur. Ôtez les premières feuilles, puis émincez finement le reste. Dans un bol, mélangez le jus de citron, la sauce de soja, le miel, l'huile de sésame, l'huile d'olive, la citronnelle et les graines de sésame.

3 Faites tremper les wakamé pendant un quart d'heure dans une grande quantité d'eau. Égouttez-les et rincez-les pendant 3 minutes sous un filet d'eau claire. Égouttez-les de nouveau et laissez-les sécher à l'air libre. Hachez-les grossièrement et assaisonnez-les avec un quart de la vinaigrette.

4 Lavez le concombre et coupez-le en très fines tranches. Salez-le largement dans une passoire et laissez-le dégorger une demi-heure. Rincez-le abondamment et essorez-le dans vos mains pour éliminer le maximum d'eau. Assaisonnez-le avec un quart de la vinaigrette.

5 Lavez et essorez les jeunes pousses. Assaisonnez-les avec un quart de la vinaigrette.

6 Coupez le cabillaud et le saumon en gros cubes. Faites-les cuire à la vapeur pendant 2 à 3 minutes.

7 Garnissez deux bols de cubes de saumon et de cabillaud, de pois chiches, de concombre, de wakamé et de jeunes pousses. Assaisonnez le poisson et les pois chiches avec le reste de vinaigrette. Servez immédiatement.

Trucs Santé

Les pois chiches sont une source de glucides complexes (18,7 g/100 g) à absorption progressive, car associés à une bonne quantité de fibres. Côté minéraux, ils bénéficient d'un bon apport en magnésium, en fer et en phosphore (132 mg/100 g) tout en étant une source intéressante de vitamine B9 et d'oligo éléments (manganèse, cuivre et zinc).

Trucs de Chef

N'hésitez pas à aromatiser l'eau de cuisson des pois chiches avec une carotte pelée, un oignon coupé en deux et une feuille de laurier. Vous trouverez le wakamé au sel en vitrine réfrigérée dans les magasins bios.

Pois chiches, maquereau, carotte, orange, salade

SANS GLUTEN

Préparation
15 minutes
(Réhydratation 12 heures)

Cuisson
1 heure

Pour 2 bowls
55 g de pois chiches secs
1/2 bouquet de coriandre fraîche
20 g de sauce tomate
1 orange
1 belle carotte
40 g de jeunes pousses de salade et d'herbes
2 cuillerées à soupe d'huile d'olive
40 g de noisettes en coques
Les filets de 2 maquereaux frais (levés par votre poissonnier)
Sel, poivre du moulin

La vinaigrette à la coriandre
1 cuillerée à café de graines de coriandre
Le reste de la coriandre hachée (voir recette)
2 cuillerées à soupe d'huile d'olive
Sel, poivre du moulin

1 Faites tremper les pois chiches 12 heures dans un grand volume d'eau. Égouttez-les et faites-les cuire 1 heure à l'eau bouillante salée. Égouttez-les et rincez-les.

2 Lavez et essorez la coriandre ; hachez les feuilles et les tiges les plus fines.

3 Dans un saladier, mélangez les pois chiches, la sauce tomate et un tiers de la coriandre. Rectifiez l'assaisonnement.

4 Coupez la base et le sommet de l'orange. Ôtez la peau et la partie blanche à l'aide d'un couteau tranchant en suivant la courbure du fruit afin de n'avoir plus que la chair à vif. Faites des incisions en V en lisière des membranes qui séparent chaque quartier pour prélever les suprêmes.

5 Pour obtenir la vinaigrette, écrasez les graines de coriandre dans un mortier. Pressez le reste de l'orange au-dessus d'un bol afin de récupérer le jus. Ajoutez l'huile d'olive, les graines de coriandre moulues et le reste de coriandre fraîche. Salez, poivrez et mélangez bien.

6 Pelez et parez la carotte. Taillez-la en lanières à l'aide d'un économe. Assaisonnez-les avec une partie de la vinaigrette à la coriandre.

7 Lavez et essorez les jeunes pousses. Ajoutez les suprêmes d'orange et assaisonnez le tout avec une partie de la vinaigrette.

8 Décortiquez les noisettes. Hachez-les grossièrement et faites-les dorer dans une poêle antiadhésive sans matière grasse en remuant très régulièrement.

9 Faites chauffer l'huile d'olive dans une poêle sur feu moyen à vif. Saisissez-y les filets de maquereau 1 minute et demie côté peau et 1 minute côté chair.

10 Garnissez deux bols de filets de maquereau, de lanières de carotte, de salade de jeunes pousses et de pois chiches à la sauce tomate. Assaisonnez les filets de maquereau avec le reste de vinaigrette. Agrémentez de noisettes grillées. Servez immédiatement.

Trucs Santé

Bien qu'étant considéré comme ordinaire et bon marché, le maquereau est un poisson doté de nombreuses qualités nutritionnelles. Riche en protéines, il constitue une excellente source d'oméga 3. Il apporte du potassium et du phosphore, mais aussi du sélénium et de l'iode en quantité intéressante. Par ailleurs, il contient des vitamines A, B3, B12 et D.

N'hésitez pas à aromatiser l'eau de cuisson des pois chiches avec une carotte pelée, un oignon coupé en deux et une feuille de laurier. Vous pouvez utiliser une orange sanguine si vous en trouvez : le résultat n'en sera que meilleur.

Crème de butternut, crabe, olives, physalis, quinoa, emmental

SANS GLUTEN

Préparation
10 minutes

Cuisson
25 minutes

Pour 4 bowls
1/2 butternut d'environ 450 g
2 cuillerées à soupe de crème fraîche épaisse
20 g de beurre
100 g de quinoa
40 g de noisettes décortiquées
140 g de physalis
160 g d'olives noires non dénoyautées
200 g de chair de crabe
60 g d'emmental
Quelques brins d'estragon
2 cuillerées à soupe d'huile d'olive
Sel, poivre du moulin

1 Lavez le butternut et retirez ses graines à l'aide d'une cuillère à soupe. Coupez-la en cubes de taille égale. Faites-les cuire 25 minutes à la vapeur : la chair et la peau doivent être tendres. Mixez-la avec la crème fraîche, un peu d'eau de cuisson si nécessaire, du sel et du poivre du moulin. Versez la crème obtenue dans une casserole, ajoutez le beurre, mélangez et gardez sur feu très doux.

2 Couvrez le quinoa d'eau dans une casserole. Salez, portez à ébullition et faites cuire de 10 à 15 minutes sur feu moyen. Égouttez et rincez le quinoa.

3 Hachez grossièrement les noisettes. Faites-les dorer dans une poêle antiadhésive sans matière grasse sur feu vif.

4 Ôtez les fines membranes qui entourent les physalis. Lavez-les et coupez les plus grosses baies en deux. Rincez les olives noires. Râpez l'emmental à la râpe Microplane. Effeuillez puis émincez l'estragon.

5 Répartissez au fond de quatre bols la crème de butternut chaude. Garnissez de quinoa, de crabe, d'emmental, de physalis et d'olives noires. Agrémentez d'estragon, de noisettes grillées et d'huile d'olive. Servez immédiatement.

Trucs Santé

Un fort potentiel antioxydant pour cette recette : le physalis, en plus de son intérêt décoratif, est un petit fruit riche en vitamine C et bien pourvu en antioxydants. Ensuite, le butternut, intensément coloré, est riche en bêtacarotènes aux propriétés vitaminiques et antioxydantes.

Trucs de Chef

Si vous utilisez du crabe en boîte pour cette recette, n'oubliez pas de le rincer sous l'eau courante dans une passoire fine. N'hésitez pas à récupérer les graines de la butternut. Lavez-les et faites-les sécher à four doux. Elles seront délicieuses et pourront agrémenter les prochains bowls.

Crabe, quinoa, fèves, artichauts, salicornes, amarena

SANS GLUTEN

Préparation
20 minutes

Cuisson
10 minutes

Pour 2 bowls
- 80 g de salicornes fraîches
- 40 g de quinoa
- 170 g de fèves surgelées (Picard®)
- 4 gros artichauts poivrade
- 1 boîte de chair de crabe (120 g poids net)
- 2 cuillerées à soupe d'huile d'olive
- 10 amarenas italiennes

La vinaigrette
- 1 branche d'estragon
- 2 cuillerées à soupe de jus de citron
- 2 cuillerées à soupe d'huile d'olive
- Sel, poivre du moulin

1 Couvrez d'eau les salicornes et laissez-les légèrement dessaler pendant 30 minutes.

2 Couvrez le quinoa d'eau dans une casserole, salez, portez à ébullition sur feu moyen et faites cuire de 10 à 15 minutes. Égouttez et rincez le quinoa.

3 Plongez les fèves dans une casserole d'eau bouillante. À la reprise de l'ébullition, égouttez-les, plongez-les dans de l'eau glacée, puis pelez-les en les pinçant entre le pouce et l'index.

4 Cassez la base des tiges des artichauts. Ôtez les premières couches de feuilles jusqu'aux plus tendres. Coupez les artichauts aux deux tiers de leur hauteur, puis en quartiers. Poêlez-les avec l'huile d'olive et un peu de sel pendant environ 10 minutes sur feu moyen à vif.

5 Dans un bol, préparez la vinaigrette : effeuillez et émincez l'estragon. Mélangez le jus de citron, l'huile d'olive, l'estragon, du sel et du poivre du moulin.

6 Égouttez, rincez la chair de crabe et égouttez-la de nouveau afin d'éliminer l'eau de conservation.

7 Égouttez les salicornes. Hachez-les grossièrement.

8 Garnissez deux bols de chair de crabe, de quinoa, d'artichauts poivrades, de fèves et de salicornes. Assaisonnez les fèves et les artichauts avec la vinaigrette à l'estragon. Agrémentez d'amarenas. Servez.

Trucs Santé

Deux produits de la mer sont ici associés : le crabe, qui offre une excellente source de vitamine B12, de sélénium, de cuivre et de zinc ; et la salicorne, bien pourvue en iode, en phosphore, en vitamines A, C et D, en calcium, en magnésium, en fer, en silice, zinc et en manganèse. Une haute densité nutritionnelle !

Trucs de Chef

Vous trouverez les amarenas, cerises au sirop, dans les épiceries fines italiennes. Les salicornes fraîches s'achètent chez votre poissonnier. Choisissez de la chair de crabe en boîte de bonne qualité, avec des morceaux de pinces. Vous pouvez également vous fournir en chair de crabe fraîche en barquette chez votre poissonnier, ou décortiquer vous-même un tourteau ou une araignée de mer.

Coquilles Saint-Jacques, riz basmati, nori, edamame, poivron, cacahuètes

Préparation
20 minutes

Cuisson
20 minutes

Pour 2 bowls
60 g de riz basmati complet
1 feuille d'algue nori
160 g d'edamame surgelés (Picard®)
1 poivron
8 coquilles Saint-Jacques
20 g de beurre
20 g de cacahuètes
1/2 bouquet de coriandre fraîche
Sel, poivre du moulin

La vinaigrette au nori
1 cuillerée à soupe de nuoc-mâm
1 cuillerée à soupe de sauce de soja
1 cuillerée à soupe de jus de citron
2 cuillerées à soupe d'huile d'olive
1/3 des paillettes de nori (voir recette)
Poivre du moulin

1 Rincez et égouttez le riz. Couvrez-le de deux fois son volume d'eau dans une casserole, portez à ébullition, couvrez et baissez le feu. Faites cuire sur feu doux jusqu'à absorption totale du liquide. Égouttez le riz.

2 Mixez la feuille de nori afin d'obtenir des paillettes. Mélangez le riz basmati avec les deux tiers des paillettes de nori.

3 Faites décongeler les edamame au four à micro-ondes avec un peu d'eau.

4 Lavez le poivron et pelez-le avec un économe. Coupez-le en deux, éliminez le pédoncule et les côtes. Taillez la chair en fines lamelles.

5 Préparez la vinaigrette : dans un petit bol, mélangez le nuoc-mâm, la sauce de soja, le jus de citron, l'huile d'olive et le dernier tiers des paillettes de nori. Poivrez.

6 Vous pouvez demander à votre poissonnier de préparer les saint-jacques pour vous. Si vous voulez le faire vous-même, voici comment procéder : ouvrez-les en insérant un couteau à plat sous la coquille supérieure (plate) et en coupant sur tout le pourtour. Retirez les barbes et le corail en veillant à ne pas abîmer la noix. À l'aide d'une cuillère à soupe, détachez la noix de la coquille inférieure. Ôtez enfin le muscle tendineux qui se trouve sur un côté de la noix. Passez les noix sous un filet d'eau pour les nettoyer. Épongez-les dans du papier absorbant. Salez-les.

7 Faites fondre le beurre dans une poêle sur feu vif. Lorsqu'il crépite, faites-y colorer les noix pendant 1 minute 30 par face.

8 Hachez grossièrement les cacahuètes. Lavez la coriandre et hachez grossièrement les feuilles et les tiges.

9 Garnissez deux bols de noix de saint-jacques, d'edamame, de poivron vert et de riz basmati au nori. Assaisonnez les edamame et le poivron de vinaigrette au nori. Agrémentez de coriandre et de cacahuètes. Servez.

Trucs Santé

Le riz apporte une grande quantité de glucides, essentiellement sous forme d'amidon. Les fibres apportées par l'enveloppe du grain qui est conservée dans le riz complet, mais également par les poivrons, le nori et les edamame ralentissent l'assimilation de cet amidon et rassasient durablement.

Si vos coquilles Saint-Jacques sont grosses, réduisez la portion à trois noix par bol.

Crevettes, haricots verts, chou chinois, riz complet

SANS GLUTEN

Préparation
10 minutes

Cuisson
20 minutes

Pour 2 bowls
75 g de riz basmati complet
160 g de haricots verts
La moitié d'un petit chou chinois
10 g de beurre
150 g de petites crevettes cuites décortiquées, surgelées

La sauce coco
20 g de gingembre frais
Une vingtaine de feuilles de menthe
La moitié d'un petit bouquet de coriandre
10 cl de crème de coco
1 cuillerée à soupe de jus de citron
20 g de cacahuètes
Sel, poivre du moulin

1 Rincez le riz et faites-le cuire sur feu doux dans deux fois son volume d'eau salée jusqu'à absorption totale du liquide. Égouttez-le.

2 Équeutez les haricots verts. Faites-les cuire à l'eau bouillante salée puis rafraîchissez-les immédiatement dans de l'eau glacée pour préserver leur vert éclatant. Égouttez-les.

3 Coupez le chou chinois en deux quartiers, puis en lanières en partant du sommet jusqu'au dernier tiers, que vous éliminez. Poêlez les lanières pendant 4 à 5 minutes sur feu moyen avec le beurre et un peu de sel.

4 Plongez les crevettes surgelées dans une casserole d'eau bouillante. À la reprise de l'ébullition, égouttez-les et rafraîchissez-les dans de l'eau froide. Égouttez.

5 Préparez la sauce : pelez le gingembre en grattant sa peau à l'aide d'une petite cuillère. Râpez-le avec une râpe Microplane afin de récupérer la pulpe tout en éliminant les fibres. Lavez la menthe et la coriandre, puis hachez les feuilles. Dans un bol, mélangez la crème de coco, le gingembre râpé, les herbes et le jus de citron. Salez et poivrez.

6 Hachez grossièrement les cacahuètes.

7 Garnissez deux bols de haricots verts, de crevettes, de riz basmati complet et de chou chinois. Agrémentez de sauce coco aux herbes et de cacahuètes. Servez.

Trucs Santé

La crevette est une bonne source de protéines, tout en étant particulièrement pauvre en lipides, ce qui permet de l'associer aux cacahuètes et à la crème de coco sans surplus de gras. Elle assure par ailleurs un bon apport en vitamine B12, en phosphore et en sélénium.

Trucs de Chef

Vous pouvez remplacer le sel de la sauce coco aux herbes par de la sauce de soja. Le résultat sera plus typique et un peu moins esthétique.

Crevettes, quinoa, fenouil, orange, pamplemousse

SANS GLUTEN

Préparation
15 minutes

Cuisson
20 minutes

Pour 4 bowls
100 g de quinoa
240 g de crevettes cuites surgelées (Picard®)
1 orange
1 pamplemousse
1 beau bulbe de fenouil
40 g de noix de pécan
240 g de carottes
2 branches de thym frais

La vinaigrette aux agrumes
1 cuillerée à café de graines de carvi
Le jus des agrumes réservé (voir recette)
2 cuillerées à café de moutarde de Dijon
2 cuillerées à soupe d'huile d'olive
Sel, poivre du moulin

1 Couvrez le quinoa d'eau dans une casserole, salez, portez à ébullition sur feu moyen et faites cuire de 10 à 15 minutes. Égouttez-le et rincez-le.

2 Plongez les crevettes surgelées dans une casserole d'eau bouillante. À la reprise de l'ébullition, égouttez-les et rafraîchissez-les dans de l'eau glacée. Égouttez-les de nouveau.

3 Coupez la base et le sommet de l'orange et du pamplemousse. Ôtez la peau et la partie blanche à l'aide d'un couteau tranchant en suivant la courbure des fruits afin de n'avoir plus que la chair à vif. Faites des incisions en V en lisière des membranes qui séparent chaque quartier pour prélever les suprêmes. Recueillez-les dans un bol. Pressez le reste de l'orange et du pamplemousse au-dessus d'un autre bol pour récupérer le jus.

4 Préparez la vinaigrette : écrasez les graines de carvi dans un mortier. Mélangez-les au jus d'orange et de pamplemousse, ajoutez la moutarde et l'huile d'olive, salez, poivrez et fouettez bien.

5 Épluchez et parez les carottes, coupez-les en fines rondelles.

6 Lavez le fenouil. Coupez la base puis émincez le fenouil en carpaccio à l'aide d'une mandoline. Dans un petit saladier, mélangez-le fenouil avec les suprêmes d'orange et de pamplemousse en ajoutant une partie de la vinaigrette aux agrumes.

7 Hachez grossièrement les noix de pécan. Effeuillez le thym frais.

8 Garnissez quatre bols de salade de fenouil aux agrumes, de rondelles de carotte, de crevettes et de quinoa. Assaisonnez les carottes et les crevettes de vinaigrette aux agrumes. Agrémentez de noix de pécan et d'un peu de thym frais. Servez.

Trucs Santé

Le fenouil fait partie des légumes les plus riches en fer avec 2,7 mg pour 100 g, d'autant plus que son absorption est potentialisée par un apport élevé en vitamine C (52 mg/100 g), complété dans cette recette par la vitamine C contenue dans l'orange et le pamplemousse. Une alliance optimale !

Trucs de Chef

Pour obtenir une version végétarienne et végétalienne, végane de cette recette, ne mettez pas les crevettes.

Crevettes, vermicelles de soja, betterave, carotte, oignon nouveau

Préparation
15 minutes

Cuisson
4 minutes

Pour 2 bowls
40 g de vermicelles de soja
120 g de crevettes cuites surgelées (Picard®)
130 g de carotte
130 g de betterave
2 oignons nouveaux
1 bouquet de coriandre fraîche
20 g de cacahuètes

La sauce
2 cuillerées à soupe de sauce pour rouleaux de printemps
2 cuillerées à soupe de sauce pour nems (nuóc cham)
2 cuillerées à soupe de jus de citron
1 cuillerée à soupe de sauce de soja
Poivre du moulin

1 Faites bouillir de l'eau dans une petite casserole. Retirez du feu, ajoutez les vermicelles de soja et laissez reposer 3 minutes. Égouttez-les et rincez-les, puis coupez-les grossièrement avec des ciseaux.

2 Préparez la sauce : dans un bol, mélangez la sauce pour rouleaux de printemps, la sauce pour nems, le jus de citron, la sauce de soja et un peu de poivre du moulin.

3 Dans un petit saladier, enrobez les vermicelles de soja d'une partie de la sauce.

4 Plongez les crevettes surgelées dans une casserole d'eau bouillante. À la reprise de l'ébullition, égouttez-les et rafraîchissez-les dans de l'eau glacée. Égouttez-les de nouveau.

5 Pelez et parez la carotte, puis râpez-la avec une râpe à gros trous. Pelez la betterave. Coupez-la en tranches puis en bâtonnets. Épluchez et émincez les oignons nouveaux. Lavez la coriandre ; hachez grossièrement les feuilles et les tiges.

6 Dans un petit saladier, mélangez la coriandre, les oignons nouveaux et un peu de sauce.

7 Hachez grossièrement les cacahuètes.

8 Garnissez deux bols de vermicelles de soja, de crevettes, de bâtonnets de betterave, de carotte râpée et de salade de coriandre. Assaisonnez la carotte et la betterave du reste de sauce. Agrémentez de cacahuètes. Servez.

Trucs Santé

On dit que pour couvrir ses besoins en provitamine A, il faut consommer des fruits et légumes colorés. La betterave et la carotte sont donc, à cet égard, des sources intéressantes. Il s'agit également de deux légumes légèrement plus sucrés que la moyenne, mais aussi riches en fibres bien tolérées après cuisson.*

Trucs de Chef

La sauce pour rouleaux de printemps s'achète en grande distribution sous la marque Ayam®. Pour obtenir une version végétarienne, végétalienne et végane de cette recette, omettez les crevettes et la sauce pour nems, car celle-ci contient du nuoc-mâm. Augmentez, dans ce cas, la proportion de sauce pour rouleaux de printemps, à base de soja fermenté.

Soba, tomates, fèves, gambas, bouillon de bœuf, pomme Pink Lady

Préparation
30 minutes

Cuisson
20 minutes

Pour 4 bowls
90 g de soba
340 g de fèves surgelées, non pelées (Picard®)
1 pomme Pink Lady
1 litre de bouillon de bœuf
320 g de tomates cerises
16 gambas
2 cuillerées à soupe d'huile d'olive
2 tiges de citronnelle
2 gousses de cardamome
15 g de gingembre
Quelques branches de basilic
40 g d'amandes grillées
Sel, poivre du moulin

1 Pelez le gingembre et coupez-le en gros morceaux. Écrasez légèrement les gousses de cardamome. Fendez les tiges de citronnelle en quatre dans le sens de la longueur.

2 Dans une casserole, portez à ébullition le bouillon de bœuf avec la citronnelle, le gingembre et la cardamome, puis couvrez et laissez infuser une vingtaine de minutes sur feu très doux.

3 Faites cuire les soba dans un grand volume d'eau bouillante salée. Égouttez-les.

4 Plongez les fèves dans une casserole d'eau bouillante. À la reprise de l'ébullition, égouttez-les, plongez-les dans de l'eau glacée, puis pelez-les en les pinçant entre le pouce et l'index.

5 Lavez les tomates cerises et coupez-les en quartiers.

6 Ôtez les têtes des gambas en retirant le boyau central en même temps. Décortiquez-les en conservant le dernier anneau et la nageoire caudale. Enrobez les gambas d'huile d'olive et de sel. Faites chauffer un gril ou une poêle-gril en fonte sur feu vif. Lorsqu'il commence à fumer, déposez-y les gambas et saisissez-les 1 minute par face.

7 Coupez la pomme en quartiers, retirez le cœur et coupez chaque quartier en fines tranches.

8 Effeuillez le basilic. Hachez grossièrement les amandes grillées.

9 Filtrez le bouillon de bœuf et rectifiez l'assaisonnement si nécessaire.

10 Garnissez quatre bols de soba, de tomates cerises, de fèves, de gambas et de tranches de pomme. Versez le bouillon de bœuf sur le tout. Agrémentez d'amandes et de feuilles de basilic. Servez immédiatement.

Trucs Santé

Quoique particulièrement maigres, les gambas sont une très bonne source de protéines. D'une excellente valeur nutritive, elles sont riches en vitamine B12, en phosphore et en sélénium.

Trucs de Chef

La marque Ariaké® propose une gamme de bouillons à infuser de très bonne qualité.

Viandes

Bœuf Angus, betterave, sauce tomate, chou rouge

Préparation
10 minutes
(Réhydratation 12 heures)

Cuisson
40 minutes

Pour 4 bowls
120 g d'avoine décortiquée
1 côte de bœuf Angus de 380 g
20 g de beurre
2 cuillerées à soupe d'huile neutre (de pépins de raisin par exemple)
60 g de feuilles de betterave
120 g de chou rouge
1/2 oignon rouge
1 betterave crue d'environ 180 g
2 cuillerées à soupe de vinaigre balsamique
2 cuillerées à soupe d'huile d'olive
200 g de sauce tomate
Sel, fleur de sel, poivre du moulin

1 Faites tremper l'avoine dans de l'eau froide pendant 12 heures. Ce temps écoulé, rincez-la sous l'eau courante à travers une passoire fine. Faites-la cuire sur feu doux avec 2 fois son volume d'eau pendant une quarantaine de minutes. Égouttez-la.

2 Sortez la côte de bœuf Angus au moins 1 heure à l'avance afin qu'elle soit à température ambiante. Assaisonnez-la de sel sur ses deux faces.

3 Faites chauffer une poêle sur feu vif avec le beurre et l'huile neutre. Déposez-y la côte de bœuf et laissez colorer chaque face pendant 3 minutes sans toucher à la viande. Baissez le feu et poursuivez la cuisson de 10 à 15 minutes en retournant la viande toutes les 5 minutes et en l'arrosant régulièrement de sa matière grasse de cuisson. Laissez-la reposer pendant 10 minutes, recouverte d'une feuille d'aluminium, sur une grille posée sur une assiette afin de récupérer le jus.

4 Lavez et essorez les feuilles de betterave. Émincez le chou rouge ainsi que l'oignon rouge. Pelez la betterave et coupez-la en fines tranches à l'aide d'une mandoline.

5 Coupez la viande en tranches en récupérant le maximum de jus.

6 Dans un bol, mélangez le jus de la viande avec le vinaigre balsamique, l'huile d'olive, du sel et du poivre du moulin.

7 Versez la sauce tomate au fond de quatre bols. Garnissez-les de tranches de bœuf angus, d'avoine, de feuilles de betterave, de chou rouge et de tranches de betterave. Agrémentez de quelques rondelles d'oignon rouge. Assaisonnez les feuilles de betterave, la betterave et le chou rouge de la vinaigrette et la viande d'un peu de fleur de sel et de poivre du moulin. Servez immédiatement.

Trucs Santé

La viande de bœuf Angus, tendre et finement persillée, est une source intéressante de protéines et de fer d'excellente qualité. Le chou est riche en vitamine C, qui favorise l'absorption du fer.

Trucs de Chef

L'avoine décortiquée se trouve dans les magasins bios. Il est préférable de la faire tremper 12 heures pour réduire son temps de cuisson.
Il existe de nombreuses variétés de betteraves : rouge, blanche, jaune, chioggia dont la chair dévoile une alternance surprenante d'anneaux blancs et rose vif. N'hésitez pas à les utiliser pour obtenir un visuel surprenant.

Bœuf, aubergine, olives, pâtes, gruyère

Préparation
10 minutes

Cuisson
25 minutes

Pour 4 bowls

280 g d'araignée de bœuf
2 aubergines de taille moyenne, soit environ 600 g
1 gousse d'ail
6 cuillerées à soupe d'huile d'olive
80 g de gruyère suisse
15 g de beurre
2 cuillerées à soupe d'huile neutre (de pépins de raisin par exemple)
110 g de pâtes intégrales de type torsette
Un gros bouquet de persil plat
40 g de noix de pécan
160 g d'olives noires non dénoyautées
Sel fin, fleur de sel et poivre du moulin

1 Sortez l'araignée de bœuf au moins 1 heure à l'avance afin qu'elle soit à température ambiante.

2 Lavez les aubergines et coupez-les en gros cubes. Fendez la gousse d'ail non pelée. Faites chauffer une grande poêle sur feu moyen avec 2 cuillerées à soupe d'huile d'olive et la gousse d'ail fendue. Faites-y revenir les cubes d'aubergine avec un peu de sel pendant 25 minutes, en mélangeant de temps en temps. En fin de cuisson, retirez du feu. Coupez le gruyère suisse en cubes. Mélangez-les aux cubes d'aubergine.

3 Faites chauffer une poêle sur feu vif avec le beurre et l'huile neutre. Saisissez-y la viande 2 minutes sur chaque face sans la toucher. Baissez le feu et poursuivez la cuisson 1 minute par face en arrosant l'araignée régulièrement de sa matière grasse de cuisson. Laissez-la reposer pendant 10 minutes, recouverte d'une feuille d'aluminium, sur une grille posée sur une assiette afin de récupérer le jus.

4 Faites cuire les pâtes al dente dans une grande quantité d'eau bouillante salée. Égouttez-les.

5 Lavez et essorez le bouquet de persil. Hachez grossièrement les tiges et les feuilles du persil, ainsi que les noix de pécan.

6 Tranchez la viande en récupérant le maximum de jus.

7 Garnissez quatre bols de tranches de bœuf, de pâtes intégrales, du mélange gruyère-aubergine, d'olives noires et de persil. Arrosez la salade de persil et les pâtes de 2 cuillerées à soupe d'huile d'olive et de jus de viande. Assaisonnez le tout de fleur de sel et de poivre du moulin. Agrémentez de noix de pécan.

Trucs Santé

Avec l'huile d'olive, l'huile de pépins de raisin, les noix de pécan et les olives, on fait ici le plein d'acides gras oméga 6 dont fait partie l'acide linoléique. Non synthétisé par l'organisme, cet acide gras est dit « essentiel ». Constituant du système nerveux ainsi que des membranes cellulaires, il protège le système cardiovasculaire en aidant à réduire le taux de cholestérol LDL.

Plusieurs marques proposent une gamme de pâtes intégrales ou complètes en grande distribution. Vous les trouverez aussi, évidemment, en magasin bio.

Bœuf, avoine, chou-rave, ananas, noix de coco, coriandre

Préparation
20 minutes
(Réhydratation 12 heures)

Cuisson
40 minutes

Pour 4 bowls
- 160 g d'avoine décortiquée
- 280 g d'araignée de bœuf
- 600 g de choux-raves
- 1 cuillerée à soupe d'huile d'olive
- 15 g de beurre
- 2 cuillerées à soupe d'huile neutre (de type pépins de raisin)
- 100 g de chair de noix de coco fraîche
- 1 petit ananas Victoria d'environ 750 g
- 1 gros bouquet de coriandre fraîche
- 40 g de cacahuètes
- 2 cuillerées à soupe de graines de courge
- Sel, fleur de sel, poivre du moulin

La vinaigrette
- Le jus de la viande (voir recette)
- 2 cuillerées à soupe de nuoc-mâm
- 2 cuillerées à soupe de jus de citron
- 2 cuillerées à soupe d'huile d'olive
- Poivre du moulin

1 Faites tremper l'avoine dans de l'eau froide pendant 12 heures. Ce temps écoulé, rincez-la sous l'eau courante à travers une passoire fine. Faites-la cuire sur feu doux avec 2 fois son volume d'eau pendant une quarantaine de minutes. Égouttez-la.

2 Sortez l'araignée de bœuf au moins 1 heure à l'avance afin qu'elle soit à température ambiante.

3 Pelez les choux-raves au couteau. Coupez la chair en tranches fines, puis en bâtonnets. Faites chauffer une grande poêle sur feu moyen à fort avec 1 cuillerée à soupe d'huile d'olive. Faites-y revenir les bâtonnets de chou-rave pendant 5 minutes avec un peu de sel en remuant régulièrement. Baissez le feu, ajoutez 10 cl d'eau, couvrez et poursuivez la cuisson 20 minutes. Retirez le couvercle 5 minutes avant la fin de la cuisson et, sur feu plus vif, faites évaporer l'eau de cuisson et légèrement colorer les bâtonnets.

4 Faites chauffer une poêle sur feu vif avec le beurre et l'huile neutre. Saisissez-y la viande 2 minutes sur chaque face sans la toucher. Baissez le feu et poursuivez la cuisson 1 minute par face en arrosant l'araignée régulièrement de sa matière grasse de cuisson. Laissez-la reposer pendant 10 minutes, recouverte d'une feuille d'aluminium, sur une grille posée sur une assiette afin de récupérer le jus. Puis, coupez-la en tranches toujours en récupérant le maximum de jus.

5 Coupez le sommet et la base de l'ananas. Ôtez sa peau et ses yeux avec un couteau à longue lame en suivant la courbure du fruit. Coupez la chair en tranches. À l'aide de la pointe d'un couteau ou d'un petit emporte-pièce rond, retirez la partie centrale ligneuse de chaque tranche. Coupez les tranches en deux. Taillez la chair de noix de coco en fines lamelles.

6 Lavez et essorez la coriandre. Hachez-en grossièrement les feuilles et les tiges, ainsi que les cacahuètes.

7 Dans un bol, mélangez le jus rendu par l'araignée de bœuf avec le nuoc-mâm, le jus de citron, l'huile d'olive et du poivre du moulin.

8 Garnissez quatre bols de ces ingrédientst, puis assaisonnez la viande, le chou rave et la salade de coriandre avec la vinaigrette. Agrémentez de cacahuètes et de graines de courge. Servez immédiatement.

Trucs Santé

Avec 52 kilocalories pour 100 g, l'ananas est un fruit modérément calorique. Sa caractéristique principale est la présence de broméline, une enzyme qui aide à la digestion des protéines et aurait également une action anti-inflammatoire, antitumorale, antiœdémateuse. Elle améliorerait en outre les systèmes circulatoire et cardiovasculaire.

L'avoine décortiquée se trouve dans les magasins bios.

Pour une cuisson un peu plus légère, vous pouvez enduire la pièce de bœuf d'un peu d'huile et la faire griller sur un gril ou une poêle-gril en fonte. Attention, cependant, à la fumée produite par ce type de cuisson.

Carpaccio de bœuf, riz complet, pousses d'épinard, pomme, physalis

Préparation
10 minutes

Cuisson
5 minutes

Pour 2 bowls
65 g de riz complet
50 g de pousses d'épinard
20 g de noisettes
65 g de baies de physalis
1/2 pomme de type Pink Lady
160 g de tranches
de carpaccio de bœuf
Quelques feuilles de basilic
Sel, fleur de sel

La vinaigrette
2 cuillerées à soupe de sauce de soja
2 cuillerées à soupe de jus de citron
2 cuillerées à soupe d'huile d'olive
Sel, poivre du moulin

1 Rincez le riz complet et faites-le cuire environ 20 minutes à l'eau bouillante salée. Égouttez-le.

2 Lavez et essorez les pousses d'épinard.

3 Hachez grossièrement les noisettes. Faites-les dorer dans une poêle antiadhésive sans matière grasse sur feu vif.

4 Ôtez les fines membranes qui entourent les baies de physalis. Lavez les baies et coupez les plus grosses en deux.

5 Coupez la demi-pomme en quartiers. Ôtez le trognon et coupez chaque quartier en fines tranches.

6 Dans un bol, préparez la vinaigrette : mélangez la sauce de soja, le jus de citron, l'huile d'olive, du sel et du poivre du moulin.

7 Garnissez deux bols de tranches de carpaccio, de riz complet, de pousses d'épinard, de pomme et de physalis. Assaisonnez de vinaigrette les pousses d'épinard et le carpaccio de bœuf. Agrémentez de noisettes grillées et de quelques feuilles de basilic. Ajoutez un peu de fleur de sel. Servez.

Trucs Santé

L'épinard se démarque des autres végétaux par une quantité plus importante de protéines de qualité satisfaisante et de lipides, dont 89 mg/100 g d'acide linolénique. Ce légume est aussi une des meilleures sources connues de vitamine B9 ; il apporte également une quantité élevée de provitamine A, de vitamine C, et de vitamine K nécessaires à la coagulation du sang. Consommé sous forme de jeunes pousses crues, il prodigue encore mieux ces bienfaits nutritionnels.*

Trucs de Chef

Achetez le carpaccio chez votre boucher le jour même de la réalisation de cette recette, car la viande finement tranchée s'oxyde très rapidement.

Jambon de Bayonne, haricots verts, tomates, pâtes intégrales, artichaut

Préparation
10 minutes

Cuisson
10 minutes

Pour 2 bowls
70 g de pâtes intégrales
2 bottes d'artichauts poivrades
155 g de haricots verts
80 g de tomates cerises
20 g de parmesan
Quelques feuilles de basilic
2 tranches de jambon de Bayonne
4 cuillerées à soupe d'huile d'olive
2 cuillerées à soupe
de vinaigre balsamique
Sel, fleur de sel, poivre du moulin

1 Faites cuire les pâtes intégrales al dente dans une grande quantité d'eau bouillante salée. Égouttez-les.

2 Cassez la base des tiges des artichauts. Ôtez les premières couches de feuilles jusqu'aux plus tendres. Coupez les artichauts aux deux tiers de leur hauteur, puis en quartiers. Poêlez-les avec 2 cuillerées à soupe d'huile d'olive et un peu de sel pendant environ 10 minutes sur feu moyen à vif.

3 Équeutez et lavez les haricots verts. Faites-les cuire à l'eau bouillante salée puis rafraîchissez-les immédiatement dans de l'eau avec des glaçons pour conserver leur couleur. Coupez-les en tronçons.

4 Lavez les tomates cerises. Taillez le parmesan en copeaux à l'aide d'un économe.

5 Garnissez deux bols de haricots verts, de jambon de Bayonne, de tomates cerises, d'artichauts poivrades et de pâtes intégrales. Agrémentez de copeaux de parmesan et de quelques feuilles de basilic. Assaisonnez d'huile d'olive, de vinaigre balsamique, de fleur de sel et de poivre du moulin. Servez.

Trucs Santé

Plus riche en glucides (7,6 %) que la moyenne des légumes, l'artichaut contient de l'inuline, un glucide non assimilable qualifié de probiotique. Fermentée par la flore bactérienne du côlon, l'insuline agit comme une fibre et possède une action bénéfique sur le transit, mais en trop grande quantité, elle peut provoquer des désordres intestinaux.*

Trucs de Chef

Outre les magasins bios, plusieurs marques commerciales et de grande distribution proposent une gamme de pâtes intégrales ou complètes.

Tomates, mozzarella, jambon de Bayonne, flocons d'avoine, roquette

Préparation
10 minutes

Pour 2 bowls
80 g de jambon de Bayonne, soit 4 tranches
120 g de billes de Mozzarella di Bufala Campana
300 g de tomates cerises
Une dizaine de feuilles de basilic + quelques petites feuilles pour la décoration
2 cuillerées à soupe d'huile d'olive
2 cuillerées à café de vinaigre balsamique
100 g de gros flocons d'avoine
60 g de roquette
Fleur de sel, poivre du moulin

1 Coupez les tranches de jambon en lanières. Égouttez les billes de mozzarella en prenant soin de conserver la saumure. Lavez les tomates cerises et coupez-les en quartiers.

2 Superposez les feuilles de basilic, roulez-les bien serré tel un cigare, puis coupez-les en fines lanières.

3 Dans un petit saladier, mélangez les tomates, les billes de mozzarella, le basilic, 1 cuillerée à soupe d'huile d'olive, 1 cuillerée à café de vinaigre balsamique, un peu de fleur de sel et de poivre du moulin.

4 Dans un autre saladier, mélangez les gros flocons d'avoine avec 8 cuillerées à soupe de saumure de mozzarella. Rectifiez l'assaisonnement en sel et en poivre du moulin, en tenant compte du fait que la saumure est déjà salée.

5 Lavez et essorez la roquette. Assaisonnez-la avec 1 cuillerée à soupe d'huile d'olive, 1 cuillerée à café de vinaigre balsamique, fleur de sel et poivre du moulin.

6 Garnissez les deux bols de tomates-mozzarella, de lanières de jambon de Bayonne, de roquette et de flocons d'avoine. Agrémentez de quelques petites feuilles de basilic. Servez immédiatement.

Trucs Santé

Des légumes crus (tomates et roquette), des féculents (flocons d'avoine) et des protéines avec le jambon et la mozzarella dont les apports, respectivement en fer et calcium, sont complétés par une juste quantité de matières grasses. Une belle recette, simple et équilibrée !

Trucs de Chef

On trouve les flocons d'avoine en grande distribution et dans tous les magasins bios. La saumure dans laquelle sont conservées les billes de mozzarella est constituée de petit-lait, d'eau et de sel. Elle entre parfois, en Italie, dans la composition de la pâte à pizza. Vous pouvez remplacer le basilic par de la sarriette fraîche ou séchée.

Chou, kale, fèves, riz complet, haricot, tomate, noix, chips de jambon

SANS GLUTEN

Préparation
20 minutes

Cuisson
25 minutes

Pour 2 bowls
50 g de riz long complet
2 tranches de jambon de Bayonne
130 g de fèves surgelées non pelées (Picard®)
100 g de chou de Savoie ou chou de Milan
100 g de kale
100 g de haricots verts
4 tomates cerises
40 g de noix entières ou 20 g de cerneaux de noix
100 g de sauce tomate

La vinaigrette
2 cuillerées à soupe de vinaigre de vin
2 cuillerées à soupe d'huile d'olive
Sel, poivre du moulin

1 Faites cuire le riz à l'eau salée pendant une vingtaine de minutes. Égouttez-le.

2 Préchauffez le four à 180 °C. Étalez les tranches de jambon de Bayonne sur une plaque à pâtisserie et passez-les au four pendant 15 à 20 minutes en les retournant à mi-cuisson. Égouttez-les sur du papier absorbant. Laissez refroidir les chips de jambon, puis émiettez-les.

3 Ébouillantez les fèves pendant quelques secondes avant de les rafraîchir rapidement dans de l'eau glacée. Pelez-les ensuite en les incisant légèrement avec les ongles et en pressant.

4 Éliminez la côte centrale des feuilles de chou de Savoie. Plongez les feuilles dans une grande casserole d'eau bouillante salée et faites-les cuire 5 minutes. Rafraîchissez-les immédiatement dans de l'eau glacée pour préserver leur vert éclatant. Égouttez les feuilles puis coupez-les en lanières.

5 Éliminez la côte centrale des feuilles de kale. Lavez les feuilles puis ébouillantez-les 3 minutes dans de l'eau salée. Rafraîchissez-les immédiatement dans de l'eau glacée, égouttez-les puis hachez-les grossièrement.

6 Équeutez les haricots verts. Faites-les cuire dans une grande quantité d'eau bouillante salée en les gardant croquants. Rafraîchissez-les immédiatement dans de l'eau glacée, puis égouttez-les.

7 Lavez les tomates cerises. Coupez-les en quartiers. Cassez les noix, récupérez les cerneaux et hachez-les grossièrement.

8 Dans un petit bol, préparez la vinaigrette : mélangez le vinaigre avec du sel et du poivre, puis ajoutez l'huile d'olive en fouettant.

9 Déposez la sauce tomate au fond de deux bols. Garnissez de haricots verts, de chou de Savoie, de kale, de fèves et de riz complet. Assaisonnez de vinaigrette les haricots, les choux et les fèves. Agrémentez de quartiers de tomate, de noix et de miettes de jambon. Servez.

Trucs Santé

Les noix sont un concentré d'acides gras de bonne qualité, dont 23 % de monoinsaturés et 63 % de polyinsaturés*. Riches en oméga 6 et 3, elles apportent plus de 10 % d'acide alpha-linolénique, précurseur d'EPA et de DHA, indispensables au cerveau et au système cardiovasculaire. Enfin, elles sont une bonne source de vitamine E.*

Trucs de Chef

On trouve aujourd'hui le kale chez certains primeurs et le plus souvent dans les magasins bios.

Pois chiches, endive, brocoli, avocat, jambon, fourme d'Ambert

SANS GLUTEN

Préparation
10 minutes
(Réhydratation 12 heures)

Cuisson
1 heure

Pour 2 bowls
75 g de pois chiches secs
2 tranches de jambon de Bayonne
150 g de brocoli
1 cuillerée à soupe d'huile d'olive (pour saisir le brocoli)
50 g de concombre
50 g de fourme d'Ambert
Quelques branches de basilic
1 belle endive
1 avocat
Le jus de 1/2 citron
20 g de graines de tournesol
2 cuillerées à soupe d'huile d'olive
2 cuillerées à soupe de vinaigre balsamique
Sel, fleur de sel, poivre du moulin

1 Faites tremper les pois chiches pendant 12 heures. Égouttez-les et faites-les cuire 1 heure à l'eau bouillante salée. Égouttez-les et rincez-les.

2 Préchauffez le four à 180 °C. Étalez les tranches de jambon de Bayonne sur une plaque à pâtisserie et faites-les sécher 15 minutes au four en les retournant à mi-cuisson. Déposez-les sur du papier absorbant et laissez refroidir. Émiettez grossièrement les chips de jambon.

3 Lavez le brocoli, prélevez les sommités. Enrobez-les d'huile d'olive et salez-les. Saisissez-les pendant 3 minutes sur feu vif au gril ou dans une poêle-gril en fonte.

4 Coupez le concombre en quatre dans le sens de la longueur, puis en tranches. Dans un bol, mélangez le concombre et le brocoli.

5 Coupez la fourme d'Ambert en petits cubes. Effeuillez le basilic. Coupez la base de l'endive ; lavez et effeuillez celle-ci.

6 Coupez l'avocat en deux et dénoyautez-le. Récupérez la chair à l'aide d'une cuillère à soupe en rasant l'écorce pour détacher les deux moitiés. Coupez chacune en tranches épaisses. Citronnez légèrement la chair pour éviter qu'elle ne s'oxyde.

7 Garnissez deux bols de pois chiches, du mélange concombre-brocoli, d'avocat et d'endive. Agrémentez de miettes de jambon de Bayonne, de cubes de fourme d'Ambert, de graines de tournesol et de quelques feuilles de basilic. Assaisonnez d'huile d'olive, de vinaigre balsamique et de poivre du moulin. Salez légèrement à la fleur de sel, mais attention : les miettes de jambon apportent déjà du sel.

Trucs Santé

Les graines de tournesol entrent dans la catégorie des graines oléagineuses. Elles contiennent 20 % d'acides gras mono-insaturés et sont également riches en acides gras polyinsaturés*, plus particulièrement en acide linoléique, précurseur de la famille des oméga 6. Ce profil lipidique est remarquable. Leur teneur en vitamine E, puissant antioxydant cellulaire, est également très intéressante.*

Trucs de Chef

Pour obtenir une recette végétarienne, supprimez le jambon de Bayonne. Dans ce cas, salez davantage l'ensemble du bol avant de servir.

Jambon blanc, aubergine, riz complet, pomme, gruyère

Préparation
10 minutes

Cuisson
20 minutes

Pour 2 bowls
60 g de riz complet
1 belle aubergine
3 cuillerées à soupe d'huile d'olive
1 pomme Pink Lady ou Cox Orange
4 oignons nouveaux
20 g de cacahuètes
50 g de gruyère
120 g de jambon blanc
Sel

La vinaigrette
2 cuillerées à soupe de sauce de soja
2 cuillerées à café
de purée de cacahuète
2 cuillerées à soupe d'huile d'olive
Poivre du moulin

1 Faites cuire le riz complet à l'eau salée. Égouttez-le.

2 Lavez et parez l'aubergine. Coupez-la en tranches épaisses. Poêlez-les avec 2 cuillerées à soupe d'huile d'olive et un peu de sel sur feu moyen pendant une vingtaine de minutes en retournant régulièrement les tranches.

3 Lavez la pomme. Coupez-la en quartiers, éliminez le cœur puis coupez-les en tranches. Saisissez-les à la poêle sur les deux faces avec 1 cuillerée à soupe d'huile d'olive sur feu vif.

4 Pelez et rincez les oignons nouveaux en conservant les tiges vertes. Émincez-les finement. Hachez grossièrement les cacahuètes. Coupez le gruyère en tranches.

5 Dans un petit bol, préparez la vinaigrette : mélangez la sauce de soja, la purée de cacahuète, l'huile d'olive et du poivre du moulin.

6 Garnissez deux bols de jambon blanc, de tranches d'aubergine, de pomme poêlée, de riz complet et de gruyère. Versez la vinaigrette sur le tout. Agrémentez d'oignons nouveaux, de leurs tiges vertes et de cacahuètes. Servez.

Trucs Santé

Fromage à pâte pressée cuite, l'emmental offre de bons apports en vitamine A, B2 et B3 mais également en minéraux : phosphore et calcium. Il vient également compléter l'apport protéique de la recette pour un bon effet rassasiant.

Trucs de Chef

La purée de cacahuète s'achète dans les magasins bios. Vous pouvez remplacer le riz complet par du sarrasin décortiqué. Choisissez un jambon blanc de qualité : supérieur ou Label rouge.

Jambon blanc, sarrasin, cheddar, champignons, tomate

Préparation
5 minutes

Cuisson
20 minutes

Pour 2 bowls
50 g de graines de sarrasin
400 g de champignons de Paris
2 cuillerées à soupe d'huile d'olive
70 g de cheddar
1/2 botte de persil
4 oignons nouveaux
100 g de sauce tomate
140 g de jambon blanc
Sel, poivre du moulin

1 Faites cuire le sarrasin 20 minutes à l'eau bouillante salée. Rincez-le et égouttez-le.

2 Coupez la base du pied des champignons. Lavez ceux-ci sous un filet d'eau, puis coupez-les en quatre. Poêlez-les sur feu vif avec l'huile d'olive et un peu de sel jusqu'à obtenir une belle coloration.

3 Coupez le cheddar en tranches. Lavez le persil et hachez-le grossièrement. Pelez et émincez les oignons nouveaux. Dans un petit bol, mélangez le persil et les oignons nouveaux.

4 Versez la sauce tomate au fond de deux bols. Garnissez de jambon blanc, de sarrasin, de tranches de cheddar et de champignons. Agrémentez de persil et d'oignons nouveaux. Poivrez selon votre goût. Servez.

Trucs Santé

Légume au sens culinaire, la tomate est, au sens botanique, un fruit riche en eau (de 93 à 95 %) et faiblement énergétique. La provitamine A constitue une fraction de ses pigments rouges. Elle y est associée au lycopène, un puissant pigment antioxydant qui pourrait avoir une action protectrice contre le cancer. Cuite, la tomate libère mieux son lycopène, lequel est par ailleurs mieux assimilé en présence de lipides.*

Trucs de Chef

Ce bowl peut également constituer un petit déjeuner complet.

Magret de canard laqué, kale, orange, riz noir, endive

SANS GLUTEN

Préparation
30 minutes

Cuisson
1 heure

Pour 2 bowls
40 cl de jus d'orange sanguine
160 g de riz noir (appelé aussi riz Venere ou riz Nérone)
1 magret de canard d'environ 400 g
200 g de kale
2 oranges
2 avocats
Le jus de 1/4 de citron
2 endives
40 g de noix de cajou
Sel

La vinaigrette
Le jus des oranges (voir recette)
4 cuillerées à soupe d'huile d'olive
1/4 de cuillerée à café de wasabi
2 branches de persil plat
Sel

1 Dans une casserole, faites réduire le jus d'orange sanguine jusqu'à obtenir un sirop épais, presque un caramel (environ 10 cl).

2 Rincez le riz noir, couvrez-le de deux fois son volume d'eau dans une casserole, portez à ébullition, couvrez, puis faites-le cuire environ 45 minutes sur feu doux. Égouttez-le.

3 Parez le magret. Incisez légèrement le gras en le quadrillant. Salez. Déposez-le, côté peau vers le bas, dans une poêle en acier inoxydable sans matière grasse et faites-le cuire 4 minutes sur feu moyen à vif. Retournez le magret et faites cuire encore 1 minute. Déposez-le dans une poêle antiadhésive avec le caramel de jus d'orange, toujours sur feu vif. Poursuivez la cuisson pendant 3 minutes en arrosant continuellement le magret de caramel d'orange à l'aide d'une cuillère et en le retournant régulièrement. Laissez reposer le magret 5 minutes avant de le découper en 20 tranches.

4 À l'aide d'un couteau, retirez les côtes des feuilles de kale. Lavez les feuilles puis plongez-les 30 secondes dans une casserole d'eau bouillante salée. Rafraîchissez-les immédiatement dans de l'eau glacée. Égouttez-les, pressez-les entre vos mains pour les essorer, puis hachez-les grossièrement.

5 Ôtez la peau et la partie blanche des oranges à l'aide d'un couteau tranchant en suivant la courbure du fruit afin de n'avoir plus que la chair à vif. Prélevez les suprêmes. Mélangez-les avec le kale dans un petit saladier.

6 Pour la vinaigrette, pressez ce qui vous reste des oranges au-dessus d'un bol afin de récupérer le jus. Lavez, essuyez et hachez le persil plat. Fouettez le jus d'orange avec l'huile d'olive, le wasabi, le persil et un peu de sel.

7 Coupez les avocats en deux et dénoyautez-les. Récupérez la chair à l'aide d'une cuillère à soupe. Coupez chaque moitié en tranches épaisses. Citronnez légèrement la chair pour éviter qu'elle ne s'oxyde.

8 Coupez la base des endives et effeuillez-les.

9 Garnissez quatre bols de tranches de magret laqué, de riz noir, d'avocat, de feuilles d'endive et de mélange kale-orange. Arrosez le tout de vinaigrette au jus d'orange. Agrémentez de noix de cajou grossièrement hachées. Servez.

Trucs Santé

Avec 14 % de lipides, on reproche souvent à l'avocat sa richesse en graisses. Cependant, il s'agit en grande partie d'acide linoléique, favorable au bon fonctionnement du système cardio-vasculaire. L'avocat contient également des traces de bêta-sitostérol, un stérol végétal qui entre en compétition avec le cholestérol au niveau de l'absorption intestinale, ce qui est intéressant quand il est associé à la consommation de canard.

Trucs de Chef

Le riz noir peut être remplacé par du riz noir de Camargue. Vous en trouverez dans les magasins bios et en grande surface sous la marque Riso Gallo®. Attention : cette marque mentionne la possibilité de traces de gluten dans son produit.

Le kale se trouve chez certains primeurs ou dans les magasins bios.

Magret de canard, soba, carotte, salade d'herbes, sauce cacahuète

Préparation
10 minutes

Cuisson
10 minutes

Pour 4 bowls
1 magret de canard d'environ 430 g
120 g de nouilles soba
4 carottes
2 gros bouquets de coriandre fraîche
1 piment vert doux
200 g de concombre
40 g de cacahuètes
Sel

La sauce cacahuète
10 g de gingembre frais
20 cl de lait de coco
3 cuillerées à soupe de purée de cacahuète
2 cuillerées à soupe de sauce de soja
1/2 gousse d'ail
2 cuillerées à soupe de jus de citron
1 cuillerée à café de miel
Poivre du moulin

1 Parez le magret. Incisez légèrement le gras en le quadrillant. Salez. Déposez-le, côté peau vers le bas, dans une poêle en acier inoxydable sans matière grasse et faites-le cuire 4 minutes sur feu moyen à vif. Retournez le magret et faites cuire encore 2 minutes. Laissez reposer le magret 5 minutes avant de le découper en 20 tranches.

2 Faites cuire les nouilles soba dans un grand volume d'eau bouillante salée. Égouttez-les et rincez-les.

3 Préparez la sauce cacahuète : pelez le gingembre en grattant sa peau à l'aide d'une cuillère à café. Râpez-le à la râpe Microplane® afin de récupérer la pulpe tout en éliminant les fibres. Pelez, dégermez la gousse d'ail, puis écrasez-la dans un presse-ail. Dans un bol, mélangez le lait de coco, la purée de cacahuète, le gingembre, la sauce de soja, l'ail, le jus de citron, le miel et du poivre.

4 Pelez et parez les carottes, râpez-les à la râpe à gros trous. Dans un saladier, mélangez les carottes avec la moitié de la sauce cacahuète.

5 Lavez et essorez la coriandre. Hachez grossièrement les feuilles et les tiges en éliminant les tiges les plus épaisses. Lavez le piment doux et coupez-le en rondelles. Coupez le concombre en quartiers, puis en tranches. Dans un saladier, mélangez la coriandre, le piment et le concombre.

6 Hachez grossièrement les cacahuètes.

7 Garnissez quatre bols de tranches de magret de canard, de soba, de carottes râpées et de salade d'herbes. Agrémentez de cacahuètes et arrosez le tout du reste de sauce cacahuète. Servez.

Trucs Santé

Le canard est souvent montré du doigt en tant que viande grasse, mais ses lipides contiennent un tiers d'acides gras mono-insaturés et un tiers d'acides gras polyinsaturés* (oméga 3 et oméga 6), favorables au bon fonctionnement du système cardiovasculaire. C'est également une source intéressante de vitamines du groupe B, en particulier B2, B5, B12 et B3 (ou PP), et pour les minéraux, de fer, de zinc, de cuivre et de sélénium.*

Trucs de Chef

La purée de cacahuète s'achète dans les magasins bios. Il ne faut pas la confondre avec le beurre de cacahuète qui est parfois sucré.

Magret de canard, riz noir, poire, pomme, champignons, fourme d'Ambert

SANS GLUTEN

Préparation
10 minutes

Cuisson
45 minutes

Pour 4 bowls
160 g de riz noir (appelé aussi riz Venere ou riz Nérone)
1 magret de canard d'environ 400 g
650 g de champignons de Paris
2 cuillerées à soupe d'huile d'olive
1 pomme de type Pink Lady
1 poire de type conférence
Le jus de 1/2 citron
40 g de noix de cajou
80 g de fourme d'Ambert

La vinaigrette à l'orange
Quelques brins de persil
1 orange
4 cuillerées à soupe d'huile d'olive
2 cuillerées à café de miel
Sel, poivre du moulin

1 Rincez le riz noir, couvrez-le de deux fois son volume d'eau dans une casserole, portez à ébullition, couvrez, puis faites-le cuire environ 45 minutes sur feu doux. Égouttez-le.

2 Parez le magret. Incisez légèrement le gras en le quadrillant. Salez. Déposez-le, côté peau vers le bas, dans une poêle en acier inoxydable sans matière grasse et faites-le cuire 4 minutes sur feu moyen à vif. Retournez le magret et faites cuire encore 2 minutes. Laissez reposer le magret 5 minutes avant de le découper en 20 tranches.

3 Coupez la base du pied des champignons. Lavez ceux-ci sous un filet d'eau, puis coupez-les en tranches. Saisissez-les dans une grande poêle sur feu vif avec l'huile d'olive jusqu'à ce qu'ils soient légèrement colorés.

4 Préparez la sauce : lavez, essorez et hachez le persil. Pressez l'orange dans un bol, salez, poivrez, ajoutez l'huile d'olive, le miel et le persil, puis mélangez le tout.

5 Lavez la pomme et la poire ; coupez-les en quartiers. Retirez le cœur et coupez chaque quartier en deux. Citronnez légèrement les fruits pour éviter l'oxydation.

6 Coupez la fourme d'Ambert en petits cubes. Hachez grossièrement les noix de cajou.

7 Garnissez quatre bols de riz noir, de magret de canard, de champignons, de pomme et de poire. Agrémentez de cubes de fourme d'Ambert et de noix de cajou. Assaisonnez le tout de vinaigrette à l'orange.

Trucs Santé

Le riz noir est un riz complet, donc riche en fibres, qui se démarque par une teneur exceptionnellement élevée du péricarpe en anthocyanes aux propriétés antioxydantes, avec des effets bénéfiques sur le cholestérol, les artères et le système cardio-vasculaire en général.*

Trucs de Chef

Le riz noir peut être remplacé par du riz noir de Camargue. Vous en trouverez dans les magasins bios et en grande surface sous la marque Riso Gallo®. Attention : cette marque mentionne la possibilité de traces de gluten dans son produit.

Magret de canard, tomates, concombre, olives, noisettes, basilic

SANS GLUTEN

Préparation
10 minutes

Cuisson
25 minutes

Pour 4 bowls
120 g de riz complet
1 magret de canard d'environ 450 g
40 g de noisettes décortiquées
120 g d'olives noires non dénoyautées
240 g de tomates cerises
240 g de concombre
1 beau bouquet de basilic
4 cuillerées à soupe d'huile d'olive
4 cuillerées à soupe
de vinaigre balsamique
Sel, fleur de sel, poivre du moulin

1 Faites cuire le riz complet à l'eau bouillante salée. Égouttez-le.

2 Parez le magret. Incisez légèrement le gras en le quadrillant. Salez. Déposez-le, côté peau vers le bas, dans une poêle en acier inoxydable sans matière grasse et faites-le cuire 4 minutes sur feu moyen à vif. Retournez le magret et faites cuire encore 2 minutes. Laissez reposer le magret 5 minutes avant de le découper en 20 tranches.

3 Hachez grossièrement les noisettes. Faites-les dorer dans une poêle antiadhésive sans matière grasse sur feu vif.

4 Rincez les olives noires. Lavez les tomates cerises et coupez-les en quartiers. Lavez le concombre. Coupez-le en quatre, puis en petits triangles. Effeuillez le basilic.

5 Garnissez quatre bols de tranches de magret de canard, de riz complet, de tomates cerises, d'olives et de concombre. Arrosez les tomates, les olives et le concombre d'huile d'olive et de vinaigre balsamique. Assaisonnez l'ensemble de fleur de sel et de poivre du moulin. Agrémentez de noisettes grillées et de feuilles de basilic. Servez.

Trucs Santé

Les olives sont des petits fruits oléagineux intéressants d'un point de vue nutritionnel pour leur richesse en acides gras mono-insaturés et notamment en acide oléique, qui a la propriété de diminuer le taux de cholestérol sanguin et d'augmenter le taux de « bon » cholestérol (HDL). Cette fraction lipidique importante est associée à une bonne teneur en vitamine E.*

Trucs de Chef

Vous pouvez remplacer le basilic par de la marjolaine ou par un peu de roquette.

Magret de canard, chou-rave, edamame, brocoli, endive

Préparation
20 minutes

Cuisson
25 minutes

Pour 4 bowls

2 choux-raves, soit environ 480 g
2 cuillerées à soupe d'huile d'olive
1 magret de canard d'environ 400 à 430 g
400 g d'edamame surgelés (Picard®)
240 g de brocoli
1 bouquet de coriandre
1 endive
40 g de cacahuètes
Sel, fleur de sel et poivre du moulin

La vinaigrette

2 cuillerées à soupe de nuoc-mâm
2 cuillerées à soupe de sauce de soja
2 cuillerées à café de moutarde de Dijon
4 cuillerées à soupe d'huile d'olive

1 Pelez les choux-raves au couteau. Coupez la chair en fines tranches. Faites chauffer une grande poêle sur feu moyen à vif avec l'huile d'olive. Faites-y revenir les tranches de chou-rave pendant 5 minutes avec un peu de sel en remuant régulièrement. Baissez le feu, ajoutez 10 cl d'eau, couvrez et poursuivez la cuisson 20 minutes. 5 minutes avant la fin de la cuisson, retirez le couvercle et faites évaporer l'eau de cuisson sur feu plus vif afin de légèrement colorer les tranches. Poivrez.

2 Parez le magret. Incisez légèrement le gras en le quadrillant. Salez. Déposez-le, côté peau vers le bas, dans une poêle en acier inoxydable sans matière grasse et faites-le cuire 4 minutes sur feu moyen à vif. Retournez le magret et faites cuire encore 2 minutes. Laissez reposer le magret 5 minutes avant de le découper en 20 tranches.

3 Faites décongeler les edamame au four à micro-ondes avec un peu d'eau.

4 Coupez le brocoli en petites sommités. Faites-les cuire 3 minutes à l'eau bouillante salée, rafraîchissez-les immédiatement dans de l'eau glacée afin de préserver leur couleur.

5 Préparez la vinaigrette : dans un bol, mélangez le nuoc-mâm, la moutarde, la sauce de soja et l'huile d'olive.

6 Dans un petit saladier, enrobez les edamame de la moitié de la vinaigrette.

7 Lavez et essorez le bouquet de coriandre. Hachez très grossièrement les feuilles et les tiges les plus fines. Effeuillez l'endive après avoir éliminé les premières feuilles. Hachez grossièrement les cacahuètes.

8 Garnissez quatre bols de tranches de magret de canard, de chou-rave, de brocoli, d'endive et d'edamame. Arrosez les feuilles d'endive et le brocoli avec le reste de sauce. Saupoudrez les tranches de magret de fleur de sel. Agrémentez de coriandre et de cacahuètes. Servez.

Trucs Santé

Le chou-rave n'est pas une racine mais une tige renflée qui fait partie des légumes oubliés. Il se distingue par sa richesse en vitamine C dont on profite particulièrement en le consommant cru. Il contient également du sulforaphane, qui combat la bactérie H pylori (Helicobacter pylori) qui séjourne dans l'estomac et occasionne notamment des ulcères.

Trucs de Chef

En saison, vous pouvez remplacer les edamame par des fèves fraîches. Dans ce cas, écossez puis ébouillantez les fèves quelques secondes avant de les rafraîchir rapidement dans de l'eau glacée. Pelez ensuite les fèves en les incisant légèrement avec les ongles et en pressant.

Vermicelles de soja, poulet, asperge, brocoli, cocos plats

SANS GLUTEN

Préparation
20 minutes

Cuisson
15 minutes

Pour 4 bowls
1 blanc de poulet d'environ 220 g
2 cuillerées à soupe d'huile de pépins de raisin (ou tout autre huile neutre)
200 g de brocoli
4 cuillerées à soupe d'huile d'olive
250 g de haricots cocos plats
16 asperges vertes
90 g de vermicelles de soja
40 g de cacahuètes
20 g de beurre
Sel, poivre du moulin

La sauce
Une vingtaine de feuilles d'estragon
4 oignons nouveaux
8 cuillerées à soupe de sauce pour nems (nuóc chấm, ou marque Ayam® en grande surface)
2 cuillerées à café de moutarde de Dijon
Le jus de 1/2 citron
2 cuillerées à soupe d'huile d'olive

1 Salez le blanc de poulet. Faites chauffer le beurre et l'huile de pépins de raisin dans une poêle en acier inoxydable sur feu moyen à vif. Faites-y dorer le blanc de poulet pendant une quinzaine de minutes en le retournant toutes les 5 minutes et en l'arrosant régulièrement avec la graisse de cuisson. Laissez-le reposer 5 minutes hors du feu, puis coupez-le en 16 tranches.

2 Lavez le brocoli. Coupez les sommités en tranches épaisses. Enrobez-les de 2 cuillerées à soupe d'huile d'olive et salez-les. Saisissez-les pendant 3 minutes sur un gril ou une poêle-gril en fonte sur feu vif.

3 Parez les cocos plats, coupez-les en biais en petites sections. Faites-les cuire à l'eau bouillante salée en les gardant croquants ; rafraîchissez-les immédiatement dans de l'eau glacée pour préserver leur couleur.

4 Cassez la base ligneuse des asperges. À l'aide d'un économe, taillez-les en lanières. Enrobez-les de 2 cuillerées à soupe d'huile d'olive et salez-les. Saisissez-les pendant 3 minutes sur un gril ou une poêle-gril en fonte sur feu vif.

5 Faites bouillir de l'eau, retirez-la du feu et plongez-y les vermicelles de soja. Au bout de 3 minutes, égouttez-les puis coupez-les grossièrement avec des ciseaux de cuisine.

6 Hachez grossièrement les cacahuètes.

7 Préparez la vinaigrette : hachez les feuilles d'estragon. Pelez et émincez les oignons nouveaux. Dans un bol, mélangez la sauce pour nems, la moutarde de Dijon, le jus de citron, l'huile d'olive, l'estragon et l'oignon nouveau. Salez et poivrez.

8 Garnissez quatre bols de tranches de poulet, de vermicelles de soja, de lamelles d'asperge verte, de cocos plats et de brocoli. Arrosez le tout de vinaigrette à l'estragon. Agrémentez de cacahuètes. Servez.

Trucs Santé

Le poulet est la principale source de protéines de cette recette. C'est une viande relativement maigre avec en moyenne moins de 7,5 % de lipides. Elle est aussi particulièrement riche en vitamine B3 (ou PP), importante dans le métabolisme énergétique, tout en étant également une source intéressante de phosphore de fer, de zinc et de sélénium. Cent grammes de poulet couvrent jusqu'à 105 % des apports quotidiens recommandés de cet oligoélément.

Trucs de Chef

Attention, certaines marques vendent sous l'appellation « vermicelles de soja » un produit composé de soja et d'amidon de pomme de terre. Cette version possède un indice glycémique plus élevé que celui des véritables vermicelles de soja, composés à 100 % de soja. Vérifiez bien la composition.

Poulet pané à l'avoine, navets, kale, haricots, fèves, sauce au yaourt

Préparation
20 minutes

Cuisson
20 minutes

Pour 2 bowls

1 botte de navets avec leurs feuilles
2 cuillerées à soupe d'huile d'olive
50 g de fèves non pelées surgelées (Picard®) ou en saison 125 g de fèves entières fraîches
110 g de haricots verts
80 g de kale
130 g de blanc de poulet fermier
20 g de farine
1 blanc d'œuf
100 g de gros flocons d'avoine
Huile pour friture
20 g de noix de cajou
Sel fin, fleur de sel

La sauce au yaourt

1 branche de romarin frais
1 yaourt
Le jus de 1/2 citron
1 cuillerée à café de moutarde de Dijon
Sel

1 Préchauffez le four à 200 °C. Coupez les fanes des navets et retirez au couteau les côtes centrales des feuilles. Lavez et essorez les feuilles puis hachez-les grossièrement. Conservez 40 g de feuilles pour la recette. Coupez les navets en quartiers de taille égale. Dans un bol, enrobez-les d'huile d'olive et salez-les. Déposez-les sur une plaque et faites-les cuire 20 minutes au four. Retournez-les à mi-cuisson afin d'obtenir une coloration uniforme.

2 Plongez les fèves dans une casserole d'eau bouillante. À la reprise de l'ébullition, égouttez-les, plongez-les dans de l'eau glacée, puis pelez-les en les pinçant entre le pouce et l'index.

3 Équeutez les haricots verts. Faites-les cuire dans une grande quantité d'eau bouillante salée en les gardant croquants. Rafraîchissez-les immédiatement dans de l'eau glacée, puis égouttez-les.

4 Éliminez la côte centrale des feuilles de kale. Lavez les feuilles puis ébouillantez-les 3 minutes dans de l'eau salée. Rafraîchissez-les immédiatement dans de l'eau glacée, égouttez-les puis hachez-les grossièrement. Dans un saladier, mélangez-les aux haricots verts et aux fèves.

5 Effeuillez la branche de romarin et hachez finement les feuilles. Dans un bol, mélangez le yaourt, le jus de citron, la moutarde et le romarin. Salez.

6 Coupez le blanc de poulet en une dizaine de bâtonnets. Versez la farine dans une assiette creuse, le blanc d'œuf dans une autre ; battez-le légèrement. Enfin, versez les flocons d'avoine dans une troisième assiette creuse. Enrobez chaque bâtonnet de poulet de farine, trempez-le soigneusement dans le blanc d'œuf, puis enrobez-le de flocons d'avoine. Une fois tous les sticks de poulet panés, faites chauffer l'huile pour la friture dans une grande poêle antiadhésive sur feu vif. Faites-y dorer les sticks de poulet sur toutes leurs faces. Déposez-les sur du papier absorbant, puis saupoudrez-les de fleur de sel.

7 Garnissez deux bols de ces ingrédients. Versez à la cuillère la sauce au yaourt au centre de chaque bol. Agrémentez le tout de noix de cajou hachées.

Trucs Santé

150 g de navet représentent au moins 5 % de l'apport quotidien recommandé en vitamines B1, B2, B6 et B9. Il est aussi une bonne source de minéraux. Enfin, les hétérosides soufrés ou glucosinolates présents dans le navet seraient bénéfiques à la prévention des cancers du poumon, de l'appareil digestif et du sein.

Trucs de Chef

On trouve aujourd'hui le kale sur les marchés, chez certains primeurs et le plus souvent dans les magasins bios.
Vous pouvez utiliser le reste des fanes de navets en salade, les faire tomber à la poêle avec un peu de beurre comme pour des épinards ou les incorporer à une soupe de légumes mixée. Ce conseil vaut aussi pour les fanes de radis.

Poulet, asperges vertes, brocoli, avocat, menthe, persil

Préparation

10 minutes

Cuisson

10 minutes

Pour 2 bowls

240 g de filet de poulet
10 g de beurre
2 cuillerées à soupe d'huile de pépins de raisin
12 asperges vertes entières + 3 pointes d'asperge verte
1 cuillerée à soupe d'huile d'olive
1/2 avocat
Le jus de 1/2 citron
80 g de brocoli
1 cuillerée à soupe de graines de sésame
Sel

La vinaigrette

1 branche de persil plat
10 feuilles de menthe fraîche
Le jus de 1/2 citron
2 cuillerées à soupe de sauce de soja
2 cuillerées à soupe d'huile de sésame
Poivre du moulin

1 Salez le blanc de poulet. Faites chauffer le beurre et l'huile de pépins de raisin dans une poêle en acier inoxydable sur feu moyen à vif. Faites-y dorer le blanc de poulet pendant une quinzaine de minutes en le retournant toutes les 5 minutes et en l'arrosant régulièrement avec la graisse de cuisson. Laissez-le reposer hors du feu, puis coupez-le en tranches.

2 Cassez la base fibreuse des asperges vertes. Coupez six asperges en deux dans le sens de la longueur. Enrobez-les d'huile d'olive et salez-les. Saisissez-les 3 minutes au gril, sur feu vif ou dans une poêle-gril en fonte. Coupez les six asperges restantes en très fines tranches, légèrement de biais. Faites cuire les pointes d'asperge à l'eau bouillante salée en les gardant croquantes, plongez-les dans de l'eau glacée pour préserver leur couleur, puis égouttez-les.

3 Dénoyautez l'avocat. Récupérez la chair à l'aide d'une cuillère à soupe en rasant l'écorce pour détacher la chair en un morceau. Coupez-la en tranches épaisses et citronnez-la légèrement.

4 Lavez le brocoli et prélevez-en les sommités.

5 Préparez la vinaigrette : émincez le persil et la menthe. Dans un bol, mélangez le jus de citron, la sauce de soja, l'huile de sésame et les herbes émincées. Poivrez.

6 Garnissez deux bols d'avocat, d'asperges vertes grillées, d'asperges vertes crues, de pointes d'asperge verte et de poulet. Assaisonnez de vinaigrette les asperges crues, le brocoli et l'avocat. Agrémentez le tout de graines de sésame. Servez.

Trucs Santé

L'asperge est à la fois pauvre en calories et riche en qualités nutritionnelles. Ainsi, cette petite pousse verte est une source remarquable de vitamine A, C et E, de magnésium, de fer et de fibres. L'avocat, lui, vient booster l'apport en vitamine E.

Dans la vinaigrette, vous pouvez remplacer le jus de citron par du vinaigre de riz.

Poulet, butternut, épinard, sarrasin, noisettes

Préparation
10 minutes

Cuisson
35 minutes

Pour 4 bowls
La moitié d'un butternut (environ 600 g)
1 cuillerée à café de graines de carvi
1 cuillerée à soupe d'huile d'olive
480 g de blancs de poulet fermier
20 g de beurre
4 cuillerées à soupe d'huile de pépins de raisin
120 g de sarrasin décortiqué
40 g de noisettes décortiquées
100 g de pousses d'épinard
Sel

La vinaigrette
2 cuillerées à soupe de sauce Worcestershire
2 cuillerées à soupe de vinaigre de xérès
4 cuillerées à soupe d'huile d'olive
2 cuillerées à café de moutarde de Dijon
2 cuillerées à café de miel
Sel

1 Préchauffez le four à 210 °C. Écrasez les graines de carvi dans un mortier. À l'aide d'une cuillère, ôtez les graines de la courge de butternut, ne pelez pas celle-ci. Coupez-la en tranches. Déposez-les sur une plaque, enrobez-les d'une cuillerée à soupe d'huile d'olive. Frottez-la de sel et de la moitié des graines de carvi. Faites cuire de 30 à 40 minutes au four en prenant soin de retourner les tranches à mi-cuisson. Testez la tendreté du butternut avec la pointe d'un couteau, qui ne doit pas rencontrer de résistance.

2 Salez les blancs de poulet. Faites chauffer le beurre et l'huile de pépins de raisin dans une poêle en acier inoxydable sur feu moyen à vif. Faites-y dorer les blancs de poulet pendant une quinzaine de minutes en les retournant toutes les 5 minutes et en les arrosant régulièrement avec la graisse de cuisson. Laissez-les reposer 5 minutes hors du feu, puis coupez-les en tranches.

3 Faites cuire le sarrasin décortiqué 20 minutes à l'eau bouillante salée. Égouttez-le.

4 Coupez les noisettes en tranches. Faites-les dorer dans une poêle antiadhésive sans matière grasse sur feu vif.

5 Lavez et essorez les pousses d'épinard.

6 Préparez la vinaigrette : dans un bol, mélangez la sauce Worcestershire, le vinaigre, la moutarde, le miel et le carvi restant. Salez.

7 Garnissez quatre bols de poulet, de tranches de butternut rôties, de sarrasin et de pousses d'épinard. Arrosez ces dernières avec la vinaigrette. Agrémentez de noisettes grillées. Servez.

Trucs Santé

Associé au poulet, le sarrasin complète l'apport protéique de la recette avec des protéines végétales d'excellente qualité. Décortiqué, il contient moins de fibres insolubles et devient plus digeste.

Trucs de Chef

Vous trouverez le sarrasin décortiqué au rayon céréales des magasins bios. Bien qu'ils n'aient pas la même saveur, vous pouvez remplacer le carvi par du cumin additionné d'une pointe d'anis. N'hésitez pas à récupérer les graines du butternut, à les laver puis à les faire sécher au four à chaleur douce. Elles seront délicieuses et pourront agrémenter les prochains bowls.

Poulet, bouillon de volaille, chou, fèves, courgette, soba

Préparation
15 minutes

Cuisson
15 minutes

Pour 2 bowls
- 50 g de soba
- 120 g de blanc de poulet fermier
- 130 g de feuilles de chou de Savoie (ou chou de Milan)
- 120 g de courgette
- 170 g de fèves non pelées surgelées (Picard®)
- 40 g de noisettes en coques (ou 20 g de noisettes décortiquées)
- 6 olives noires
- 50 cl de bouillon de volaille
- 1 branche d'estragon
- Sel, poivre du moulin

1 Plongez les fèves dans une casserole d'eau bouillante. À la reprise de l'ébullition, égouttez-les, plongez-les dans de l'eau glacée, puis pelez-les en les pinçant entre le pouce et l'index.

2 Éliminez la côte centrale des feuilles de chou. Plongez les feuilles dans une grande casserole d'eau bouillante salée et faites-les cuire 5 minutes. Rafraîchissez-les immédiatement dans de l'eau glacée pour préserver leur vert éclatant. Égouttez les feuilles puis coupez-les en lanières.

3 Faites cuire les soba dans un grand volume d'eau bouillante salée. Égouttez-les et rincez-les.

4 Coupez le blanc de poulet en morceaux de 2 cm de côté.

5 Lavez et parez la courgette, coupez-la en quatre dans le sens de la longueur, puis en tranches épaisses.

6 Portez le bouillon de volaille à ébullition dans une casserole. Pochez-y les morceaux de poulet pendant 5 minutes à frémissement. Récupérez-les à l'aide d'une écumoire. Pochez ensuite la courgette dans le bouillon pendant 2 minutes.

7 Décortiquez les noisettes et hachez-les grossièrement. Rincez les olives noires. Effeuillez l'estragon et émincez finement les feuilles.

8 Garnissez quatre bols de soba, de chou, de fèves, de courgettes et de poulet. Versez le bouillon de volaille sur le tout. Agrémentez d'olives, de noisettes et d'estragon. Servez immédiatement.

Trucs Santé

Il s'agit ici d'un plat complet bien équilibré. La courgette et le chou sont riches en potassium (230 mg pour 100 g) et pauvres en sodium (3 mg pour 100 g), ce qui les rend bénéfiques à la santé cardio-vasculaire : une alimentation riche en potassium possède des effets antihypertensifs reconnus.

La marque Ariaké® propose une gamme de bouillons à infuser de très bonne qualité.

Poulet, riz basmati, algue, chou-rave, carotte, pamplemousse

Préparation
20 minutes

Cuisson
25 minutes

Pour 4 bowls

1 gros chou-rave d'environ 320 g
2 cuillerées à soupe d'huile d'olive
120 g de riz basmati complet
65 g d'algues wakamé au sel
260 g de blanc de poulet
10 g de beurre
2 cuillerées à soupe d'huile de pépins de raisin
1 pamplemousse
2 belles carottes
40 g de cacahuètes
Sel, poivre du moulin

La vinaigrette

Le jus du pamplemousse (voir recette)
Quelques pluches d'aneth
2 cuillerées à soupe de sauce de soja
2 cuillerées à soupe de sauce Worcestershire
2 cuillerées à soupe d'huile d'olive
Poivre du moulin

1 Pelez le chou-rave au couteau. Coupez la chair en fines tranches. Faites chauffer une grande poêle sur feu moyen à vif avec l'huile d'olive. Faites-y revenir les tranches de chou-rave pendant 5 minutes avec un peu de sel en remuant régulièrement. Baissez le feu, ajoutez 10 cl d'eau, couvrez et poursuivez la cuisson 20 minutes. 5 minutes avant la fin de la cuisson, retirez le couvercle et faites évaporer l'eau de cuisson sur feu plus vif afin de légèrement colorer les tranches. Poivrez.

2 Rincez et égouttez le riz. Couvrez-le de deux fois son volume d'eau dans une casserole, portez à ébullition, couvrez et baissez le feu. Faites cuire sur feu doux jusqu'à absorption totale du liquide. Égouttez le riz.

3 Faites tremper les wakamés pendant une quinzaine de minutes dans une grande quantité d'eau. Égouttez-les et rincez-les pendant 3 minutes sous un filet d'eau claire. Égouttez-les de nouveau et laissez-les sécher à l'air libre.

4 Salez le blanc de poulet. Faites chauffer une poêle en acier inoxydable sur feu moyen à vif avec le beurre et l'huile de pépins de raisin. Faites-y dorer le blanc de poulet pendant une quinzaine de minutes en le retournant toutes les 5 minutes et en l'arrosant régulièrement. Laissez reposer le poulet, puis coupez-le en tranches.

5 Ôtez la peau du pamplemousse au couteau en suivant la courbure de l'agrume et en prenant soin de ne pas laisser de partie blanche. Prélever les suprêmes. Coupez-les en petits morceaux.

6 Pressez le restant du pamplemousse au-dessus d'un bol afin de récupérer le jus. Hachez les pluches d'aneth et ajoutez-les ainsi que la sauce de soja, la sauce Worcestershire et l'huile d'olive. Poivrez et mélangez.

7 Coupez les wakamés en lanières. Dans un saladier, mélangez-les avec la chair de pamplemousse et un tiers de la vinaigrette.

8 Pelez et parez les carottes, râpez-les à la râpe à gros trous.

9 Garnissez quatre bols de ces ingrédients. Arrosez les carottes et le chou-rave du reste de vinaigrette. Agrémentez de cacahuètes grossièrement hachées. Servez.

Trucs Santé

La composition de l'algue wakamé révèle une grande richesse en protéines végétales de bonne qualité et en calcium, avec 1 300 mg aux 100 g. On lui prête ainsi des propriétés tonifiantes et reminéralisantes. Il semblerait qu'elle soit également utile pour détoxifier le système digestif des métaux lourds et des toxines grâce à l'alginate (sel) qu'elle contient, et le fucoïdane présent dans ses feuilles contribuerait à renforcer le système immunitaire.*

Trucs de Chef

Le riz basmati complet se trouve dans les magasins bios et en grande surface sous la marque Taureau Ailé®. Vous trouverez le wakamé au sel en vitrine réfrigérée dans les magasins bios.

Vermicelles de soja, bouillon de volaille, céleri branche, champignons, carottes

Préparation
10 minutes

Cuisson
30 minutes

Pour 4 bowls

15 g de gingembre frais
2 gousses de cardamome
2 tiges de citronnelle
1 litre de bouillon de volaille
32 g de vermicelles de soja
240 g de carottes
200 g de champignons de Paris
320 g de blancs de poulet
1 petit bouquet de coriandre
240 g de jeunes pousses de céleri branche
2 cuillerées à soupe de graines de sésame
2 cuillerées à café d'huile de sésame
Sel, poivre du moulin

1 Pelez le gingembre et coupez-le en gros morceaux. Écrasez légèrement les gousses de cardamome. Coupez les tiges de citronnelle en quatre dans le sens de la longueur.

2 Dans une casserole, faites chauffer le bouillon de volaille avec la citronnelle, le gingembre et la cardamome. À ébullition, baissez le feu et laissez infuser 20 minutes. Filtrez le bouillon et rectifiez l'assaisonnement.

3 Faites bouillir de l'eau dans une petite casserole, retirez du feu et ajoutez les vermicelles de soja. Laissez-les gonfler pendant 3 minutes. Égouttez-les et rincez-les, puis coupez-les grossièrement à l'aide de ciseaux de cuisine.

4 Parez et épluchez les carottes. Coupez-les en deux dans le sens de la longueur, puis en tranches.

5 Coupez le pied sableux des champignons. Lavez-les soigneusement puis coupez-les en deux ou en quatre selon leur taille. Pochez-les 5 minutes dans le bouillon de volaille et récupérez-les à l'aide d'une écumoire. Réservez.

6 Coupez les blancs de poulet en cubes de 2 cm de côté. Pochez-les 5 minutes dans le bouillon de volaille frémissant. Récupérez-les à l'aide d'une écumoire. Réservez.

7 Lavez et essorez le bouquet de coriandre. Hachez grossièrement les feuilles et les tiges.

8 Garnissez les quatre bols de carotte, de vermicelles de soja, de morceaux de poulet, de champignons et de jeunes pousses de céleri branche. Versez le bouillon de volaille sur le tout. Agrémentez de coriandre, de graines de sésame et d'un filet d'huile de sésame. Servez immédiatement.

Trucs Santé

Le céleri branche, particulièrement riche en eau et en potassium mais pauvre en sodium, est un des légumes frais les moins énergétiques. Jusqu'à la Renaissance, il fut employé comme plante médicinale pour ses vertus diurétiques et son action stimulante sur le système nerveux.

Trucs de Chef

La marque Ariaké® propose une gamme de bouillons à infuser de très bonne qualité.

Table des recettes

Index par produits

Définitions*

Acide aminé
Acide organique constituant l'unité de structure des protéines.

Acide ellagique
L'acide ellagique est un polyphénol* antioxydant que l'on trouve dans divers fruits et légumes comme les châtaignes, les framboises, les fraises, les noix, les canneberges ou les grenades, par exemple.

Acides gras saturés
Ce sont les acides gras issus du règne animal (beurre, crème, fromages, graisses de porc, de bœuf, de canard, d'oie, etc.) ou du règne végétal (huile de noix de coco, huile de palme). Solides à température ambiante, ils sont moins fragiles que les acides gras insaturés, car ils supportent mieux la chaleur de la cuisson. Cependant, consommés en excès, ces acides gras augmentent la synthèse de mauvais cholestérol, le risque de diabète, l'hypertension et donc les problèmes cardiovasculaires. Les acides gras trans sont à proscrire.

Acides gras insaturés
Qualifiés de « bons » gras, ils se divisent en deux sous-catégories : les monoinsaturés et les polyinsaturés.
Les acides gras monoinsaturés sont les oméga 9. Liquides à température ambiante, ils supportent relativement bien la chaleur. On peut donc les utiliser pour cuisiner. La principale source d'oméga 9 est l'huile d'olive, mais on en trouve aussi dans les noix, l'avocat et les arachides.
Les acides gras polyinsaturés comprennent les oméga 3 et les oméga 6 (huile de tournesol, de soja et de maïs). Ces deux acides gras sont dits « essentiels » car ils ne peuvent pas être synthétisés par l'organisme. Ils doivent donc être obtenus par l'alimentation.

Alcaloïde
Composé organique azoté et basique tiré d'un végétal (nom générique).

Anthocyane
Pigment végétal rouge, violet ou bleu des feuilles, des pétales et des fruits, situé dans les vacuoles des cellules.

Dégénérescence maculaire
Dépression de la rétine, appelée aussi tache jaune, située au pôle postérieur de l'œil et où l'acuité visuelle est maximale.

Fucoïdane
Il permet d'augmenter le flux sanguin soit l'oxygénation au niveau des organes.

Hypercholestérolémie
Augmentation anormale du taux de cholestérol dans le sang.

Hypocholestérolémiant, hypolipidémiant
Se dit d'un médicament intervenant dans le métabolisme des lipides et visant à normaliser le taux des lipides sanguins, des triglycérides et du cholestérol.

Probiotique
Se dit d'un micro-organisme vivant (bactérie ou levure, notamment ferment lactique) qui, ingéré en quantité suffisante, a un effet bénéfique sur la santé en améliorant l'équilibre de la flore intestinale.

Provitamine
Toute substance présente dans les aliments que l'organisme transforme en vitamine.

Végétalisme
Régime alimentaire excluant tout aliment d'origine animale (œufs, laitage, miel, etc.).

Végétarisme
Régime alimentaire excluant toute chair animale (viande, poisson), mais qui admet en général la consommation d'aliments d'origine animale comme les œufs, le lait et les produits laitiers (fromage, yaourts).

*Les définitions sont extraites du *Dictionnaire de français Larousse*.

Achevé d'imprimer en décembre 2017
par Macrolibros (Espagne)